ISLAND DOGS

+1

Island Dogs

A Novel

B.M Simpson

ISLAND DOGS
A NOVEL

bmsimpson@LIVE.com
www.facebook.com/BMSimpson.author

ISBN-10: 0-9863954-0-4
ISBN-13: 978-0-9863954-0-6

PRINTED IN THE UNITED STATES OF AMERICA

Book Design by Mads Berg, Mads Berg Illustration

DISCLAIMER

Island Dogs is a work of fiction. Names, characters, businesses, organizations, places, events and incidents are either the products of the author's imagination or used in a fictitious manner. Any resemblance to actual persons, living or dead, or actual events is purely coincidental. The reader should consider the words on these pages to be much like stories told in an island bar, which are typically made up of threads of imagination woven into blankets of disillusion... and mixed with rum.

ISLAND DOGS

PROLOGUE: FROM THE CORNER

They were all lost souls looking for a place to hide and a place to heal. Desmund was simply there to serve them drinks and help them find that place in the sun. Island music played as customers laughed and yelled to each other across the bar. Waves splashed onto the shore just a few feet away while Desmund, the Rasta bartender with long dreads and a warm smile, cruised from one customer to the next. He poured Rum Punch and set beers in front of them just as he had done countless times before. Mostly he provided an easygoing island vibe that was a safe haven from the rest of the world.

From his table in the corner, Helmut watched as customers blew smoke into the air while telling stories, mostly lies. He watched as they mingled, keeping each other company; keeping themselves company. He listened to them laugh at each other's jokes as they drifted seamlessly from one conversation to the next. They were loud and gregarious; he was quiet and introspective. They lived as a group while he lived in self-imposed solitude—but he knew that deep down in the hidden places they all were very much alike. They were broken, if not beyond repair, at least to the point of never being new again. He was certain if they didn't have each other, then they probably wouldn't have anyone. Behind their laughing, beyond all the joking, there was loneliness kept silently buried in the past, a past that never completely faded away.

They more or less mirrored each other's personal histories and there was usually no need to share the details. Like so many others who had moved to the Caribbean, they all had a story. In some ways, most of them had similar stories: Their pasts were gone and their dreams had slipped away. Somewhere along the way, their options in life had become limited. For each of them, running had become the best of what seemed like all bad choices.

Helmut knew he was just like the rest of them, even if *they* didn't know it. He didn't belong anywhere, so he ended up here. He had always done a poor job at envisioning what the future would be like. When it finally arrived at his doorstep, he just wanted to close the door and go back inside. But there was no inside. There was no warm safe place to go to, to kick his feet up while dreaming about a brighter future. The future had arrived, done its damage, and become part of his past. The past that he regretted had left its deep, ugly scars. The past that he longed for was unattainable. It was never coming back.

So he sat and he watched. He watched as others struggled with their existence, while he barricaded himself from his own. He stayed in his safe place in the corner while he kept his distance from everyone. Not once did he realize that this small gathering of would-be friends, this little pack of island dogs—they were mutts, really—were slowly creeping into his private world. They were becoming part of his life. Despite what he believed, he was still alive.

His heart was not yet dead. And they were tugging at it.

PART I

CHAPTER ONE

THE MORNING AFTER

With his eyes closed, Pellet listened to the early morning surf splashing onto the sandy white shores of Anguilla, and felt the warm Caribbean breeze barely moving the soft sea air across his face. The rhythm of the waves was soothing as always; but they sounded closer than normal. It was apparent whatever events had transpired late last night, when it was all said and done, did not go well. He did not go to sleep, nor was he waking up, in his own bed.

As he began to stir, and felt the jagged edges of rocks and shells jabbing into his rib cage and against his cheekbone, it was obvious he was not waking up in a bed at all. Last night was a blur of smoke, alcohol and a vague memory of kissing some tourist named Tina, or Trudy or some name that started with a *T*. "Please God... tell me it was not Tim or Truman," he mumbled to himself with a lingering suspicion that it was. He remembered taking shots of Jägermeister around one a.m. as "Sympathy for the Devil", cranked on the bar stereo while Desmund repeatedly screamed, "Yeah Baby!" But those were the last things he vaguely remembered.

Waking up on mornings like these were always a bit strange and a lot hung-over. Not knowing if what he vaguely recalled was a moment of heavenly bliss or shameful embarrassment—which would likely become a legendary story

for bar friends to tell and retell for months or years to come—
was an unsettling feeling. And wondering if the beautiful woman
he hazily remembered kissing was in fact beautiful, or ugly, or
God help him, a woman at all, was a scary thought. For some
reason, it also seemed as if he might have taken a whiz on the
floor in the bar. Hopefully, he only *thought* he was in the bar and
Desmund would not be looking to give him hell the next time he
showed his face at Da Limin Hut, or what the locals had come to
know as *da Hut*. No matter what happened last night, the
realization that regret would settle in shortly after the hangover
began to recede was unnerving. It seemed as though both events,
the kissing and the whizzing, probably happened. But no matter
what actually occurred, there was one thing he was certain of.
All details would be cleared up and amplified once the island
gang sobered up and reunited for the post-game summary.

Not wanting to see the world around him yet, Pellet
refused to open his eyes. His hands began to stir and touch the
ground, trying to determine what he was lying on. For one
disillusioned moment, he believed he had a kind of native Carib
power with unique island tracking and nature-sensing abilities,
but as his hand felt the ground within his reach... nothing. He
was disappointed to realize he didn't have a clue about where he
was lying, and he definitely did not have any native Carib
tracking abilities. Clearly he was lying face down in the dirt. His
foggy brain, still not functioning correctly, thought it best to
attempt one more time to piece together what might have
happened the second half of last night before he received any
visual confirmation of his condition or location. Try as he might,
there was no hope of retrieving the lost memories. So with one
deep, nauseous breath and one tiny micro-prayer, hoping he was
not waking up on the side of the road with cars driving past, he

opened his eyes to see what awaited him in the early morning island sun.

Lying in the dirt not six inches from his face was the wet, dirt-covered nose and furry face of one of the local flea-infested, lazy island mutts. He wondered for a moment how bad his own breath must smell, if he couldn't smell the dog's breath so close to his own nose. As they both lay face down in the yard of the Hut, perhaps fifty feet from the bar he had been drinking at just a few hours ago, all he could mumble was, "Damn, two island dogs waking up face down in the dirt. Maybe it's time for one of us to make a change."

The dirty, scrawny mutt looked as though the sleepy island life was the life he had chosen for himself right from the beginning of his existence. It also appeared he lived in complete contentment, lying around in dirt, doing nothing, free from hangovers, free from regret or any other dark emotion mankind had to deal with. More to the point, he seemed happy with the status quo; it appeared Pellet was going to be the one who was going to have to make the change.

"Damn... I hate change," he mumbled as he once again closed his eyes and hoped the situation would be better the next time they opened. At the very least, maybe the dog would be gone.

It somehow seemed to Pellet his condition could have appeared worse than it actually was if there was another living creature lying beside him and a comparison could be made by anyone who happened upon the site. It was not too unrealistic to imagine that a mangy old mutt probably looked better than the bearded, dirt-covered white man lying next to him in the sand between the palm trees.

"Who am I kidding?" Pellet mumbled. "I'm either face

down in the dirt beside a dog, or I'm face down in the dirt by myself. Not too flattering either way." Without moving his body or his head, he scrunched his face in a futile effort to restore blood flow to the vicinity of his brain. He tried wetting his lips with his tongue, but his tongue was dry and sticky, and his lips were covered with sand. He ended up with a nasty, sticky tongue covered with sand that crunched between his teeth as he tried to take back his effort to wet his lips.

"Damn... I hate change," he mumbled one more time.

A half-hour later he woke up again, still hung-over, still full of the knowledge that this morning was going to be a regrettable morning that would lead into a painfully regrettable afternoon. He was also wondering why his back was all warm and wet. Opening his eyes to the painful rays of the morning sun, he struggled to turn as he looked over his shoulder just in time to see the scraggly island dog walking off, fully contented with his self, and fully relieved since he had just peed on Pellet's back. Apparently he wanted to make it clear to the intruder that he was crashed out on native island dog turf. As far as Pellet was concerned, the territory was marked. The message was received.

As Pellet struggled to get onto his hands and knees in an effort to eventually get to his feet, he heard someone stirring around on the porch of the bar. When he at last got upright on his wobbly legs, he turned and saw Desmund standing on the porch with a cup of coffee in his hand and a grin on his face.

"Now dat's some poetic justice for ya, mon. You piss in me bar, n' me dog pisses on you. Guess we be even," Desmund said as he raised his coffee mug up in a toast. Pellet searched his foggy brain for a quick, witty response, and soon realized there was no quick, witty comeback to be made after passing out, sleeping face down in the driveway, and last but not least, being peed on by Desmund's scraggly old dog. Resigning himself to defeat, he hung his head in throbbing shame as he headed to the sea for a much-needed swim and rinse. It was going to be a long day.

Pellet stumbled as he misjudged the first slight drop-off hidden beneath the morning surf. Catching his balance required a bit more energy than was available to him, so once he started to fall, he flinched for only a moment, and then fell like a tree, letting the cool water absorb his pathetic existence. The salty water washed away the dry, sticky sand that covered his lips and tongue. For a split second he felt a splendid instant of relief, immediately followed by an extended period of death-defying nausea. "Please, take me now and stop this suffering," he silently prayed as he stared at the bottom of the sea. But God did not instantly kill him or give him relief from his self-inflicted pain. Once Pellet resigned himself to the reality that he was not going to die today, he simply began telling the lie he had told a hundred times before: "God, if you end this painful suffering, I promise I won't ever drink this much again."

Unfortunately for Pellet, God knows all, and God knew with absolute certainty that Pellet was lying to himself and to God. The suffering did not cease for several more hours, when the hangover was cured through the normal bodily purging process.

***

It was late in the afternoon when Pellet picked up the cold beer, took a gulp and tossed a couple of peanuts into his mouth.

"Shit... what a night," he said to Desmund, who was standing behind the bar, not surprised by Pellet's late afternoon arrival.

"You never fail to put on a show," a short, stocky white guy with a strong island accent said as he bounced into the bar, looking thirsty and eager to drink as always. Oscar was born and raised in Anguilla and had been hanging with Desmund, the Rasta bartender, longer than either of them could remember.

"I don't want to hear it yet," Pellet said, glancing over his shoulder.

"It's good to have a dream, my friend, but I'm afraid that dream just is not going to come true," Oscar answered as he plopped onto the stool next to Pellet and slapped his hand onto the bar. "Beer, please!"

CHAPTER TWO
ANTIPODAL POINTS

In geography, the antipodes of any place on EARTH is its antipodal POINT; that is, the region on the EARTH'S surface which is diametrically OPPOSITE to it. In simpler terms, it is the other side of the world.

***

Growing up, Wayne Francis Pelletier—known to his friends as Pellet—was a quasi-dysfunctional kid, from a somewhat dysfunctional family, in a nondescript little town, in a gray dreary county, in a state that had one hundred and eighty days of rain, snow, and other assorted forms of moisture each year, along with sixty days of black flies mixed in with mosquitoes. To add insult to injury, his parents insisted the entire family—which included two brothers, three sisters, a cousin who was a bit too creepy for comfort, various cats, dogs, a miniature pig, and of course, his parents—live in a dilapidated old house all together until they were all grown up and could more or less take care of themselves. This final issue, more than all the other issues, left him scarred with emotional wounds.

To be honest, there was no reason for him to believe his future was going to be any brighter than the weather that continually loomed over his head, or the weather that was almost always on the near horizon. Up to that point in time, the history of his life consisted of years of stagnant and unhappy bleakness. The future looked to be more of yesteryear, recycling itself day after day after day, for as long as it took until there were no more days left.

Despite the hand that life had dealt him, which any good poker player would have taken one look at and said, "I fold," Pellet still managed to scrounge up a few dreams and hold them near and dear to his heart. He clung to his dreams like a Christian holds on to Jesus, or a drowning man holds on to a life ring. Quite frankly, his dreams were about the only thing for him to hold on to. And the dream that was the key to his salvation, was the dream of one day running as far away from home as possible. His one and only hope for a bearable, if not blissful, future was to start a new life in a strange and very distant land. It never entered his mind that the destination he would eventually reach could possibly be stranger than the one he started out from. But as the old saying goes, "Ignorance is bliss," and his dream, or more importantly, his ignorance of all its details, big and small, made him about as blissful as they came.

In its infancy, his dream was simple and good, but lacked all the components that would enable the dream to become a reality. At sixteen he started thinking, or rather dreaming, about packing up and hitting the road. But the dream had no form, the road had no end, and the destination did not exist. To be specific, he didn't know where to go. His original plan was to simply go *away,* but illusion and reality were often difficult to separate from each other. At sixteen *leaving* and *going* seemed to be the same thing. As time passed, he realized the difference between leaving and going was that *going* had a destination; *leaving* was just wandering aimlessly to points unknown. So as the plan very, very slowly evolved, it went from leaving, to going, to going away, to going far away, then the Eureka moment! To go as far away from his starting point as humanly possible. And he meant it literally when he said *as far away as possible*. At last, his plan began to clarify itself. He decided that going to the other side of the earth would be just about an acceptable distance from his current life.

For the next three years he muddled his way through drab days at work, and tolerated hopeless family functions. All the while, in the back of his mind, he dreamed of finding the exact point on the other side of the world that was geographically as far away from his home as he could travel. Then he would allow his life to evolve from there. He imagined what it would be like to find the antipodal point of wherever he happened to be standing at any given point in time. Finding that specific place on earth that would take him right to the mile, foot, and inch on the other side of the world, and going as far away from his current existence as possible became his life-nurturing quest. Building a new life became an obsession, and he could not imagine how the plan could possibly get any better.

As if life wasn't as bleak, bland, and hopeless as one could possibly imagine, his considerably large family was eccentric and eclectic beyond any reasonable description, and they seemed to be ratcheting up their odd personalities as time went by. They were not a group who would inspire one to say *There's no place like home*. At least not in a good way. Pellet was a quiet, somewhat reclusive individual, while they were... not. Pellet was one of those people who blend into the woodwork. He was a single piece of wheat in the middle of a field, or a not-so-impressive oak tree in the middle of a thick forest. On the other hand, the brothers, sisters, cousin, and parents would be described as loud, flamboyant oddballs.

Between the drama queens, barroom brawlers, political activists to the extreme degree, womanizers, man-chasers, holy rollers, and whatever else you can think of, his family had them all.

In what seemed an eternity of monotony, absurdity, and oddities, Pellet's job, his family, and his life had all taken their toll on his rapidly fading sanity. It was unavoidable that he would soon need to make a drastic move or get sucked up into the hopeless void he had been trying to escape from for as long as he could remember. He knew he was nearing the time when his plan needed to take form. He had dreamed about it for as far back as he could recall, but now it was time to lay out the specifics of the plan, to set a timeline for the implementation phase. The hour to take action was quickly approaching.

***

It was another cold, rainy, dreary Saturday morning when Pellet walked from his fading teal-blue mobile home down the muddy sidewalk, and climbed into the rundown Volkswagen Beetle. After starting its chugging VW motor, he turned on the defroster that barely cleared the fog from the windshield, and drove to the Waldoboro Public library. A few minutes later, as he once again walked through the cold rain from the car to the library, his spirits began to lift. Even though he wouldn't be starting the trip for a few weeks or months, today the exact location on the world atlas was going to be pinpointed. Today, his finger would touch the spot on the map that would one day soon become his new home.

Walking into the small library, he headed straight for the section that had a table with a four- by eight-foot world map under a quarter-inch-thick piece of glass and a two-foot globe of the planet earth sitting in a heavy metal stand on the floor right beside it. The map and the globe were sitting there when he was in grammar school, they were there when he was in high school; he had been certain they would still be there now.

So there he stood looking down at the world. No need to worry about feet or inches at this time; the exact location could be pinpointed later. Today all Pellet needed to do was to get a good feel for where he'd be living, and start answering some of the questions that were racing through his mind. What country would it be? What's the climate like? Hot? Cold? Dry? Wet? What clothes and equipment were going to be needed? What kind of food would he be eating? Clearly, since it was much further south, it was going to be much warmer than the cold Maine winters. As his anticipation grew, the questions and unverified answers raced through his mind. The moment of truth was at hand.

And then it happened. As he stood there looking down at the mass of land and water on the table in front of him, reality slapped his face... hard. He started at Waldoboro Maine. Then he went to the other side of the world to the approximate location where his new home was supposed to be. But there was no land within a thousand miles of the antipodal point of Waldoboro Maine. As a matter of fact there was nothing but water, water, and more water. And it was not just any water. His dream home was located on the fringes of the Antarctic Ocean, a few thousand miles southwest of Australia.

"Holy f'n mother of God." He mumbled loudly enough for all five people in the library to hear him and look in his direction.

"How could this be? What am I... stupid?" he mumbled even louder than the first time. He had never really put two and

11

two together as he pondered where the other side of the world actually was. It was just much simpler and far more uplifting if he clung to the dream that it would be some faraway place with neighbors who didn't speak English, but loved him just because he had moved to their strange, exotic land. It never dawned on him that his neighbors might be penguins, walruses, and whales. It absolutely never dawned on him that he might have to live on a houseboat with a heater if he wanted to live on the other side of the world. It appeared that if he had any neighbors that weren't swimming, they would be living on icebergs.

Embarrassment came in a huge rush, even though he was actually the only person who knew about the big dream. Depression soon followed. The dream crashed down around his head like a truckload of mud.

He immediately settled back into the dull, gray life of merely existing from one day to the next. Up in the morning, one cup of coffee, off to nine hours of work in the eraser factory, home again, one drink, supper, TV, bed; repeat it four more times a week for fifty weeks a year. Two weeks of camping each year, then more self-loathing and wondering why the hell the other side of the earth was a thousand miles south of Australia, in the Antarctic. Then back to the eraser factory. More years of dreariness to look forward to, death to follow at some undetermined point in the future; then of course there would be the wake, funeral, cemetery, and finally, the end. He was living the dream!

Even his job was empty beyond words. He got out of bed every day, made a product whose sole purpose was to take things that had been previously written, and then make them go away. If he at least made pencils, or hammers, or something constructive, he could say, "This pencil might write the next great novel," or "This hammer might build someone's home." But he made erasers. All they did was erase things. Theoretically, the item that Pellet made every day of his life could actually erase another person's life's work. If that happened, then he would have literally accomplished less than nothing during his time here on earth—his entire life's accomplishments would have to be measured in negative numbers. Over the next several months, his existence consisted of the job at the eraser factory and a drab, foggy dampness filled with enough crazy relatives to fill a loony bin. To add insult to injury, his antipodal point from the mobile home, which everyone knows is just a better sounding name than *trailer*, was in the Antarctic Ocean. O happy daze.

Then it happened!

On a Wednesday morning exactly one hundred and seventy-four days after the great library wake-up call, or *the slow death sentence*, as he liked to call it, everything changed. For reasons far too mysterious for him to understand, God, or the Universe, or whomever the elusive creature is that lurks out there in places that we can't see and messes with our heads and hearts and lives on a sporadic basis, decided to rekindle his spirit. It must have happened in his sleep, because from what he remembered of the previous night, nothing eventful happened. No life-changing events took place. The Tuesday night bowling league wrapped things up at about ten o'clock with one last pitcher of beer split among the Epic Surf's Up bowling team. They lost again, just in case you were wondering, and no... there is no surf up, down, or any other manner, in Waldoboro Maine. Then he drove home, watched a few minutes of completely fake reality TV, and went to bed.

He remembered having a dream about riding a huge

bullfrog that was saddled up and harnessed like a horse. After the frog hopped off a giant lily pad and trotted down Main Street, the dream suddenly shifted to a new dimension as they darted through the Catholic Church, which was holding a mass at the time. He remembered stopping for a moment so the priest could give him and the frog Holy Communion, washed down with a gulp of wine. The priest seemed strangely calm to Pellet as the frog's long tongue darted out and snatched the wafer from his hand, giving the frog at least momentary absolution from whatever frog sins he may have committed. Suddenly they—the frog and Pellet—were standing in the shoe department at Macy's in New York City. He was whispering to the frog about the beautiful woman who was trying on the spiked-heeled work boots. The frog smiled, looked at him with great big buggy frogeyes and nudged Pellet to go over and talk to the stunning mystery woman. The last thing he could remember from the dream was taking a deep breath and starting to move forward. As with all his great dreams, Pellet woke up without actually seeing the woman's face. But for the first time in a long time, he got out of bed with a smile on his face. Whether it was because of the dream or the beer, or simply because sometimes enough is enough, and he was sick and tired of being sick and tired, the next chapter of his life was about to begin, and he knew it.

As he stood in the bathroom looking into the mirror, with hair flattened on one side and sticking straight up on the other, with stubble covering his face and little sweaters covering un-brushed teeth, it was completely clear in his mind that there would be no more days at the eraser factory. Not even one. There would be no more family fiascos; the local rainy weather was going to be a thing of the past. Today, before the sun went down, he'd be leaving town and not coming back.

Within minutes of making the decision, he began packing his one suitcase and a duffle bag, then immediately started to formulate and activate a plan all at once. The two bags were more than enough; he owned almost nothing worth taking. He finished packing, then called his landlord and told him he could have whatever was left behind. He called his most sane sister, not to be confused with a completely sane sister, and told her he was leaving and would write soon. Minutes later he hopped into the VW Beetle and pulled out of the muddy driveway one last time. A quick stop for coffee to go at Dinkin's Diner, a stop at the bank to withdraw his substantial savings of $2,481.27, which had only taken four years to accumulate, and then the great adventure commenced.

Clearly the Antipodal Point Plan had crashed and burned, so it was time to activate the next best thing. It was time to begin a quest for thrills and adventure that had called out to so many young American men who had gone away to seek their dreams. It was time to start the journey that was going to take Pellet to a new life in a new place. He was heading to a strange new land filled with sun and fun and excitement. He was going to a land where people—where *women*—from all over the world gathered, celebrated, and reinvented themselves. Shangri-La was at hand. He was heading to Florida.

CHAPTER THREE

THE JOURNEY BEGINS

Insanity: Doing the same thing over and over again and expecting different results.

—Albert Einstein

***

It's possible that Pellet's moral compass may have been skewed a bit from pointing north, and he'd been told more than once that he should question his judgment a bit every now and then. The simple truth was that he had not grown up yet and adulthood did not seem to be looming on the near horizon.

It was also plausible that a little introspection would have made him question why he spent so much time sitting in the Hut or any other bar. Unfortunately, he did not question his judgment and no such introspection had yet taken place. Quite predictably, while the bar may have provided him shelter from the storm, it also encouraged frequent moronisms, which Pellet clung to like a kid with his tongue stuck to an icy metal flagpole in the middle of a long cold winter. Sticking the tongue on the pole and hanging out in bars might have seemed like good ideas on the front end, but the pain always came later, and it came in spades. As usual, he hoped for a better outcome tonight.

Pellet sat at the bar, running his fingers in the grooves a tourist had made when they scratched a poor rendition of a dolphin into the dull lacquered bar top. Shaking his hanging head back and forth, he mumbled to himself and stared blankly at the island art, mulling over his current state of living a somewhat dysfunctional, mildly absurd life while the sound of a dozen warning bells rang in his head. The alarms constantly going off were nothing unusual, but the fact that he was acknowledging their presence was definitely something new. All he could think of was the robot on the old TV show *Lost in Space* calling out, "Danger! Danger! Run, young Will Robinson! Danger!" as his scrunchy-tube robot arms flailed all about. "Danger, young Pellet! Danger!"

Blurry recollections of the events of just a few nights ago kept bouncing around in his mind; kissing a stranger of unknown gender, passing out in the yard, being peed on by an island dog, and last but not least, the day long hangover that ensued. They had all come together to create a perfect storm of shame, remorse, regret, and, most importantly, self-loathing.

"How the hell did I end up here?" he mumbled as Desmund walked over and leaned on the bar.

"Dat a rhetorical question?" Desmund answered as he attempted to play down the remorse. Clearly the shenanigans of a few nights ago did not damage Desmund's psyche anywhere near as much as they damaged Pellet's. "Tings happen, mon. Jus let em go and move on to da next. Can't undo what's been done, but dey fade away."

"So you think everyone will just forget about the other night, huh?"

"Oh hell no! We be talkin bout it for years, but wacha gonna do, huh?" he said with a grin as he turned to wait on a customer who was waving an empty bottle at him.

"Oh hell no! We be talkin bout it for years..." The words ran through Pellet's mind again and again. For a moment

he considered slamming his forehead on the bar while screaming as loud as possible, *"Oh hell no! We be talkin bout it for years..."* His brain was stuck in a perpetual loop. For a moment he flashed to the future and envisioned himself years from now, sitting at the bar with some woman he hoped to sustain a real relationship with—something that had eluded him for years, by the way—and then he hears some congenital malfunction that he's known for nearly an eternity call from across the bar: "Hey, Desmund, do you remember..." and the entire story is retold. A roar of laughter follows, then a loud hissing sound, as his once proud ego quickly deflates, followed by the woman easing out of the bar and out of his life.

Oh hell no! We be talkin bout it for years... ran through his mind again as he finished drinking the beer in his hand out of sheer desperation, then waved to Desmund to bring another. One might think drinking alcohol at a time like this would be ill advised and counterproductive; it was after all how the initial set of circumstances had begun in the first place. But for the moment it seemed as if there were no other logical solution—other than to drink and think. But mostly to drink.

"Man, I'm a mess," Pellet mumbled as he looked up and saw Desmund standing in front of him again. "I think I'm broken," he said, with the sarcastic smirk growing larger on his face, but not hiding his depression.

"How'd you end up down here anyway?" Desmund asked as he puffed on a joint and sipped his fruit punch.

"What?"

"In da islands. How'd you end up in da islands? Ain't you from Maine or Canada or one of dem cold places filled with white folks?"

"Yeah," Pellet answered. "Once upon a time I was from

one of them cold places filled with white folks." Sitting at the island bar and thinking that far back seemed surreal. That life was so long ago it felt like he was trying to remember the details of an old movie he'd watched as a stoned teenager. Friends, family, and home had all become faded memories he rarely thought about these days. To be honest, he didn't feel much like strolling down Memory Lane tonight either, but his lack of enthusiasm didn't seem to dissuade Desmund one little bit.

"So what got da ball rollin? Why'd you leave home in da first place?"

"Seemed like a good idea at the time," he said, drifting back to where it all started, where it had all taken him, and the shitload of life that had occurred between the two points. "On the other hand, you know me. I might have just been a little wasted and made a snap decision. I can't really remember it all that well."

"Maine, right? You started in Maine?" Desmund continued, even though he already knew the answer. He'd heard him talk about Maine nearly a dozen times over the past couple of years.

"About a million years ago, Desmund," Pellet mumbled, and took another swig from his beer bottle.

Just a few months ago, on a perfect Caribbean night in February, a light sea breeze gently caressed his face while he sat at a beach bar, sipped a rum drink and watched a perky, pudgy weather girl wave her arms and point at sub-zero temperatures and a blizzard in the Buffalo area, he felt as if he had chosen the right path in life. He vaguely recalled saying, "I must be a fucking genius," as he raised his beer, toasting his good life in the islands while another snowstorm pounded the northeast. But sitting here right now with the hot, humid August air suffocating

19

him as if it were almost too heavy to breathe, his spirit worn, battered, and broken, things didn't seem so clear. He did not feel like a fucking genius any longer.

Desmund blurted out a few more questions as he expertly worked to maneuver Pellet away from his woes and ease him to a place where the bleakness of today was put aside, while the hopes and dreams of yesteryear were restored. Bartenders are not by nature fortunetellers other than to say things like "It'll get better, just give it some time," and most of the time they don't believe their own advice. Good bartenders like Desmund knew how to work people, and knew enough not to try to sell that "Tomorrow will be a better day" crap. There's no reason for anyone to believe a potentially broken-down drunk, who is sitting at a bar ordering a drink, is heading in the right direction. The truth was at this point in time, almost any advice from anyone would be good advice. That is, any advice except "Have another beer." Desmund was smart enough to know that the past was the best place for Pellet to focus his attention for the time being.

"I'll take another one," Pellet said, wiggling his empty bottle toward Desmund.

"So when you lef Maine, you drive or fly?"

"What?" Pellet answered with a puzzled look.

"Drive or fly?"

"Now that's a story," Pellet said as his mind began to drift back to where the journey all began.

Desmund sat back on his stool with a look of satisfaction on his face, listening to yet another discouraged customer as he began to leave his current woes behind.

"Lay it on me, baby!" he said as he opened another ice-cold Carib and set it down in front of Pellet. Number four.

***

On a cold, dreary, late September morning that was like so many other drizzly, lifeless days in Waldoboro Maine, the journey began. The backseat of Pellet's beat-up VW Beetle was loaded with the little bit of stuff he owned. The front seat was arranged to hold a wrinkled map he'd found stuffed in the glove box, and a cardboard cup-holder he found on the garbage-covered floor. With a little creative stacking and some not-so-precise engineering, he set them flatly on the passenger seat so his coffee cup would be easily accessible and would not spill. As it turned out, his engineering feat didn't work, and the first time he hit a pothole, half the coffee spilled all over the wrinkled map.

Suddenly it was official. The journey south had begun.

All in all, the trip commenced quite uneventfully, as leaving Waldoboro wasn't exactly like leaving a place the size of New York or Miami. He was beginning from nowhere and heading toward somewhere, so it would seem only logical the excitement would be at the far end of the trip, as opposed to the Waldoboro end. The forty-five minute drive down US 1 was a postcard picture of green Maine forest and rolling pastures dotted with occasional century-old New England farmhouses. Small run-down homes and trailers sporadically popped up along the side of the road, with TV dishes big enough to pick up porn from Mars on their front lawns, and old broken-down cars abandoned beside dilapidated garages which were apparently being saved for... well... for something. Not so sporadic gnomes or fake black bears stood in front yards next to shiny balls that sat on three-foot-tall concrete pedestals. These balls signified absolutely nothing except at least one person who lived in these homes or trailers liked shiny balls that sat on pedestals beside other characters that were as pointless as the shiny balls. They were classic Maine yard-art lawns.

All those scenes were about to be history as he scooted a mile or so down the Blue Star Highway toward I-95 South. He glanced at a memorial plaque and small parking area on the edge of the road where they used to drink beer on Friday nights back in their high school days. A smile came to his face as he recalled bringing Susie Lockhart up here for his first sexual experience. "The best fifty-five seconds of sex I had ever had," he said out loud, with a grin on his face. He took one final look before saying farewell to his old stomping grounds. With that last comment, he hit the Volkswagen's accelerator, pulled onto the on-ramp, and headed down I-95 toward Portland Maine and the great unknown.

It turned out there was much more to life than he had imagined, and it was a lot closer than he had anticipated. The trip started off completely uneventful—other than a couple of cups of coffee, a few gallons of gas, and a traffic jam on the outskirts of Boston, which was something that he was not prepared for. Who knew there could be more than twenty-five cars on a highway at one time?

After a couple of hours of stop and go, and stop and go, and stop and sit, and sit some more, and go, he at long last got to be one of the lucky winners who was given the opportunity to rubberneck for a few seconds and take a good look at the tractor trailer that had lost control and crashed across the median on the northbound highway. The cause of the accident was unclear, but what had been a load of caged chickens on the trailer, many of which were now successfully running toward freedom with all the hazards that came along with it, was clearly the main cause of the stoppage of traffic. Watching the chickens scurrying around, Pellet thought it was strange that even though virtually everyone in America is willing to eat chicken, nobody is willing to kill one with his or her car. He took his obligatory gander at the wreck and caused his own personal fifteen-second traffic jam—and if you multiply that by several thousand cars, it quickly became apparent why there was a two-hour backup. Pellet slowly accelerated and worked his way back up to an acceptable cruising speed, as he continued on his journey south.

Five miles past the big jam he spotted a hitchhiker on the shoulder of the road with a cardboard sign with *NYC* written in big black Magic Marker letters. He figured, what the hell, he'll only be in the car for a little while. If he's a good guy, then great! It's good to have company. If he's an ass, well it's no big deal because he'll be gone soon enough anyway. Pellet pulled the VW to the shoulder of the road, started throwing trash and the questionably crafted cup-holder into the backseat while the hitchhiker jogged up the shoulder of the road to where the car had come to a stop.

***

"Since you tellin me dis story I'm guessin you ran into problems, huh?" Desmund said as he grabbed an old wooden stool and prepared to make himself comfortable for the story that was becoming a saga.

"You think?" Pellet said as he reached for his beer and puffed on a newly lit cigarette.

***

23

The guy, the hitchhiker, was fairly clean-cut, in his early twenties, wearing blue jeans, a T-shirt, and a denim jacket with a small backpack thrown over his shoulder. He jogged up to the car and stuffed the backpack on top of the stuff in the backseat, climbed into the front passenger seat, stuck his hand out, and said, "Hey, I'm Shaun." They shook hands, Pellet introduced himself, put the car into first gear, and down the road they went.

"Where you headed?" Pellet asked in an attempt to get a conversation rolling. Shaun pointed to the sign that he'd thrown down by his feet and didn't say anything more.

"Oh yeah, I guess you were holding a sign, weren't you. Live there, or just visiting?"

"Just visiting," he said as he looked out the passenger window, appearing not all that interested in jumping into a conversation.

"Friends or family?"

"Friends."

"So, where you from?" Pellet asked.

With this question Shaun quizzically looked at Pellet as if he were trying to decide whether he was being interrogated by the Gestapo or examined by a curious onlooker at a zoo. A few highly caffeinated hours in the car, followed by the long slowdown in the traffic jam, had gotten Pellet slightly more high-strung than he had realized. He glanced at his newly acquired traveling companion with a big grin on his face and realized he had asked him four questions within the first ten seconds of his arrival in the Bug.

"I'm not an axe murderer or rapist, if that's what you're getting at," Shaun said with a crooked smile. "Plus New York is a big place, so finding out if my family lives there or not won't really help you all that much if the police are trying to locate me during the follow-up investigation... if you were alive to tell the police anything. I mean, telling the cops a guy who said his name was Shaun, whose family presumably lives in Manhattan, tried to kill you probably wouldn't be a lot of assistance in the attempted-axe-murder investigation."

Pellet smiled and realized the absurdity of the rapid-fire questions he'd thrown at the guy. At the same time, he felt a little strange about how comfortably his passenger had jumped right into the axe murderer thing and the impending investigation. It was hard to tell what the expression on his face was saying, but the thoughts running through Pellet's mind were *Man, I was a bit rude nailing him with all them questions,* quickly followed by *He seems awful comfortable talking about killing me and the cops looking for him and his family.* Finally he found himself back to the somewhat unanswered question, *So, where you from?* After all of that ran through his over-caffeinated brain in the span of a split second, Pellet simply nodded and said, "Huh," then looked back at the road as he headed toward Hartford.

The conversation may have gone from full speed to full stop in a matter of seconds, but the flow of traffic was by no means letting up. It was three in the afternoon, and they were less than an hour and a half east of Hartford on a weekday. Jumping right into new experience number two for the day, it appeared Pellet was going to get introduced to his first brush with rush-hour traffic, and it wasn't going to be the Down East-style rush hour. The caffeine was still operating at peak efficiency when a truck with two trailers came flying by at what seemed to be a hundred miles an hour, and almost blew the little car off the road. Pellet's forehead wrinkled as his eyes locked on the road in front of him. At the same time he tried to keep an eye on each and every vehicle that surrounded him. He was overwhelmed, his driving judgment was questionable, and he swore out loud on more than one occasion as cars on both sides appeared to purposely see how close they could get without actually crushing the little VW along with Pellet and his newly acquired passenger.

Watching Pellet must have been uncomfortable for this unsuspecting hitchhiker, who eyed him as he maintained the concentration and intensity of someone trying to defuse a bomb. His knuckles almost glowed white as he gripped the steering wheel so tightly that it was difficult to control the car and not jerk it one way or the other every time he twitched ever so slightly. Against any reasonable odds, his level of intensity actually increased as the occasional car beeped or blared its horn when it blew past at near the speed of light.

"I take it you don't get much traffic like this where you're from," Shaun said, as he pondered the wisdom of having gotten into the car.

"Not too often... ever," Pellet answered without taking his eyes off the road, as if peering forward hard enough would control all the vehicles around them.

"Well, let me give you a couple pointers. First of all, try to drive the same speed as the rest of the cars. I know you think they're going real fast, but the truth is you're going so slow we're lucky one of them big trucks hasn't run us over yet."

Pellet immediately stepped on the gas. Even though he didn't quite get up to the prevailing speed, he at least got going fast enough that it seemed as if the cars were slowly passing him instead of blowing the doors off.

"The next thing you ought to do is stop squeezing the steering wheel so tightly. Sooner or later you're going to need some blood to flow into your fingers, and that's probably not going to happen as long as you continue crushing the steering wheel with that death grip you're using."

He loosened his grip a bit as the VW's speed continued to inch its way up to somewhere near the same speed as everyone else.

"Last but not least," Shaun added, "you might want to start breathing again. I'm not sure how far you're going, but this traffic is going to stay like this for the next couple of hours. You guys do breathe where you're from, right?"

With that last comment they both laughed. Pellet breathed.

"So you're from Manhattan, huh?" Pellet jokingly blurted out as he returned to the earlier interrogation.

"Actually I live in Boston, but I thought I better throw you a curve, just in case you get away," he said.

"You're a funny guy," Pellet answered, trying to convince himself that Shaun was in fact joking. After all, what were the chances of picking up an axe murderer on the first day of his great adventure?

"I'm just messing with you, man. Boston is home, but most of my friends live in the city. I bus down or hitchhike down there a couple weekends a month. Good party scene in New York. Lot of good clubs, good people, and a damn good time. You go clubbing much?"

Until just a few hours ago, Pellet had spent his entire life in Waldoboro Maine. When he and his friends wanted to hit the big-city clubs, they ventured way up to the metropolis of Bangor, which was their version of New York City, without all the people, clubs, entertainment, or restaurants. And the Bounty Tavern, the Sea Dog, or the Red Barn were just about the entire club scene to be found. Clearly there was no big choice of what *kind* of clubs they could pick from. Pellet and his friends just called them bars, and they weren't good or bad or anything else. They were simply the only places they had. They also didn't have a huge ethnic, social, religious, or any other kind of diversity in their local community. Breaking the local population down into the major groups would consists of lumping them into groups like male or female, young or old, fat or skinny, good looking or not so much. Other than what Pellet considered to be "regular Mainers" the only diversity that existed were some Native Americans—and, of course, Canadians.

"You like to party?" Shaun asked.

"Sometimes. Not really much of what you would call a club scene where I'm from."

"No... I mean do you like to *party*?" he said again, as he pulled a joint out of the pocket of his denim jacket.

"Ohhh... *party*. I smoke now and then, but I'm guessing this may not be the best time for it. You may have noticed that I'm already showing signs of being trafficly-challenged, and adding more obstacles in my path might not be the wise way to go."

"*Au contraire,* mon ami. I believe it's exactly what the current situation calls for. It appears to me that the biggest issue at hand is that you're concentrating much too hard, and your intensity exceeds any reasonable level. But Dr. Shaun has a cure for what ails you. I'm like one of those miracle workers that you see on Sunday morning TV. I'm like a VW Bug, I-84, stoner version of a televangelist," he said, as he popped the joint into his mouth then reached into his pocket and pulled out a box of wooden matches. He extracted one match from the box and struck it on the flint strip, all in a smooth, effortless motion that clearly displayed that he had repeated this sequence a few thousand times before. As he held the match up to the end of the joint, he gave a momentary glance that convinced Pellet he might turn toward him as if he were a tuxedoed spy and say, "Shaken, not stirred." Pellet had a kind of homespun charm that enabled him to warm up to most people with little or no effort, but Shaun was one of those guys who seemed to take it to a whole new level. He had an air that said he was the kind of guy who possessed a stoner *savoir-faire* that not only made it easy for him to warm up to people, but people were drawn to him like bugs to one of those black-light bug zappers. He was a sort of modern-day "James Dean combined with a little James Bond and a smidge of Brad Pitt smoking a joint in a VW Bug" kind of guy.

Smoke quickly permeated every inch of the little car as Shaun took a small puff, followed by a long drag on the expertly rolled joint. Pellet waited for the lung explosion after Shaun inhaled deeply, but he had no trouble holding the smoke in as he handed the joint to Pellet. Looking away from the traffic for just the length of time that it took for him to snatch it out of his fingers, Pellet quickly snapped his head forward with the attentiveness of a fighter pilot landing on an aircraft carrier during a raging storm. Pinching the joint between his fingers, he took two quick puffs and tried handing it back to Shaun without taking his eyes off the road.

"You're gonna have to do better than that, Bumpkin," Shaun said, without reaching for it. It seemed that Pellet had already been assigned a name that would probably stick with him for the duration of their time together. Against his better judgment he took a long drag, held it in as long as he could until he burst out into a coughing fit, and then handed it back to Shaun as he continued to struggle to prevent bringing them to a tragic end.

"Easy there, Bumpkin. I wouldn't want you to hurt yourself," he said, as he smoothly took another long drag and held it in his lungs, obviously savoring the moment not only for enjoying the smoke, but also for the satisfaction of showing Pellet just how it's done.

The minutes turned into miles, and the miles turned into more smoke. Somewhere along the line, Pellet commented it seemed like this joint was lasting forever.

Shaun laughed so hard he had tears running down his face and kept gasping for air. "Man, I gotta pee," he said as he tried to breathe, talk, and laugh, all while concentrating on not peeing his pants. Pellet had no idea what was so funny; but being stoned, he didn't have the need to know. He laughed just as hard as Shaun did until he finally composed himself long enough to ask what they found to be so hilarious.

"We've smoked three joints, man. You bumpkins must think us city folks have slow-burning pot and that our joints just keep going until we can't smoke anymore." He tried to compose himself and wipe the tears off his face.

Pellet sat for a moment as he tried to remember him lighting the other two joints, but his concentration was sporadic. He quickly moved on to thinking about something else. For the next fifteen minutes they rode in silence, interrupted only by the occasional "Man, I am stoned" coming from one of them, followed by "Yeah!" mumbled by the other. An abrupt end to the silence came when they both saw the big pink-and-white sign sticking high into the air at the end of the upcoming off-ramp.

"Dunkin' Donut!" Pellet yelled. He immediately hit the blinker.

Shaun quickly began reciting a list of great and

memorable places that could be compared to their destination. "Shangri La, Xanadu, Emerald City, Camelot... Dunkin' Donuts!" he proudly proclaimed in a tone that clearly stated that the last magical place on his list, at this very moment in time, ranked up there with all other mythical kingdoms of peace and harmony and joyful fulfillment.

Thirty seconds later, as they continued to drive toward the off-ramp, Pellet grinned and looked at Shaun. "Perhaps I put my blinker on just a tad early."

Once again, they both laughed so hard that when they finally reached the exit, Pellet had a difficult time turning off the highway and pulling into what at the time seemed to be the parking lot of Stoner Heaven.

They climbed out of the Bug and stumbled into the shop. The pimpled seventeen-year-old doughnut clerk looked at them, rolled his eyes and said, "Welcome to Dunkin' Donuts. How may I help you?"

"I'll take a large coffee with cream and sugar, one of those chocolate doughnuts, one of them jelly things, a dozen of the munchkins, and... that Boston cream thing right there on the end," Pellet said, pointing at the Boston cream thing. "Anything for you?" he said to Shaun with a classic stoner grin on his face.

Not to be outdone, Shaun ordered about as much as Pellet had ordered, except he got a large Frozen Mocha Coffee Coolatta topped off with whipped cream, in lieu of regular old coffee. After being handed two bags and large cups, they promptly headed out toward New York City, at a somewhat acceptable speed, while feasting on their junk food with lightning speed. Well, that is after they went back inside to pee, which was something they both forgot to do when they went in the first time.

It took a while, but eventually they came back down to the general vicinity of earth and began having a composed conversation once again. The Bug was now cruising along at a steady fifty-five mph; only slightly limping behind the flow of the neighboring traffic. Pellet's knuckles were no longer white from the perpetual death grip, and it seemed highly likely that he was not going to die in the Connecticut or New York traffic, at least not today.

"So what are the clubs like in New York? Must be pretty wild."

"Doubt they'd interest you much," Shaun responded, while looking out the passenger window.

Pellet's brain was not operating at peak efficiency and he didn't really give his answer much thought. Staying in his perpetually curious mode, he immediately moved on to the next question. "What else do you do? I mean, you can't hang out in clubs the whole weekend."

"You're a nosy little man, aren't you, Bumpkin?" He looked in the bag to see if there were any Munchkins left, then sighed in mild disappointment.

"I feel like we've bonded, Doc. After sharing a good smoke, wolfing down about a hundred and fifty thousand useless calories and a massive amount of sugar, there are simply no secrets between brothers like us," he mumbled, and watched the next trailer truck blow past them in the left passing lane. "But if you're going to start talking about that axe murder shit again, I've got to tell you, you freaked me out a little the first time around."

"If I tell you what I do in the city, you'll probably wish we were back on the axe murders."

"Well, if I'm safe, then lay it on me, but if you're going

to kill me or something... I'd just as soon not know."

"I'm going to the city to hook up with some friends, get another tattoo, and hang out at gay bars for the weekend," he answered, while looking directly at Pellet.

Pellet pondered: It wasn't like nobody had heard of gay people in the 1990s, and they were starting to move onto the edge of mainstream; on the other hand it wasn't like too many people in Waldoboro Maine were running around and bragging about being gay either. The problem was that Waldoboro hadn't yet moved onto the edge of mainstream.

"Tattoos and gay bars, huh? Well, Doc, I've got to tell you, I didn't see that one coming."

"Why's that?"

"Well, I suppose I didn't think about the tattoos because I can't see any tattoos. And the gay thing... I guess you're not acting gay enough for me to catch the tell tail signs. No pun intended," Pellet said with a sarcastic grin that unequivocally stated that the pun was indeed intended. His quick wit, and his ability to banter back and forth with the first gay guy that he'd ever hung out with, left him quite pleased with himself.

"You mean since I wasn't wearing frilly clothes and a boa, flailing my hands in the air, and singing 'YMCA,' you just presumed I was straight?"

"Exactly!" Pellet proclaimed with a grin of satisfaction on his face.

"Well, surprise, surprise, Bumpkin. We come in all shapes, sizes, and colors. Hell, *you* might even be gay and just don't know it yet." Shaun believed he could make Pellet feel more uncomfortable about the outside possibility of being gay than he did about the axe murderer thing.

"Well, I do get excited when I jerk off, and even though

I am technically sexually servicing a male, I have to say that as far as I can remember I have always thought about women when the deed was taking place. As a matter of fact, if I stopped long enough to think about my own body parts I am quite certain that I'd have difficulty performing... if you know what I mean. Does that qualify or disqualify me?"

Shaun sat looking out the passenger window again and thought for a minute without responding. He stared at some cows grazing in the field and momentarily lost track of the conversation, as he thought of the irony that those dumb creatures stood knee-deep in green grass, eating to their hearts' content, and getting fat for the sole purpose of becoming a hamburger patty. Then he began to wonder why it's called hamburger when clearly there was no ham involved in the process. He quickly deduced that once upon a time there must have been some poor pigs eating their way into blissful oblivion as they worked their way toward a hamburger bun covered with mustard and relish. Then of course he began to get hungry again. Once he had pondered this great mystery of the universe long enough, he drifted back to thinking about the conversation at hand. He was not as convinced as Pellet as to what Bumpkin's orientation might be, and Shaun felt at least a slight obligation to help his driver explore his true sexual identity.

"Holy shit," Pellet mumbled in mild disbelief. "I haven't even gotten past New York and I've experienced my first traffic jam, first rush-hour traffic, got stoned out of my gourd, and have made friends with a tattooed gay guy. Not bad for the first day. I wonder what's next?" Pellet asked of nobody in particular.

"The judge is still out on your sexual status," Shaun blurted out. "You country bumpkins are sometimes a bit slow to come around. Time will tell... time will tell," he said as an afterthought.

"Hey, have you ever considered that *I* might be an axe murderer?" Pellet asked in an attempt to make the situation uncomfortable for Shaun.

"Naw. No respectable axe murderer would drive a VW Bug. And besides, you couldn't even fit a decent size axe inside this car," he replied.

"Well then, maybe I'm a hatchet murderer."

"See, now you're just embarrassing yourself. If you keep this up, when it finally comes to you that you're gay, we're not going to let you come out of the closet for fear you'll cast shame onto the gay community. What would a hatchet murderer even be considered? A minor league axe murderer? Do they let anyone from the minor leagues actually kill anyone, or do you just get to scare people for a while until someone gives you the go-ahead to move up to the proper size weapon?" He jabbed with enough arrogance to send the message that he wasn't buying into Pellet's violent self-incrimination, not even as a joke.

"Since you got me stoned I guess I'll let you slide by without an attack. Looks like the hatchet gods are giving you a break today," Pellet added, as he chugged on toward New York City. Of course as always, stoned or not, he couldn't go too long without conversing, and as often is the case, this conversation should have fallen by the wayside.

"So you're into tattoos, huh?" There was no need to ask this question, and there was less reason for Shaun to answer it, but the ball was rolling forward again. "How many tats do you have?"

"Got a couple," he mumbled and said nothing more.

"How many is a couple?" Pellet persisted.

"According to Webster's it's two, so technically I guess I've got more than a couple," he said as he once again gazed out the passenger window, this time looking at a horse pasture, wondering if they would be called *hamburgers* also.

"Big ones? Little ones? Or what? Do you have a tattoo of a really good-looking gay guy on your bicep, sitting on a heart with an arrow through it? Maybe it says the guy's name under it?" he asked with another big grin on his face. Pellet continued to be pretty impressed with his gay wit, being that it was new to him. He supposed it was just his competitive nature, but he was fully determined to be a little quicker and wittier than Shaun.

"Yeah, I think it's a tattoo of your dad. It says Big Bumpkin right in the middle of a purple heart," he shot back, making it clear one more time that Pellet would not outgun him. This could have been and should have been the end of the conversation. Obviously Shaun was indifferent about discussing his tattoos, and it didn't seem like there was any point in trying to outwit him any longer, so one would think Bumpkin would have just let it go. It would have been a perfect time for peace and quiet.

"So, you gonna show me one or what?"

"Jesus Christ, man!" Shaun finally stopped looking out the window and looked toward him as if he were a parent who was irritated by a child that wouldn't sit still. "You're not what they'd call a laid-back stoner are you?" he asked.

"Well?" Pellet answered without hesitation.

"You want to see the smallest, the biggest, or the best tattoo?" he asked, as if they were on *Let's Make a Deal*.

The problem was Pellet didn't realize he was on a game show that he might regret playing, and more importantly there was a door that should have remained closed. "The best, man!

Always go with the best."

Shaun smiled a smile that should have announced, "Change your answer... Quick... Change your answer!" But like every other sign that had been sent his way over the past hour or so, Pellet missed it—except for the Dunkin' Donuts sign, of course.

The VW continued to chug down the road. Pellet waited for Shaun to show his *best* tattoo. Shaun was wiggling around in the cramped quarters as he fought with his denim jacket, pulling on the sleeves and trying to create enough space to slide it off one arm, then the other. What Pellet presumed he would do next was to either take off his shirt or roll up one of his sleeves, but he was wrong. As he drove on, Pellet felt a smidge of satisfaction that he had kept after him until he finally decided to show his tat. However, it appeared that once again, satisfaction might be short-lived and Shaun might once again have the upper hand, when it became clear that he was not taking off his shirt, but was pulling down his pants... underwear and all. A few minutes earlier Pellet was thinking quite highly of himself, since in his own mind he had suddenly become an open-minded and worldly man who could comfortably not only accept, but also befriend, a gay man riding in his car. Of course, when he was feeling confident about his newly discovered enlightenment, Shaun was wearing pants and underwear.

"What the hell you doing?" he asked, feeling a little of that axe murderer paranoia returning once again.

"Showing you my *best* tattoo," Shaun answered with his Dean, Bond, Pitt smile on his face.

"Where the hell is this tattoo?" The words came out of his mouth and hung in the air as if God himself had reached down and momentarily frozen time. Before Shaun could even think about shooting his next sharp comeback, Pellet's eyes widened and he seemed to forget he was driving.

"Holy mother of... what the hell is that?" The Bug must have been on autopilot because it seemed like an eternity from the time he looked down at Shaun's crotch until the next time that he looked back up at the busy highway. His driving had apparently improved, because he could now manage to drive down the road in heavy traffic with absolutely no awareness of the road or those around him.

"I know things are probably different up in Bumpkin Land, but I'm certain that you guys have penises. Don't you?" he replied, as he sat in the passenger seat with his dick in his hand.

"Hey, I got a penis, but it doesn't look anything like that monstrosity. Holy shit, are all you gay guys hung like that?" The question sounded as stupid to Pellet as it did to Shaun, but he was in shock and couldn't help himself. He couldn't even begin to imagine how many inches the thing was, and it dawned on him that he probably didn't want to know. But that curiosity thing was spinning again. If he felt a little inadequate at first glance, one could only imagine how nebbish he would feel once it was confirmed that Shaun's penis was two and a half times the size of Pellet's.

***

Desmund, who had been sitting on the serving side of the bar and smoking cigarettes for the past half-hour while Pellet spun the story of how the journey started off, awkwardly began to sit up a little straighter. He cocked his head to one side, while looking at him as if there might be a bird or something sitting on top of Pellet's head getting ready to take a shit. He was wondering if there was something about Pellet that he had never realized, and certainly had never thought to ask. First there was his drunken escapade a few nights ago when he kissed some tourist guy, and now this. Desmund was bracing himself for a twist to the story that he just didn't see coming. If the story had ended with Pellet befriending a bunch of gay guys and partying all night in the gay bars of New York City, leaving him with a bunch of colorful gay-bar stories, Desmund would have smiled and said, "Great start to your trip, huh?" But right now the story was hanging in limbo with Pellet in absolute awe of Shaun, who was half naked with his huge penis in his hand in the passenger seat of the little car. After a few more moments of awkwardly looking at Pellet, Desmund took a deep breath and asked what happened next. Pellet motioned for another beer, lit another cigarette, and continued.

After the initial shock of realizing that Shaun was pant-less and had a dick the size of a horse it had finally dawned on Pellet that there was something even more bizarre about *it*, other than its size.

"Remember... this story was leading up to showing his best tattoo. Well, in case you haven't guessed it yet... *it* was tattooed."

"Get da hell outta here," Desmund said in disbelief.

"I'm telling you, the whole damn thing was one big tattoo that probably took a gallon of ink to create. From one end to the other there were tiny scales, colored lines going around the thing every inch or so, and finally, when it got all the way up to the head, there were two little beady eyes staring up at me. And from what I could see, it was a pretty damn good tattoo."

"What da hell you talkin about? A tattoo of what?"

"It was a snake, man! A Goddamn snake! Done to

perfection right down to every scale, stripe, crease, eyes, and last but not least, fangs."

"On his cock?" Desmund nearly yelled. A tourist on the other side of the bar gave them a strange look.

"Damn right. And the eyes and shit were on the head of his dick."

***

As the VW continued to chug down the road, Shaun sat motionlessly looking at Pellet, clearly pleased with himself as it became obvious the battle of uneasiness was over; he had won by a landslide. Pellet stared and drove in silence for a long time, when Shaun finally reminded him that he had better at least occasionally glance up at the road.

"A snake?" Pellet rhetorically asked.

"ANACONDA!" Shaun bellowed as if he were announcing the arrival of a superhero. His trance, finally broken, was reduced to frequent glances between ANACONDA and the highway. The steady stream of questions had stopped, as he tried to absorb what had been revealed to him.

"You tattooed your thing?" Pellet finally blurted out.

"ANACONDA!" he bellowed once more in a proclamation of pride.

Pellet shook his head in disbelief as the two continued to sit beside each other with Shaun's pants and underwear pulled down to his knees. Eventually Pellet's mind began to process what was lying in the lap just one seat over, and once again the questions began to formulate in his already overwhelmed head. First he wondered, Who would tattoo a penis? Then he thought, he supposed it would be a gay tattoo artist, but then again, maybe it was just some straight guy who was real good at what he did, and didn't mind holding a guy's penis while he worked on it. The next thing he wondered was whether it was hard or soft when the tattoo was being done. It would seem like if he was gay and some guy was holding his thing in his hand while an electronic tool was vibrating against it, he would probably be hard. But tattoos are supposed to be painful so maybe it wasn't hard... unless the guy was into pain. He thought all of this to himself as his face contorted and showed all the signs of someone who was silently asking countless strange questions of himself, then silently answering them as best he could. Suddenly his eyebrows rose up as the next question jumped into his head. With all the holding, stroking, and vibrating, he wondered, did *Anaconda* spew venom as it was being created? If it did, did the tattoo artist like it or did he charge even more than he originally quoted due to unforeseen complications and a mess that needed to be cleaned up. In complete exasperation he looked over at Shaun, then shrugged and laughed, "I got nothing," he said, shaking his head.

"In that case I'll presume you're impressed with my tattoo and I'll put my pants back on," he said with a smile of satisfaction.

Pellet may have been awestruck up to this point in time, but as Shaun thrust his hips into the air with his penis flopping around as he pulled up his pants, for the first time since he revealed his... stuff, Pellet felt completely uncomfortable. He cringed sheepishly.

"Hey... keep that thing over there. I don't want to get snake bit."

"It seems you may not belong in my closet after all," Shaun said as he zipped up his jeans.

"That's quite a tattoo, but I'm confident I won't be petting your snake anytime soon."

"So what do you think?" Now Shaun was enjoying asking the questions.

"I think if you got any more pot you'd better fire up another one. That thing more or less killed my buzz."

Once again, Shaun flipped a joint into his mouth and quickly lit it. Smoke rolled up in the air and filled the car. All that Pellet could think was, "Man, what a first day."

Shaun looked toward him, handed over the joint, and to Pellet's surprise, said, "Bond, James Bond," as if he knew what he'd had been thinking a while back. For a moment Pellet froze and looked at him as if he were asking, "How the hell would you know what I was thinking?" It took a minute for him to recall he'd called him Bond somewhere during the first round of smoke, before they'd made the Dunkin' Donuts pit stop.

***

A tropical breeze blew through the bar and by now Pellet had long forgotten that he had come to the Hut for the sole purpose of wallowing in self-pity. Desmund had long forgotten that the story had started because he was trying to cheer up his friend and frequent customer. Seemed Dez's mission was accomplished.

"So what da hell happened?" he asked, making it clear that Pellet had left him in limbo.

"What do you mean?"

"Wit da gay guy? Anaconda? New York City?" he blurted out in exasperation.

"Oh... that. We drove a while longer, then pulled off at some rest stop along I-84 and he called a friend to come pick him up. An hour and one more joint later, they asked if I wanted to party with them, but I'd had enough for the first day. I drove a couple more hours and crashed for the night in a rest area."

"Holy shit," Desmund mumbled.

"Oh yeah, there's one more thing."

"Good God," Desmund said in exasperation.

"When Shaun was leaving, just before he climbed into his friend's car, he stopped and yelled, 'Hey, Bumpkin!' When I turned to see what he wanted, he reached into his backpack and pulled out a hatchet and waved it in the air like some sort of crazy guy. By that time, I just shrugged and shook my head."

Desmund sat in stunned disbelief.

It was getting late. Once again Pellet had had enough to drink, plus a couple of extras for good measure. He tossed some money on the bar then nodded at Desmund and another couple sitting at the end of the bar before he wandered up the long driveway toward the road. He strolled beneath the starlit Caribbean sky and smiled at the thought of Shaun yelling "ANACONDA" all those years ago. For a moment he wondered whatever happened to him and wondered if he survived the AIDS onslaught that had likely taken so many of Shaun's friends. Then once again, he quickly flashed back to him yelling "ANACONDA!" Pellet laughed out loud and blew cigarette smoke into the warm night air. He continued to smile until his face hurt from smiling so much.

"ANACONDA!" he yelled loudly as he strolled beneath the Caribbean stars.

Chapter Four

The End of the Beginning

Three years after being introduced to and parting ways with Anaconda, Pellet sat on the back veranda of the small single-level Florida home on the outskirts of Royal Palm Beach where he had lived since arriving in the Sunshine State. As it turned out, Royal Palm Beach did not actually have a beach any more than Waldoboro Maine did; nevertheless, it was warmer than Maine and the construction work was better than the factory work. The women? If they weren't better, at least there were more of them, making the odds of having an actual relationship, and sex, slightly better than in Waldoboro. To top things off, he had nothing to go back to Maine for. Like most northerners who stray into the far southern stretches of America, he came to Florida and he stayed in Florida, for a time.

He sat in a foldup lawn chair, the kind with the plastic straps for a seat, and had his feet propped up on another as he methodically popped Peanut M&Ms into his mouth. He chomped on each M&M until it was gone, then tossed another in, and chomped again like a cow feeding in a pasture, while he blankly stared out at the long grass. Pellet looked down at his flabby bare belly that hung over the belt of his raggedy cargo shorts, then rubbed it in slight disgust that he had put on at least ten pounds over the past four or five months. A few too many beers, too much sitting in front of the TV, with way too little exercise of any kind, including in the bedroom, had begun to take its toll.

Zoe, the woman he once thought to be the love of his life, his faithful wife, mother of his child, and the woman whose love and tenderness had won his heart only two years ago, stuck her head out the sliding glass door and snapped at him, "I thought you were going to mow the grass."

"I'm going to do it in a while," he mumbled without looking away from the grass that he had no intention of mowing.

"And you're going to finally fix this damn door today?" she snapped again, as she fought to close the slider that was sticking just like it had for the past six months.

"Yup, gonna fix that right after I mow the grass," he replied.

What Pellet was in fact going to do on this particularly hot, muggy Florida day was exactly what he had been quietly planning for the past two months. About fifteen minutes from now Zoe was going to leave for work. When that happened, he was going into the bedroom to throw a few things into a duffle bag, the same duffle bag that he tossed into the back of the VW a few years ago. Then he was calling a taxi to take him to the airport. Just before walking out of the house he was going to drop an envelope on the kitchen counter with Zoe's name on it, and he was going to lay his keys and his cell phone on top of the envelope. After that, he was walking out the door, out of her life, and would not be looking back. The Florida years—which turned out to be far more interesting yet considerably more painful than all his years in Maine—were coming to an end. Pellet was heading to a job in the Caribbean and taking one more step closer to his antipodal point.

A few minutes later Zoe came back to the porch with their seven-month-old son, who was half dressed, crying, and thrashing about in her arms.

"I'm heading to work and dropping Justin off at Mama's house. I told her you'd pick him up around five. Be on time for a change, please," she snapped. "I'm getting tired of constantly apologizing because you screwed up again." Without a kiss, or "I love you," or even feigning the slightest bit of intimacy, she slammed the door and headed off to work.

***

Around midnight Zoe whipped her car into the driveway and stomped into the house, slamming the door behind her, ready for a blowout. Justin was spending the night with his grandmother, and Zoe expected an answer from Pellet as to why he didn't pick up his son—or even answer his phone for the past six hours. His truck was parked next to the curb in front of the completely dark house when she got home. Without slowing down when she stormed through the front door, she switched on the entryway light as she goose-stepped straight for their bedroom. To her surprise he was not in bed, and his dresser drawers were open and empty. She momentarily stood looking around the room like a confused puppy that was watching itself in the mirror for the first time. Then she wandered back to the kitchen where she found the letter, keys and phone. She opened the letter and began reading it. None of it seemed to quite register until after she read the last line.

Zoe,

We've had some ups and downs over the past couple of years, but it's all gone to shit now, hasn't it. I've known for a long time that you make a lot more money then you let on, but I justified it in my head by telling myself that you're just looking out for yourself. Can't hold that against you, I suppose. As it turns out, I suspect trust is not one of your stronger traits. A few months ago someone whispered in my ear I might want to get a paternity test to ensure that my son is in fact, my son. Guess what, Justin seems like a great kid, but he's not mine as you can confirm by the paternity results I left under your pillow. I thought you and his dad might want to share the results the next time you're screwing him in my bed. You wore me out just about everywhere except the bedroom, but no more. I'm done, I'm gone, and I won't be back.

With Warmest Regards,
Pellet

He had considered telling her to be good to Justin or to give him a hug and kiss on his behalf, but then he decided it would be pretty weak to walk out of the kid's life but whisper "I love you" on the way out the door. So instead, he just left and hoped Justin's life didn't suck too bad with the selfish bitch he had for a mother. He also considered telling her to go to hell, but decided against that as it would be a waste of good ink and precious time. Besides, she'd probably take a small amount of pleasure in knowing he was irritated enough to swear at her.

Zoe stood in the kitchen with her mouth hanging open. "Son of a bitch!" she said, to nobody. It had never entered her mind that she might actually get caught being a lying, she-devil. Of course she didn't bother to check the paternity test results. She already knew that Ron, one of the bartenders from work, was Justin's father, and she knew she was going to have to take him to court if she hoped to get child support. Ron was not the easy target Pellet had been. As she slumped against the kitchen counter, her mind was numb.

***

Meanwhile, Pellet was sitting at Da Limin Hut in Anguilla sipping on a beer. He hadn't felt this weightless in years.

The first beer went down quickly and he motioned to Desmund for another.

Desmund, always good at reading customers, didn't take Pellet to be a tourist. "Jus visiting?" he asked.

"No, just got here today. Starting work at the Blue Wave Project in a couple of days," Pellet answered.

"OK, OK. Dat's cool. Be seein you around, den." Desmund set the beer on the bar top and reached to shake hands with his new regular. The construction expats usually got paid good money and a lot of them had little intention of taking much of it with them when they left. They worked hard and played hard. That was just fine with Desmund and all the other bar owners on the island.

"Dey call me Desmund," he said as they shook hands.

"They call me Pellet."

"Pellet?" he asked with a puzzled look on his face.

"Yup, that's it. Pellet," he answered, picking up his new beer.

"Like a goat turd?" he blurted back, still looking confused by the name.

"What?"

"You know, goat turds are like... little pellets. Dat da kind of pellet we be talking bout?"

"I suppose my life has been like a goat turd for a while

48

now, but I think things are beginning to look up, so I'm afraid not. I'm talking about Pellet, short for Pelletier. Wayne Pelletier," he answered, still a little surprised by the question. "So, there are a lot of goats and goat turds on the island?" Pellet asked.

"Ya, mon. Good eatin." Desmund smiled.

Pellet sat looking at the Rasta bartender and cocked his head to one side, but didn't respond for a few seconds. Clearly there were a lot of things he was going to have to learn.

"Goat turds?" Pellet asked, then straightened up and set his beer back down.

"What?"

"You eat goat turds here?"

"No, mon! Don't nobody eats no damn goat turds. What da hell is wrong wit you, mon? You eat turds where you're from?" Desmund asked with a tone of sarcasm.

Pellet smiled and looked a little relieved. For just a moment he thought maybe he had gotten into more than he had anticipated.

"No... we don't eat turds either. Guess we're on the same page with that, huh?"

Desmund walked away to attend to other customers while Pellet sat and began to reflect on the past few years of his life. He thought about the cold rainy months in Waldoboro and the endless days at the eraser factory. He laughed to himself when he recalled finding out that his antipodal point was in the middle of the Antarctic. Then he got sad thinking about when he first found out that Justin was not his son. He held him for hours that night and cried while Zoe was at work—or maybe she was off screwing Ron, for all he knew. Pellet had been so proud to become a father, and as much as he wanted to stick around for the boy's sake, he knew it wouldn't work. The smile returned to his face when he looked down at his watch and realized Zoe had come home by now and was probably standing in the kitchen with the letter in her hand at this very moment. She was going to be pissed. Since he was not there to receive the brunt of it, it made him feel good.

For the first time in a long, long time, Pellet felt at peace. Everything seemed to feel right, as though he had finally found the place on earth where he belonged. For his entire life he had felt as if he was always in the wrong place at the wrong time. But not now. Not here. His mind began to wander and he searched for words that would describe exactly how he was feeling, when Desmund walked back over to him.

"Everyting cool?" he asked.

Pellet looked at him as a smile came to his face. "Yeah, man. Everything is very cool," he answered.

Pellet was home, and he knew it.

CHAPTER FIVE

HELMUT BRANDT (PART 1)

Old, smoothly worn dominos slapped loudly on the rickety weather-beaten table as four island men played an afternoon game which had lasted the better part of their lives. They gulped beer while they intermittently ranted and mumbled about how much better island life used to be back when they were young island boys. Never once did they consider that almost everyone's life was better when they were children, no matter where one spent their childhood days. For all intents and purposes, a child's world is quintessentially far better than the world created by grownups. Innocence lost and all that stuff. But the old saying, *Youth is wasted on the young,* did not appear to apply to this particular situation, which in itself was not all that unusual in the Caribbean. One of the good things about island life was that a significant number of the men, locals and expats alike, wasted much of their adulthood with the same joyful naiveté as they wasted on their youth. When they were boys, they wanted to be men. Yet now that they had become men, they all continued living the carefree demeanor of island boys—with no sign of making a change any time in the foreseeable future. It often appeared that the only difference between island boys and island men was height, weight, perhaps a few gray hairs, weathered skin, and whiskers.

Chatta, the oldest of them, the one who rarely shut up, sat with a domino in one hand and tugged his scraggly gray beard with the other. He had earned his nickname fifty years ago for obvious reasons, and with a huge victory smile on his face,

51

he slammed a white square of ivory down on the table as if driving a nail with a mighty hammer.

"Take that n' stop ya whining, ya lil babies. Young, old... it don't matta. Either way, I be beatin you at da domino table since da beginning of time!" The other three men laughed, talked some trash talk, as they began mixing the dominos for the next game just like they had done an hour ago, yesterday, last week, last year, and as far back as any of them could recall.

The afternoon heat lingered in the air without enough breeze to move a single palm. A short, solid-looking white man in his mid-thirties, who could have easily passed for his mid-forties, sat at the same corner table where he sat almost every afternoon. On the left side of the table there was an ever-present glass filled with melting ice topped with a slice of lime. His laptop sat directly in front of him, and a satchel containing writing tablets and pens stuffed inside its pockets sat in one of the empty chairs. A worn and nearly full Moleskin journal lay open beside the laptop, with a pen lying on the half-filled page where he had just finished adding a note. From his vantage point in the corner of the open-air bar, he sporadically watched people as they busied themselves doing what people do in island bars. Giving them only a little attention, he listened as they laughed, and cried, and romanced in the island way. But mostly he wrote, and he wrote incessantly. He watched, he listened, he wrote, he thought, he edited, and then he did it all some more. This is what he did late in the afternoon, every day of every week.

Locals barely noticed the well-tanned German who had spent so much time blending into the woodwork that he had more or less become part of the Hut décor. The chairs were old, the wobbly tables were covered with white tablecloths that hid the scratched and weathered tops, and Helmut Brandt sat in his corner wearing cargo shorts, sandals, and a colorful T-shirt as if he had long ago been placed there by an interior decorator who wanted to give the bar an Ernest Hemingway look. And as always, the Moleskin and the laptop were being filled with thoughts, stories, poems, notes, and irrelevant drivel. It was widely believed by most who knew him that there was more drivel than anything else.

Desmund paid little attention to the semi-permanent figure who wasn't a big spender, but who consistently spent just enough to cover the rent on his second home in the musty corner. The German always started off with ice and lime, which was free, but sooner or later he moved on to beer, along with something to eat. A couple of times a week, he had two, or perhaps three, glasses of Chianti. The writer was cordial enough to say hello, but rarely sociable enough to strike up an actual conversation with anybody. Even though nobody knew what he wrote, there were volumes of it that were growing by the day. If a passerby happened to be intrusive enough to ask what was going into the volumes of journals and what perchance was being tapped interminably into his laptop, he simply smiled and said, "It's personal," then returned to his writing with no further acknowledgement of their existence. Truth be told, the only two things anyone knew of him was that he was a German who wrote a lot, and he had worked as an engineer in Anguilla for a while now. Most noticeably, he apparently didn't feel the need to enlighten anyone about any of the details of his past life.

***

Helmut Brandt was the only child of a father who was a renowned neurologist and a mother who was an electrical engineer of solid reputation in Hamburg, Germany. His childhood days had been highly structured and obsessively motivated. He lived under the constant pressure of the great expectation that he would one day surpass one or both of his parents on the intellectual scale of life. He would dazzle the academic world with his quite predictable and genetically acquired brilliance. Both of his parents believed, or at least hoped, he would one day academically and intellectually rule the scientific world like some sort of divine cerebral being from the Fatherland.

As it turned out, despite their best efforts, the experiment showed no notable success. Both parents lamented for years about the apparent failure of their attempt to give Helmut, their one and only living legacy, the cranial jump-start that they both agreed was much needed. They forever clung to the idea that, if they had found a way to begin the boy's education nine months before he first breathed fresh German air, he would have likely surpassed Albert Einstein's noteworthy intellect. In the end, Helmut did not surpass him.

While he may not have achieved the level of academic grandeur that his rigid, emotionally desolate parents might have hoped for when the less than romantic act of combining the genetic fluids of two intellectual freaks of nature first took place, he was not a raving dimwit either. That fact did not stop his father from, at one point, considering using his son as the basis for a study to explain how combining the reproductive products of two academic gifts from God—not that the German neurologist believed in any god—could come up with a product that was only slightly above average. The good doctor could not wrap his head around the possibility that the result of creating this boy was less than the sum of the two donors' IQs. After conferring with his colleagues, he decided the study would have likely been tainted due to the father-son relationship, and he moved on to other research projects outside of his genetic pool. Helmut would have likely testified that there was absolutely *no* father-son relationship to taint the study. However, since he didn't want to be emotionally, physically, and mentally probed and prodded in order to explain his supposed intellectual deficiency, he let the matter take its natural course and go away.

His mother, every bit as loving and supportive as his anally rigid father, left their new son of yet unknown mental capacity in the loving hands of Helga, his nanny, from the ripe old age of two weeks. Helga, a consummate professional, was efficient, clean, obedient, and punctual. She ensured that the boy completed all required task such as his studies, sports, and whatever else was placed in his highly structured life, on time and to a satisfactory level. Those early years were the formative years of his life when he learned all things, big and small, that his parents and Helga believed he needed to know. The things he did not learn to do were to love, to feel, or to express emotion in any manner whatsoever, other than to work harder and focus more on the task at hand. What he learned about emotions was that they were altogether counterproductive; more important than suppressing them, he should completely avoid having them at all, a feat that both his parents had apparently mastered. While Helga did quite well at suppressing most of her own emotions, she frequently displayed just enough anger to make Helmut aware that he was straying outside the emotional and intellectual lines that were the prison walls of his world.

It was the belief of the Brandts that emotions were nothing more than a psychiatric roller coaster that would in no way encourage intellectual growth or academic excellence. They firmly believed that within the general human population, emotional highs were always followed by harrowing lows. Lows eventually returned to highs, and in between there were miniscule glimpses of the normality separating the highs and lows where a young boy could be efficiently productive. It was their extraordinarily educated opinion that people were not productive during high periods because they were experiencing euphoria and they were too happy to feel the need to accomplish anything. This type of joy was simply not acceptable. They also believed people were unproductive in painful low periods because once the roller-coaster mentality was the chosen path, people spent far too much of their time and effort trying to pull themselves out of the deep emotional valleys that quite predictably followed the euphoric highs. Flat line was the way to go. Steady and even, not too low, not too high, never happy and never sad. The Brandt version of the desired emotional pinnacle of life was summed up in the phrase, "Always keep steady and remain focused on the task at hand." From the very beginning of his life, this mantra is what they instructed Helga to drive into their son's head, and she was more than willing to comply with the orders from above. From the time of his birth until he was thirteen years old and sent off to Heidelberg Military Academy for Boys, a very expensive, very exclusive private school that was slightly less structured than a Nazi indoctrination camp, "Always keep steady and remain focused on the task at hand" was everything Helmut had learned about how to cope with feelings, emotions, and love.

The Academy, of course, was not a place where young men were encouraged to blossom emotionally or express themselves, anymore than Helmut was encouraged to do so at his boyhood home. It was a military academy where the importance of standing in a straight line, doing what he was told to do, and being a good little soldier and student were his only real purposes in life. At eighteen years old, after a lifetime of pretending that passion, heartache, euphoria, and misery were states of mind that one chose to have or not have, Helmut Brandt graduated from the military academy and headed off to the University of Freiberg to begin work on his Engineering degree. Filled with an endless stream of book knowledge, a work ethic that was second to none, slightly above average intelligence, and absolutely no idea how to cope with the world filled with love, hate, joy and pain, Helmut continued his education. He would soon find out that the real world was not as emotionally sanitary or controlled as his parents, Helga, and the Heidelberg Military Academy for Boys had led him to believe.

At the University, life took its natural course; he was introduced to all things his parents believed to be unproductive and wasteful. Helmut drank to excess, vomited on his shoes, passionately vowed to never do it again, and quite naturally did it a few more times before graduation day. He dabbled in pot every now and then, but smoking made him feel much too lethargic. It was in total conflict with the years of being indoctrinated into a world of hard work and efficiency. Last but not least, Helmut discovered women while in college, and more than alcohol or pot or any other possible catalyst to the emotional roller coaster of life, women seemed to be an area that could cause a problem for him in his never-ending quest to remain steady and focused on the task at hand. At the very least, they clouded the issue of what the actual task may be.

Helmut was a small but muscular German boy with the typical blond hair and blue eyes. He was good looking, smarter than most of the guys he hung out with, surprisingly creative given his excessively structured past, but most importantly in the world of male/female relationships, he had "it." Whatever "it" was, the girls gravitated to this quiet, shy boy who didn't seem to fit any description one might apply to a young man who always had an attractive girl at his side. He wasn't what one might call physically sexy; he didn't ooze charisma; he didn't wine and dine and dance his way into their hearts or, more to the point, into their beds. In the end, he didn't usually affect their hearts all that much and they rarely sparked his heart one little bit, but they always ended up between the sheets. And Helmut, ever disciplined to remain steady and focused on the task at hand, consistently left his partners smiling and satisfied with the results of a job well done. Good conversation, good sex, and good relationships on a casual level filled his college years. Studying was so easy for him it often seemed as if he had gone to college to have a constant stream of sex partners, while studying was just something he did to fill the time between the blondes, brunettes, redheads, and all other shades imaginable.

Only once during his time at the University did he become emotionally attached to any of the girls he had befriended. Only once did he actually discover someone he could more or less refer to as a girlfriend. Inga was a tall beauty from Sweden who had surprisingly sparked Helmut's heart, or at least that was what he had thought, from the first time they kissed. They laughed together, ate together, had lots of sex together; and for the first time in his life, Helmut believed he had become emotionally attached to another human being. When she walked into the room his spirits lifted. When they kissed he found himself enjoying the passionate pleasure of her taste, the texture of her lips, and the feel of her tongue against his mouth—far more than simply concentrating on being a thorough and considerate lover. Their lovemaking came naturally, with no effort whatsoever. They satisfied each other's desires, leaving each other breathless and covered in sweat as they lay in bed, drifting off into the warm peace of sexual satisfaction.

Then one chilly November afternoon he skipped his advanced calculus class and wandered back to his dorm room to find her in bed with his roommate.

Inga was horrified to see him. She knew she was his first love; and not only had she betrayed him, but he'd caught her in the act.

Helmut's roommate, an arrogant lacrosse boy, rolled over and leaned his back against the wall, keenly aware that this was probably going to get ugly pretty damn fast. He could handle himself in a fight, but he knew that Helmut was tough and would likely inflict some damage. In his head, the roommate considered what he would do if Helmut charged him; he was well aware that his balls and penis were in full view, and fair game if a fight broke out under these circumstances. He momentarily considered covering his groin with his hands, but then decided that he shouldn't draw any extra attention to this region of his body at this point in time.

"Hey man..." Jock Boy mumbled as he looked toward Helmut, but not directly into his eyes, as if eye contact might inflame the situation.

There was an awkward stillness as Helmut stood looking at his two naked friends, one with high-spirited nipples on her small, perfect breasts, and the other with a quickly dying hard-on, with both betrayers half covered in a white sheet. The room was tense as they waited to see what was going to happen. After ten seconds of silence that seemed like an eternity, Inga began to speak. With her young breasts exposed and only one leg covered by the linen, her ivory white skin gave her the appearance of being an angel who was blushing with shame. She stared in shock at Helmut. She glanced at the roommate as if to ask what they were supposed to do—and quickly realized that she no longer mattered to him. From the look on his face, defending himself was the only concern on his mind. Finally she hung her head in shame as she looked down at the sheets and awkwardly caught a glimpse of the once hard penis that she did not quite get the chance to experience.

"Helmut, I am so sorry. We didn't mean for this to happen." She was being honest on her own behalf, but the roommate of course had wanted it to happen from the first time Helmut had brought her back to the room. She paused for a moment and then started to speak again.

Helmut held up his hand. "I'm going to grab some schnitzel and a beer. You guys want to come along?" he asked, very matter-of-factly. He surprised himself, not with the question, but with the absence of the pain, which he presumed would have been the correct feeling in this situation. He'd believed he had found someone he actually bonded with emotionally. He thought he had stepped into a world that was unknown to him; a relationship that would consist of the highs and lows that he was so aggressively warned to stay away from, a relationship where lows would surely come and he would have to expend precious time and energy climbing out of the dreaded, painful valleys. Much to his surprise, and even more to the surprise of Inga and his roommate, he did not feel the heartbreak that he expected to feel. He did not experience the sense of betrayal by finding the woman, the girl, he thought he loved in the arms of another. And perhaps most disappointing to Helmut, he realized she was just another girl in a long line of girls he had a good time with. She was a better time than he had had with others, but still she was just another good-time girl. What he did feel was hunger mixed with a mild thirst for a good German beer. So as the two unfaithful friends sat staring at him with puzzled looks on their faces, with breast and genitals exposed, Helmut said, "Well, schnitzel. Yes or no?"

Inga had never been so callously disregarded in her life. She was sitting naked on a bed, still half wrapped in a sheet, with her boyfriend's roommate. And she was hurt. She tried to figure out why Helmut didn't love her enough to be heartbroken, or at least saddened, when she cheated on him. She looked at him with a puzzled look on her face, curiously wondering why he was not even mildly irritated by the event. To this question, she would not find an answer. She could not know that he wasn't capable of being in love or having his heart broken. Whether the Brandt ancestry had actually managed to genetically remove the love gene from his DNA, or whether he had simply never learned to love anyone or anything, didn't seem to matter all that much. The powerful truth manifested itself in complete emptiness. As far as Helmut was concerned, there was nothing to date that resembled even a trace of evidence that he was capable of an emotional commitment that could make the angels sing or cry. He had mastered all the mechanics, but none of the passion. Strangely enough, it was his lack of ability to have his heart broken that disturbed him—much more than finding Inga in all her nakedness entwined with Jock Boy.

"I'll wait for you outside, OK?" he said as he turned and walked back out the door he had just entered.

"What the hell was that?" Inga asked the roommate after Helmut closed the door.

"I think he was giving us his blessing. Shall we get back

to business?"

Inga paid no attention to his weak effort to restore the sexual energy. She climbed out of bed and slid her panties on and reached for her T-shirt. In a strange twist of events, it seemed the unexpected reaction, or lack thereof, from Helmut had broken Inga's heart just a little bit. For the first time since she had met him she realized that perhaps Helmut was special. He was different from the other boys.

University life continued for Helmut in the same steady manner for the next three years. Classes, girls, sex, skiing, some drinking, an occasional trip to visit the mausoleum he referred to as *home* to spend some time with the undertakers he referred to as his *parents*. Then without fanfare or any great expectation for his future, graduation day arrived. He did not surpass the academic excellence of either of his parents, and he certainly didn't surpass the genius of Albert Einstein. Even though they attended his graduation, Mother Engineer and Father Neurologist sat in the back row and kept their heads low, concealing their mild shame and embarrassment, and not so mild disappointment in their only son. Late in the afternoon on a damp, cloudy Freiberg day, Helmut Brandt walked onto the stage, grasped his diploma which he had been forever informed would be the ticket to his future, and walked off. He wondered if work would be as unfulfilling as his college classes, and if women of the world would be as enjoyable as the girls at the university.

After graduation Helmut pulled a monotonous stint as a junior engineer working for a small firm in Berlin. For two long years he endured the mind-numbing months of calculating the bearing loads of I-beams for office buildings that were soon to be built. These buildings would be filled with cubicles and human mice scampering around in mazes, doing whatever it is that office people do. The absurdity of it all hit him one day, as he realized he was designing cubes filled with cubicles exactly like the one he dreaded working in each and every day of his uneventful life. After sipping the last few drops of his morning coffee, Helmut quietly slipped out the back door into the alley and did not return. Within a month he took a job with another engineering firm in Pula, Yugoslavia. This is where he first fell in love. This is where his emotions were born, and this is where his spirit died.

CHAPTER SIX

HELMUT BRANDT (PART 2)

In those days Yugoslavia was at war. While much of the country was trying to survive through the dark days of death and blood and bombs, Pula was left in an awkward peace, which is often the norm for cities and towns that lie just outside the fringes of hell. While it would have been an exaggeration to say Pula was continuing a normal existence, it was still a relatively safe place to live, all things considered. Like all wars that had come before it, this war would end someday. When the end arrived, there would be businessmen who had positioned themselves to move the new nation forward and to do what businessmen do: make money. During the war these men could be found in Pula while bombs were flying and blood was spilling not far to the east.

Helmut went to work for a company that designed warehouses and apartment complexes that were to be used by refugees who migrated from the war-torn parts of Yugoslavia. During the day he worked hard and enjoyed the challenges his new job brought to him. He relished the excitement of surviving and thriving in the outskirts of such a turbulent place. In the evenings he ate, drank, and dallied about at the Barcelona Bar, just a short walk from his apartment. As he sat in the bar smoking cigarettes, he saw what he considered to be the real world with real people who had real problems and true passions for the first time in his life. This is where he met Samira.

Women in Pula were not all that different from women in Germany, as far as Helmut could tell. They were short, tall;

fat, skinny; smart, not so smart; friendly, unsociable; good in bed, or not so much. They were women just like all the other women he had ever known. He liked them, he enjoyed them; as always, there was a steady stream of them. One-night stands were the most common, with a relationship thrown in every now and then that lasted one or two weeks. They lasted as long as both of them were enjoying the sex and not complicating their lives. The women were almost always someone he met at the Barcelona Bar, and the relationships never seemed to end badly. In truth, they never really had an end. They just were what they were; then they weren't.

From the time they opened until the time they closed, all of the bars in Pula were filled with cigarette smoke thick enough to asphyxiate non-smoking humans. Helmut sat at a corner table of the smoky bar and sipped a locally brewed version of Budweiser as he chewed on a panino and scribbled notes in his Moleskin. He had kept a journal off and on over the past few years, but before landing in Pula he had often gone weeks at a time without writing a word. But things were different in Pula. From the first time he sat and drank in the dirty, rundown bay-front bar, he began writing prolifically, while soldiers, women, and dockworkers hovered, smoked, and drank in search of at least a temporary reprieve from their brownish-gray reality. He thought, perhaps for the first time in his life, he was in a place that was worthy of recording.

Days, work, women, cigarettes, beer, and writing came and went in a steady, uneventful stream—until she appeared. Hung-over days followed by mind-numbing evenings at the bar, followed by sweaty nights with passionate women whose names he could not or chose not to remember, led to more hung over days at work. For a time, this was the norm; all in all, he had no real complaints other than moaning and groaning about the self-inflicted alcohol-related sufferings. While Pula was a glimmer of hope in an otherwise bleak and bloody country, it was still a dirty suburb in a nation busying itself with the cruel business of war. War had brought out the best in writers since the first war and writers consummated this cruel marriage thousands of years ago. Helmut seemed no different from the countless writers of days gone by, who found inspiration in the most destructive acts of mankind. Suffering and death seemed to inspire words of wisdom that created lines of hope. Death, it seemed, created life, or at least it did in the written word. The soulless vacuum of war inspired heart-felt passion.

As soon as he met her, he realized Samira was a solitary daffodil surrounded by all things dark and dirty and lifeless. She was hope where there was no reason to have hope, love in the face of logic, forgiveness of the unforgiveable, beauty and life in an otherwise ugly scene of pain and suffering. She was the anti-Helmut. She believed in everything. He believed in nothing. Where he consisted of the overtly structured logic that was ingrained in him since his youth, she was an artist of the truest form. The foundation of her life was completely based on the creative process, only mildly touched by what one would consider to be a thread of logic—but only to the minimal degree necessary to create life in her artistic world. He believed the world was what it was, He could logically explain why and how each event took place, or how it had come to be. War, peace, poverty, or prosperity; he could explain it all—except for love, of course.

She believed the world was good, because she said that it was, and that's all she needed to know. All things in her world were rooted in love and hope and charity. In her world, all bad things were temporary blemishes that would eventually be conquered. Or as she liked to proclaim in her words, "They will be inspired by love." In his world, things were possible if logic dictated them to be so. In her world, everything was possible as long as she believed them to be possible, as long as she pronounced them to be possible. Goodness and love were what she was, and she didn't have the option to be anything else. She painted her paintings, she smiled for the world and for herself, she danced her dance of life, and she sang to and loved everyone whether they liked it or not. If Helmut had lived to be a thousand years old, he could not have adequately explained to her why mankind would ever choose to go to war. There were not enough words in all of the languages of the world that could conceivably explain to her why someone would destroy homes, rape women, kill children, ruin men, snuff out the flame of life, and shatter entire nations, in the hope of making the world a better place. Helmut could methodically explain how and why these things happened, but his words would fall on deaf ears. Love conquers all. She knew this to be true every bit as much as Helmut knew that two and two equaled four. In the end, his logic would have no effect on her, and her love would conquer him.

He glanced up as she strolled across the bar in his general direction on the day they met. She was tall and slim, with an attractive figure, nice breasts. Her face was thin with a sharp nose, full lips, pale blue eyes, and short black hair. The way she looked at people she knew and people she didn't know as she crossed the bar, the way she nonchalantly waved to the bartender, all of her movements and actions, her very presence, oozed of confidence, easiness and sexuality. Her white, short-sleeve T-shirt was covered with smudges of charcoal from whatever picture she had been working on up in her apartment studio. Her faded, frayed blue jeans, covered in multiple colors of paint from projects both new and old, gave her the calm, comforting look of someone who could create life with her own hands. When she reached his table, she glided into the spare chair as if she belonged there, as if she thought he was anticipating her arrival. Without hesitation she picked up his Marlboros, flicked a cigarette out of the pack and into her mouth, and in one smooth motion, grabbed his lighter to light it.

"Don't you know you're supposed to light a lady's cigarette?" she asked as Helmut sat and glanced at the ray of light that had just planted her slender body at his otherwise dreary table. Smoke drifted up into the air as she blew out what she had just inhaled. She tossed the lighter back onto the table. Helmut said nothing.

"So, what do you write in this book?" she asked.

"It's personal," he replied, barely looking up from his journal, trying to pretend she hadn't completely caught his attention.

"Are you going to write about me?"

"I don't know. Are we going to get personal?" he asked, this time looking up with a cocky smile on his face.

"You wish," she said, reaching over and gently squeezing the back of his hand with her long, slender, painted and charcoaled fingers. She got up and walked away, acting as if she had already forgotten his very existence the moment she turned her back on him.

For the first time in his life, Helmut thought, *So this is what love at first sight feels like!* His heart wasn't racing, but it certainly had picked up its pace when she sat at his table. And he, who was never at a loss for words when it came to conversing with beautiful women, had found himself speechless when she commented about lighting her cigarette. When she blew him off while softly squeezing his hand, the combination of reaching out to touch him at the same moment when she turned her back on him actually made him blush. He wasn't sure, but thought that this may have been the first time a girl, a woman, had ever made him feel this way.

"You owe me a cigarette!" he called to her as she moved, tall, slender, catlike, through the crowded bar. He couldn't see her face or the smile that came upon it, as she pretended she didn't hear him and slipped out the front door.

At seven o'clock two nights later, she easily walked through the crowded bar and again sat in the empty chair beside Helmut. She picked up his cigarettes and once again flicked one out of the pack; but as she reached for the lighter, she saw he was holding it, ready to light her cigarette. He smiled, mildly pleased with how smooth he had been, but before he could relish the short-lived victory, she blew a stream of smoke into the air and said, "Are you going to buy me a drink, or should I go sit at the bar?"

He closed his eyes momentarily; she had beaten him to the punch once again. This would be something he was going to have to get used to, as her wit was more impressive than her artistic talent, a talent he would come to find was by no means lacking. The first time they met he was surprised at how his emotions rose to new heights. The second time they met he was even more surprised. He felt even higher than the first time.

"This could be the beginning of something special," he said, smiling once again with his ever-present cocky smile.

"We'll see," she said, smiling back at him. Her smile made his heart race a little more. A few more cigarettes, a few more drinks, and some dance-like conversations, eventually ended up with them walking out of the bar, into the warm damp night, together.

Stepping into her apartment through an old door barely hanging on its hinges and covered with blue paint, curling in chips and peeling from the cracked wood, he entered a world far removed from the dirty, busy streets or the docks of Pula. Paintings hung everywhere, full of color, full of life. Children playing in fields of golden wheat, dogs splashing in the water near riverbanks covered in ferns, old men playing checkers in the park, and old women cooking in old-world kitchens with food and wine sitting on the tables. Her paintings portrayed nothing but life being lived to its fullest. In one corner there was a portrait of a beautiful woman wearing only a look of utter contentment, curled up in the arms of a very white, almost sickly-looking skinny man, who had probably waited his entire life to make love, to give love, to this woman. In another corner sat a large portrait of a new mother standing in a dark red nightgown in the middle of a snow-covered field and holding a baby wrapped in a brilliant blue blanket. Darkening skies of orange, pink, and blue silhouetted this angel holding a smaller angel.

Helmut slowly turned clockwise, taking his time to absorb the colors and passions on every wall. Her entire one-room apartment was a kaleidoscope of life. Three easels of varying sizes held pictures that were all completed to one degree or another. Cans of paint were scattered about the floor, some open, some closed, all messy and spilling brilliant colors wherever they happened to be sitting. There was a small table in another corner with a half-bottle of red wine, and a piece of cheese wrapped with brown paper sitting beside the butcher's knife she had used to cut it. Old white curtains hung down on each side of the single window in the middle of the south wall, curtains that had been used many times as hand rags to wipe rainbows of paint off her beautiful, talented fingers. As he completed his long, slow, clockwise tour of her gallery home, he finally reached the spot where she was standing, naked, with a small crooked smile on her face, and her hand reaching out to him.

"Come on. I'll give you something to write about," she said to the man, who for the first time in his life was afraid that he might not be good enough for a woman—for this woman. For the first time ever, he was worried that a woman might not be satisfied and would not want to be with him another time. This woman, he knew beyond any doubt, was special. She was different from all the others. He didn't know why she touched him so deeply, but he recalled reading a line of a poem once that said, "When she's the one, you will know." For reasons he could not explain, he was in love, and he knew it.

CHAPTER SEVEN

HELMUT BRANDT (PART 3)

The small paved road was barely as wide as a single lane as it wound down through the mountains two and a half hours to the east of Pula. Tall trees covered steep banks that ran high above where the car was driving. More trees and even steeper-looking banks dropped off far into the valley below. Antonio slowly drove the beat-up old Fiat covered with mud from driving on even more remote mountain roads, with Samira riding in the passenger seat. A scared, elderly man huddled together with his elderly wife sat silently in the back seat as they rode through the darkness en route to the safe haven of Pula. They found little comfort in Antonio's reassurance that they would be out of danger in just a few more minutes.

***

Helmut and Samira had argued the day before she headed out of Pula to make another of her ill-advised rescue trips into the badlands. It was the only thing they had fought about in the four months they had been in each other's company. When he wasn't working, Helmut spent every spare moment with her. He watched her paint, they made love, they drank and they smoked at the Barcelona, he wrote, she painted, and then they made love some more. He tried to no avail to explain to her how the business of politics kept the world moving forward, and that she should not ignore the dangers that came along with the progress of war. She told him about playing with little children and spreading love to strangers. She told him how sacrifices such as going into a war zone to help scared, old people in need of a safe passage out, were necessary actions to show the world that someone still cared.

"I don't think you understand how dangerous what you're doing is," he pleaded as they laid in bed after making love. "There are very bad people out there who do very bad things. Not all things are good, you know?"

"I don't think you understand how dangerous it is if I *don't* do it. What kind of world would we have if those who would kill and destroy are willing to take the time and energy to do what they do, while those of us who believe that someone should help the old or the weak don't put the same time and energy forward? Living is not always safe, but it's what we're supposed to do with our lives. We're supposed to be strong. We're supposed to live!" She was passionate about art, about people, about love and making love, and she was passionate about her convictions. His arguments, his lessons about politics, his concerns for her safety, they all fell on deaf ears.

"And for the record, I don't agree with you. All things are good because I say they are good. That's all I need to know," she added.

When Antonio had come to her with word that there was yet one more elderly couple in the mountains who needed help to escape, Samira knew instantly they would go to get them. Quite naturally, even before he told her about them, Antonio knew they would go. With little discussion or planning, they would make one more trip to help souls in need. Helmut could be as outraged as he liked. She would not waver from what needed to be done.

She was committed to living life the way she saw fit.

***

The car slowly wound its way down the dark and curvy mountain road at three o'clock in the morning. They didn't count on being hidden from the soldiers, as much as simply traveling in the middle of the night to avoid them. This was the fifth trip in the past few months, and so far so good. Antonio down-shifted as he neared a sharp curve in the road and then navigated at a crawl through the corner to ensure he didn't lose control and skid on the dirt-covered pavement that was bordered by the steep sloping drop-off of thick bushes and boulders that disappeared deep in the dark ravine hundreds of feet below.

"A few more turns, and then we'll be able to travel faster and get you into a safer area," Samira said, turning to the couple in the back seat.

The old man smiled at his wife and squeezed her hand in an effort to show her he was confident they would be out of harm's way soon. But years of life in a war-torn nation had long ago eroded the arrogant confidence he had when he was young and strong, and had the answers to life's tough questions.

The comforting words had no more than rolled off Samira's lips when Antonio slammed on the brakes, bringing the car to a skidding halt.

Parked in the middle of the road, directly in front of them, sat an army jeep with its lights turned off and two soldiers standing with their rifles aimed at their car. Another soldier sat behind the wheel of the jeep, prepared to follow any order that was barked out by the sergeant, who was holding a rifle and yelling at the car full of refugees. As soon as the Fiat came to a stop, the lights of the jeep came on.

"Turn your lights off and get out of the car!" one of the soldiers yelled as they stood fast, guns aimed. Antonio sat staring straight forward in a moment of sheer panic. His hands tightly squeezed the steering wheel while he tried to figure out what to do next. His mind raced as if he had options to consider, as if there were a choice to be made on his part. The old woman whimpered slightly; she suddenly missed the comfort of her home. The home hadn't been safe in recent months, but was likely safer than the situation they currently found themselves in. The old man sat up straight and felt his shoulders rise and his jaw clench. For one futile moment he wished he were young and strong and had at least a fighting chance in this war; but those days were long gone. He now found himself completely at the mercy of God and the men with the rifles.

"Stay here," Samira said. "I'll go talk to them."

"Don't go. This is not good," Antonio said as he switched off the headlights. But Samira knew, just as he knew, they had no other choice. The only way down the mountain was by convincing these men to let them pass, and that wouldn't happen if she didn't go to plead with them. The passenger door creaked as she opened it and climbed out into the jeep's headlights. Dirt crunched under the soles of her work boots as she slowly walked toward the man aiming the rifle at her. Once again she was wearing the same blue jeans and white T-shirt that Helmut had first seen her wearing in the Barcelona Bar. As always, she looked appealing; in this particular war that might not be a good thing.

"What is the problem?" she asked with one hand shielding the light from her eyes and the other placed on her hip, looking as if she had no idea why someone might be stopping them on a mountain road in the middle of the night in the middle of a war.

"Everyone out of the car!" the soldier standing directly in front of her yelled. He motioned with a wave of his trigger hand to the other soldier to go and get everyone out of the car. His rifle was still aimed directly at her.

"I have just come to pick up my grandparents so I can bring them to my home," she continued. "They are old and cannot take care of themselves. I only came for them. I have no politics." Her eyes were beginning to adjust to the jeep's headlights as the soldier moved slightly to the side so she was no longer blinded. The other soldier was short and fat with a scraggly beard. He kept his gun pointed at Antonio, who was helping the frightened old couple climb out from the backseat of the Fiat.

"We wish for no trouble. We only wish to take my grandparents to our home. That's all we want. That's all we need," she continued.

But she knew. Like flowers know to turn toward the sun, like animals know to take cover before a big storm rolls in, like children know when something is wrong even when their parents tell them everything is all right, she knew. She knew what he was going to do before he knew himself, and she felt sorry for him. She had pity for this man, this angry soldier, who was once a little boy who did little-boy things, but was now old and tired and full of hatred. He had long ago forgotten what it was like to be a small boy who was full of life and to have small-boy dreams. Once, when he was cocky and arrogant and filled with the desires and confidence of a young man, he would have made a valiant effort of trying to seduce a woman like Samira. He would have dreamed of kissing her lips and making love to her.

He would have imagined her soft skin as he dreamed of tasting her breast. He would have tried to talk smoothly, make her smile and laugh, take her to dinner or buy her a drink at a local café.

But as they stood on the mountain road on this cold, dark night, he recalled none of the boyhood days he had spent playing with his friends. He didn't remember any of the young women whom he had courted when he was a bit older, nor did he have any memory of the soft lips he had kissed or how they kissed him back. As he stood in the bitter cold that bit at his face beneath the lifeless cloudy sky hanging over his head, there was only the war and death and strangers looking at each other. He no longer had any dreams or desires. There was only a gun, some bullets, and a soul that had been hardened by death, destruction, and heartbreak. These days, even shattered dreams no longer existed, not even in a faded memory.

Antonio was slowly helping the old couple move in front of the car as the fat man slowly walked backwards toward the jeep with his gun aimed in their general direction, but at no particular person.

Samira closed her eyes for a moment and drew in a deep breath so she could smell and breathe and taste the crisp, clean night air of her homeland one last time. Then she opened her eyes as she smiled a warm smile. "Everything will be all right. Life is good. Love is good. You'll see."

The moment she spoke the last word, the soldier standing in front of her gripped the wooden stock of the gun tightly with his left hand, and pulled the trigger with the index finger of his right hand. The bullet struck her in the forehead. She was gone before her beautiful, lifeless body tumbled unceremoniously to the ground. The single gunshot startled the fat man who immediately pulled the trigger of his gun without aiming. The bullet ripped into the old man's shoulder. He stumbled backward onto the hood of the Fiat with blood spraying from the exit hole in his back. His wife froze where she stood as the skinny soldier turned toward her and Antonio. She looked at the soldier in mesmerized horror, realizing this is how her eighty-three years on earth was going to end. Her hand squeezed the warm, strong hand of her old, best friend one last time.

Antonio, by reflex, dove off the embankment. He tumbled over and over through the rocks, trees, and bushes, down the long, steep hillside as he heard gunfire in the background. The fat man ran to the bank, wildly shooting into the dark, but there was little hope of hitting Antonio with no light to show where he was. When the soldier turned back around, Antonio's friend and the two passengers lay dead on the ground for reasons even the shooters could not explain.

Moments later, the two dispassionate soldiers loaded the dead bodies into the car, pushed it over the bank, then climbed into their jeep. The driver turned the key and started the engine. Antonio listened to the Fiat, which he had been driving less than five minutes ago, tumbling loudly through the forest hundreds of feet below. He heard the army jeep drive away. The car, mangled and mashed from rolling end over end before slamming into trees and rocks, finally came to rest far below where he sat in a state of shock. Fate or God or luck had spared him, but without Samira's undying belief in love, he would have much difficultly ever again believing in the goodness of life or the strength of love.

He sat crouched behind the tree, which had abruptly stopped him when the back of his head slammed into it. Quickly, he had scampered to the backside of the tree and taken cover while the frantic hail of bullets whizzed, clicked, and thumped among the branches and nearby tree trunks. As his mind raced frantically while it processed all possibilities of what had just taken place, he momentarily clung to the absurd idea that somehow all would end well. After a few seconds he regained control of his faculties and came to grips with what he had just seen happen. Samira was dead. He had seen her head jerk back, and then he saw her seem to float to the ground in slow motion. In a frame-by-frame re-run in his mind, he watched the old man's body jerk and twist to the left as the bullet struck his shoulder. Blood sprayed into the air as the bullet exited through the back of his tan flannel shirt, speckling the hood of the dingy white car with dozens of dark red spots. And he didn't have to see what happened to the old woman to know her fate. Closing his eyes, he leaned back and rested his head against the rough bark of the tree trunk. Tears flowed down his face. Blood seeped from the scratches and gashes he had received in his long, painful journey down the hill. Perhaps in a vain attempt to hold onto one more moment with his dearest friend, he recalled going to pick her up a few days earlier.

He had sat at the small round table in the corner of her apartment as the morning light filled the room and she danced across the floor with coffee cup in hand. Wearing only her boxer shorts, one of Helmut's button-up shirts, and a sweet smile of contentment on her face, she wished Antonio a good morning and offered him some coffee.

"You're happy today," he said, motioning for her to bring coffee. "New perfume? It smells nice; but a bit strong, don't you think?" he added as she handed him the cup.

"Well, probably a little too much was applied. Helmut brought me some massage oil with a lovely scent, but he may have gotten carried away while putting it on me," she responded with a devilish grin like a teenage girl who had been bad. They both laughed; she sat on the edge of the bed and began to slip on her blue jeans.

"I didn't know it was possible to use too much massage oil," Antonio teased, then let it go when she pretended to ignore him. Truth be known, he loved her as much as, if not more than, Helmut loved her. He felt a surge of exhilaration followed by jealousy as he momentarily imagined massaging oil onto her beautiful body, and then instantly faced a vision of Helmut having the honors. She was simply the most beautiful woman, and the loveliest human being, he had ever known. On that morning, while sitting in her apartment, he snapped out of his momentary trance when she stood up and walked across the room.

Tonight he snapped out of his trance when the car that had rolled far down the hill, the car that they had been riding in side by side less than ten minutes ago, suddenly erupted in a ball of flame. Antonio hung his head and wept while Samira turned to smoke and ash, drifting toward heaven. As the flames began to die, he knew with certainty his friend was gone.

After a time, the sound of the soldiers' jeep faded off into the distance. He opened his eyes and came to grips with the realization that he was in a dangerous place with no way out except to walk.

For the next four nights he walked in the dark, and hid during the day.

On the fourth day he felt safe enough to flag down a truck heading into Pula. He sat alone in the back of the beat-up flatbed half filled with piles of useless junk that had likely accumulated over the past decade while the old farmer had gone about the business of fixing things and saving the broken parts for reasons unknown to anyone, as there were very few working farms that had survived this long war. Once Antonio arrived in Pula, he went straight to the Barcelona Bar.

***

Almost a week had passed since Samira had gone east into the angry jaws of war. Helmut sat at his table, jotting notes in his journal. When he looked up he saw Antonio standing in front of him. His face was pale white, covered with dirt and dried blood. He hadn't taken the time to change or clean up before going to find Helmut, and tears were once again streaming from his red, tired eyes. He looked exhausted, like someone who had been trying to survive a war for no other reason than to be the deliverer of heartache and sorrow. He said nothing as he stood looking at the German. Helmut looked up at him and momentarily waited for Antonio to say something. No words were spoken; the silence confirmed Helmut's worst fears. Over the dull music and murmur of voices in the bar, he wailed in pain then screamed a blood-curdling scream of agony.

His heart was enraged and shattered beyond anything he had ever imagined possible. He suddenly wished he had stayed off the roller coaster of life. He wished he had never experienced the emotional highs that were predictably followed by emotional lows. Never in his well-disciplined, always logical mind had he remotely considered a valley that was this dark, this deep, and this full of pain. Without thought or reason, he lunged toward Antonio, throwing the table out of the way as he attacked the man standing in front of him. Antonio did nothing to protect himself as the enraged, heartbroken friend plowed into him, driving him to the floor with more force than Helmut ever could have mustered without death fueling his rage. He began throwing wild punches as the men in the bar, the rugged construction workers, the dirty dock workers, and the weathered soldiers who knew the pain that was rushing through the German's veins, jumped in to grab him and haul him off Antonio. They pinned him to the floor until the flailing, clawing, and punching subsided. His rage was replaced with feeble moans of agony.

Antonio lay flat on his back on the floor, physically and emotionally spent. Blood ran from fresh wounds on his face, a rib was newly cracked, and an old gash had re-opened when his head slammed against the floor just as it had slammed against the tree trunk four nights earlier. But he was unaware of any of it. His last few threads of hope or concern for anything or anybody, including himself, had died on a dark mountain road, and there was nothing he could do about it. There was no purpose in continuing, no reason to breathe or think or feel. For the first time he thought that Samira had been wrong. Everything was not good. He saw nothing good in her death. Or in anything else.

Helmut was curled in a fetal position, sobbing uncontrollably with no hope of ever returning to the emotionally managed life he had known since his boyhood days in Hamburg.

In Pula, Helmut Brandt had been born.

A few months later, life came cashing down and he died.

***

For the next several years he drank. He worked, he drifted, he drank. After Pula, he went to a construction project in South Africa, then on to another in Madrid. There were a couple of jobs back in Germany for a short time, but he couldn't handle the structure or the sobriety of living in such a make-believe, homogenized world. Eventually he landed in Jamaica, followed by Saint Maarten, and then for the past five years the small, peaceful, blue-water island of Anguilla. His life had become much more sober, as he found comfort in existing in a self-inflicted exile in an emotionless state on the small under-populated island where he had tucked himself away. He lived a flat line existence that consisted of working during the day, writing in the afternoons and evenings, and then sleeping without dreams at night. It had become a life that kept him safe and it kept him stable; there were no highs and, more importantly, there were no lows. He never formed any real relationship with anyone, certainly not with a woman. Most importantly, he took great comfort in clinging to a life free from the possibility of losing anything. It didn't matter to him that he didn't really have anything to lose. It had been a long time since having a woman to love, or even wanting to make love, or simply to have sex with a woman, had entered his mind. In his flat line world there was no need for it. The truth was he didn't really care about sex, or much of anything else, after Pula. After Samira there was a chain of meaningless women, but she had ruined him for life. His heart, his soul, and apparently his penis were fully committed to a woman who was gone and was never returning. He had long ago given up on ever finding or even wanting another, and firmly believed that none would come close to the only woman he had ever loved.

***

Da Island Hut was filling up with the regular late-afternoon, early-evening crowd as Helmut sat working at his corner table, more intently writing than watching people.

He paid little attention as Pellet strolled in and sat down at the bar and began his own evening ritual of searching for the bottom of more than a few bottles.

"What'll you have?" Desmund asked as he tossed a coaster onto the bar in front of Pellet's stool.

"A cold beer and a woman who understands me," he shot back.

"Lots of women understand you, mon. Dey jus don't want you." Desmund set a newly opened Carib on the coaster he had just tossed down.

"Good point. Perhaps I should have said I'm searching for a woman who loves me for who I am."

"So... you're looking for a blind deaf woman?" Desmund asked.

"Only if she's good looking and lustfully willing," Pellet answered with a smile and took a swig from his bottle.

"Well, as dey say, timing is everyting and hope springs eternal," Desmund mumbled as he nodded his head toward the woman approaching the steps.

Fatisha strolled across the lawn that sloped up from the beach to the steps of Da Island Hut. The sun was just beginning to set on the distant horizon of the blue Caribbean Sea, and red and purple colors danced on the water behind her. Unfortunately for Pellet, she was not deaf or blind, but that didn't dampen his spirits in the least. He had spent the last several months in a noble, albeit fruitless, effort to get her to go on a date with him. Among other things.

Fatisha was the only woman in Anguilla who ever so slightly caught Helmut's attention, not that he was the least bit aware of what was stirring inside him. Up until now, he had managed to keep all emotions barricaded deep behind the thick walls he had erected after leaving the accursed city of Pula.

Fatisha reached down and scratched the old island dog's head as she stepped over Shlomo, who was once again sleeping on the top step leading into the bar. It was the most inconvenient place he could find to collapse and pretend to die. Standing up, she noticed a friend on the other side of the room; she smiled and waved, then drifted towards the bar.

Pellet shamelessly watched the tall, slim, strong-looking island woman as she glided barefoot across the sand-covered wooden floor. Her long dreads, tipped with colorful beads, were pulled back into a loose ponytail that hung far down the back of the white spaghetti-string T-shirt she wore. The cotton shirt hung comfortably loose with a pink-blue-and-green Peace sign on the front of it, highlighting her firm, perfect breasts. Pellet appeared to either be infatuated with her womanly figure or overly impressed by the colorful Peace sign; his eyes were shamelessly glued on them as she approached. Her light green cargo shorts fit loosely, but hung perfectly from her waist down to her knees. Her skin was light brown, flawless and almost glowed. Her smile and her eyes were so brilliant that Pellet was certain they actually did glow.

Meanwhile, Helmut sat with his fingers lying motionless on his keyboard, not aware that he had once again stopped typing, as he almost always did when she graced the Hut.

"How's life?" she asked, leaning over the bar, giving Desmund a kiss on the cheek.

"Cool," he said, holding up an empty wine glass to make sure that she wanted one before he poured it.

"Please," she answered with her always-radiant smile.

"So, have you come to your senses yet?" Pellet asked.

"Are you ready to let me treat you to dinner and an evening out on the island?"

"Not yet, Pellet, but stranger things have probably happened. I can't think of one at the moment, but there must be something," she said, as if they were talking about the weather or something even more trivial. The truth was he had asked her out so many times that it had become less eventful than actually talking about the weather, and it would have surprised her more if he hadn't made his routine pass at her. But in the end, an island snowstorm was more likely to occur than Fatisha ever going out for a night on the island with Pellet.

"Thanks," she said to Desmund as she took a sip of the sweet white wine he had just handed to her. A glint of a small, teasing smile rose from the corner of her mouth; she brushed her long, slender fingers across Pellet's shoulder when she turned to walk away. The fact that she had no interest in him did not deter her from being what she was, which was a highly flirtatious, beautifully cool, calmly seductive, enchantingly artistic island woman who flowed through life as smoothly as one of the local sailboats cutting through the bay between Anguilla and Saint Maarten.

"What if I can't live without you?" he asked in mock desperation.

"Better live while you can, Pellet. You'll be dead soon enough and it will last a long, long time." She continued to walk away without a care in the world.

"Man... This is just no good, Fatisha. You're killing my pride," he said, with another mock look of pain on his face, which this time was only a partially mock look. He was rough around the edges, or perhaps rough a bit deeper than that, but he was desperate for a date with her, and he was relentless in his quest to win the Fatisha lottery. She, being perceptive of all things in her world, was well aware his heart did not long for her anywhere near as much as another body part longed for her. She would not be filling his heart's desire—or any other of his desires—any time in the foreseeable future.

She turned back. "Pellet, you are a funny man. Tings just aren't that bad, ya know. Everyting is cool. Everyting is good."

"Cool? Good? What makes everything good?" he asked with fast-fading enthusiasm. After months of relentless effort, he was not ready to give up, but his self-respect was beginning to waver. Never in his life could he imagine taking so much rejection from one woman. On the other hand, Fatisha was special and Pellet knew it.

"I do, Pellet. I say what's good in my world. And I say everyting is good." She hesitated for a moment before adding, "And because I say it is, that's all you have to know." Raising her wine glass to him and all things good, she turned away and continued her catlike dance across the bar and broke out into an angelic *a capella* version of "One Love" by Bob Marley.

Helmut, who had been watching and listening from his corner table, suddenly felt sick and turned pale white as the blood ran out of his face. He was dizzy and the room began to spin; beads of sweat started to stream over his entire body. For just a moment he thought he might pass out. He firmly planted the palms of his hands on the table in order to steady himself. Closing his eyes, he took several slow, deep breaths in an effort to regain his physical composure. His heart, in a state of total confusion, momentarily raced with excitement then tragically crashed as he was immediately struck with horrifying panic. He had carelessly allowed himself to remember the single high point in his life when his heart soared, when love conquered all, when

Samira was still alive. A split second later he unwillingly recalled the dark, cavernous, pain-filled valley that followed. He felt the icy dagger drive deep into his fragile heart, ruthlessly tearing away at the flesh. He felt the joy and the rage all come together to form a perfect storm of agony. Nauseated, he shivered as he recalled the void left in his world when Samira died. These thoughts had been locked away for a long time and he had no intention of ever revisiting them. Not for the past several years; certainly not this evening. Frantically, he closed his laptop, threw everything into his bag, and scurried out of the bar.

"You OK, mon?" Desmund asked as he watched the German darting toward Shlomo and the steps with his eyes focused on the floor in front of him.

"Not feeling well. Pay you tomorrow," Helmut answered without looking up.

"Cool, mon. Take care." Desmund watched him leave the bar, keenly aware that something was wrong. He didn't know what it was, but he had never seen Helmut be anything other than steady and focused on the task at hand, whether it be writing or simply eating dinner.

The last time Helmut had heard those words, the great proclamation of love and all things good, his naked body was lying entwined in Samira's arms in her magical, colorful apartment in Pula. After dinner at the Barcelona Bar they had returned to her apartment, drunk wine, then made love. Helmut held her close and asked her why her world was such a wonderful place.

"My world is good because I say it is, and that's all I need to know. That's all *you* need to know." She kissed him on the cheek just before she went to sleep in his arms. That had been a long time ago. He didn't dare to contemplate the idea that Fatisha might just give him something worth writing about again. Something more than irrelevant drivel.

CHAPTER EIGHT

A QUEEN IS BORN

"So let me get dis straight. Some white guy from France come to Anguilla and says dat you are part of some French royal family... just like dat?" Desmund asked Astra with a disbelieving look on his face.

"Dat's right, old man. I tell you forever I was someting special, but you never listen. Now you know," Astra answered, smiling her bright white smile, with her round body jiggling all over. She was being honest when she said she had always claimed to be *someting special*, but even Astra didn't suspect she was a distant heir to the throne of France—perhaps the heir to a small, dirt-poor village somewhere in Africa, but definitely not Paris.

"So da man jus marched in n' say, hey woman, you be French royalty, jus like dat?" Desmund demanded again. "Dis gotta be some kinda scam. Ain't no way you're French *or* royal. Even if you was, why would some white guy come all dis way, find a black woman like you n' say, Hey... we owe you someting? I'm telling you someting ain't right." He shook his head back and forth as he rambled on to himself.

"Mista! Don't you be cloudin me sun! Me ship is come in n' you ain't sinkin it," Astra yelled, as she threw an old frying pan in his general direction. "N' don't you be forgettin, your boat is hooked to my boat. If I sink, you sink," she added. Desmund ducked the pan and stood, contemplating the slim odds of him getting the upper hand with Astra.

"What's dat make me? Duke? King?" Desmund demanded.

"It makes you an old worn-out bum. Nothing has changed on your end."

"Maybe I'll have a little chat with da French dude," Desmund said, as if he was throwing a bomb her way.

"He'll be talkin to you soon enough. You jus be youself," Astra shot back. An uneducated, unambitious Rasta would play perfectly into the Frenchman's plan. More importantly, she knew it would work even better in her own plan.

"Lawd! If I thought you gave me a headache before, you gonna be unbearable now," Desmund mumbled, as he sat down at the dining room table.

"Maybe you should have listened when I told you to stop chasin dem skirts all over da place. You tink dey gonna take care of you like I can? I told you I was special."

"Maybe when dey crown you, you can have someone chop me head off n' end da misery," Desmund sighed.

"Ain't nobody choppin you head, old man. You stuck with me even worse now," Astra said, smiling and giggling even more.

As it turned out, they were both right. Astra was going to become French royalty, and something was definitely wrong with the Frenchman's story.

***

The Frenchman they referred to was Pierre Doyon, Directeur de Sovereign Legacy Royale de Frances, or SLRF (pronounced *slerf*), as it was referred to among its pompous and clueless members. The SLRF's sole purpose was to restore lost members of royal families, who had fallen by the wayside over the centuries, back to the titles bestowed upon their families by God or someone of near god-like power. Their reasons for doing this were wide and varied, but the truth was there was strength in numbers—and the royal herd was shrinking fast. Simply put, they enjoyed hanging out with other royal blood-liners, and increasing the size of the pack dramatically improved royal social events.

For over twenty-five years the organization had successfully restored honor to dozens of royal families throughout France. Some were wealthy, and had simply let their titles slip away with the passing of generations. Others had fallen on hard times and more or less unofficially lost their status and position. Either way, rich or poor, the royal numbers grew, for a time, through the diligent work and generosity of the SLRF.

The SLRF did what it could to lift up the poor souls who had temporarily fallen from the grace of God and the Kingdom. The problem was that elevating and restoring, much like their expensive French champagne, cost money and a lot of it.

Unfortunately, modern-day royals, much like their ancestors, were virtually useless folks who had no legitimate means of making money. This was becoming a problem for the royalty-restoration fund, as the bottoms of the coffers were becoming visible. Another regrettable problem for the SLRF was, unlike the glory days of times gone by, they were not allowed to simply tax and pillage peasants, forcing them to support a king and his court. Modern-day governments had already laid claim to that money. They were not about to share it with the SLRF.

This was one of the few areas where the French were jealous of the English Queen and her family, who had found a way to survive, or daresay, even prosper in these God-forsaken times of rob from the rich and give to the poor. What all of this nonsense meant was that contemporary French royals had to come up with more creative solutions to solve their financial woes—other than the historically accepted method of brutally pillaging the masses—if they hoped to survive into the future.

"It's marketing, Pierre. If you want to raise funds for the SLRF, then you must show the world we are more diverse and less controversial than we've appeared in the past," Jacques said, as he pled his case to his old friend while sipping Cognac on the rear terrace of his summer villa on the outskirts of Paris. "Our traditions, our heritage, and our very existence are fading. Soon it will be too late to salvage any living legacy of our rich past. If we hope to restore the royal line, we will need significant funding. It simply is not coming in." He rose from his seat, walked to the edge of the terrace and leaned against the weathered marble railing that stood guard over the intricate maze of hedges. For three centuries his ancestors had come to this same terrace, sipped Cognac, and leaned on the same worn marble while discussing their self-preservation issues. The issue had always been the same: How do we get someone else to pay for our opulent lifestyle without turning them against us in the end?

Pierre listened with aloofness as he blew a stream of smoke into the air while swirling his Cognac around in the small crystal glass in the palm of his hand. He held it up and watched the sun shine through it like some kind of intoxicating prism. Jacques, his oldest and dearest friend, was well educated and confident, but spoke with agitation that seemed to have little effect on Pierre.

"In order to raise money," Jacques continued, "we are compelled to show we are enlightened to a degree that commoners will appreciate. We don't want bad publicity these days Pierre, but we can't afford to have no publicity at all." After a brief hesitation, he said, "As our crude friends in America say, it's time to shit or get off the pot." He sat back down in his chair with slouching posture, which clearly showed he was not convinced that Pierre was going to have the solution to their economic woes.

Pierre spoke with his typical pompous attitude. "Don't worry, my friend. I have a marvelous idea that I'll be unveiling soon. I assure you everyone will be delighted with the cure-all I have come up with for our financial misery. It's very low risk, and the potential for superior PR is phenomenal. I assure you there is no downside to my plan. In a phrase, all pleasure and no pain is the way I like to think of it," he continued, with absolute confidence. He would eventually come to realize he had never spoken less true words in his entire life than when he said, "all pleasure and no pain." He would also come to loath the moment when he was appointed to the much-sought-after Director's seat, but for the moment he was basking in the glory of his infallible plan and title. It was his brainchild, or so he claimed, and it would forever leave his mark on the SLRF. In this presumption, he was correct.

Shortly after Pierre became the Director, and the organization's restoration finances began to dry up, he initiated his grand plan to market SLRF to the world. In keeping with the tradition of almost all royalty, the grunt work was done by someone of less prominence, while the credit would go to the man in charge. In this case, Pierre's assistant, Claudette, was the one who came up with the idea of finding a commoner—preferably someone of African decent, as that seemed to be the most marketable demographic— then find a way to connect this person to his or her French royal lineage. It was an eureka moment when she laid out the plan to Pierre of using an overlooked, poverty-stricken soul to line the pockets of the SLRF.

Finding someone who was not only seen as a commoner, but also a minority, would likely draw even more positive publicity, and hence more money. To add more spice to the recipe, they quickly decided to look outside of France for the perfect candidate, thus increasing the chance of raising international donations. Pierre and Claudette believed that, if they could put the right spin on the perfect candidate, the donations would flow like the water in the French Riviera, thus ensuring the monarchy would live on long into the future. They were both pleased as well as proud of themselves for creating such a masterful plan.

Keeping in line with royal tradition, Pierre gave Claudette a small token of appreciation by allowing her to take a week of paid vacation, a week he was required by law to give her anyway. With Claudette away, he promptly took credit for the entire idea. When she returned from her week of rest and relaxation, he immediately sent her back to her office and put her to work searching for the ideal candidate. Three weeks later she came back to him with the good news. Once again, Pierre gave her a small reward, and once again, he immediately took credit for continuing to develop and implement the ingenious plan of finding the perfect individual to restore the royal line. Later on down the road, Claudette would finally be given due credit for coming up with this idea and finding the girl named Astra. When that day arrived, Pierre walked into her office uttering the words, "Vous êtes licenciée. Sortez!" Which translated to, "You're fired. Get out!"

***

The Lancaster family members were humble descendants of slaves on the tropical Caribbean island of Anguilla. The three remaining survivors were purportedly attached by a thread that somehow connected them to a long, skinny, meandering branch of the French Monarchy.

Mama, as everyone on the island called her, was a well-fed, happy woman with a heart of gold. She was a perfectly contented soul who wanted no big changes in her life. She had no dreams or desires to have more, do more, go more, or be more. God and Anguilla had blessed her for an entire lifetime and she saw no reason to change her lot in life at this point in the game. Technically, she was heir to the throne by marriage to her long since deceased husband who had passed the bloodline along with her assistance, but as far as the SLRF was concerned the connection was sufficient enough to be official. When the funny-sounding Frenchman showed up in her kitchen with the grand news, she was mixing dough to make Jonny Cakes. After he called her Madame several times while explaining her good fortune to her, Mama laughed so hard she fell off her kitchen chair and almost peed her panties. The very thought of her being a Marquis, or Duchess, or whatever title they had for her, was too much for her to comprehend. When she finally composed herself, caught her breath, and climbed back onto her chair, she smiled her bright island smile and thanked the polite, yet disillusioned Pierre, who had come a long way to bring the glorious news to an old island woman. After spending a lifetime living a full and simple life, she thought there was no reason to do anything else.

The son, Alfred Lancaster was a banker; he smiled politely when he received the news of his royal bloodline. He was very candid with Pierre, thanked him for the SLRF's interest, but declined all invitations to participate in the enthroning process. Alfred was an exceedingly quiet and proper man who thought if the whole thing went badly, he didn't want to be tied to any part of it. He decided to protect his name and reputation and avoid possible embarrassment, even at the risk of giving up the throne of France.

Last and by no means least, there was Astra, who was Mama's daughter and Alfred's sister. She almost immediately understood the opportunity being laid at her doorstep. She seized it with the ferocity of a tigress biting into a baby gazelle that had wandered away from the safety of home. Astra was a rotund island girl, with a smile that shined as bright as the Caribbean sun, and a voice that sang out "Praise the Lord," like a brown angel sent from heaven. She was also a tenacious woman with razor-sharp wit, which was well known to anyone who had ever spent much time in her company. The poor Frenchman, who thought he was the bearer of good news to the simple island girl, had no idea whom he was dealing with.

Astra Latisha Lancaster-Kingston d'Aumont-Villequier, the last added after the Frenchman discovered her and claimed her for the French Monarchy, would later become *Queenie* for short. She was supposedly a long-lost descendant of the Marquis d'Aumont-Villequier. The family history that was discovered— then likely embellished—and the legend that was soon spun and spread throughout France and Anguilla, was astonishing. There was a tale of a man of royal blood falling in love with a beautiful slave girl on the small Caribbean island over three hundred years ago. In almost no time at all, he married her, but then was suddenly called back to France on urgent business. It was a heart-wrenching saga, which didn't clarify why he was never able to return to the islands to live out his days with the love of his life, although there were rumors of an untimely death. But like all legends, the story was largely based on threads of truth woven into blankets of illusion and myth.

A more accurate retelling of history was that the Marquis d'Aumont-Villequier was the father to a son of questionable character, who was of little use to anyone. René was a burdensome derelict who brought nothing but pain and shame to his family. As good fortune would have it, the young man managed to find himself island-bound as he sailed with Captain Lobeau on the ship *Le Triomphant*, heading toward Puerto Rico and surrounding islands, back in the late 1700s. In all likelihood, he was taken on the ship by the good captain as a favor to the Marquis—or more accurately, the Captain was paid handsomely to take such a useless malcontent on a long, time-consuming journey, thus giving the family at least a temporary reprieve from his embarrassing antics. In truth, the family would have gladly mourned the son's heroic death, if he managed to get himself killed while exploring the outer reaches of the world and defending the empire on behalf of God and King and France. Unfortunately this did not happen. The family's mourning was once again over his misdeeds as opposed to his untimely death.

At some point on the journey, there was some frolicking. Not long after the frolicking, there was a wedding of sorts, which could be construed to form a shred of legal bond between René, the regrettable son, and an alluring slave girl named Nkiruka, which allegedly means, "The best is still to come." Her mother frequently told her when she was a child, "You, Nkiruka, are the path to our family's future. I've seen it in a dream. Great things will come of you and your children." The heated romance and following nuptials led to more frolicking. It was not long before their son, who could be traced through the centuries to the present-day Lancasters of Anguilla was born; hence his grandmother's premonitions began to take form. Eventually, the lineage landed at the feet of Astra Latisha Lancaster-Kingston, who was many generations removed from the woman whose mother said she would take the family to greatness.

Astra soon attached d'Aumont-Villequier to the end of her island name so the world, or at least Anguillans, would know she was indeed the fulfillment of an African-Anguillan prophecy.

The publicity ball began to roll forward. The first step in the process was a press release in Anguilla that tastefully described the Lancaster family of Crocus Bay along with their royal bond to France. The story was then sent to a small newspaper in Paris, which lead it to being promptly reprinted in a larger paper. Everyone loved the real-life Caribbean Cinderella tale. Soon the news was buzzing throughout social circles, where everyone was told the heartwarming saga of how it was brought to Pierre's attention that a humble and long-forgotten island family were descendants of the French royal bloodline. All this was done thanks to research done by the noble and charitable organization called the SLRF.

Initially the plan was a grand success. The photographer was summoned from France to document the existence of the Lancaster family, Astra in particular. The truth was the Lancasters were not particularly bad off. Mama was a happy, old-world island woman who owned her own home and shared home cooking with friends and neighbors. Alfred was a banker of quite notably successful reputation. And Astra was a bookkeeper at one of the local grocery stores. Her husband Desmund Kingston was a local fisherman/ part-time construction worker. Their home was modest, but a good enough home to be happy in, or at least good enough for Desmund—but not Astra— Astra always had her eye on more.

In order to meet SLRF's needs, their photographer took shots that, at best, made the Lancaster situation look bleak. At worst made all of them, Astra, Desmund, and Mama, look to be near destitute. Alfred was left completely out of the pictures and story, with the exception of one brief mention of his existence in the original article. Mama was disgusted by the article and angrily mumbled about being portrayed as a poor, dumb old island woman. Desmund was furious that he was portrayed as an uneducated laborer who dared not dream of a better life due to the blight handed down from his enslaved African descendants. But Astra gave a humble smile for the world to gaze upon. The "amount due" column, which was an undetermined amount when the SLRF first contacted the family, was slowly growing; and Astra was apparently the only person who realized it, although Alfred was familiar with Astra's ingenuity, and suspected it.

The entire plan could have been a limited but profitable success if SLRF had discovered the long-lost royal Lancaster family, released a heartwarming story about reaching out to them, and then capped it off by bestowing a title or two and giving some sort of mildly generous, but strongly symbolic, gift to the family. Perhaps a book showing the family tree, with a golden crest on its ornate cover, would have been seen as a spectacular gift for all the locals to admire when they came to Astra's house and oohed and aahed, as they ran their fingers over the gilded cover. That plan would have had some small expenses, and would have almost certainly generated more income than the project actually cost. But like so many venturers in the bold modern-day business world, Pierre went with the "go big or stay home" attitude. He forsook a conservative plan for a grandiose plan with a substantial payday for the SLRF if all went as planned. If all went bad, it would have ended up as not much ventured, not much lost. However, after he weighed out the risk/reward factor, he decided bringing Astra to France to live for a few months would be where the real payoff was going to take place.

He had flown to the island on two different occasions and found her to be photogenic, personable, and charismatic. Best of all, she didn't seem too bright. The world would love her, but more importantly, the world would devour her story. In the spirit of wanting to be part of something bigger than life, celebrities, fiscally tight royalty, and hopefully even some corporate organizations would climb aboard the giving train. All the while, Astra would sit quietly smiling like a dumb, humble island girl, who was simply unspeakably grateful for such wonderful news brought to her and her little island world.

Before getting on the plane and heading off to France, Astra calmed Mama by telling her that when she did more interviews in Paris, she would make sure the truth was told. Of course this was a little white lie, as she planned on embellishing the poverty and lack of education even further once she had the eyes of Europe cast upon her. She pacified Desmund by telling him she was going to France without him for an extended visit. The thought of her leaving the island for any length of time instantly offset his resentment over any beguiling comments written about him in the papers. Last but not least, Astra called Alfred to reassure him she would keep his name out of the whole situation, but mentioned he may want to begin creating some sort of investment portfolio for her in the near future. Alfred, ever the banker, was immediately torn between staying away from the entire affair, or obtaining a new and substantial client. Astra never doubted for a moment he would most certainly go with the latter. With peace restored, off to France Astra went.

CHAPTER NINE

A BAR IS OPEN

"What's shakin?" Oscar blurted out as he climbed up the first two rickety wooden steps. He hesitated as he attempted to maneuver his way over the last step and into the Hut. As usual, Shlomo was lying in a spot that somehow encompassed the entire top step and then some.

"Don't move on my account, Shlomo," Oscar mumbled as he took one large step over the top of the lazy mutt. Shlomo did exactly what he'd been doing for most of his life since he was a pup: nothing.

"Desmund was just telling me the saga of Marie Antoinette of Anguilla," Pellet said.

"Ah, yes... the infamous Queenie. Whom has she beheaded today?" Oscar asked as he continued heading to a barstool. "FYI, she's more like Henry the Eighth than Marie," he said.

"Don't know n' don't care who she's beheaded today, as long as it's not me n' she stays on da other side of da great big ocean dat lays between us." Desmund replied. He reached into the cooler and pulled out another cold Carib, popped the top off, then held it into the air as a toast to her royal highness. "Long live da Queen!" he said with a smile, followed by a long gulp.

"So I take it that she stayed in France?" Pellet asked.

"Stayed? I tink she owns da damn place by now," Desmund answered. "Boy, Frenchy didn't know what he was grabbin when he reached in dat bag of fire. I'm guessin he was tinking dis be da islands n' everyting is cool, all laid back, no worries. He was listening to too much reggae tunes."

Oscar slid onto the stool next to Pellet and picked up the beer that was set in front of him. Over the years, Desmund had told the story with conflicting amounts of pride and shame. He was more than happy to allow Oscar to jump in to continue with the never-ending saga. Oscar reached into the side pocket of his cargo shorts, pulled out a wrinkled pack of Marlboros, and tapped out one of the cigarettes. As he lit it, he watched the smoke roll into the hot Caribbean air and continued with the story, as if he were reminiscing about the '67 revolution, when Anguillans tossed the Kittitians off the island. Britain promptly sent paratroopers to crush the small Caribbean uprising that consisted mostly of rum and music. Astra d'Aumont-Villequier would go down in local island legend as the Anguillan woman who stormed Paris and singlehandedly defeated the French monarchy. British paratroopers had nothing on her.

"Astra navigated the waters of the French PR machine like the local fishermen navigates these warm, blue Caribbean waters," Oscar began poetically, in keeping with the spirit of telling an island legend.

"She went to France and they put her up in a modest, but nice, little apartment. She oohed and aahed and humbly thanked Jean or Jacques or Pierre, or whatever his name was, three or four times for every little thing he did. They'd give her five dollars worth of stuff, she'd do a little TV or radio interview, and then they'd give them a thousand dollars' worth of publicity. Their *God Save the Queen* organization started getting rave reviews for saving the poor, black princess from the islands. People who like being involved in that sort of stuff started paying attention and promtly began giving money. Strange world, isn't it? Rich people giving money to rich people in order to help poor people become rich people so they can look down on other poor people."

He stopped for a minute and took another long drag on his cigarette then a sip of beer before continuing on. Oscar wasn't one of those guys who could talk and smoke in a seamless conversation. When it came time for him to take a drag, the talking stopped for twenty or thirty seconds while he filled his lungs with tar and nicotine, held it for a short time, then exhaled the entire toxic cloud into the clean air before starting up again.

In the long run, as irritating as the smoke delays seemed to be, they somehow added to the mystique of his storytelling. Pellet found himself leaning forward in anticipation of the next line each time the talking stopped and the puffing started.

Recharged, Oscar continued. "When she got to France she didn't ask for anything. They gave her a place to stay and made sure she had food to eat. For the most part they didn't take her out shopping much because they didn't want to ruin the poor-island-girl image. Some of the old royal cronies loosened up the purse strings just a bit and made donations to the Save the Queen club in an act of showing how enlightened they had become in the racially challenged times. Pretty soon the celebrities joined the party. All the French papers and networks were carrying the story to one degree or another. As much as they wanted to mock the whole thing for the joke that it was, there was something captivating about taking a short, fat, poor, semi-uneducated island girl and raising her to the status of being the Queen of France. Especially since it was rich, white French guys orchestrating the whole damn three-ring circus. As soon as a couple of French pop stars made donations, other celebs began noticing them being showered with loads of cheap publicity. After that, everyone jumped on the Save the Queenie train. Then an American movie star who had an apartment in Paris had lunch with Astra, which of course was done in a manner that the paparazzi couldn't miss, and made the French-Caribbean-princess story a worldwide event. She had her picture taken with politicians, businessmen or anyone else who wanted to be seen with her; they all wanted to be part of the campaign to open opportunities for minorities to become the Queen of France. Not that they actually had a Queen anymore. Astra continued to play the poor, dumb island girl routine as good as any Hollywood actress could have played the role."

"How long has she been there?" Pellet asked.

"How long has it been, Dez? Fifteen, sixteen years?"

"Bout dat, but I don't count em. Jus keep tanking God dat she still loves France, n' dey've given up on trying to get rid of her."

Oscar continued, "Anyway, after she'd been there about six months, some rapper in the UK wrote a song about her and it took off all over Europe. Even made a little airtime in the US. It was sort of a reggae-rap thing called "Queenie," and it was the last piece of the puzzle she needed. From that point on, her new name stuck like honey. The royal club was raking in the cash and doing whatever it was that they did, while Astra, who was no longer a peasant accountant in a grocery store, continued living in her little apartment in the semi-rundown part of Paris, getting little more than grocery money on the side."

Oscar stopped again, did the whole cigarette routine. He smiled as he said, "That was all about to change, though."

"How so?" Pellet threw in, as if prompting Oscar would

make him smoke quicker.

"Turns out, some Hollywood movie company had been negotiating the movie rights with the French guys and she found out about it. She called Pierre, the guy who had taken credit for coming up with the whole brilliant island girl princess scheme in the first place, and asked him to come by her humble abode for a visit. He jumped to the conclusion she was getting homesick and figured that this would be his chance to send her back to the warm, blue waters of Anguilla. He was so wrong."

"How so?" Pellet asked again.

"The short version? When he got to her apartment she gave him some wine and cheese. Then told him the gig was up. She let him know things were going to change or she would go to the press with the whole truth. It seemed her *I'm jus happy to be getting whatever you throw my way* demeanor, had been replaced with a *Where's the stuff you owe me?* attitude."

"Frenchy went for it?" Pellet blurted in disbelief.

"He tried to call her bluff for about five seconds," Oscar said. "Until she picked up the phone and began calling a reporter she had befriended when she first arrived in Paris."

"Holy shit. She had the whole damn thing worked out?" asked Pellet.

"Oh, she wasn't done yet. Not by a long shot. Before he left the apartment she handed him a piece of paper with a name written on it along with a room number at some high dollar hotel in Paris. There was an Anguillan attorney waiting there with papers he'd drawn up on her behalf. She made it clear that she expected them to be signed that very day. If that didn't happen, she'd be meeting with the reporter the following day. Poor bastard left the place not knowing what the hell had hit him. The contract covered the costs of a better place to live, new clothes, flying in her personal assistant from Anguilla to live with her, and of course her fair share of the song and movie rights. "

"So she's been living in France ever since?"

"Long live da Queen," Desmund said once again as he held his beer high in the air with an almost genuine toast to the French Monarchy.

"And that's how Desmund became the owner/operator of Da Limin Hut."

"OK, you've lost me," Pellet said.

"Well, after the dust settled, after the organization found a more appropriate place of residence for a woman of her stature to live, after they bought her the appropriate clothes, after they agreed on a proper size for her slice of the pie, and after they paid for her best friend Majare to be flown over to become her personal assistant, Queenie had one more card to play."

Pellet continued to listen with his mouth hanging open like a kid listening to "'Twas the Night Before Christmas" for the first time.

"A few months had passed since their wine and cheese meeting at her starter apartment, and it was still a win-win situation for everyone, albeit that Queenie was winning more than Frenchy had anticipated. His efforts made a lot of money, but most of it ended up going to the new royalty as opposed to the old royalty. According to Queenie, the whispers in the SLRF were that she had gotten the best of him. Then she heard that there were rumors that perhaps she was not even of royal line at all. Announcing to the world that the black princess thing had all been a ruse was a card they wouldn't dare to play, even if it were true. Frenchy eventually resigned in shame without lining the pockets of his royal gang. Despite his lingering bitterness for being played, he was still civil to Queenie. Then one day at lunch she brought out a bunch of pictures of her poor, pathetic, uneducated, dirty, foul, crude, womanizing fisherman loser of a husband, and handed them to Frenchy, with a look of despair on her face."

Pellet said nothing as he glanced up at Desmund, who was now blankly looking out to the sea. Despite the passing of time, and despite the fact that he had gotten a bar out of the whole deal, Desmund was never quite able to accept that he personally profited from the fact that someone would actually pay a good sum of money to ensure he stayed away from their continent. No matter how many times he kicked this idea around in his head, and no matter how many times he counted the money that came into his till, he couldn't quite understand what made him so repulsive to the good people of France.

Oscar continued on with his version of the Legend of Queenie. "She announced he should be brought to France, cleaned up, educated, and... and... and... anything that she could think of that would cost money and cause embarrassment to the SLRF. Frenchy just sat there and stared at her.

"'Or... ' she blurted out, 'maybe da rum drinkin, skirt chasin island man won't play so good in da press.' She sat silent for a few seconds allowing Pierre to stew in his exasperation, then she added, 'Perhaps we would all be better off if he stayed right where he is, but da man's gotta eat, dontcha know.'

"So Pierre surrendered to her and asked her what she wanted this time.

"'A bar,' she says. 'You need to buy a bar, dat would allow the destitute but nevertheless royal Desmund, to prosper in his homeland. After dat, no need for him to journey all da way to France to be fed and housed and dressed and educated by my friends at da SLRF. Mostly, no need for da good people of Paris to meet my Desmund.'

"Brilliant isn't she?" Oscar said as he ended the legend of Queenie.

"Damn... sounds almost charitable or patriotic," Pellet said, raising his bottle to Desmund.

"Hear, hear!" Oscar answered as they all raised their beers in reverence to God, Queenie, France, and Anguilla. "Plus I think she dislikes living with him as much as living with her scares the heebie-jeebies out of him," Oscar threw in.

"So, your woman and the French are both willing to pay you to live in a land far, far away from them," Pellet said to Desmund. "I'm not quite sure if I've ever known anyone who was so disliked."

"Fifteen or so years later," Oscar continued, "Queenie is still taking France by storm, the French are still taking in royalties from the movie and the song, then promptly turning most of it over to Queenie. Most importantly, Desmund, Duke of our humble but apparently royal bar, is serving us peasants ice-cold beers and allowing us to drink in his royal presence."

"So that's why you have a small French flag hanging up on the wall," Pellet said.

"God bless France," Desmund added. Three more beers were opened and the celebration continued late into the night.

CHAPTER TEN

AN EVENING WALK

Iggy Srebotnik had spent most of her childhood days running around the dirty pig-poop-filled yard of her grandmother's farm near a small town in southeast Slovakia. As a grown woman, she often shared her youthful stories of taking baths in a metal tub sitting out in the backyard only a few feet from the pen where the stinky snorting pigs lived their carefree existence, deprived of the knowledge that they would soon become salt pork, bacon, and prosciutto.

Meanwhile, far beyond the rocky, snow-covered mountains, past breathtaking ice-covered lakes, and even further past quaint European villages that lay to the west of Slovakia; and finally across the cold, dark, deep Atlantic ocean that led to the warm blue island waters of the British West Indies, Oscar Duncan lived a carefree existence as a chubby white island boy. He had little concern for anything other than playing in the warm Caribbean Sea and hanging out with his best friend Desmund Kingston, the son of a Rasta, but mostly, like Oscar, a son of the Carib.

Growing up, Iggy had no recollection of being born in the Soviet Union, nor did she have any knowledge of what the Iron Curtain was other than what she had read in history books. As a matter of fact, since she was a poor and only slightly educated girl and not all that bright to begin with, there were a lot of things she did not know or understand. But one thing she clearly knew, understood, and recalled with sickening clarity, was her father staggering home from the bar night after night, stealing what little money she had earned at her waitress job, then promptly spending it on more cheap vodka and cheaper whores. She recalled his feet clumsily tripping over almost everything in her dark bedroom as he rummaged through her things. Even as a full-grown woman, on quiet nights when she couldn't sleep, she could still recall his mumbling voice as he prowled around her room, ferreting out what did not belong to him. Worst of all, she could not forget the stink of booze on his breath when he leaned over her bed and kissed her forehead, thanking his little girl for her donation to his dereliction fund.

Even though his pathetic routine of stealing and drinking disgusted her to the bone, she rarely showed any emotion about her father's transgressions. Over the years it seemed easy, if not natural, to love and hate him at the same time. After all, he was her father. He was her only role model, as father roles go. Through the years he had stolen from her so many times that it hardly seemed to matter any more.

But like many things in life, there is a point where enough is enough. From the time she was twelve when she got her first job, until she was a lovely young woman of eighteen years, she dreamed of escaping the rural poverty that had slowly consumed the lives of so many generations of her ancestors. Her father the drunk had never particularly weighed into the picture of escaping, one way or another.

What Rostek Srebotnik did not know was that, in an act of desperation and self-preservation, his daughter had been making two stashes for the past six years. The smaller stash was the one he pillaged two or three times a week. The second stash had continually grown, and was almost large enough to buy a ticket to Berlin—perhaps even enough to get her all the way to London. She kept this larger stash in a small coffee can hidden in the loft of their ramshackle barn. Her mother and her brother knew she was robbed on a regular basis and they, or at least her mother, suspected she had a second stash hidden somewhere. Fortunately, her father never did the math. It hadn't ever dawned on him that his little cash cow was probably tucking money away in order to escape to greener pastures at some point in the future.

Though she had never been too bright, what she lacked in intelligence she more than made up for in beauty. Even Iggy was smart enough to know she was as attractive as any young woman around, and her natural good looks and raw sexuality could be her ticket out of the rustic rural Slovak poverty, if that was the road she needed to travel. More than a few men, "talent agents," as they called themselves, who had come in to the café where she worked, tried to sell her on a dream of wealth and travel if she would only join their agency. But she was a good girl. That option had always been Plan B. Plan A was to work, scrimp, save and keep her eye on the goal.

On a hot July afternoon, Iggy sat in the hay on the barn floor, sobbing, while holding the empty coffee can in her beautiful hands. After years of tucking away a little bit from here and a little bit more from there, it suddenly seemed as though her first option, saving money for her escape, had just come to a tragic end. Plan B, for the first time ever, suddenly looked as if it were going to be her only real choice, even though her mother had warned her that the promises of talent agents were no more valid than her father's promises to sober up. Not surprisingly, Iggy had remained loyal and in love with her father. She had always forgiven him for his life choices. But slumped over on the dirty barn floor, Iggy felt the pain of betrayal far worse than ever before. Her heart ached as she realized the money was gone and her dream of leaving with dignity had gone with it. She sobbed in absolute agony as tears flowed down her cheeks and onto her blouse.

If Iggy had a violent bone in her pretty little body, she would have considered killing her father when he eventually staggered home and crashed through the front door. But she didn't have any violent bones, nor did she have the ability to hate. She simply cried as she felt the weight of her dreams and her future crashing down from the sky.

The barn door creaked as it opened and the bright sunlight blinded her momentarily. She knew it was far too early for her father to be coming home. With the amount of money he had stolen he would be gone for days. The next few days would bring a lot of drinking, a lot of screwing, along with a fight or two. She shielded her eyes from the bright light and began to focus on the silhouette of her mother as she came closer. Iggy wiped the tears away with her sleeve, trying in vain to hide her obvious pain. Her mother had problems of her own with no dream of escaping them, and Iggy did not want to add to her pile.

"Stop your crying, little girl. This is a good day for you," her mother said in a very matter-of-fact tone.

"Mama, he stole from me again, but this time he took a lot of money. He took everything. He got it all, Mama," she whimpered through the sobs. There was no holding back now.

"No, Iggy, I took the money. Your father began mumbling that he thought you had a stash hidden from him. He swore he was going to find it, so I threw a coffee cup at him and told him to stop being stupid. When I told him you had nothing more to give, he took the money from your bedroom and went to the bar." Mama took a big sigh before adding, "But I knew he was right."

"How?"

"I am your mother. I am supposed to know what my little girl is doing. I may not have finished school, but I can do math. I knew you had more hidden somewhere. After he left I decided I better find it before he did. I came out here and looked. You don't hide things so good."

Iggy felt a wave of relief flow through her body and for a moment it seemed like the world was right. Perhaps she wasn't fighting the battle to escape all on her own.

"So can I have it, please?"

"No," Mama answered as she turned and walked to the corner of the barn. Iggy hadn't noticed the suitcase sitting in the corner until Mama picked it up and headed back to her. "Stand up and come over here," she snapped.

Iggy got up, not quite understanding what was happening. For a moment she thought perhaps Mama had taken the money for herself and was going to escape and leave everyone far behind. In a sad sort of way, Iggy would not have blamed her for doing it. As she stood in front of her mother, Mama reached into the pocket of her old dress and pulled out an envelope and handed it to her.

"There's train tickets in here that will get you to London. I've written down the names and addresses of some cousins who live there. They probably don't have any money either, but perhaps they can help you to start a new life."

Mama was a tough farm girl who had grown up during times that were even tougher than what Iggy had seen. When she was young, there were no dreams of going west to start a new life. There was only hard work and no hope, day after day, year after year, decade after decade. Yet in all of her eighteen years, Iggy had not heard so much as one complaint, or seen so much as one tear flowing from her Mama's eyes.

But as they stood there facing each other in the old barn on this warm summer's day, Mama's voice began to quiver. Her eyes became watery. "Iggy, go live a life. Go find some dreams for yourself. Live some dreams for me." She momentarily lowered her head as she searched for the right words. She reached deep to be strong while saying good-bye to her daughter. "I packed your suitcase and put a little money in the envelope, but there's not much, so be careful with it. And, little girl, you must make two promises to your Mama."

"Whatever you want, Mama," Iggy said as she choked on her words and again wiped away the tears with her sleeve.

"First, do not trust everyone, Iggy. It can be a bad world out there. Trust your instincts and do only what you think is right. Second, do not come back. I will always love you, but you cannot return to a prison once you escape."

With those final words, they hugged and kissed each other on each cheek, then Iggy bent down and took hold of the handle of the suitcase. As she walked down the dirt road toward the train station, the pain in her chest was overwhelming and the lump in her throat grew so large she could barely swallow or breathe. She knew if she turned to wave good-bye to her mother, she probably would not be able to bring herself to turn back around to continue walking towards the train. With no other choice, she hung her head and walked until she was out of Mama's sight.

That was ten years ago; she had never returned home.

Oscar's family on the other hand did not survive aggression, oppression, depression, or poverty. As a matter of fact, even though his family wasn't exactly British royalty, they were not peasants either. His ancestors, who were from the bottom layer of the upper crust of London, way back when stuff like that mattered, had done well enough to be given land in order to establish British cotton plantations in Anguilla. Plantations in Anguilla turned out to be a bust since the island had very little rich soil and even less rainfall. Plantations or not, the Duncans were still Lords of the Land over this small, desolate island kingdom.

Sadly even though the Duncan family moved to the island of Anguilla during times of slavery, and even though they had been given land free of any debt, and despite the fact they had been one of the founding families, they somehow managed to survive for a couple hundred years on this tiny little Caribbean island without prospering. Another oddity was that, despite their living in Anguilla for over three hundred years, the family history remained somewhat obscure.

The good news for the Duncan clan was they still owned a lot of what was once considered to be worthless land on a scrub-brush Caribbean island. The even better news was that in the age of fun in the sun, when the rich bought homes in every exotic location on the face of the earth, the land was no longer worthless. The question remained, however, as to whether the current Duncan family would manage to squander away one more incredible business opportunity, or would they finally prosper.

Oscar had met Iggy a few years back while he was on a trip to visit his family in London. Almost instantly they fell in love and got married. The rest, as they say, is history.

Iggy's childhood hardships had long since gone away and her dreams were coming true. Other than adding Iggy to his life, Oscar's life remained much the same as it was when he was a child with Desmund, who was never too far away.

***

It was early evening when Oscar and Iggy were walking down the beach to the Hut. Iggy abruptly stopped and asked Oscar to sit down on the sand so they could talk about something important. As usual, five minutes into the conversation, Oscar was struggling to comprehend just what it was they were talking about, as Iggy continued her somewhat directionless conversation.

"All I'm saying is I've heard drinking alcohol is bad for a baby's brain," Iggy said with her strong Slovakian accent while watching her toes scrunch up sand between them.

Oscar, her loving, doting, and typically alcohol-consuming husband, listened cluelessly and was confused as to where this conversation was going. He sat beside her with a beer in his hand, not sure if he should continue drinking while they talked, or just pour the remaining beer on the ground then begin getting undressed in order to start making babies. "Well, I suppose you're right. I mean, if we had a baby I don't think I'd let him drink beer until he was at least eight or ten. Seems like a bad habit to get him started on right at birth."

Iggy sighed in frustration before responding. "No, Oscar. I'm not talking about a baby drinking alcohol. I'm talking about the mother and father drinking while trying to make a baby. Gawd, do I have to explain everything to you?"

Oscar smiled at her question and said nothing for a few seconds as he watched the waves splash near their feet. Conversations like these were nothing new to him. He was well aware of the interrogation process he was going to have to gently apply in order to extract the pertinent information she had clearly forgotten to share with him.

"Iggy, may I be so bold as to inquire... are you pregnant?"

"No!" she shot back as if surprised by the question. "And it's a good thing too, the way you've been drinking lately. The poor child would be as dumb as a rock."

"Hmmm. Well then, are we planning on making a baby in the near future? Is that where this conversation is going?"

"Oscar, we talked about this."

"No... No, I would definitely remember talking about creating a new life and bringing it into our world, changing our lives forever and ever," he said with his ever-present British-Carib accent. "I'm certain I'd remember that conversation."

"Oh, maybe you're right," she said with a slightly puzzled look on her face. "Maybe I was going to talk to you about it, then I forgot to, but now I want to talk about it," she said as she wrinkled her nose, which was something she did when she was thinking really hard.

"OK then. Now we're getting somewhere. What are your thoughts on the subject?"

"I wanna have a baby," she blurted out.

"All right," he said, while pondering how this might affect his life. "And how soon would you like this to happen?"

"Now."

When he heard that, Oscar hung his head in solemn resolution that they were in fact going to begin the blissful process of making a baby. For all of her faults, despite the fact that her wits were so dim a flickering candle burned brighter, Iggy was beautiful and had a heart of gold and he loved her more than life itself. He could never say no to her, at least not on the big issues like "I wanna have a baby." On top of all of that, he knew he'd be deceiving himself if he thought he was going to try to convince her, or himself, that he could say no to her when she slid into their bed and cuddled her sleek body up against his stump of a torso. All signs pointed to the obvious; The Duncans were going to make a child, whether the world was ready for it or not.

Oscar and Iggy Duncan were about as unlikely a couple as you could ever find, and it was difficult to determine if that made them a great couple or a terrible couple. Oscar was light-skinned, ivory white like a white whale, except for some red-rash pimply blemishes splattered about here and there. He clearly had no business living anywhere that had as much sun as a Caribbean island. A daily dose of Carib sun was probably more than he should have been exposed to in an entire year. But such is life. Or as Oscar would say, "Ya can't help lovin the place ya love, can ya now?"

He was short, squat, and somewhat round, with a compact physique that gave him the look of being a slightly oversized hobbit who had spent most of his life eating fried foods, drinking beer and rum, and lifting weights. Perhaps Bilbo Baggins on steroids, following a hearty diet washed down with a lot of beer, would have been a good description of what he looked like. The fact that he smoked a lavish amount of ganja was simply a side note that had little to do with his appearance, other than the constant redness of his eyes.

Iggy, in contrast, had a nearly perfect bronze-olive complexion with flawless skin, long dark silky hair, and eyes that gave a hint of some Greek or Italian ancestry. Her body was tiny, but strong-looking at the same time—like that of a ballerina, or a Greek-goddess version of Tinker Bell. This all made her nothing short of breathtakingly beautiful and the exact opposite of Oscar. To accentuate their differences even further, Oscar was a quick-witted, sharp-minded intellect of sorts, always reading, researching, and studying anything that caught his interest. One week he'd be reading everything he could get his hands on relating to the history of Anguilla or Peru or New Guinea. The next week he would be researching various techniques on becoming a successful trader in the stock market. Not that he had any money to invest in stocks, nor did he think he ever would, but one day someone sitting at the bar mentioned they weren't doing too well in the market, and Oscar became obsessively curious about how the whole stock market thing worked. Inevitably, not too far down the road, after that conversation, something else would catch his attention and he would once again unconditionally commit himself to learning the new topic with zest, like how to bend the wood to make the curvy parts of a rocking chair, or the side effects of taking Viagra. As long he was learning about the side effects of Viagra, he would probably need to find out how long they took to create it, how much the research cost; and of course he would need to try it out just so he could give his opinion on how well it did or didn't actually work.

Iggy, however, was what one might call dimwitted. She was the classic case of the girl who would continue to write checks as long as there were blank checks in her checkbook, never quite grasping the connection between writing checks and needing money in the bank to cover them. Iggy was the girl who opened magazines to look at the pictures, and never seemed to notice there were stories written that accompanied the pictures of the women in the great dresses with matching shoes. But with all that said, she was still the most compassionate and the most beautiful person Oscar had ever met.

Despite their differences, they somehow happily maintained a uniquely healthy relationship. She was slow-witted, he was quick; she read nothing, he read everything. She survived completely on her exceptional good looks, her petite figure, her obvious sex appeal, and her heart of pure gold, while Oscar was as attractive as she was intelligent, and had a personality as blunt as he was round. They were perfectly mismatched.

The world would be blessed if they ever decided to have children, and if—*if* being the key word—if they were fortunate enough to combine their best attributes. Any child, male or female, who inherited Iggy's charm and exceptional good looks, combined with Oscar's intellect and thirst for knowledge, would be like a god or goddess sent from the heavens to be a blessing to mankind.

On the other hand, if the poor child combined their worst features, he or she, or whatever it turned out to be, would be nothing short of a hideous abomination. To imagine Oscar's short chubby build, kinky dirty-blond hair, complimented by rashy red patches on ultra-white skin, not to mention his complete lack of social graces, put together with Iggy's obvious moronic intellect and indescribable gullibility, had more than once caused Oscar to ponder whether or not they should ever take a chance on having children at all. Clearly, if they decided to reproduce, the risk/reward factor would have to be carefully weighed, as they would have to decide if it was worth the risk of ending up with a troll-like abomination instead of an angelic gift from God. He considered the whole idea to be unsettling and had even once tried to calculate the odds of coming up with Beauty versus Beast. As it turned out, no matter how much he researched and factored in variables, and no matter how many genealogic trends he brought into the equation, it always turned into a 50-50, hit or miss deal. It was like playing Russian roulette with his sperm.

"So what do you think?" she asked Oscar as he now stood above her with his hand reaching down to help her to get up from the beach.

"About alcohol and babies, or about making a baby?"

"Oh, we don't even need to talk about the first one. You're going to have to give up the drinking. My father was a drunk as far back as anyone remembers. They say it kills the brain cells in babies. You just don't take a chance on something like that," she replied with a tone of knowledgeable confidence that surprised Oscar. This was clearly an issue near and dear to her heart, and it sounded as if she may even have done some research that included reading actual words and pages on the topic. If this was the case, Oscar's party days were numbered.

Oscar listened, and as always, he thought. He wondered if her father's drinking had anything to do with her slow intellect, then he wondered if *she* thought about the same thing. Most of the time he presumed she didn't really contemplate her IQ and probably didn't realize just how challenged she actually was. Ignorance is bliss. But other times he could sense her frustration. He wondered if she connected the dots between her learning curve and the enormous amount of alcohol her father had consumed over the years. While Oscar was a dedicated party boy-man, her father was a full-on hard-core alcoholic. They were both drinkers, but the old man was in a completely different league. On the other hand, Oscar was a self-centered human being who instantly connected the dots between his carefree party life and the changes that must come to his immediate future if they were going to procreate.

If, he thought to himself. Iggy was making a request. He knew he was going to submit to her. He always did. There was no *if*.

A twinge of anxiety rushed through his veins as he pondered sober days and nights, along with the thought about breaking the news to the bar gang. For just a moment, he felt as if he were back in high school, contemplating informing Alice Spillman that he didn't want to date her anymore. The big difference, of course, was that while he really didn't want to date Alice any longer, he still wanted to date his friends at the Hut. Then he realized sobriety was going to be more like a teenage boy giving up porn. Alice had been heartbroken but prideful; when she received the news she simply called him some names, insulted his sexual prowess, and then went along on her merry way. The gang was going to be more like a copy of *Penthouse*, always lying there, waiting for him to take just a peek, that would likely lead to something more. Unlike Alice, the gang would be there as a constant temptation. That was something he was certain of.

"So when you say *now*, could you be just a bit more specific? I mean, do you want to start this week, or this month, or this year?

"Tonight would be good. We could blow off the Hut and go home to start right now if you want to," she said with a mischievous smile on her face.

"Hmmm. Well, perhaps we could just stop by for one drink, say hi to the gang, then we could head home. Nothing strong, mind you. Just a beer, then off we go. What do ya say?"

Iggy smiled and leaned her body firmly against Oscar's and slid her hands in the back pocket of his jeans, pulling his hips tightly against hers. He breathed in the scent of her perfume. Her long hair brushed against his face as she leaned in to kiss him. When their lips touched, he was surprised to feel the tip of her tongue ever so lightly flick into his mouth, enticing him and making him wonder if blowing off the Hut might be the way to go. But bad habits are not that easily broken, and after a long, hot, passionate kiss, they strolled arm in arm towards their friends waiting at the bar.

Four hours later, they walked with three feet between them. Iggy's arms were tightly crossed across her chest in disgust, sending the message that she was clearly blocking any possibility that Oscar might be touching her perfect body tonight.

"Come on, it—"

"Quiet!" Iggy snapped, cutting him off in mid-sentence as she continued her brisk pace, staring straight forward.

"I didn't drink—"

"Don't talk to me!" she snapped again.

"If I had known about the baby-making earlier, I—"

"SHUT UP, OSCAR!" This time the yelling did not stop. "You had the choice of being in our bed with my legs wrapped around you, my body doing whatever you wanted it to do. You could have made love with me, or... idiot... you could get drunk with Pellet and the morons and sleep on the couch by yourself. Well, I guess I don't have to tell you, I will not be wrapping my legs around you and you won't be sleeping with me tonight!"

In retrospect, even Oscar wondered what his reasoning could have been when he decided drinking with the morons was a better idea than lying on clean cotton sheets in the warm Caribbean night, exploring Iggy's body while trying to create a new life. In his drunken stupor he convinced himself that despite his obvious bad judgment, it would not happen again.

"Iggy, I'm sorry that—"

"SHUT UP, OSCAR!" When she was on the beach, before he drank seven beers, the thought of making a baby, creating a new life, beginning a family with him, had made her feel whole. It filled her with warmth and a newfound contentment. In the heat of the moment, she was surprised by how sexually excited she had become. Every inch of her body tingled with erotic exhilaration as she impatiently waited while Oscar drank his first beer of the night.

The tingling arousal was long gone now, and had been replaced with the scornful anger that only a rejected woman could vindictively cling to. Earlier in the evening she had intended to screw the hell out of the man she loved with every inch and ounce of her lovely body. She had intended to have sex with him until they were both exhausted.

Now he was simply screwed. There was little doubt he'd be exhausted by the time Iggy stopped being angry with him. "Really Iggy, I'm—"

"SHUT THE FUCK UP, OSCAR!" This time she not only yelled, but her face was contorted in rage.

They walked the rest of the way home in silence. After climbing the small stairway onto their porch, Iggy stormed through the front door, marched down the hall, and slammed the bedroom door. Oscar heard the door lock turn as he plopped himself onto the couch with no blanket and no pillow. The last thing he thought of, before drifting off into a hazy drunken sleep, was Iggy's naked body lying on the white sheets, behind the locked door.

CHAPTER ELEVEN

WHAT'S IN A NAME?

In 1828, Charles M. Stodgy considered himself to be a visionary, an explorer, a new, improved and enlightened version of Ponce de León. For most of his adult life, Charles dedicated nearly every available moment to finding the Fountain of Youth—along with running the Stodgy Trading Post at the south end of Main Street in Savannah Georgia. He avidly believed that somewhere in the great land of America, the elusive Fountain flowed like a river from God himself. He also believed that it was his calling, his obligation, his destiny to find it, thus allowing his name, if not his very life, to go down in history to be remembered for all time to come, and for all mankind to admire. In his mind, Charles Stodgy, much like Peter the Great, Christopher Columbus, and Ponce de León himself, would go down in the annals of history and become a household name to such an extent that streets, parks, towns and cities would proudly claim the Stodgy name.

After years of studying everything he could find from the seemingly endless volumes written by or about Ponce de León, and the elusive Fountain and its possible location, Charles drew a conclusion. Using his self-proclaimed razor-sharp wit, his keen investigative abilities, his admittedly limited education, and most importantly, his unwavering faith in God and the Fountain, he deduced that the Fountain was located somewhere in the southwest area of what would later become the State of Arkansas. All that was left to be done was to work out a few details, raise some additional funds to support a quest, and put an expedition party together. Then history would be made.

Many decades and several generations later, Matty Stodgy sat on the rickety front porch of her small home on Brisbane Road in downtown Stodgy Arkansas. Not surprisingly, the Fountain of Youth was nowhere to be seen. The truth was that after months of traveling while enduring the hardships of the journey, this was the very spot where the original group as a whole had decided to say, "Enough is enough." They were tired, worn out; a couple had died along the way, the food was running short, and winter was coming. It was time to make camp for a season. Charles in his infinite wisdom decided it would be good to rest until spring. After a season of recuperation they could resume the expedition once they had recovered from their hardships.

By spring they had begun to settle in. Cabins were being built and gardens were being planted. They decided that this location, which was promptly named Stodgy, would become the home base for the never-ending search for the Fountain. The Fountain of course would not be found, at least not the way Charles had imagined, but his search, which continued sporadically for the next thirty years, kept him young at heart and helped him to survive into his late sixties. That was quite an accomplishment in those days, especially for a Stodgy man.

A century and a half later, Matty who did not share his vision of eternal youth, was keenly aware that the definition of the word *stodgy* was "boring, dull, uninteresting, dreary, turgid, tedious, dry, unimaginative, uninspired, unexciting, unoriginal, monotonous, humdrum, prosaic, or staid." In her mind, those words aptly described what Charles had created in southwest Arkansas.

As if simply living in Stodgy wasn't mundane enough, and the word *living* could be considered somewhat of an exaggeration, Matty's Aunt Rita threw an additional twist into her otherwise uneventful life. Rita, who was destined to be a spinster librarian from the time she was fifteen years old, had moved in with her brother, Matty's father, thirty-some years ago while studying for her degree in Library Science, and she simply never left. Aunt Rita was a woman of few passions, but the few interests she had were pursued with a feverish zealousness that could not be denied.

First, it appeared she would be a spinster until the end of time: No man could come close to penetrating her tweed-covered exterior barrier, since the tragic time when Ralph Nelson broke her heart in ninth grade. The high school Romeo and Juliette love affair, coupled with the devastation that ensued when poor Ralph told her he was asking Darlene Smith to the school dance, were enough to inspire Rita to swear off all men, except for Jesus, for all eternity.

Rita's second passion, which was a close second right behind Jesus, was the love she had for Matty. Over the years Rita had become a sort of mother/big sister character and she flipped back and forth between the two roles as naturally as a woman who had been there since Matty was born, which was exactly how long she had been there. Becoming a permanent household resident for the rest of her life had never been the plan in the Stodgy residence. But given her past reputation for not being able to handle rejection very well, as well as the distinct fact that she had never offered to move out, the family never broached the conversation. After thirty years of visiting, she was still visiting.

Other than Jesus and Matty, Rita had only one other interest and she clung to it tightly. What had originally inspired her to begin going to the library, and to eventually become the town librarian, was her never-ending quest to map out her family history, right down to the most mundane, miniscule, and absurd detail. As if digging up and no doubt embellishing legends about her long-deceased ancestors wasn't enough, she also insisted on rekindling the search that Charles Stodgy had started back in the 1800's.

By the time she was six, Matty could recite dates and facts about his expeditions and endeavors as if she were reciting history lessons about the Revolutionary War or other authentic American history. Rita had shown her the maps and the journals that had somehow survived for a couple of centuries without producing so much as one drop of life from the eternal Fountain of Youth. Somewhere along the line—Matty couldn't quite say when it actually happened—Rita came to the conclusion that old Charles was not crazy for searching for the Fountain, but he and Ponce had simply misread a key element of the search. While both men were considered to be Godly men, who had prayed for strength and guidance as well as anything else He might provide, Rita saw quite clearly what they had missed. After years of reading journals, maps, notes, and the Bible, she realized the documents were all intertwined. It was obvious to her that Jesus was the Fountain of Youth, but not in the conventional Biblical way. Like Charles, she believed the Fountain existed. But she believed the Fountain *was* quite literally Jesus, who was most certainly located somewhere near Stodgy Arkansas. Like Charles, once she had dug her holy fingers deep into this pietistic thought process, she committed the remainder of her life to finding the sacred Fountain.

So growing up in the small, dingy town in southwest Arkansas, Matty spent much of her time with a woman who was devout beyond words, a Christian, and a woman who thought herself to be a sister/mother to her niece. She also wholeheartedly believed that Jesus had converted himself into a pool of water that lived in an eternal spring, river, pond, or lake somewhere in the vicinity of Stodgy. Being a woman who evangelized as a way of life, Rita would not consider keeping all this good news to herself. So as luck, fate, or the Fountain would have it, she spent an absurd amount of time reminding the locals that she and her family, which included Matty, were direct descendants of the legendary Charles M. Stodgy. After a hundred plus years of the dream being dormant, the search had resumed. The quest to find liquid Jesus was underway.

At twenty-eight years old, Matty sat on the front porch of her small Stodgy home, contemplating her life and the strange series of events that had brought her to this point in time; to this place in the universe. While she sat on her front porch in a slightly drunken stupor, she wondered what it all meant. Over the years, Aunt Rita had bored her with so much family history and so much of the family name that Matty had actually gone to the library to look up the derivation of the word *stodgy*. She was quite certain that when she found the reference it would say something to the effect of "See Charles M. Stodgy and his descendants." When she finally completed her research, the only thing she knew was what she had already known. Stodgy meant dull or uninspired, or if applied to food, it meant heavy; but there was no reference to its origin. She wondered if the family was named after the word *stodgy*, or did someone who knew the Stodgy family long, long ago create a new adjective based on what they knew of them. She took a long drag off her cigarette then leaned back in the rickety old rocking chair, as she watched the smoke roll out of her lungs and up into the air while she regrettably began to accept the fact that Stodgy was going to be her last name once again.

Matty Stodgy dated Carl Savall for the last two years of high school. Their young love grew deeper while she went to nursing school and he went to four years of college. After college things got serious. She started a nursing career and he went to three years of med school. After he graduated they tied the knot, moved to Little Rock where he did his internship. That was where Matty thought he would open a private practice, settle down and live happily ever after, more or less. Needless to say, she was more than a little surprised when he came back to their small apartment one afternoon and announced he wanted to return to Stodgy to open his practice in a place where they already knew the good people of the town. She would have been lying to say she wanted to return to the place where her family legend was still being kept alive and well by Aunt Rita. But home was home. It was hard to generate a valid argument for not returning to the place where they both were born and raised.

The real shock came about a year after their return to their hometown. Carl walked into the kitchen one warm, muggy summer evening as Matty was slicing a pork roast and suddenly blurted out, "Matty, I know this is going to be hard to comprehend, but I'm gay. I'm moving out."

She stood at the kitchen counter with her left hand holding the large fork that was sticking into the roast and her right hand holding the carving knife that was sliced halfway through the pork. Her mind could have simply gone blank once he made his announcement and she could have stood there at a loss for any meaningful words. Or she could have hysterically screamed a dozen or more phrases or profanities. But in the shock of the moment she simply stood there for a few seconds with her head motionless as she struggled to process the unbelievable statement Carl had just heaved upon her.

"You're gay? A gay proctologist? You're a gay proctologist? Are you fucking kidding me?" Her tone started out at a calm level, almost a whisper when she began talking, but ended up loud enough that anyone passing on the sidewalk outside the house would have heard her yelling voice.

"I don't see why being a gay proctologist is any bigger of a deal than being a heterosexual gynecologist," he replied weakly.

"WE'RE MARRIED!" Matty screamed back at him.

"Well... yes. I suppose there is that," Carl answered with a sheepish look on his face. Clearly he had said all that needed to be said for now. He hung his head as he slowly turned around, and walked towards the front door to pick up the shoulder bag he had set down on his way into the kitchen. He had thought about his escape plan prior to the conversation starting, but as the carving knife flew across the kitchen, and glanced off his shoulder, barely missing his head, he realized that breaking this kind of news to Matty while she was holding a butcher knife was probably a strategic mistake. Fortunately he managed to escape the evening without serious bodily injury, and the rest, as they say, is history.

As is often the case in life, everything became crystal clear in hindsight, and this situation was not the exception to the rule for Matty. Once they began dating in high school, Carl had never, not even once, showed interest in another girl or woman. He got along with all of her friends; despite valiant efforts by some of her less than loyal sorority sisters, he had never even flirted with any of them. The nurses loved him, the office girls loved him, hell... all the women loved him. But Carl was as steady as a rock. He was well on his way to becoming a successful doctor, he was a good husband, he had a lot of friends, and he was by all means a kind and wonderful human being.

Despite the bomb he had dropped on Matty while standing in the kitchen that fateful summer evening, she was still somewhat taken aback when he moved out of their house and moved in with Steve Baker. Steve was a childhood friend who was proudly, flamboyantly, flamingly gay, and who wore his homosexuality like a badge of honor. She could not quite put her finger on how she could have missed that relationship or the signs that pointed to it. Needless to say, the failed marriage, and the speculation that Matty was the one who turned such a fine, young specimen of a man to desire such an unnatural relationship, was the talk of Stodgy.

Over the next few months, Matty spent most of her days hanging around the house trying to figure out what to do with the rest of her life. She spent most of her evenings sitting on the front porch smoking cigarettes, a newly acquired habit, and sipping Riesling, an old habit that she was increasingly practicing and coming to cherish.

In the end, she was surprised that the death of their holy matrimony wasn't the most devastating part of the entire fiasco. Without ever realizing it until it came time to give it up, one of the best things about marrying Carl, other than that he was the catch of the town, was that his last name was Savall. She loved the name Matty Savall almost as much as she loathed the name Matty Stodgy. Once the dust had settled, she realized she was probably going to have to revert back to her maiden name or be forced to repeatedly tell the story about Carl, her gay proctologist ex-husband, and how she was pretty sure, but not one hundred percent certain, he was gay before they dated, and she was not the cause of his sudden unveiling. As much as she disliked the name Stodgy, it was clear she was headed back to her original title of Matilda Bethany Stodgy, the living, breathing legacy of the town founder and the descendant of the seeker, or seekers, of the Fountain.

The late October nip was biting at her cheeks as she sat, wrapped in an old blanket, on the front porch. It was a cold, drizzling Stodgy evening and smoke drifted out of the dirty ashtray as her cigarette slowly burned itself out. An almost untouched glass of wine sat on the table beside the ashtray. The routine had become a nightly routine and Matty had no problem justifying her self-pitying mode. But last night when one of the neighborhood boys walked by, he stared at her with a long, puzzling look. That was when she suddenly realized she was talking quite loudly… to herself. A few too many glasses of wine motivated by too much bitterness, mixed with self-pity and nicotine, had caused Matty to slip into a strange inebriated world where conversing out loud to herself somehow seemed normal — or, at the very least, acceptable. She snapped, "What are you looking at?" in the direction of the young boy who quickly hung his head and moved on; but even in her stupor she knew that perhaps it was time to make a major life change. Tonight she was only sipping, not drinking, while she was re-reading a brochure that Alice Graham had given to her a couple of weeks earlier.

Alice was one of those crusty antique RNs who seemed as if she had been born an old gruff battle-axe. She had been the Head Nurse in the Little Rock clinic where both Carl and Matty had worked right after college. Matty had been a full time nurse while Carl came in to work as an assistant to help pay their bills. Most people didn't know too much about Alice; certainly her staff knew nothing other than what she believed they needed to know. The truth was, Alice was an enigma to most people and rarely did anyone hear of the adventures that she had experienced in another lifetime before Little Rock.

News of Matty's separation and divorce, coupled with Carl's change or revelation of his sexual preference, spread fast through Stodgy and among their friends and colleagues back in the Little Rock medical community. Shortly after the separation, a knock came on Matty's door. Much to her surprise, when she opened the door, the Rock of Gibraltar, the worn old battle-axe, stood there with a warm smile on her face and instantly reached out to give Matty a big hug. Even more surprisingly to Matty, she nearly collapsed into Alice's arms like a little girl cuddling up with her mother after having her heart broken in junior high. They spent the afternoon talking, as they sipped tea, not wine. Alice told Matty about her younger nursing days when she was a lieutenant in the Air Force. She shared stories about what it was like living in Japan and Korea. She told her about working in a Los Angeles trauma center and how every day seemed like she was working in a war zone. Then there was her own divorce, that was much less colorful than, but probably just as traumatic as Matty's. There were no flamboyant stories that led to her divorce, just too much work by both parties. They were two people married to their careers, and a person can only have one true love at a time. Being a nurse had always been Alice's first love. After her six-year military career, after the war years in LA, and finally after the weight of her own divorce had taken its toll, Alice decided to make a life change. Through an old friend she had heard about a nursing job in the Caribbean island of Anguilla. The pay was lousy, the work was somewhat unrewarding, the rotations were long, supplies were sparse; but the water and the skies were blue, the weather was warm, and the people were peaceful and loving. It was exactly what she had needed at that time in her life. She had come to Matty's house to pass on the gift of Anguilla.

"I knew something wasn't right with that little son of a bitch, you know?" Alice said as they sat on the couch.

"Is that right?" Matty replied with a tone of skepticism.

"Look, Andrea Smith might be a lousy nurse and a worse human being, but she's as sexy of a woman as either one of us have ever seen. While I would normally commend a man like Carl who repeatedly ignored her come-ons, I have to say he didn't even feign a hint of carnal interest. That poor woman almost had a breakdown when she couldn't get a response from the unflappable Dr. Savall. Believe it or not, one day when she gave one of her gallant attempts to catch his eye, and he simply ignored her once again, she actually mumbled, 'The man has to be gay,' as he walked out of the nurse's station. It was probably the first time in her life she figured something out before anyone else."

Matty sat emotionlessly on the couch. She had gone through the different levels of denial and depression and rage. She was now at the point of wondering what the hell had happened to her dream life. She was not happy to come to the realization that she was at the very beginning of trying to figure out what was to be next in her life, which she thought she had already mapped out. She took pride in her nursing career and looked forward to starting a family soon. She liked being married to Doctor Carl; her life seemed orderly and blessed. But that was then and things had drastically changed. That's where Alice came in. She handed Matty a tourist magazine with pictures of the little island that showed plush resorts, luscious restaurants, and elegant, graceful, filthy rich expats. None of which would be the part of the island life Matty would experience, unless of course one of the ultra-neon-white New Yorkers laying out in the sun too long without proper sunscreen, came into the clinic demanding that she make the pain go away so they could enjoy their much-needed vacation far from Madison Avenue.

"Ignore all the fancy stuff and pretty people, and look at the water, the beaches, and the humble-looking locals in the background. Then understand it's too hot most of the time, you run out of water on a regular basis, electricity is intermittent, and everything is too expensive. You will work too hard, get paid too little, and wonder what you're doing there half the time. You need to trust me when I tell you, you'll love the experience, you'll hate the experience, but most importantly, you need this experience. There's more to life than Arkansas Matty. There's life after Carl the gay proctologist."

Matty looked down at the magazine without actually paying attention to the pictures. More than anything, having Alice in the house comforted her, and she was relieved to be talking to someone who wasn't from Stodgy. Moving to a little island in the Caribbean seemed a bit extreme, but then again, the whole Carl thing was more than she could have ever imagined. Years later, when she told a friend her life story, he would simply smile and say, "Man... you couldn't make this shit up." He would be right. She not only couldn't have made it up, why would she have wanted to?

"I didn't know your home town was named after your

family," Alice added into the silence. Matty cringed and instantly thought maybe moving to an island would be a good change for a while. Alice laid the brochure about the island hospital down on the coffee table. Before she left she told Matty to give it some thought and to call her when she was ready.

This all led up to the cold rainy night when she sat on the porch, rocking in the old rocking chair, with the brochure in her hand. She was physically, but more importantly, she was emotionally drained. It seemed like it might be time to do something drastic before she started yelling at the neighborhood children on a regular basis. Taking a deep breath, she dialed the phone. After four rings a voice on the other end said hello. Matty closed her eyes and hoped she wasn't making a mistake.

"Alice, this is Matty. I'm ready for Anguilla. What's the next step?"

CHAPTER TWELVE

SEVEN WINDS

Jasper's Seven Winds Junction was a dirty, dismal little gas-station town, located on a long stretch of road on the outskirts of nowhere. For the most part, the town consisted of the gas station and Betty's Diner, an unappealing, dilapidated breakfast place, whose owner was bold enough to call it a diner despite serving almost nothing fit to eat. Several years ago, Betty had decided that if this was a good place for a gas station, then it was surely a good place for a restaurant. Betty and Jasper were both wrong, as the new entrepreneurs had failed to take into account the lack of living, breathing, and—most importantly—paying customers. In due time they would find a remedy for that problem.

***

In what had become the norm in his ill-fated life, Clive Higgins was the lone forlorn-looking customer parked on the victim's side of Betty's foul-smelling lunch counter. Over the years, Clive had experienced his share of greasy spoons and was accustomed to the unappealing smells of stale burger grease and the pungent aroma of the current 'Daily Special.' But Betty, a seasoned grill master, had taken the roadside diner experience to inconceivable gastronomical levels, creating a peculiar odor even the battle-scarred road warrior would struggle to identify. After a few meals he had given up on trying to figure out what freakish combination of ingredients could possibly cause the powerful, gaseous cloud that seemed to engulf the diner.

In some kind of make-believe world, Clive would have liked to think this was his first and last meal at Betty's, but it was neither. He would also like to believe he was simply waiting for his pickup truck to be repaired at Jasper's Garage, so he could leave this grimy nothing of a town later in the day. Regrettably, the sad truth was his truck had been under repair for more than two weeks now, yet he was still sitting here at Betty's, as if he were some dried up old bug stuck on a filthy sunbaked windshield with no hope of changing locations anytime in the foreseeable future. He also would have liked to convince himself that he was sitting at Betty's because the coffee was fantastic, the food was delicious, and the company was even better. The unfortunate truth was the coffee was quite possibly the worst he had ever had, he rarely ate more than the minimum amount his body required, and compared to Betty's charming personality, the coffee and food were the selling points of the diner. In a way he couldn't possibly understand, Clive had been drawn to this little spot of dirt like a cockroach being sucked into a vacuum cleaner and he couldn't seem to pull himself away from the draw of the sucking force. Clearly he was going to be stuck here until the vacuum was shut off, or a stronger force pulled him away. Or perhaps he would be stuck here until the vacuum literally sucked all the life out of his beaten-down existence before it simply spit him out the backside, thus enabling his dusty carcass to blow down the road and out of town, like the useless piece of dirt he had come to feel like in recent days. He could only hope that he was nearing the point in time when he could bid farewell to Betty, her daughter Tina, and the conniving old mechanic named Jasper.

After spending five years in a marriage to a woman who could have passed for the bride of Satan, he was overdue for a break, but the break hadn't come yet. Staying true to form, he promptly followed up that relationship by getting involved with another woman who simply smiled at him when a picture of her ran across the TV screen while they were watching *America's Most Wanted*. The narrator dramatically announced, "Nicole is wanted for armed robbery and attempted murder. She should be considered armed and dangerous." As her unflattering mug shot came up on the screen, Clive glanced back up at her with that *oh shit* look on his face one more time.

"Clive, I'm going to do you a favor. I'm not going to shoot you with the gun I keep in your nightstand because you're a good guy. Now, you're gonna do me a favor and not call the police for a while. Tell them whatever you want when they eventually get here, just don't call them anytime soon, OK?" she said as she got dressed.

Clive sat in the bed in a mild state of shock as Nicole, with her long sexy legs, smiled and winked at him as she reached for her bra on the foot of the bed. *How appropriate,* Clive thought to himself. *She gets busted five minutes before we have sex instead of five minutes after we finish. Just my luck.* "OK. Well, I guess we're not really going to Kentucky to visit your family next month, huh?" Clive mumbled as he watched her get dressed.

"Nope, we won't be taking a vacation, Clive, but I will need to take the vacation money with me... if you don't mind. Something to hold me over."

"By all means," Clive added. "Can't see being broke would negatively affect my life all that much, all things considered."

Nicole smiled then leaned over and kissed him on the cheek. Then she ran her fingers through his hair with one hand, while holding the pistol in the other, before turning and walking out of his life, hopefully forever. Several weeks later he scraped up a little cash, climbed into his pickup truck, and headed out for a few days away from life as he knew it. He had never bothered to call the police.

***

There was no real explanation for the draw to this spot in America, to this place with the sign on the gas station that said, "Jasper's Seven Winds Junction." There was no scenic view, or any view at all for that matter, unless you consider miles and miles of flat, brown fields, occasionally dotted with a dust-devil, to be a view. And it wasn't like this void in America was a point halfway between two significant places. In fact, in the middle of nowhere would be a misnomer, because it was actually quite a ways from the middle of nowhere, or anywhere. A more accurate description would be to say that Jasper's Seven Winds Junction was remotely located on the faraway, barren fringe of nowhere, which was even more remote than the middle of nowhere. In truth, there were no good reasons for anyone to come to, or even drive through, Seven Winds. Yet as bewildering as it may seem, some still came. Not many, but just enough to keep the fringes of nowhere alive. Barely alive, but alive.

Forty-one years ago, Jasper, the first and last mayor of the Junction, was driving west on his way to visit a brother-in-law who apparently lived somewhere beyond the badlands. When he hit this particular spot, the spot with the vacuous pull, he stopped to pee on the side of the road and smoke a cigarette.

While puffing on his Camel non-filter and relieving himself at the same time, he glanced at a falling-down *land for sale* sign on the side of the road. He began looking around at the remotely located vortex that was discreetly sucking him into his yet unforeseen and bleak future. For reasons that sounded completely valid to him at the time, he came to a life-changing decision. He promptly got back into his old Buick and announced to his wife, who has been his ex-wife for the last thirty-nine years, that this location would be an excellent place for a gas station and a store.

"Why, there aren't any gas stations for miles," he said to her while giving her his ill-advised sales pitch. The fact that there weren't any customers for miles didn't discourage his enthusiasm one little bit. As a matter of fact, not only was this vortex lacking customers, there wasn't anything for miles. Before the pitch had even begun, he had made up his mind that this location, this insignificant little patch of dirt, this dismal abyss, was the answer to his dreams. Jasper had found his utopia where he immediately and incorrectly knew he had found the place where his riches were to be made. He promptly turned his car around, went back home, sold everything, and returned to the fringes of nowhere, to embark on the quest of creating his future empire, thus accelerating his impending divorce.

History had spun at least a dozen half-baked stories about the origination of the town's name. The un-glorious truth was that, when Jasper opened his new business station, he needed a name better than "Jasper's" to put on the five-cent postcards he was ordering. Using the same thought process which had brought him here in the first place, Jasper thought "Jasper's Seven Wind Junction" was as good a name as any. The summer months were long and hot and the winter months were long and cold, but none of the months had so much as one wind, never mind seven winds. The *winds* part of the name was as much sarcasm as marketing. Adding the *seven* in front of *winds* simply made it sound more appealing, more magical. He had justified the word *junction* with the rumor that he constantly perpetuated, that the state was slated to someday build a north-south highway in this region, thus creating a major four-way junction. The current east-west highway seemingly came from and went to nowhere. Adding the new north-south highway would simply create another identical road connecting different points of nowhere to this 'No Place Junction,' which didn't sound marketable at all. In retrospect, it would have been a fabulously accurate name. But back in those days, Jasper was convinced this small patch on the map would be the next Reno or Salt Lake City, and he was also convinced it wouldn't be 'No Place Junction' for long. Once he ordered the thousand postcards with a picture of his brand-new empire to be, along with the name "Jasper's Seven Winds Junction" printed in bright, bold orange letters at the top of the cards, the name was carved into history and there was no turning back. A few years later he had a guy come up from Greenville who painted a billboard at the edge of town that was a large replica of the postcard. With the oversized postcard planted far from what most people would call civilization, it was official. The town had been named.

Whichever word or combination of words that were sporadically used as the town's name, it was highly unlikely anyone else would ever officially rename the place. There was no one, other than Jasper and his band of twelve citizens, who wanted anything to do with Jasper's Seven Winds Junction in the first place. Logic would have dictated that when the locals eventually shortened the name, it would simply become

"Jasper's" or "Seven Winds," but again, if this had been a place where logic prevailed there wouldn't have been a gas station, diner, or town in the first place. So, when the name was shortened it became "The Junction" or "Winds Junction." A few people called it "Jasper's Junction" along with other assorted labels. In the past couple of years the locals, all thirteen of them, including Jasper, had bastardized the name even further. Some had begun calling the town "Seven," and others were calling it "Winds," with the occasional "Seven Winds" thrown in just to keep the infrequent lost person who was passing through town, confused as to what the name of the town really was—since the billboard had long ago rotted to the ground. The strange pull of the Junction and the thought processes of this peculiar little spot seemed to live eternal in the place that had almost as many names as it did people.

**

Clive Higgins was passing through town when he decided to stop at Betty's for lunch and coffee. It was a mistake on so many levels, but Clive's life had become so abundantly mistake-filled over the past couple of years, that "Damn, this was a mistake!" had seemingly become his life mantra. In the end, the food, the coffee, the company, and worst of all, hiring the mechanic who apparently vandalized his truck while he was being distracted by the strange-looking abomination that Betty had served him on that first day, were all mistakes and they were beginning to pile up. It never dawned on him to consider what the odds were of his truck breaking down at a diner that sat next to the only gas station within fifty miles. If he had given it any thought, he would have realized the odds were pretty damn slim. But try as he might, the truck engine just wouldn't fire up after he finished staring at his greasy, greenish-brown, inedible pile of meat that was alleged to be "meatloaf" on Betty's menu. After tinkering with the truck for a while, he was left with no choice but to walk over to the garage and ask the mechanic to take a look at it. What he should have been asking the mechanic was, would he take "another" look at it, but Clive was not going to figure that out any time soon. Jasper scratched his grey head and said he supposed he could take a look in a few minutes as soon as he finished what he was working on. Clive looked into the garage bay behind Jasper that appeared to be filled with auto parts that hadn't been worked on in fifteen years. He almost asked the unscrupulous old fart what he was working on that couldn't possibly wait just a few minutes, but then decided against the idea of offending the only known mechanic in this region of nowhere. As the decrepit old con man shuffled back into his dirty, unorganized garage with his back turned to his newest customer, Clive could not see the crooked little smile turned up at the corner of his mouth with the knowledge that he had just drummed up another mildly desperate soul who would soon become a temporary cash cow of sorts for the town businesses. As Clive stood in front of the garage and looked around, his heart sank when he realized there was no place to go other than the wretched place called Betty's Diner. He took a deep breath of resignation, mumbled "Shit," and headed back across the dirt parking lot toward the dilapidated building.

He kicked some dirt in Betty's parking lot and hoped his truck wouldn't take too long to fix. Shaking his head back and forth in disbelief of yet one more unfortunate incident to add to a long string of catastrophes that were the sum total of his current life, Clive stood and lit a cigarette in nearly the same spot that

Jasper had smoked, forty some years ago. Taking long drags of toxic smoke into his long ago nicotine-polluted lungs, he looked around one more time to see what there was to see. Strangely enough, other than his experience of being exposed to the inedible food, undrinkable coffee, miserable hospitality, and then his truck breaking down, it seemed as though there was actually something genuinely appealing about this desolate place. He couldn't quite put his finger on it, but there was something almost comfortable, if not inviting, about Jasper's Seven Winds Junction. The pull of the illogical vacuum was taking hold.

After smoking his cigarette, he tossed it on the ground, turned the old brass knob of Betty's front door and headed back inside. When he opened the door, he froze momentarily as he immediately noticed Betty was gone and someone much more preferable had replaced her. At the very least she was better on the surface. The chubby, pale, thin-haired, crotchety old bitch with yellow smoker's teeth and a raspy smoker's voice, and even worse, smoker's cough, was nowhere to be seen. The first time he'd entered, about an hour ago, he sat at the counter in front of the archaic wench who tossed a menu at him and barked, "Let me know what you want when you're ready." Then she promptly turned and waddled her fat ass back into the kitchen to see if there was anything she could possibly pass off as edible food. But right now as he stood in the doorway, the nightmare of the diner had been replaced by the dream of the diner. Clive looked around to see if Betty was somewhere crouched in a corner, perhaps preparing to lunge back into action as soon as he let his guard down, but she was nowhere to be seen.

"Hey, come on in and have a seat," the new girl said in a sweet voice. "I see you been talking to Jasper. Looks like you got truck troubles."

"Yeah, it doesn't seem to want to start," Clive answered as he headed back to the same stool where all his dishes still sat. He wondered momentarily if the same dishes would still be sitting there if he came back for dinner tonight.

"Can I heat that coffee up for you?"

"No, maybe just a Coke," he said, remembering what the coffee had tasted like.

Strange day indeed, he thought to himself as the thirty-something redhead, who was far too good looking to be working here, turned her back to him while she poured a drink from the Coke machine sitting directly in front of him. As if driving through this god-forsaken place hadn't been bad enough, it got worse when he stopped for food, and went one step further downhill when he gave the truck keys to Jasper. But now his luck had seemed to change direction and he suddenly felt good about being here in Seven Winds. It was as if midnight had struck and the evil stepmother had turned into a redheaded Cinderella. *My luck could actually be taking a turn for the better*, he thought quietly to himself.

"I'm Clive," he said, sticking his hand out for her to shake as she handed him his glass of Coke. Over the years, Clive had endured tenuous relationships with several women. None of them had ended well. At some point in the distant future he would come to realize that the beauty of the woman whom he was dating, at any given point in time, was almost always directly proportional to the size of the impending disaster that would eventually end the relationship. Unfortunately, today was not the day Clive was going to discover that tidbit of information; to make the situation even worse, Tina was drop-dead gorgeous.

"Tina," she said, reaching out and grasping his hand

with a nearly perfect handshake. Her hand was soft, but strong. Her grip was exactly firm enough to exude self-confidence, but not in the least bit overpowering. Her vibe... It was sexy and it was all good, and her perfume was even better.

"Nice to meet you," Clive said as he reached for his glass and flashed a friendly smile. "Could have been under better conditions, but I guess fate works magic in its own way, huh?"

Honey, fate's got nothing to do with it, she thought silently to herself as she leaned against the counter and said, "Fate is a good thing." She flashed a smile that could have melted the rusty ice in his glass. But the top two buttons of her blouse were undone, exposing an abundance of cleavage, so Clive barely noticed her smile.

"So what do people around here do for excitement?" he asked in an effort to drum up some kind of conversation.

"Honey, there's not much excitement here in The Winds," she said with another smile as she cleared away his dirty lunch plates filled with food that had been stirred, not eaten. She took the dishes into the kitchen, then quickly returned. It appeared she was anxious to strike up a conversation with the new man in town.

The two of them talked, then laughed and eventually ended up sitting together in a booth, chatting for hours. Tina told Clive about growing up in Jasper's Seven Winds Junction and Clive told her about his life or lack thereof, about his job at the factory where they made concrete septic tanks, and how he was heading to see a cousin who lived a couple of days' drive from here. After he told her where he was from and where he was going, Tina explained if he had turned north three hours earlier, it probably would have shaved about a day off his trip. A more accurate truth would have been, if he had turned north three hours ago, it would have shaved about a couple weeks off his trip, but Tina was not in full disclosure mode when they first began courting each other. The simple fact that someone was traveling through Jasper's Seven Winds Junction almost automatically threw up a flag that the obviously lost stranger had missed a turn somewhere along the line.

None of that mattered to Clive right now. He had already decided that fate had finally dealt him a favorable hand when it brought him to Betty's Diner. Then good fortune had delivered him to a wonderful world where he was sitting in a booth talking to a beautiful, red headed, warm hearted, friendly, and enticing woman named Tina. If he had taken a few minutes to clear his mind and evaluate the situation, he would have come to the obvious conclusion: This was too good to be true.

But she was intoxicating. He didn't take the few minutes—or even a few seconds—to think it over. He was grateful for the company and he was seizing the moment.

A few hours quickly passed in no time at all. When an eventual lull came into their nonstop conversation, it dawned on Clive he needed to go check on the progress of his truck. He presumed, incorrectly presumed, it had long since been repaired and now there would be the small matter of haggling over the cost of the repair before heading down the road. When he wandered into the miniature junkyard of a garage, the old man was sitting on a rickety stool smoking another cigarette.

"Can't seem to find the problem, but that ain't the worst news. The worst news is I gotta go to church tonight and won't be able to work on it anymore till tomorrow morning," he mumbled through the smoke.

In all likeliness, Jasper hadn't been to church in forty years. But Clive hardly put a heartbeat between his disappointment of his truck still being broken down and his excitement that he might be able to spend the evening with Tina. "There a hotel anywhere around here?"

"Go back over and talk to Betty or Tina. They'll get you fixed up in a room," he mumbled, as he got up and strolled through a screen door that led into the part of the building that was a store once upon a time.

***

All those events had taken place over two weeks ago. Betty had set him up in a room for twenty bucks a night. He and Tina had hit it off so well that they even worked up a pretty good sweat between the sheets a few times. Despite the unfortunate state of his truck, Clive was pleased with the current state of his life... for a time. But eventually her redheaded charm began to run out. As a matter of fact, it began running out just about the same time he mentioned his cash was beginning to run low. Jasper had been working on the truck off and on for the entire time he had been staying there. The truth was that Clive had been in no hurry to leave. Now that his cash and Tina's passion were fading, and given that neither Betty nor Jasper took credit cards, it seemed the hospitality Betty had extended by renting him a filthy room with a lumpy mattress while charging him top dollar to serve up almost inedible food was also fading fast. He had gotten into a little run-in with Jasper yesterday morning about the never-ending repair, when it was going to be complete, and how much it was going to cost. The old-timer said he thought the young buck was having a good time with Tina, but if the honeymoon was over, he could probably have the truck running by morning. Clive thanked him and felt sick as he wandered back to Betty's.

He could scarcely stomach the thought of eating more of her cooking, but he was hungry. There was no other choice.

At 7:30 the next morning, Clive wandered out of his room behind the diner. Tina was standing on the back porch already smoking her third menthol cigarette of the day and Jasper was standing in front of the garage talking to a confused-looking county constable and pointing towards Clive.

"What's going on over there?" Clive asked as he neared Tina.

"Daddy said someone stole your truck last night."

"What? Wait! What are you talking about?" he snapped sharply. "What do you mean someone stole my truck? There's nobody within fifty miles of here, and it hasn't started for three weeks. And who the fuck is Daddy?"

"Jasper," she said as she blew a puff of smoke into the air and turned to walk into the diner. Clive didn't see her crooked little smile any more than he had seen Jasper's crooked little smile the day that he had agreed to work on the truck.

Marcellus Ingram was a gray-haired old black man who owned the third and final business in "JJ," as he called it. Marcellus had arrived in town twenty plus years ago, had lunch at Betty's Diner, decided he liked the place, and bought the old run-down shack across from the diner. Once upon a time when Jasper still held on to the dream of creating the "No Place Empire," he had managed to sell a few spots of land to potential founders of the impending kingdom.

Owen Labrie, the original owner of the house, had completely convinced himself, with some encouragement from Jasper, that some day soon his piece of land would be a prime location for a hotel that would surely be needed to accommodate the travelers who streamed through the new highway junction.

With the lack of any nearby intersections, and with the presence of Marcellus sitting on his porch, it was clear that Owen hadn't stayed. With his money nearly gone and his hopes of a bright future dashed, Owen eventually drifted out of town as clueless as he was upon his arrival; minus his investment, of course.

Marcellus, on the other hand, was not a disillusioned entrepreneur. He had enough cash to buy the old place, a government pension to allow him to exist in some menial sort of way, and a taxi business that gave him an excuse to sit on the front porch and read *The Wall Street Journal* while patiently waiting for his next customer. It wasn't as if the *WSJ* had any impact on the world he lived in, but he found the stories to be interesting, and for the most part well written, even if they were about as relevant to Jasper's Junction as a weather report from Russia. Two half-rotted wooden posts in the front yard held the old, faded, hand-made sign that said "MIT" in barely legible ten-inch high red letters. Below the letters, written in a smaller size, were the words "Marcellus Ingram's Taxi."

Today was a typical day for Marcellus. Sitting on the front porch with his inbred mutt that he affectionately called Jasmine, named for the woman whom he abandoned a few decades back, he took no notice of the air that was hot but no hotter than normal. Every once in a while a smidgen of a breeze, which would have to be considered one of the Seven Winds, would puff a tiny momentary cloud of dust into the air, rustle the leaves just a bit, and then settle back into the silent existence that had become Marcellus' peaceful life far from the hectic, crime-ridden city he grew up in. It went without saying that "MIT" had very little taxi business other than the occasional call to take someone to Greenville or Franklin. Even then it was usually a one-way fare, as the customer would likely be one of the thirteen locals going to catch a bus to visit a distant relative who lived somewhere, as opposed to nowhere. To add insult to injury, he rarely charged more than the cost of gas, as he found it difficult to take money from the dirt-poor people who had become his extended family over the past couple of decades. Besides, there really wasn't anywhere to spend money in JJ, so he didn't really see the need to make a profit. Of course, every once in a while a stranger needed a ride somewhere and he would charge them as much money as he could possibly extract from them while they fought to remedy their desperate condition of being stuck at Seven Winds Junction, or even worse, at Betty's Diner. Having no competition for business was pretty much the only perk of owning a taxi business in The Junction.

Sitting in his old rickety chair on the front porch, he used a two-foot tall pile of *Wall Street Journal*s as a table where a plate of half-eaten toast and an almost empty cup of coffee sat beside a charred and haggard corncob pipe and an ashtray that looked as if it hadn't been emptied in twenty years. The paper he was reading was a couple of months old, but since Marcellus interpreted the stories more as fantasy than reality, it didn't matter whether the story was current or not. Every Saturday he received the weekend edition, and sometime over the next year or so, every last word would be read. The journal would eventually become part of the coffee table or starter paper for the fire in his wood stove that he lit when it got cold enough to need additional heat. This morning, however, he wasn't actually reading the paper as much as just holding it up like a disguise as he listened through the perpetual silence of the town to the voices of the three men having a heated conversation in the parking lot across the street.

"Well mister, I understand you're upset, but as I told you

before, these things happen," the deputy responded to Clive's yelling. Randy was a short, chubby little county deputy who always spoke in a high shrill voice that made him sound as if he were in a state of unremitting stress and eternal puberty.

"These things happen my ass!" Clive yelled back as he pointed and shook his finger at Jasper. "This con man kept my truck until my money was all gone, then stole it from me and sold it in the middle of the night!"

"Now you can't just make blind accusations like that, mister. You gotta have some proof before you go blabbing that kind of thing in public," Randy shrilled back at him, as if Seven Winds actually had a public who could overhear such things.

Jasper silently stood with the two men and calmly smoked his cigarette and acted as if he were genuinely concerned about the theft of the truck and hurt by the unfounded accusations that were being so recklessly hurled at him. Clive wondered what public Randy could possibly be talking about and who the hell Jasper had sold his truck to. Since he couldn't see the truck from where he was standing, he presumed someone from Greenville must have worked out some sort of deal with Jasper. After taking another long drag of smoke, he quickly concluded that the truck sale negotiation probably started weeks ago while he was being distracted by the sexy young redhead who had recently referred to Jasper as "Daddy." It was the correct conclusion. Clive looked down at the dirt and recalled the sickening wave he had felt when he first encountered Betty's cooking, then he remembered his heart sinking even further when his truck inexplicably refused to start. Finally he recalled returning to the diner and discovering the soft curves, and irresistible charms of Tina. It suddenly dawned on him that the phrase "Damn, this was a mistake!" should have been the first words that popped into his overly pleased brain. Unfortunately those words had not popped into his brain—now, in the light of day, with hindsight being 20/20 and all that, he could clearly see the words brightly flashing like a neon sign, with all the bells and whistles that typically accompany dangerous, life-threatening hazards. Now that the damage was done, all he could do was pick up the pieces and move on... again.

Marcellus continued to hold *The Wall Street Journal* in front of his face, but just low enough to see the three men across the street trying to solve the crime of the century. He was calculating in his head how long it would be before Clive would come across the street and hire MIT to take him to the bus stop in Greenville. He also wondered how much money the poor boy had left to pay for the ride. If he didn't have enough, Jasper was going to have to kick in a little cash for the taxi ride or else Clive would be hanging around JJ long enough to make everyone just a tad uncomfortable. Thirty minutes later Marcellus saw a beaten man walking across the street with a duffle bag hanging from his slumped shoulder, a cigarette hanging from his mouth, and his head hanging low. It appeared the pull of Jasper's Seven Winds Junction and Tina were no longer tugging at his heart.

"How much for a ride to Greenville?" Clive asked as he tossed his half smoked cigarette on the ground. He couldn't see the crooked little smile on the face of the owner of MIT, as the old driver remained buried behind *The Wall Street Journal*. Ironically, the headline at the top of the page read "Small Business Picks Up." Clive momentarily looked away from Marcellus as a dusty gust kicked up and he noticed a dead piece of tumbleweed blowing down the road, heading out of town. He wondered if there was much difference between him, the dust, and the tumbleweed.

Three hours later Clive found himself in Greenville, slouching down in a dirty, worn-out seat on a bus taking him back to his old life. Sitting next to him was a guy with dreads hanging down his back, covering half the picture on the Bob Marley T-shirt he was wearing. Clive was heading back to Lincoln for one reason and one reason only. He had no place else to go. His satanic wife was long gone and in all likelihood creating a living hell for some other poor bastard. His felon girlfriend with legs that went on forever was ancient history. And as it turned out, Tina, the smoking hot redhead in cutoff blue jeans, who turned out to be a grifter, stayed right where she was, but he got tossed out with nothing but a duffle bag full of dirty clothes. His truck, which wasn't the greatest truck in the world, but at least ran all right prior to pulling into Seven Winds, was now gone, and last but not least, he presumed his job in the septic tank factory was also gone since he hadn't reported for work in the past three weeks. The last one was actually a bit of a relief—with the exception that he was nearly broke, couldn't pay rent, didn't have money for food or a new vehicle, and there were no prospects on the horizon.

The bus was less than half full and he wondered why the Bob Marley guy sat in the adjacent seat as opposed to one of the many completely empty rows. He considered for a moment asking him why he did it, but then thought the Rasta-looking guy might get insulted, or worse, take it as a sign that Clive wanted to strike up a conversation. As the roaring bus pulled out of the station, Clive put his head against the window, closed his eyes, and slouched down.

Just as he was about to fade off to sleep, the Bob Marley guy began talking to him. "How you doin, mon?" he asked, looking directly at Clive.

Clive opened his eyes and looked at him with a puzzled expression on his face. Wasn't it obvious he was about to go to sleep? Wasn't it clear that he wasn't looking for a conversation?

"Everyting cool?" the island man continued.

"Well, I was about to go to sleep, but you woke me up. I guess everything else is all right," Clive answered with an irritated look on his face. He readjusted himself in his seat and closed his eyes again.

"You sure?" the Bob Marley guy shot back.

Clive's face scrunched up and he cocked his head a bit while he tried to understand what the guy was talking about, or more importantly, why he was talking at all.

"You don't look like everyting is cool, mon. Looks like da whole damn world be beatin ya down. Know what I mean?"

"What are you, some kind of fucking Rasta psychic or something?" Clive grumbled.

"No mon. I jus a guy on da bus, but I ain't no psychic. On da other hand, I ain't got no problems either. You... you look like you got a boat fulla dem. Why do you tink I sat with you, mon? Da whole damn bus is empty, but I see you need an ear. You need a change n' maybe I can help. I'm a helpful guy, you know."

"I got a boat the size of the Titanic full of problems that life's been throwing at me for too damn long. But what can I do, huh? Shit happens and then you die. Isn't that how the saying goes?" Clive responded in a moment of carelessness.

"Not in da islands, mon. When tings go good we say everything is cool, when tings go bad, we say da same ting. It's all cool, mon. You should try it sometime."

"Trust me. Saying it's all cool will not fix my life."

"No mon, not just sayin it. You gotta come to da islands

n' live it. It's not just a place, mon. It's a way of life. No traffic, no mail, no worries."

"So what are you trying to tell me? You saying you guys don't have bills to pay or jobs to work and all that other shit? I mean, you do have to pay for electricity, right?" He wasn't really sure how it happened, but Clive had been drawn into the conversation. Now it seemed that unless he got up and changed seats, he was probably stuck in the conversation.

"No, mon. We got jobs. We got electricity to pay for. But in da islands when da current gets turned off, da house jus gets dark, da world don't end. Jus gets dark n' we get it turned back on, n' everyting is cool. No worries."

Clive looked at the Bob Marley guy for a few more seconds, this time with a tad of suspicion as to why this guy sat with him in the first place, and wondered what his motivation was.

"Who the fuck are you anyway? Why are you sitting beside me?"

"I am Mole from Anguilla," he said, with a big smile on his face. "Maybe your luck is changing, huh? Maybe I bring some island vibes n' everyting will be cool for you too."

"So... Why are you sitting by me?" Clive threw back at him.

"Seen you getting on da bus lookin all beat up, n' said to myself, 'Sit with dat guy, Mole, n' see if he needs a friend.' Den I tought about it for a few seconds n' said, Why not? Why not sit next to dis white guy who looks like tings are going bad n' see if I can help? I got no money or nothin, but... you know... I can listen n' stuff. I can do what I can."

Clive shrugged in a gesture that implied, *Why not? What can it hurt?* Then reached out to shake Mole's hand. Mole smiled and grabbed his hand, palm to palm, and then interlocked palms and thumbs, then slid loose and kind of interlocked the ends of his fingers with the ends of Clive's fingers, then let go. Clive stared down at his own hand trying to figure out what it had just done.

"So... What's the deal, mon? Why you be so beat up? Maybe it'll make you feel better to tell da story," Mole said as he relaxed and sat back in his seat. Clive took a deep breath and began venting his frustrations as he described what it was like to live with his first wife. After that, he went on to describe living with Nicole, the tall brunette with the endless legs. That story was actually pretty good until he got to the part about her being wanted for the attempted murder of her husband, a guy she was apparently still married to. Finally he told Mole about Tina, the luscious redhead who had recently swept him off his feet and into her bed, and then promptly stole all his money and his truck. He ended the saga by giving a rundown of what there was to look forward to when he got back home to Lincoln. All in all it sounded as if Clive was about to give up on life; for a moment Mole sat in awe of such a long stretch of bad luck.

"You ever tink bout given up women?" Mole blurted. "I mean, I like sex as much as da next guy, but damn, mon... You can pick em. Maybe you should be a priest or someting," he added as an afterthought then shook his head in disbelief.

"Well, to be honest, every time I think about starting over with a clean slate and staying away from trouble, I meet another one. Then I think, you know, this one seems better. This could be the one. And I'll be damned if the same crap doesn't happen again. What about island women? Think I'd do better with them?"

"No, mon. I tink dey'd see you comin. On the other

hand, island women are cool. Better be careful, though. Ain't no place to run on an island. When dey get mad, dere ain't no place to hide."

"Someplace to hide. That's what I need. A place to hide."

"Da islands, mon! Come to da Caribbean. People are cool. The sea is good. Life is good. Lots of white folks come down to hide from tings."

"Warm breezes and rum drinks, huh?" Clive added.

"No, mon. I don't tink you need no rum drinks. Maybe jus a cold beer n' a little smoke to cool da nerves. Time to relax, mon. Can't do much relaxin if you drinkin rum. Trouble follows hard liquor. You don't need more trouble, huh?"

For the next couple of hundred miles they joked around and told more stories about themselves. Clive talked about growing up as a poor country boy in a big family on a small farm. Mole talked about his dozen or so half-brothers and half-sisters living throughout three or four islands; seemed his father got around just a bit. He described what life was like in the islands and how it had changed over the past decade. But mostly, he talked about the love he had for his homeland of Anguilla. When he described the fresh fish, Clive's mouth watered. When he talked about Goat Water, which was some sort of goat stew, Clive cringed. He spoke of strong, beautiful island women and how they were the most amazing women in the world. Then he described the stubborn crazy island women who were probably the most dangerous women in the world.

"Life ain't good when my woman gets stirred up, Clive. Need to sleep with one eye open when she gets mad," he said, shaking his head back and forth in the same exact manner as way too many women had caused Clive to shake his head back and forth.

By they time they had reached Lincoln the two men had exchanged phone numbers and addresses. Mole had told Clive about some construction projects where he might be able to find work on the island, then he had offered to put him up in a room for a bit if he needed a place to stay. Clive, who had been irritated by the presumptuous black guy who had intruded on his pity party, was now intrigued about the possibility of a fresh start in a world that was completely new to him.

Six months later, after he had scraped up some money and landed a construction job, Clive walked down the stairs of the small island-hopper that had flown him to Anguilla from San Juan. As he stepped onto the tarmac, the sweet evening breeze blew the aroma of island flora, mixed with soft Caribbean air, into his face. Mole threw a wave and a big island smile through the chain-link fence. Clive thought, *What the hell am I getting myself into now?*

PART II

CHAPTER THIRTEEN

THE CONGREGATION

Desmund barely noticed the blue and white fishing boat that was the first of two boats that cruised by the bar. A few minutes later a bright yellow cigarette boat eased through a narrow channel that led into the bay where the sailboat *Aqua Vita* had been anchored for the past twenty hours. Neither boat went near or seemed to pay much attention to the sailboat, or to the Latino man sitting with his feet hanging over the edge of the deck on the starboard side. He had motored the fifty-foot sailboat into the shallow waters and dropped anchor in front of the Hut late in the afternoon yesterday. Since then, other than his coming out on deck a couple of times for just a few minutes, there was almost no sign of life aboard the boat that rocked back and forth like a piece of driftwood floating in the bay. Desmund knew a boat dropping anchor in front of the Hut was not an unusual occurrence, but it was abnormal when no one came ashore once they got everything onboard squared away. After all, the reason people generally sail to shore is to go ashore. Whether for food, fuel, or fun, they always leave the boat and head to dry land. If they wanted to stay at sea, they wouldn't have come to land in the first place.

Julio fidgeted as he sat on the south side of the boat, facing away from land, so no one on the beach could see him. He nervously tapped the deck with the flip-flops he was holding in his left hand while he smoked a joint that he held in the other. It was the third time today he had ventured topside, with the plan of heading ashore, and more importantly, to the island bar he could plainly see while peeking through one of the boat's portholes. The first two times he made it only as far as the deck where he sat down, smoked, and contemplated his choices before going below again. As the fishing boat chugged past, he watched men moving around the deck. One of them looked his way and nodded as he worked to organize his fishing gear. Julio nodded back but then quickly looked away. He didn't want to appear unfriendly, but on the other hand he didn't want to encourage anyone to ease on over his way. He wasn't looking for company to visit the *Aqua Vita*.

A few minutes later the cigarette boat sped to the channel and abruptly slowed down as it eased its way into the bay. Julio pulled his hat down, covering most of his face, as he took another drag from the joint. Once through the channel, the yellow boat accelerated and quickly moved away from Julio. From what he could see, no one onboard had looked his way or even noticed that he was anchored in the harbor. As it disappeared around the stone jetty to the east, he stood up and tossed the last bit of his joint into the water.

"Fuck it. Can't stay out here forever. I'm getting thirsty," he said to no one as he worked his way to the back of the boat, grabbed the rope and pulled the Zodiac close enough to climb aboard. On the fourth pull of the cord the small boat's motor started up and he headed to shore. A chill ran through him as he glanced one last time in the direction of the cigarette boat before his thoughts drifted off to cheeseburgers washed down with rum drinks.

After a day of having his curiosity piqued, Desmund watched the tall lanky guy, in worn-out cargo shorts and a ragged T-shirt with a picture of a sea turtle on his chest, hop out of the small boat and walk through knee-deep water onto the beach. Once he had pulled the boat out of the water, he did what any respectable sailor would do when coming ashore. He headed straight for the bar and ordered a drink.

"What can I get you?" Desmund asked the thirty-something year old guy who strolled in and hopped onto a barstool.

"Rum Punch. May as well keep it tropical," he answered as he took off the floppy hat that protected his head from long hours in the sun. "And may it be the first of many."

"I see you come in on da Zodiac. Dat your sailboat?" Desmund asked as he poured the premixed punch into a glass of ice and rum, and nodded toward the *Aqua Vita*. It wasn't like he didn't already know the answer, but keeping true to form, Desmund liked to get the conversation rolling. Talking customers were typically drinking customers.

"Yup. Been cruising around for a few months now. Air's getting pretty dead lately, though. Thought I might just park it for a few days and see if I could find a bar to hang out at."

"Name's Desmund," he said as he set the drink in front of him and stuck out his hand. "Looks like you found your bar," he added with a smile.

"Julio," he responded. "Nice to be here." He reached into the side pocket of his dirty cargo shorts and pulled out a half-smoked pack of cigarettes. He tapped the pack to get one out and a joint slipped out and landed on the counter. He nonchalantly picked it up and dropped it into the pocket of his T-shirt. Desmund tossed him a book of matches with a little 'Limin Hut' logo on the side and then turned to move on to the next customer, paying no attention whatsoever to what Julio may or may not have been smoking.

"Screama! We need beers," Chatta yelled out as he and a couple of other locals walked in and headed directly for the domino table. Desmund nodded and opened some beers and set them on the bar. One of them would come and get them when they got thirsty enough.

Throughout the islands, most Caribbean men have at least two or three names, sometimes more. Desmund was not an exception to this unwritten naming rule. Desmund Isaiah Kingston was the name given to him at birth, and even though his parents believed it was the best of all names they could have chosen, the only thing for certain was it was the first of many names that would be given to him over the next several decades.

Almost immediately after he was born, Desmund's list of names began to expand when his family started calling him Dezzy. All in all, life was simple and life was good and everyone knew his name was Desmund or Dezzy. By the time he was four or five, his Aunty Labricia began calling him Screama, because if he wasn't upset and screaming about something, then he was happy and screaming about something. Either way, Dezzy was a Screama and that's what Labricia would call him for the rest of her long life.

Island names almost always stick, but they only stick within a particular group of friends. While nearly everyone knew his given name and the shortened versions of it, not everyone knew he was also called Screama.

When Desmund was a teen he developed a reputation as a ladies' man. One afternoon as he and his friends were watching old reruns on TV, the *I Love Lucy* show came on, and Oscar quickly converted Dezzy into Ricky Ricardo. Ricky, played by Desi Arnaz, was the suave Cuban who always had a tribe of little hotties chasing after him. Somewhere along the line, Ricky was dropped and the name was shortened to Ricardo. Hence, one more name was added to the ever-expanding list of aliases. To this day, more than a few island cuties smile and say, "Hey Ricardo," as they pass by.

Of course there are always those on the island who refer to almost all their male buddies by their last name, which can be quite confusing in a small country with a limited number of last names. Nonetheless he was also known as just plain old Kingston or King by some of his friends, as were his father, grandfather, two uncles, three brothers, and a few cousins.

Shortly after Pellet had claimed the Hut as his home turf, he strolled into the bar one afternoon and called out, "Barkeep, a cold beer please." A few minutes later, Boatmon, one of the local boat captains, decided the name suited Desmund just fine, and he called out, "Keepa, another one," holding up his empty glass. From that moment on, one more name was added to what appeared to be an ever-growing list of names. Depending who you were talking to, the friendly island Rasta bartender was now known as Desmund, Dezzy, or Dez for short, Kingston, or King for short, Screama, Ricardo, and last but not least, Keepa.

In keeping with island tradition, no one knew him by all of his names, and like so many island men, when his name came up in a conversation, the next few minutes would be dedicated to deciphering just whom they were actually talking about. If a tourist like Julio sitting at the bar for an hour or two was paying attention to all the people who called out to Desmund upon their arrival, there's a relatively good chance he would have absolutely no idea what the Rasta bartender's name really was.

"Keepa... what's going on, mon?" Boatmon mumbled in a raspy voice as he climbed onto the stool at the far end of the bar nearest the ocean. "Appleton, no ice," he added as if Desmund wouldn't already know what he drank.

"Make it two, King," a tagalong fisherman added as he leaned up to the bar next to Boatmon.

Desmund nodded and reached for the half-empty bottle of rum and poured generous shots into short glasses and handed them to his friends, who began to hash out the island news. The big story of the day was that a local fishermen had fallen out of his boat about ten miles offshore while fishing all by himself. The boat was still running and for the next five hours it ever so smoothly idled large circles round and round, taunting the fisherman as he treaded water and watched the boat perpetually circle him. To aggravate an already bleak turn of events, the poor fisherman had filled both tanks just before heading out to sea. With the engines running barely above a slow idle, the chugging would likely continue for a day or two before the boat would eventually run out of gas and sputter to a halt. The good news was he had a life jacket—but to add insult to injury, like every other fisherman in Anguilla he never wore it. So as he swam helplessly in the water, his boat circling him like a taunting shark, his life jacket was safe and dry under a pile of ropes and fishing gear, still in the plastic bag it was in on the day he bought it two years ago.

"He got lucky, mon. Some Frenchman from Saint Maarten was cruising around in his sailboat and saw him flapping his arms in the water. Pulled him out and saved his ass," Boatmon said as he sipped his rum.

"Same idiot fell outta his boat a couple years back, ya know?" Boatmon added. "Needa give up fishin. Maybe he could drive a taxi or someting." They both chuckled and shook their heads in mild disbelief.

"He catch any fish?" Desmund asked.

"Don't know, but I bet a couple big fish was eying his sorry ass," Boatmon shot back. "After Frenchy got him outta the water, catching the boat was a whole new problem. The dumb bastard fell back in two times, trying to hop from one boat to the other."

"Everyting OK now?" Desmund asked.

"Think so. Happy and dry and back on land. You probably get a good buy on a fishing boat if you're looking for one," he added with a smirk.

The crowd began to grow. Helmut the scribe drifted in and anchored himself in his corner table just as always. Clive, quite predictably looking for love and a cold drink, cluelessly, dropped onto a stool just like he had done a hundred times since his arrival on the island. Pellet, much like Clive, enjoyed his drinks. And he also loved women, or at least dreamed of making love to women while he desperately imagined finding one who would love him back. More important than drinking or loving, just like when he first left Waldoboro Maine, Pellet was still searching for what he commonly referred to as "a life." Regrettably he spent an absurd amount of time searching for love and life while perched upon the barstool directly beside Clive. His odds for success were not increasing with each passing day.

Matty, good looking, tan, friendly, and damaged from an eternity of being the living legacy of Charles M. Stodgy and being hitched to what turned out to be her gay proctologist husband, was simply trying to heal while tanning her lean body on the white beaches of Anguilla. Unfortunately, she was also spending what some might consider far too much of her time at the same bar as Pellet and Clive. While she had often discussed breaking that unhealthy habit, clearly today was not going to be the day it happened, as she strolled along the beach toward the Hut.

Oscar, always the last to arrive, was right on schedule. He thought of himself as an island native, an enlightened white man who was every bit as carefree as his black island friends, perhaps even more laid back than they were. These men were the boys he'd grown up with, and he was the poster child for *the color of your skin does not define who you are*. Like most of his buddies, if he could escape an exhausting conversation with his wife and go have a drink or two with his friends, play some dominos and talk some trash, then life was good. Today his life was good and he chugged along the dirt road in his beat-up old island car, with dust kicking up into the air.

Having been on the island since his early boyhood days, Oscar had seen expats come and go. But this group was a collection of high-spirited, mischievous rascals, far more so than the folks of days gone by. They were a band of friends who had evolved into a group of island dogs, and they formed a camaraderie that would become legendary on the island. The hands of time, the fingers of fate, their circumstances, the beer, pot, rum, and sun, all the ingredients that were needed to create the perfect storm of friendship, pleasure, mischief, and eventually...disaster, fell into place for this small group of friends to evolve into a Caribbean version of *the Island of Misfit Toys*.

Desmund, who oversaw the group, was frequently drunk and stoned; like some delinquent black version of Father Time he had been there when they all arrived, except for Oscar, and would likely be there when and if they all left the island for good. Like Oscar, he was keenly aware this group was extraordinary. They laughed more than most. They cried more than most. They loved and fought more than most. They absolutely drank and smoked more than any of the groups that had come before them. They were in or near disaster more than most, and they were tighter with each other than any group of friends he had known since he was a young boy. They were the group of people who come along once in a lifetime, if you're lucky.

There were other locals and expats, and an occasional tourist, who hung on the fringes of the diehard partying comrades, but these five were the core of the bomb, the nuclear material that made the Hut explode into levels of absurdity that would not be possible without their presence. Iggy quite naturally came and went as the wind blew her warm heart and pretty face in and out of the blue-water bar. And Queenie continued to rule France with an iron fist, while giving no sign of relinquishing her throne or ending her tyranny any time soon. Fatisha was the cool breeze in the warm bar. To know her was to love her. Pellet dreamed of her a lot.

"What are we drinking to?" Clive asked as he picked up one of the shots of rum that Pellet had just ordered.

"Desmund's pretty face." Pellet said, tossing back his own shot.

"Better make it a double." Clive said as he mockingly examined Desmund's face.

Desmund poured three doubles and passed two of them to his friends and marked them down on their ever-present tally sheet. Sometimes he added his own drink to the tab, sometimes not. Boatmon and his friend were sitting at the end of the bar, and Chatta and the boys were loudly banging dominos on their table. Julio sat on the other side of the bar, and of course Helmut was parked at his table in the corner. They sipped on their rum in silence for a few moments until Clive decided he needed to make another toast.

"To Thomas!" he said, raising his glass.

"Thomas who?" Pellet said while already raising his shot glass into the air.

"You peed on his foot and then kissed him to make up for your rudeness and now you don't even remember his name? What a shame."

"Well... I guess I knew this was coming. I just thought you'd let a few drinks settle in before we discussed the details."

"Dem not really the details," Desmund added. "Details would be reminding you dat you offered to take him back to his room, or dat you told him you knew he was a closet gay because of how ugly his wife was, or dat you told her she could watch, but not join in because she would ruin da mood."

"Or..." Clive added, "details would be that we had to almost drag him and his wife out of the bar to keep him from killing you. Or here's a good detail, the guy was about six and a half feet tall, two hundred and fifty pounds and built like a fucking rock. Pretty sure he could have killed you. Plus his wife was hot and she was pissed. I think she would have enjoyed watching him beat the crap out of you, and she probably would have kicked you a few times once you hit the floor."

"Holy shit! I don't remember any of that," Pellet answered as he knocked down the double rum Desmund had poured. "How the hell did things end?"

"You came to you senses and offered to pay for everyting. Dinner, drinks... tip."

"Shit! How much did that cost me? I presume they took up the offer."

"Bout two hundred for dinner and drinks, and he gave

me a fifty-dollar tip. U.S. dollars. Didn't want him to think you was cheap. You'll see it on your next Visa bill," Desmund said with a smile.

"Give me a Carib," Pellet said as he reached for his pack of cigarettes. "What's a couple more bucks on top of the rest of it?"

"Make it two," Clive chimed in. Desmund opened three and handed out two of them. This time all three went on Pellet's tab.

"So how many people saw my public display of intoxication?"

Clive smiled and sipped his beer. "Well, there was me and Matty, and Desmund, of course. The guy and his wife, Oscar, and I think Iggy had already left. Helmut was sitting in the corner, and... Oh yeah, there were about thirty tourist here. You may want to stay away from the beach near the resorts for a few days. At least until this current batch leaves."

"What about Thomas and his wife? Anyone know their schedule? They leaving anytime soon?" Pellet asked with a sigh, hanging his head in regret and shame. Before anyone answered, it dawned on him that he may want to glance over his shoulder and make sure Thomas was nowhere to be seen.

"If you're thinking about pursuing a relationship with him, I have bad news. Dey left dis morning. Headed back to New York."

"Well... I guess I'm back in the closet for now," Pellet added as he drank some more.

The surf spilled up onto the white sand covering Matty's feet as she neared the bar. Another quiet day at the hospital. A couple of sunburns, one bad cut that needed stiches on the leg of a tourist who had swam into a coral reef, and one severely dehydrated guy who had drunk way too much rum and followed it up with way too much sun needed an IV. Quiet days were good days at the clinic.

She lazily walked across the lawn, up the stairs and over Shlomo, and eased her way onto the barstool beside Pellet.

"So, should I presume you are no longer going to hit on me anymore, or do you go both ways now?" she said without looking at him. "I mean I'm glad you're going to stop trying to get me in the sack, but I'm going to miss the attention." She smiled and motioned to Desmund for a drink and added, "I suppose Clive is going to have to fight off your pathetic one-liners now too, huh?"

Pellet said nothing as he feigned a glance at her and sipped his beer. She was hot. He had no intention of giving up on project Matty. She had always been the more realistic backup plan to landing Fatisha.

Matty said, "You know, now that I think about it, the last time we were in St. Maarten, the guy in the pastry shop was giving you the eye. You're probably going to have a much better sex life now that you're out of the closet."

"Keep it coming," Pellet finally said. "Your day will come, you know? And when it does, I'm going to be the one dishing it out."

"Not today," she retorted as she picked up the beer that Desmund slid her way.

"Lady and Gentlemen!" Oscar barked out as he bounced in like a beach ball caught in a gust of wind. "How is everyone this fine day? Ricardo, beer please," he spouted out as he waved at Desmund. "And what, pray tell, is today's topic of conversation?" As if he hadn't already presumed correctly what they were talking about.

"We were just discussing Pellet's newly revealed sexual preferences," Clive answered.

"Ahhh yes, the homoerotic sexual urges of Mr. Wayne Pelletier that have surfaced as of late. I must say, as intriguing as the recent events appear to be, I believe an excessive amount of alcohol, combined with some sort of childhood trauma, left an emasculated and somewhat damaged psyche that likely caused him to act out of character. Not to mention an irresponsible amount of smoking may have added to his questionable judgment of the night. In short, I am confident that he is not actually gay, but was simply shitfaced and stoned out of his gourd," Oscar said as if he had spent the past several hours researching why someone would act the way Pellet had.

"I thank you for your vote of confidence in my sexual preference," Pellet said and offered a half-hearted toast.

"However," Oscar added, "just in case I am wrong I wore this shirt on your behalf." He quickly turned around so everyone could see the large, colorful rainbow on the back of his shirt with the words "be proud of who you are" written in curly pink letters below the rainbow.

"Kiss my ass!" Pellet barked at him.

"Easy now. Someone could take that the wrong way," Oscar replied.

Helmut sat quietly in the corner, listening and writing. He showed no outward sign of interest, or of having an opinion on the conversation that was taking place. He just listened and wrote whatever it was he was incessantly putting down on the paper.

Julio sat quietly on the other side of the bar and listened to the strange conversation; he waved to Desmund to ask for another drink and to inquire as to what they were rambling on about. "I'm sorry," he hesitated. "First of all, what is your name?"

He had already told him he was Desmund, but that was a few names ago. "Too many to say. Just call me Desmund or Keepa."

"OK. Now the other thing is, I don't mean to be nosy, but did this man just 'come out' or did something else happen? I am a bit confused," he quietly asked Desmund.

"Pellet, da man wants to know if you just came out?"

"No, I did not come out. I believe I passed out, and I seem to have been down and out, but I did not come out."

"Ohhh. I understand." Clearly not understanding in the slightest degree. "I'll drink to that," Julio said as he held up his Rum Punch and toasted whatever it was that everyone was talking about. "As a matter of fact, I'll buy a round if nobody minds."

"Man wants to know if you mind if he buys a round," Desmund said in the general direction of the regulars sitting together in a row.

"You know, I once read that when interviewed, the number one drink of choice amongst millionaires was *free* drinks," Oscar retorted.

"Ahh, you're a man of wealth?" Julio said with a slightly surprised look on his face.

"No, I'm just pointing out the similarities between all people, and letting you know this group of would-be millionaires has never turned down a free drink." And with that little conversation, and his offer of free drinks, Julio—the confused Latino guy on the other side of the bar—eased his way across the room and found a seat among the group of island characters.

CHAPTER FOURTEEN

THE SONG LIST

It was late for Chatta to still be hanging out at the Hut. He and the boys had just finished a marathon of nine hours of banging dominos and talking trash. The sun had set two hours ago and the typical medium-sized Friday night dinner crowd was beginning to thin out. Clive had been leaning on the railing facing the water and had been half-watching Chatta push the dominos into a small velvet Crown Royal bag. He also half-watched a couple of doves just outside the bar, cooing their last couple of times before they settled down in the bushes. It was all a typical Friday evening.

"There sure are a lot of doves in Anguilla," Clive said to Chatta, not really expecting a response, as he wasn't really trying to have a conversation. He was simply making an observation and for some reason, he had felt the need to say out loud what he was thinking.

"Don't talk to me bout no doves," Chatta shot back, catching Clive by surprise.

Clive looked at the domino king for a minute before deciding to ignore the instruction. He was just making small talk before. Now he was actually curious about the doves. "That's a little harsh, Chatta. What happened, you get attacked by a pack of mad doves when you were a kid or something?" he asked, taunting the old man into a conversation.

"Naw, didn't get attacked. In fact, I like doves," he

snapped. "Don't like talkin about dem. One of them times where government gets involved and ruins every damn thing it touches."

The thing about living in the Caribbean is that just when you think you've heard it all, you hear the next story that tops the last. Sometimes the stories are unbelievable, other times they're just entertaining, but you never know exactly what you're going to get until one of the locals spills the beans and fills in the details. Chatta was not in the mood to fill in any details tonight. "Damn politicians," he mumbled as he picked up his bag of dominos and walked out of the bar.

Desmund was wiping the bar down and listening to the brief conversation. There was no doubt in his mind he'd be telling Clive about the Great Dove Fiasco. Clive wandered over and took a seat on a stool, then said, "Well, you gonna fill in the blanks or what?" as he reached into his pocket and laid his iPod on the bar.

"Suppose I'm gonna to have to now. Not as interesting as you might tink."

"I'll be the judge of that, and I'll take a rum and pineapple."

Desmund poured ice into a plastic cup along with enough rum for two drinks before reaching into the cooler and pulling out a container of pineapple juice. Setting the cup in front of Clive, he took a big sigh before telling the tragic Dove tale.

"Back in the sixties we had the big revolution here n' Anguilla separated from St. Kitts n' Nevis. You probably heard bout the revolution by now."

"Yeah. You'll be impressed to know that I actually read one of the local books about the whole thing," Clive answered.

"Well, here's the ting. A few years later someone

decided that we had to have all the same stuff that everyone else has. You know, like a national tree, n' a national flower, n' all them tings."

"That's cool," Clive interjected and then sipped his rum drink. In truth he had no real thoughts about whether it was cool or not. It just seemed like the right thing to say.

"So here's what dey did," Desmund continued. "Someone who organizes dat kind of stuff made a form, kinda like a ballot, n' circulated it all over da place. All the schools had da kids fill em out. Churches had their congregations fill em out. Just about everyone on the island filled one out. Some folks filled out more than one."

"Cool," Clive said again, and sipped.

"Anyways, when dey got to the bird part, da form said, 'What is your favorite bird?' Everyone, n' d I mean jus about every last person, wrote down dat dove was da favorite bird. Now da reason we all loved doves so much was because dere was plenty of em, dey were easy to catch, n' dey taste great when you cook em up right. Good eatin!"

"Ohhh, I'm guessing you guys didn't quite get what the whole Official Bird thing was," Clive replied.

"No mon. Wasn't nobody too happy when da government came out a few months later n' said, "No more eatin doves."

"So how many years has Chatta been pissed off about this?"

"Long time now. We would have voted for the pelican if someone had said we couldn't eat da official bird. Don't nobody eat pelican."

"You know, somehow I thought the story was going to be more interesting, but I was wrong. Rum please," Clive said, pushing his already empty cup across the bar. "Time to pick out my songs. I've procrastinated this week," he added as he picked up his iPod.

Friday nights were unique at the Hut. The dinner crowd was generally gone by nine o'clock, ten at the latest. Once they were gone, the bar was officially closed, but unofficially remained open for Pellet, Clive, Matty, Oscar, and an occasional invited guest. Desmund would of course be behind the bar. Helmut often stayed in the shadows. He would hang around but he didn't participate in Friday nights any more than any other night. Once in a while Iggy would pop in for a while, but Friday was typically a relatively hard-drinking night, so she rarely stayed long. On a good night, Fatisha would stroll in for a drink and maybe a little smoke, then she would drift away, leaving Pellet useless and dreaming about her for the rest of the night.

The only rule—unwritten—of Fridays at the Hut was to pick six songs on your iPod without telling anyone what your picks were going to be. Every week, the drinking, smoking, talking and laughing were accompanied by a typically well-thought-out play list. Tonight Clive had decided that, for no particular reason, his list was going to be songs with one-word titles. Sipping on his rum, he scrolled though his songs and scanned his music until he stumbled on "Smooth" by Santana, "Sweat" by Inner Circle, "Jaded" by Aerosmith, "Blues" by HPCrazy, "Tush" from ZZ Top, and finally, "One" by U2 and Mary J. Blige. He was on his third rum drink and had considered sticking "Conga" by Gloria Estefan or "Africa" by Toto on the list, but decided to shy away from the certain harassment that Pellet—who had not arrived yet, but was sure to shortly—would inflict on him.

The fun about each of the gang picking out music, with

no input from the others, was the eclectic mix created. Somehow listening to a handful of obscure rock songs, followed by a half-dozen reggae tunes that quickly transitioned into a mix of pop-rock that would occasionally end with a song like "It's Raining Men," all flowed together like the rum and pineapple juice, mixed with smoke.

"You're looking sweet and perky tonight," Clive commented to Matty as she came in, all smiles, and sat down beside him.

"I am very sweet and perky tonight, as a matter of fact," she fired back, with a smile on her face that said, *I've got something to tell you, so please ask me what it is*.

"Well, lay it on me, baby. I mean you got good news, right?" Clive shot back. Then he interrupted before she got a word out. "Wait! Let me guess."

Matty waved to Desmund who knew to bring her a beer, as she waited for Clive to brainstorm.

"You got a promotion."

"Nope."

"You're moving out of that dump you call home and moving into a beach house."

"Nope."

"Ahhh, you've decided to have sex with me," he said as if it were the obvious answer.

"Then *you'd* be smiling."

"Well then, there's only one thing left. You found a man!" which was the obvious guess from the beginning. She was radiant.

"Yup," she said and she actually blushed. Most days it was hard to bring any of the schoolgirl signs out of Matty's beaten-up psyche, but tonight she was a happy girl.

"And?" Clive added. Matty, for all intents and purposes, was one of the guys. Even though clearly, Clive, Pellet—and even Desmund—would have slept with her given the opportunity. Luckily she had somehow made partying friendships with all of them early on, and the sexual window was closed before they even tried to get through it. Once that happened, she was just one of the guys. Except other guys paid a lot more attention to her than she did to them. So when Clive asked *And?*, it meant what it meant to all comrades in a bar: *Did you have sex yet?*

"Oh hell yeah," she said and tapped her bottle against his plastic cup.

"And?" This, of course, meant *So how was it?*

"Ohhhh hell yeah," she added, and blushed before toasting again.

"Well, well, well. Our little sister has found a friend to play with. When is this guy coming in for his screening, and approval or rejection, from us?" Clive asked.

Matty squirmed and chose her words carefully. "Well, he's what you guys would refer to as civilized. I don't suspect he'll be coming to the Hut for iPod Fridays."

"Oh, that's just not cool." Clive seemed genuinely hurt that he was being snubbed by a guy he'd never met, and possibly wouldn't like anyway. "So what's the deal, you up scaling your friends?" he added, only half joking.

"Clive! That's not fair. He's just not much of a drinker. I told him I had plans for tonight, and he was very nice about me leaving him to hang out with you guys. Besides, I've been thinking about cutting back on my drinking anyway," she threw in as an afterthought.

"Hmmm... I'll have to kick this around a bit and get

back to you," he said as he waved for his fourth rum drink.

"What's he whining about?" Pellet threw in as he made his appearance.

"Clive's mad at me because I'm seeing someone who won't get drunk with us."

"Don't worry about it. He acted like a jealous little bitch when I got a dog. Thought he was gonna cry," Pellet said as he pulled out his ever-present cigarettes. "We say the dog ran away, but to be honest, I think Clive may have done something drastic in a jealous rage."

"We're just a funny man tonight, aren't we?" Clive mumbled.

"So who's the lucky fella?" Pellet asked.

"One of the doctors who comes down here on rotation. He comes for a couple months at a time then goes back to Charlotte for a couple of months."

"Name, please." Pellet continued the interrogation of his little sister.

"John—and that's all you're getting."

"And... have we played doctor yet?"

"OK, I'm not having this conversation again. What's on your music menu for tonight?"

"Mine's a smidge loud tonight so I'll be one of the later venues. And yours?"

Matty handed her iPod to Desmund who had been listening to the two knuckleheads display their class. He plugged it in and hit Play. "Steal My Kisses" was the first song, immediately followed by "What a Wonderful World" by Louis Armstrong.

By now Pellet was already nearing the bottom of his first drink and he raised his glass in her direction.

"Must be love," he said with a wink and a smile.

"You never know," she answered back.

"Not a proctologist is he?" said Clive.

"Fuck you, Clive!"

Even Clive knew he'd taken it too far. "Sounded funnier in my head," he mumbled.

"Like I said, I might be cutting back on drinking with you anyway."

The truth was, this was typical. The gang laughed and fought like an old married couple. As quickly as spats began, they went away.

Matty's list was still playing when Oscar strolled in looking like he'd had a long day. "Bartender, a book of matches and a bottle of beer if you don't mind."

Desmund glanced around to make sure his last real customers had left and then tossed a box of matches to Oscar who was already standing there with a joint in his mouth. "You know, it's a good thing they pay us money, because I'm sure I wouldn't go to work if I didn't get paid." To that comment, there was a "Hear, hear!" from the trio at the bar as they raised their drinks and Oscar lit his joint. "Hey, you gonna give me a beer or not?" he said to Desmund as he let the smoke out.

Desmund put the beer on the bar and said nothing as he took the joint from Oscar. After taking a long drag and holding it for a minute he blurted, "Matty's in love, mon. Ain't that cool?"

Oscar raised his eyebrows as he smiled at her. "And?"

"Jesus Christ!" Matty said. "What's wrong with you guys?"

"Hey, we're guys," Pellet answered as he got up and kissed her on the top of her head as he walked away to get some smoke.

"It's all that matters, Matty," Oscar interjected. "Why do you think we let you hang out with us?"

"I know these three are hoping to get me in the sack, but I suppose you just want to hear the details."

"Exactly." Oscar replied with a grin. The truth was they all knew none of them would ever sleep with her, she'd never give up the juicy details of her love life, and she was the sugar in an otherwise sour tasting group. Most of all, she was one of them. She was a perfect fit.

Julio lumbered up the beach from his Zodiac. He'd now been anchored in the bay for eight days and would probably leave soon, but he had temporarily become one of the regulars, even though he didn't have an iPod.

"Ahoy, mate. Welcome aboard," Pellet called as Julio strolled up to lean against the bar. Pellet had formed the habit of talking to Julio as if they were pirates. It had started off as a drunken joke and sort of stuck over the past few days.

"Ahoy, sea dog," Julio called back as he reached for the Red Stripe that Desmund was already putting in front of him.

"Bilge rat," Oscar corrected, when Julio said *sea dog*.

"What's a bilge rat?" Pellet asked, presuming it wasn't a promotion.

"The appropriate term," Oscar replied, and left it at that.

Julio didn't feel the need to explain to Pellet that it basically meant the lowest form of a sailor, a rat in the bottom of the boat. Nor did he care whether Pellet figured it out on his own. Joining the party, and socializing with people for a few more days before he left, was all he cared about.

The next few hours went by like they did every Friday, in a blur. Matty proudly proclaimed this would probably be her last iPod Friday and that tonight would be her last big blowout.

After tonight she was going to calm down and spend her evenings with Dr. John. With every dead soldier, she swore the next would probably be her last.

"Matty," Julio called out over the music, "I have a proposition."

"No thanks, I found a doctor," she proudly responded.

"Calm down, little sister." Even Julio had already adopted her as a little sister. "I'm not talking about that kind of proposition." He seemed to stop and consider putting in a disclaimer just in case that kind of proposition was a possibility, then he went back to his original conversation. "I was thinking: If you're serious, you know, serious about going sort of straight, then we should all have one last blowout. On the *Aqua Vita*."

"Tonight?" Pellet asked, thinking maybe they were too far along to go sailing tonight.

"Oh, God no. I'm not even sure if I could make it back out there in my Zodiac tonight, never mind trying to sail. I'm talking about next weekend. Let's take off next Friday and go out for a couple of days. We can be back by Sunday or Monday."

"I'm in!" Oscar yelled before any of the details were talked about.

"Sounds good to me, too," Pellet chimed in.

"Three days on a boat with you guys!" Matty said. "How could a girl turn down an offer like that? I'll have to check my work schedule first, though."

"Afraid I've got a bar to run," Desmund said. In truth he looked a little relieved to have an excuse to avoid a three-day bender at sea.

"I'm afraid I've got a bar to patronize," Clive added. "Not to mention I get deathly seasick. I get nauseous looking at your boat. Standing on it would be out of the question."

"Then it's settled," Julio announced with a look of excitement on his face. He'd been sailing around the Caribbean for almost two years and had people out on his boat only a couple of times. Both times it was just for an afternoon. The thought of having Oscar, Pellet and Matty with him for three days on the sea sounded like a blast. "Next Friday we're heading out and you'll be sailors by the time we get back."

"If we make it back," Matty added with a laugh.

"Pellet will still be a bilge rat," Oscar added. Sailing terminology was yet one more thing he had studied, even though he didn't own a boat and rarely sailed.

"What the hell is a bilge rat?" Pellet asked again. Oscar smiled and said nothing more.

CHAPTER FIFTEEN
THE PLAN

"Why so quiet tonight?" Desmund asked Pellet, who was sitting at the bar clearly lost in thought.

"Working out the final details of a plan in my head. Just getting ready to kick it into action."

Desmund shook his head slowly. He didn't want to hear even one detail of Pellet's plan, or the hoped-for outcome.

Hesitantly, he finally asked, "So, what you planning now?"

"Faaateeshaaa..." Pellet answered in a long, drawn-out voice only slightly louder than a whisper.

"Lawd, you jus ain't gonna let dat stick go, are you?" Desmund responded, shaking his head back and forth with purpose this time.

"I'm telling you, I got a plan, and I'm about to get some help."

"From who?" Dez asked with a surprised look on his face. He couldn't think of anyone who would be willing to help Pellet land Fatisha, or at least not anyone who could really be of any assistance. Clive was the only person who came to mind—and Dez couldn't imagine what help Clive could possibly be.

"Just give me two beers and watch me make this thing happen. I'm telling you that somehow or another, Fatisha and me are hooking up. You'll see."

Desmund opened two Red Stripes and set them on the bar. Pellet immediately snatched them up and eased his way over to Helmut's table, the table where conversation did not typically take place. This was the place where Helmut quietly and contentedly minded his own business. He bothered no one, and no one bothered him. When Pellet reached the corner sanctuary, he immediately set one of the beers down in front of his friend, of sorts, and then promptly sat down without an invitation. He looked at Helmut as if he were a puppy who had just been given a treat. Pellet was waiting for him to wag his tail.

"Guten Tag! Vie geht es dir, Helmut?" Pellet said with the expertise of someone who had practiced greeting Helmut in German at least twenty-five times before he actually tried it in person. When he finished talking, he smiled from ear to ear as if he was supposed to be given a trophy, or at the very least, a cordial welcome.

Helmut sat and looked at Pellet without speaking for an awkward length of time, long enough to make Pellet feel a bit foolish, and long enough that he began to wonder if he had actually said, "Hello, how are you, Helmut?" in his native language. When the silence had reached the point where Pellet looked physically uncomfortable, Helmut sat back and looked at him as if an old friend from his native land had joined him at the table.

"Nun, ich war wohlauf vor ihrer Ankunft, aber da du schon hier bist, na ja, die Dinge ändern sich. Jetzt ist es nur noch eine Frage der Zeit, bis Sie mir sagen, was Sie wollen. Sie wollen etwas von mir oder? Nach all—"

"Hey man! I don't actually speak German. I just thought I'd learn to say hello in your language and then ask you for a favor."

Helmut had suspected as much, and did not particularly like the interruption while writing. Perhaps more importantly, he disliked the intrusion while he was sitting in his own little corner of the world minding his own business. What Helmut had said in his response to Pellet's question was *Well, I was doing fine before your arrival, but now you're here, well, things change. Now it's only a matter of time before you tell me what you want. You do want something from me right? After all—*

"Surprise, surprise," Helmut added in English. "Who would have guessed that after two years of saying almost nothing to me, the first time you buy me a drink or sit at my table you want a favor?"

"Damn, man, this isn't working out anywhere near as cool as I had pictured it in my head. Maybe I should have learned how to say, 'Fuck you Helmut.'"

"Fick dich Helmut," Helmut answered as if he were giving a German lesson. "But then again, you did bring me a beer. That's worth something, isn't it?" he added.

With that, they both smiled and took a drink from their beers. Pellet wasn't sure if a friendship had actually been formed or not, but things seemed to be getting civil. He thought that they were possibly moving in the right direction.

Helmut knew he didn't ever make friends or enemies. He just minded his business and that was what he intended to keep doing. Then again, almost everyone enjoys a free beer. To this, Helmut was no exception.

After sitting in more silence, which was not quite as awkward as the first silence, Pellet finally spoke up and began with his proposal—or his "plan" as he had called it when speaking to Desmund. "Here's the thing. I need to write something, but I'm not all that good at writing and I thought you could help me."

"You can't write? How can you be a construction

manager if you can't write?" Helmut asked with a straight face. "How about reading. Can you read?" he added.

"No… I mean yes. I can read, and I can write too, but I can't write creative stuff, if you know what I mean."

"Hmmmm," Helmut said as he took another sip and continued watching Pellet.

"So anyway, I'm sure you know, hell the whole island knows, I've been trying to get a date with Fatisha for the better part of two years."

"With less than no success," Helmut added with a bit of satisfaction and perhaps some solace.

"Thank you for noticing," Pellet said. "But with your help I think I can change the course of destiny."

"Hmmm… ." Helmut said again. On the surface he appeared to be, at best, uninterested. At worst, slightly irritated by Pellet's continued presence. The truth was that in a strange sort of way he enjoyed watching Pellet and his nightly routine at the bar. It was kind of like watching a live sitcom at the Hut, or maybe more accurately, like being at a comedy dinner theatre. Tonight he felt as though he was part of the show, except his own part was clearly improvisational.

"You wanna hear what I need or not?"

Helmut said nothing. He knew he was going to hear the plan whether he wanted to or not, and whether he responded or not.

He stopped writing again, laid his pen down and rubbed the two-day-old whiskers on his face as he looked out to sea. He and Pellet had never really had an actual conversation due to Helmut's insistence on keeping to himself, but the truth was that Pellet was one of those guys that grew on people with time, despite his refusal to grow up. Today was apparently the day the two men from different worlds were going to have a heart-to-heart.

"I'm gonna take that as a yes," Pellet said as he lit a cigarette and leaned forward, resting his arms on the table. "It's like this. I've been hooked on Fatisha since just about the first time we met. And I've tried everything to get her to go out with me."

"This may sound crazy to you, but have you ever imagined perhaps she just may not have any interest in going out with you?" Helmut asked. He thought that the best favor he could do for Pellet in regards to Fatisha was to get him to give up hope.

"Yes. And that's the problem. But you can help me with that."

Helmut was surprised by Pellet's inability to connect the dots and see that he and the lovely island girl Fatisha would not make a great couple. He was also slightly surprised; perhaps even a little impressed that Pellet would show such determination and perseverance. To be honest, he never would have believed that Pellet had it in him to do anything more than throw bad pick-up lines to her from his bar stool and then shamelessly accept rejection again and again.

"So, you've got a plan," Helmut mumbled with a slight smile showing a little more enthusiasm than when he said, *hmmmmm*. "I'm not really interested in being part of it, since Fatisha seems to be a lovely woman, and you... well, you are you." It was the first time he had shown any sign of being even mildly cordial.

It was also the first time he had ever said Fatisha's name out loud, or the first time he had actually spoken of her at all. It felt nice.

Pellet continued, "So here's the deal. I've tried everything. I've bought her drinks. I've sent her flowers. I even sent her a bottle of wine on her birthday. I've invited her out and been rejected in every way imaginable. She, on the other hand, has consistently turned me down with very little imagination."

Pellet took another drag. "You know, you'd think she could at least be nice enough to put a little effort into her rejections. All she ever does is laugh and smile as if I asked her the most absurd question in the world. Then she says no."

"Did you ever ponder the idea that, to her, it may *be* the most absurd question in the world?" his new friend responded.

"If you don't mind, I'm going to ignore your skepticism."

"Pellet, let me give you some honest advice and save you from more pain."

"Thank you. That's what I want to hear," Pellet answered.

"Listen to me carefully, Pellet, and try to absorb what I say. You are you, and I'm not going to bother to explain what I mean by that. I suppose you know yourself better than anyone, so why would I try to improve on your understanding?"

Pellet said nothing.

"Fatisha, on the other hand," Helmut continued, "is like a warm fire on a cold winter day. She is a beautiful woman who, from what I have seen, is loved by everyone who knows her. She lights up a room when she walks in. When she speaks, her voice sounds like an angel from above. She glides when she walks, she shines when she smiles, and she moves about with grace."

"That is what I'm trying to tell you," Pellet answered. "You got a way with words and you could help me."

Helmut considered telling Pellet to go back to the bar

and leave him alone. He took another sip from his Red Stripe and smiled in amusement. "What can I do to help you, Pellet?" he asked with a strong tone of sarcasm.

Another big grin came to Pellet's face and his confidence instantly grew to absurd levels. He could already taste her kisses and feel her soft touch. It was just a matter of time now. "Like I said, I've tried everything, or almost everything. Then last week I saw her on the beach and I went over to get shot down one more time. We talked for a few minutes before she went back to reading her book, which I presumed was my hint to leave, but I ignored it. I asked her what she was reading and she told me she loved reading poetry at the beach. That's when I got an idea of how to win her over," he said with a look of pride. "Then she said, 'Go away, Pellet,'" he added.

"So the plan is?" Helmut asked.

"Well, the plan was going to be that I was going to start reading poetry so we'd have more in common, but I tried to read a couple different books. All I can say is me reading poetry just isn't going to happen."

Helmut smiled politely. He understood that, for once, Pellet was right.

"Then I decided if I couldn't read a book of poetry, I could at least write her a poem. I mean how hard could it be to write one poem?" he asked rhetorically and then answered, "It turns out that it's pretty damn hard to write something that's any good. And I suck at writing poetry."

Helmut now understood where all this was going and how he, Helmut, was going to fit into the picture. He was also leaning toward not doing it, but he wasn't sure why. After all, he presumed Pellet was going to offer to pay him and it sounded like easy money. It hadn't yet dawned on him that the visceral feelings that had ripped through him just a few weeks ago at the Hut could have been valid emotions. Almost immediately after leaving the bar that night, he had quickly buried those feelings back into a deep-seated place where they could do no damage. His subconscious took control and reminded him: No highs, no lows. Stay steady, stay focused. Perhaps he hadn't noticed that the refuge he had remained hidden in for a long, long time was solitude. Nobody ever came into or left his world anymore, and his heart was safe. The morning after the incident, he convinced himself he had eaten something that made him feel ill, and that was that. Since then, he hadn't given that night, or Fatisha, any further thought.

"So here's the thing. I need you to write me a poem. You know, a poem about Fatisha. I'll pay you to do it."

Helmut had not written a poem, or any other thoughts about love or sex, for years. Not a word. No inspiring lines of passion or heartache. No youthful tales of love and lust. No romantic sagas. There were no stories of sweaty bodies in cotton sheets or old couples walking off into the sunset holding hands. In the thousands of pages he had written since the day his world turned black, love was a taboo subject, whether he realized it or not. The wall he had unwittingly built around that emotion had been impregnable since Samira had left him all alone in a world where she had been the only light he ever felt who had truly shined on him. It wasn't likely he would re-enter the world of love just so Pellet could enter the world of sex. Not that he believed that Pellet could pull it off.

"What was it Fatisha said about you a couple of weeks ago?" Helmut asked, then answered: "'You're a funny man, Pellet.' I think that's what she said... you know... when she was shooting you down at the bar one night. That's what I heard her say, 'You're a funny man, Pellet.'"

"She's said that a bunch of times, but she's always been good-spirited about it, so I'm taking that as a good sign. You know, she hasn't ever been a bitch to me or anything like that."

"Your optimism is fascinating. Unrealistic, but fascinating," Helmut mumbled. He looked down at his notebook as if to begin writing again, and not a poem.

"So what do you think?"

"What do I think? I think God himself couldn't write a poem inspiring enough to convince Fatisha to make love to you." His sharp tone surprised Pellet, but it surprised Helmut even more. He was beginning to feel strange talking about her so much. Not as overwhelmed as he had felt on that night when she came in, but still, something was changing. Talking about Fatisha and her grace, and making love—even if seeing Pellet in the picture kind of made it all seem bizarre—was like nibbling on something he hadn't tasted in a long, long time. He was talking about things that didn't exist in his world anymore, and they were things he presumed would never exist in his world again. But she was creeping in ever so gently. Samira had stormed into his life and left him a wreck. Fatisha was easing into his world like the blue Caribbean tide easing its way onto the beach. He was beginning to get scared, perhaps even working his way to another panic attack, but he was not trying to keep her out.

That worried him.

"I don't believe that I'd be interested in being a part of your failed plan," he said, after regaining his composure.

"Don't be such a downer, man. This could work."

"In that case I don't believe I could live with the guilt of corrupting such a beautiful woman as Fatisha," he shot back with more sincerity than humor. "It would be like pouring cheap tequila into a sacred chalice."

"You're looking at it all wrong, man. Instead of ruining her, maybe it would make me a better person. Did you ever think of that?"

"I'm an atheist. I don't believe in miracles."

"A hundred bucks. I'll pay you a hundred bucks for one little poem. Fifteen or twenty lines. You write it, and I'll rewrite it in my handwriting and say it's from me. That's easy money, Helmut. Damn, man, five bucks a line. That's good money."

"First, it's not that easy to write a good poem. Second, a hundred dollars isn't that much money. If it was, you certainly wouldn't have offered to pay it to me."

"Two hundred. I'll pay you two hundred and throw in an extra hundred if it works."

"So you'd be paying me two hundred, and no bonus," Helmut replied. "Even if the poem is spectacular, you're still in the equation, aren't you? I can't write you away." Helmut still wasn't sure why he didn't want to write the poem. Pellet was right; it was easy money.

"Come on, man. I got no other plan," he pleaded in a tone of desperation. "This is my last-ditch effort. If the poem doesn't work, I got nothing else. After that, I'm out of ideas. Even I have a certain amount of pride. If I can't at least get a date out of her with a romantic poem, then I give up."

That statement alone didn't immediately inspire Helmut to start writing the poem, but it certainly nudged him in the direction of considering it. He could consider it a personal favor to Fatisha, if he could be part of a plan that got Pellet to leave her alone.

"Five hundred. Cash, US dollars, all due on the day I give you the poem." The words involuntarily slipped out. Helmut couldn't believe it when he said it.

"Are you nuts?"

Helmut shrugged and picked up his pen then started writing in his notebook again.

"Three hundred and a hundred-dollar bonus," Pellet said in response to Helmut's apathy.

Helmut stopped writing as he took a sip of his beer and looked at Pellet as if he were going to say something. Then he put his beer back down and started writing again.

"I'll make it four hundred and a hundred-dollar bonus."

Helmut stopped writing again and looked at Pellet. "Five hundred dollars. And if you convince her to sleep with you, then I'll carry the burden of guilt silently for the rest of my life."

Pellet lit a cigarette then blew smoke into the air, took a drink and then another long drag.

"Shit, she better be worth it. Five hundred it is," he said, sticking his hand out to shake the hand of his last hope. Helmut hesitated, then shook Pellet's hand. For just a moment he felt a bit like Judas betraying the light of the world. He presumed the plan would fail and Fatisha would remain untainted, but if the plan worked her metaphorical blood would be on his hands.

Chapter Sixteen

The Poem

Pellet sat at the bar like always, but tonight he was a man on a mission that wasn't alcohol related. He was wearing cargo shorts as usual, but they were new and clean and ironed for a change. His rubber flip-flops had been replaced with new leather sandals. His normal T-shirt was gone; he was wearing a button-up light pink Polo shirt with a button-down collar and a pocket that had a little polo horse with a rider on it. His hair was washed and combed. His face was cleanly shaven, and he was wearing aftershave. He looked downright respectable, if not actually dateable.

Helmut, originally opposed to the plan of writing a poem, had eventually come around. The five hundred dollars didn't really play into his decision to write it, whether he realized it or not. The god's honest truth was that the idea of writing about Fatisha was what ultimately drew him into 'the plan.' Once he got going, it was the most enjoyable writing he'd done in years.

It seemed like he'd been hiding in the shadows for a long time. For the first time in ages a woman was drawing him back into the light. In his mind, Samira had made him a promise she couldn't keep. She had invited him into her world, the world she proclaimed to be wonderful, the world where love trumped all, and then she abandoned him and took all her goodness with her. Before meeting Samira, he was not aware of the great void that existed within. Once she was gone and the vast emptiness was exposed, the pain was too much to deal with. It took a long time before he could function as a stable human being again. Helmut was not the type to make the same mistake twice. But without his being aware of it, Fatisha was bringing some of the wonder back into his life, even if it was from a distance and only in his writing. Still, she was in his life and she was the first since Pula.

"You sure she's coming?" Pellet asked.

"No," Desmund bluntly responded.

"No? What the hell do you mean, no? You said you took care of everything," Pellet snapped.

"Look mon, all I know is dat she said she would be here bout nine. Can't say for sure dat she'll actually do it. I told you dat you should have just surprised her. Givin her heads up dat you have someting planned is like telling a fish dat you're tryin to catch it."

"Yeah, well I considered that, but then I thought it might be better if I didn't blindside her. I haven't fared all that well with her spontaneous rejections."

"Forewarned is forearmed," Oscar interjected from his seat down the bar.

"You're not helping."

Pellet nervously smoked a cigarette. He'd tried not smoking in order to keep the fresh smell of his cologne alive, but in the end he was too nervous to go without the nicotine. "I've gotta keep my confidence up and put my best foot forward if this thing is going to work."

"I've been around for a while, and I've got to tell you, the odds are not in your favor, best foot forward or not," Oscar added.

"Hey... you got Iggy. What were the odds of that happening?"

"Touché. I suppose anything could happen."

Helmut sat at his corner table, pretending to write. But the truth was he wanted a front-row seat for the show. If he had thought watching Pellet in the past was like watching a sitcom, then for tonight's show he was one of the staff writers, and he was curious to see how the audience would react.

At 8:55, Pellet looked down at his watch and mumbled, "Zero hour, nine p.m."

"You're gonna be high as a kite by then," Oscar sarcastically chimed in.

"It's lonely out in space," Matty sang only slightly out of tune, with a smirk.

"I gonna cut all of you off if you don't start makin some sense," Desmund grumbled. He looked at them a bit strangely while he washed some glasses.

"They're flipping between an Elton John and a David Bowie thing," Oscar said. "Pellet's trying to inject some kind of cosmic karma into his Fatisha Space Oddity plan. He's hoping to be the Rocket Man."

"Better try 'Dream On' by Aerosmith," Clive threw in and they all cracked up. All of them except Pellet.

"I thought Elton John was gay," Desmund said.

"I thought Pellet was gay," Matty added.

The night was already starting off on the wrong foot as far as Pellet was concerned.

At 9:30, which is early in the Caribbean for someone who was supposed to show up at 9:00, Fatisha strolled into the bar. All the regulars were there, plus a half-dozen tourists. The music was turned low; "Sweet Child of Mine" hummed in the background. With the exception of the tourists, everyone was discreetly or openly watching The Pellet Show as the starlet entered stage right.

"Why Pellet, you clean up kind of nice," she said as she leaned over the bar to give Desmund their customary kiss on the cheek.

"I thought I'd clean up for the occasion," he replied. It suddenly dawned on him that he'd never taken an honest shot at getting a date with her; he'd always been drinking or already drunk. Being sober, and having an outside chance of success, made the entire situation more stressful than he'd counted on.

"Ahhh yes, 'the occasion.' Dez told me that you have something special planned and that he would consider it a personal favor if I'd show up here tonight. You understand he's the reason I accepted the invitation?"

In an almost unheard-of moment, Pellet was at a loss for words. After sitting with a foolish grin on his face while everyone waited for him to put his plan into action, he finally invited her to take a seat on the stool beside him.

"If you don't mind, I appreciate the offer to sit, but I think I'll just stand here next to you, all right?" she asked and told him at the same time.

"Sure. That's cool. As long as you stay and hear me out, I'm good with you standing," he said. As if he had a choice.

As usual, her long dreads were tipped with colorful beads, and large gold-hooped earrings hung down against her long, slender neck. She was wearing a baggy yellow linen shirt and a bright red, loose-fitting linen skirt. Fatisha was the living embodiment of a portrait of a Caribbean woman. A stunningly beautiful Caribbean woman.

"Wine?" Desmund asked her. He had waited for a

minute or two in the belief that Dumbass would have offered, but that didn't happen.

"Not yet, thanks. I haven't decided if I'm staying or not." She stood in front of Pellet and placed her hands on her hips and raised one of her eyebrows as if to say, "Well?" After a few more moments of waiting, she rolled her eyes and said, "Pellet, Dez said you had something you wanted me to be here for?"

Pellet licked his lips. "OK, here's the thing. I know you really like poetry, so I thought if I wrote you a nice poem that you might just give me a chance to take you to dinner or something. You know... go on a date." He stopped talking and took a deep breath as he tried to muster up the courage to go through with reading the poem.

"You wrote me a poem?" she asked, half in disbelief and half flattered by his effort. Not that she was moved anywhere near the point of going out with him. After all, she knew the real Pellet.

"Yes I did," he proudly responded. "And I've practiced reading it and I memorized it, but no matter how hard I try, even though it sounds good on paper, it sounds not so good when I read it." He reached into his shirt pocket and pulled out a folded piece of paper. "So what I was hoping was that since your voice is so beautiful, and you're so cool under pressure, I thought you might read it... out loud."

"You want me to read your poem out loud in front of all these people?"

"Yes please," he answered, sounding like a small child.

"That's brave, Pellet. What if I don't like it? What if nobody likes it? I'm not going to have to put up with a temper tantrum, am I?" Now she was talking to him as if he were a small child.

"I'll take my chances," he answered as he reached for his cigarette pack. He had no illusions of this being easy if the plan failed.

"And I'm not going to be mad at you for some inappropriate language in the poem or anything like that?" she asked.

"It's all on the up and up, Fatisha. I'm trying to get a date with you. So what do you think? Are you going to read my poem?" he asked as nicely as possible, as the pressure began to build and he considered, for the first time, that the plan could actually fail. Foresight was not one of his strong suits.

Fatisha looked down at the folded piece of paper still in his hand and then looked around at the patrons in the bar. She really had nothing to lose, and she did owe Desmund more than one favor. He had been a good friend to her over the years, and he had asked her to do this for him.

"Give me the paper," she said, sticking her hand out to Pellet.

Pellet grinned as he handed her the paper. "Hey man, can you turn the music off?" he asked Desmund.

Desmund shut the music off and loudly banged a spoon against a thick glass beer mug. "All right, all right, listen up. Most everyone knows Pellet is on a quest to date Fatisha. For dose dat are visiting, dis is Pellet, n' dis beautiful creature is Fatisha," he said, nodding toward each of them. They both in turn gave slightly embarrassed nods before he began to speak again. "Tonight da man is trying again, n' he has written a poem for her n' asked her to read it out loud. She ain't never read it before, so... let's quiet down n' listen to Miz Fatisha read... whatever he wrote." When he stopped talking, Fatisha took the cue that it was her time to take center stage.

She smiled at the patrons and then boosted herself up so she was sitting on the bar top, facing most of the audience. After making herself comfortable and picking up the paper, she warned Pellet that she'd better not be embarrassed by this as she unfolded it. Speaking loud enough so everyone could hear, she began reading Helmut's plagiarized words in her angelic voice.

"*Island Girl*, by Pellet," she said and glanced up at her captive audience. "That's the title of his poem," she added.

> *Warm exotic raindrops*
> *dripping sweet from island skies*
> *gently landing, easing pain*
> *on salty, sun drenched lips*

> *Tropic breezes caress the blue*
> *As blackbirds lightly skim*
> *then gently kiss the rising mist*
> *of the foaming white capped world.*

She stopped reading for a moment and looked up at Pellet in mild disbelief. She was pleasantly surprised by the first few lines of the poem, but even more amazed that he had put forth the effort or had the talent to write them. Taking a deep breath, she continued to read the poem with more sincerity and the slightest bit of passion.

> *Complicated yet simple*
> *tangled blurry clarity*
> *her long and slender fingers point*
> *to angels in the stars*

as whispers cut the silent dark
and temptation lingers on

She paused for a good ten seconds without looking up, and then continued reading words that were clearly stirring her emotions.

Fragrant scents of Jasmine light
dance thinly in the air
While enchanting tones of coffee bronze
flow richly through her skin
And salient flavors of passion fruit
hang enchanting from the limb

Cool nights set in
the warmth remains
Dreams are vivid, yet come and go
reality's perhaps illusion
imagination perchance to know.

Fatisha sat staring down at the paper for a long few moments, as she tried to recall if anyone had ever written something so beautiful just for her. The audience clapped lightly. Those who knew Pellet sat in a state of shock. Those who didn't know him thought he had written a passionate poem for a woman by whom he was smitten. It was hard not to be moved by the words and the gesture. Helmut was still on the fence in reference to their—or more importantly, her—reaction.

"A glass of Chianti, please," she whispered softly, looking back over her shoulder at Desmund. As he poured, she slid down off the bar with the grace of a cat, then turned and took the glass of wine from his hand. Without so much as a glance at Pellet, she eased her way over to Helmut's table. He sat with his fingers on his keyboard as if he was writing something, but his eyes were locked on Fatisha. When she got to Helmut she laid her long, slender hand on his shoulder as she leaned over and placed the Chianti in front of him.

"I could love a man who writes words like the ones I just read," she whispered softly into his ear. Helmut was mesmerized and said nothing. Only once in his life had he been in love. He was as smitten and speechless this time as he was in the bar in Pula. Fatisha reached down and picked up his pen and wrote her phone number in the middle of the page of the notebook he had been writing in. Without another word she kissed him gently on the side of his face, then turned and walked away, after whispering "warm exotic kisses," quietly enough that nobody except Helmut heard.

"Call me," she said after taking a few steps without looking back at him. Helmut could not see the smile on her face, but he knew it was there.

Passing the bar, she wagged her index finger at Pellet and shook her head.

"What?" he said, as if he were an innocent bystander.
Even with what just happened, she couldn't contain her flirtatious ways, and she nonchalantly ran her hand across his back on the way by. "Pellet, if you live to be one hundred years old, you'll never write words or love a woman like that," she said on her way out of the bar.

"Damn," he mumbled as she strolled away, humming a tune to herself. The poem had worked and she had fallen in love. Just not with Pellet.

"And shame on you for trying to deceive me," she yelled

as she crossed the yard.

"I was wrong. She can be kind of a bitch when she wants to be," he said quietly enough that she did not hear him.

"Dat da way you seen your plan workin out?" Desmund asked as he poured a shot of rum and set it in front of Pellet.

"What the fuck just happened?" he yelled in Helmut's direction as Fatisha and his plan slipped away into the darkness.

"I suppose you'll want a refund?" Helmut answered and gave a little shrug of false indifference. It turned out that he had been wrong. It seemed he could write Pellet out of the picture.

Desmund turned the music back on and Clive began singing along with "Me and Bobby McGee" playing in the background. *Busted flat in Baton Rouge, waiting for a train, And I's feeling nearly as faded as my jeans.* He stopped singing and raised his beer to Pellet at the appropriateness of the lyrics.

"Well that's just fucking brilliant," Pellet growled. "Just fucking brilliant," he added one more time.

Helmut sat motionless with his fingers on the keyboard for the next ten minutes. When he wrote *Island Girl*, he dreamed of Fatisha, he envisioned her, he heard her and smelled her, he felt her touch, but none of it was real. More importantly, he hadn't imagined any of it would become real. The poem may have been written about a nearly perfect woman, perhaps as perfect as Samira, but the words had been written from a safe distance. There was no thought of actually reaching the sacred highs. There was no danger of plummeting to the forbidden lows. They were just words. It was all fiction based on observation. But when Fatisha leaned over his shoulder to write her number, he was consumed by her fragrance. When she kissed him on the cheek she sent electricity through his skin. When she whispered, "warm exotic kisses," she took his breath away.

212

When she said, "Call me" without looking back over her shoulder, she sealed the deal.

Snapping out of his trance, he tried to appear composed as he closed his notebook and laptop. Once everything was packed in his satchel, he sat for another five minutes and sipped the glass of Chianti. It wasn't so much that it was great wine or that he was particularly thirsty, but it was the first thing that she had ever offered to him. He was going to savor every last drop of everything she offered. After taking one last sip, he stood up, shouldered his satchel, and headed toward the bar.

"You headin out already?" Desmund asked as Helmut approached.

"Got a phone call to make," he said with a smile and tossed a fifty on the bar as he walked by. In all the times that Helmut had come to the bar, he had been two things: predictable and cheap. This was the first time he had ever dropped a big tip, and more importantly, this was the first time he looked like he was going to float all the way home. As Helmut walked away, the Eagles were playing on the bar stereo in the background, *I like the way your sparkling earrings lay, against your skin so brown. I want to sleep with you in the desert tonight, with a billion stars all around. I got a peaceful easy feeling...*

Three shots and two beers later Pellet made a proclamation. "I'm swearing off relationships cold turkey," he said with complete authority.

"OK," Desmund responded. "And I'm going to stop being white."

After stewing in his misery for a few more minutes, Pellet mumbled, "Maybe another time, another place," in an effort to pacify the sting of this final and scathing rejection.

"Naw, it was never going to happen, anytime,

anywhere," Oscar retorted. "But I gotta tell you, we all watched you doing this thing like we were watching a car race. You know, just watching you going round in circles so we could be there to see the big crash. My friend, you did not disappoint us. I suggest we drink to the plan, the poem, but mostly to the monstrous crash and burn."

Nearly everybody in the bar cheered and raised their glasses to Pellet. He was the only person that left the Hut disappointed on the warm, starry Caribbean night, but there was much drinking before he finally left.

Chapter Seventeen

Pleasure Cruise

The winds, much like the rum and the smoke, had been moving moderately steady since the crew had pulled anchor in Rendezvous Bay, left Anguilla, and headed out on their little sea excursion two days ago. The skies were clear, the stars had shone bright all last night, and their cruise, which had been Julio's idea back when they were bonding at the Hut, had been uneventful. At first they headed south towards St. Maarten and then down to St. Barths. Just offshore St. Barth they dropped anchor for the first night. Julio told them that, if they sailed at night, somebody would have to stay awake all night long. Since none of them believed any of them could be trusted to stand watch, they happily dropped anchor, cooked dinner, and immediately moved on to after dinner drinks—which were a continuation of the before dinner drinks, after lunch drinks, lunch drinks, and before lunch drinks. All that, of course, took place after the morning Bloody Marys that kicked the day off on the right foot.

On the second day, after another Bloody Mary breakfast, they headed north, skirting St. Maarten again, past Anguilla, and then turned northwest to the Sobrero Lighthouse. The plan was to sail to the northeast side, go around Anegada, then loop down to Tortola.

They had passed the lighthouse and made a slight turn to the west when Julio, without saying why, brought Pellet to the helm and began giving him a crash course on how to sail. For the most part, Pellet smoked, did his best captain-in-training impersonation, and heard almost nothing that Julio had to say.

"You really should pay attention, you know. Shit happens out here. When it does, you need to be ready."

"Aye aye, Cap'n," Pellet growled as he stood with his hands on the wheel, more to keep himself upright than to actually steer the boat.

"This is the compass right over here. Do you know how to read a compass?"

"Aye aye, Cap'n," he growled again.

"Hey man, I'm not fuckin around here. You need to listen to me."

Pellet had been smoking for the better part of the past day or so, and as usual, he was claiming his share of Red Stripes.

"You need to get at least a little grasp of how to get to someplace if you need to take over. This is a big damn ocean. If you get headed in the wrong direction, you're screwed, man." Julio followed up his little speech by rambling on in Spanish for thirty seconds. Pellet presumed he was being insulted or sworn at, but he didn't really care. It was all getting just a bit too serious for his liking.

Oscar and Matty were sitting on lawn chairs they had set up on the forward deck. The seas were calm, the winds were mild, and fortunately the chairs weren't sliding all over the place.

Pellet stood with his hands still on the wheel, but even in his slightly drunken state he was beginning to realize something was wrong. "Dude, you're getting a little intense. I know you think someone should be able to take over if a shark eats you or something, but I gotta tell you we're really counting on you remaining in charge of the vessel all the way to the end of the journey."

"Count on it all you want, but there might be a change of plans," Julio said as calmly as if he were predicting the weather.

"What are you talking about?"

Julio glanced forward at Oscar and Matty, who were laughing about something and passing a joint back and forth. Once he confirmed they weren't paying attention, he reached into the console beside the helm and pulled out a pair of binoculars.

"Remember that cigarette boat you guys were kind of freaked out about early this morning? The one that Oscar was absolutely convinced was filled with pirates?"

"Yeah..." Pellet answered with his voice trailing off as though he was asking something as much as answering. "You don't think they're really pirates, do you?"

Julio scanned the horizon through the binoculars and came to a stop. He pointed straight south and handed the glasses to Pellet.

"I've got some things to tell you, but first let me give you the good news. They're not pirates."

Pellet took a cautious sigh with full knowledge that some kind of bad news was going to follow. Taking the binoculars, he looked in the direction that Julio had pointed and saw in the distance the cigarette boat headed straight towards them.

"So there's a couple things I've got to tell you. First, I'm not the son of a diplomat who bought me a boat. The truth is, my friend, I was a courier for some drug runners. About eighteen months ago I was given a briefcase with a little over a million dollars in it. All I had to do was go from point A with the case and drop it off at point B. I didn't even have to pick anything up.

Didn't have to negotiate anything. I didn't have to do anything at all except be a delivery boy. I was just making a payment."

"What the fuck did you do?"

"I didn't show up at point B. It seemed like a good idea at the time. But you know, the funny thing is that once I decided it was a bad idea, it was too damn late. Cartels are funny like that."

"So who the hell is in the cigarette boat, Julio?" Pellet said in a voice just below a yell.

He didn't answer. He simply reached over, took the binoculars out of Pellet's hand and looked at his associates on the speedboat.

"I hope you listened to a little of what I've tried to teach you for the past few minutes. If you're lucky you'll get to use your sailing skills. If you're not lucky... Well, I guess it don't matter much then, does it."

With that last comment he turned and walked to the stern of the boat. As if he were getting ready to go ashore, Julio began reeling the small Zodiac in. "They're coming for me. I'm going to try to put some distance between us. You never know... it might help."

"What the fuck are you talking about, man?" Pellet yelled as he stood looking at Julio. Nobody was steering the boat.

By now Oscar and Matty had gotten up; they began working their way to the stern, where their two friends were having a heated conversation.

"What's going on?" Oscar blurted with a clueless grin on his face, a joint in one hand, and a beer in the other. The smile quickly disappeared as he watched Julio climb into the Zodiac, pull a switchblade out of his pocket and cut the rope that kept the two boats attached to each other.

"Where's he going?" Matty asked. Clearly he was leaving, but even more clearly there was no place to leave to. There was no land in sight and she couldn't possibly believe that he was headed out to sea in a fourteen-foot Zodiac.

"Vaya con dios, mis amigos," Julio added quickly while pulling the cord three times before starting the small engine and speeding off to the east. He turned back as he looked at Pellet and nodded at him as if he were telling him that he could do it. He could get them home if he had to... if he was given the chance.

Pellet turned and looked back at Julio. Then he looked back in the direction of Julio's business associates, and thought it wasn't likely he would need to retain the sailing lesson. The distance between the Zodiac and the *Aqua Vita* quickly expanded while the hum of its small engine faded into the sounds of the sea. But even more quickly, the gap between the cigarette boat and the *Aqua Vita* closed. It was just hitting Oscar and Matty that their pirate friends had returned.

"Holy shit!" Oscar yelled. "It's the fucking pirates!"

"Afraid not," Pellet answered with no further explanation. Matty and Oscar looked at him, surprised he had information they were not privy to. Before he could begin to explain, the cigarette boat was roaring too loud and too close for them to talk to each other.

The boat came within a few feet as it sped past. A large Carib man nodded at them and gave a quick wave. It wasn't so much as a wave as a salute, and as soon as they passed they turned in a big loop, making it clear they were coming back around.

Oscar began to panic and scurry around the deck in

search of a weapon. Matty was completely confused as to what was happening and was still clinging to Pellet's words, "Afraid not." Pellet stood quietly watching the boat and taking note that five men were onboard. They looked to be armed with pistols and a couple of shotguns or rifles. There was nothing on the *Aqua Vita* that was going to stop them, not even Oscar.

"What did you mean, Pellet? What's going on? Who are those guys?" Matty asked as Oscar continued on his mad search.

"Apparently our friend Julio, if that's his real name, ripped off some drug runners and they've come to collect their debt."

"Holy shit!" Oscar said as he momentarily interrupted his scavenger hunt.

"And he thinks he's going to outrun them?" Matty asked in disbelief.

"Nope," answered Pellet. "I think he's hoping they'll just take him and leave us alone. He's trying to save us. You know... a last noble act sort of thing."

Oscar stopped running around for a moment and all three of them stood staring at Julio and the Zodiac as he continued journeying out to sea at about one third the speed of the cigarette boat.

Coming from the west again, the cigarette boat approached a second time as it completed its loop back to the *Aqua Vita*. The three island dogs stood like statues as they braced themselves for the worst. But instead of pulling up alongside the boat as they anticipated, the driver throttled up and roared off toward Julio.

Within thirty seconds the boat pulled up beside the Zodiac and motioned for him to shut off his engine. But instead of stopping his little boat, Julio reached into the pocket of his cargo shorts as if he were going to pull out a note from his mother telling them he was to be excused from this hijacking. When he pulled his hand from his pocket, all he had to show them was his middle finger, that flashed one last gesture of rebellion and an obvious response to their request for his surrender. They instantly opened fire on Julio and the engine of his small boat.

Mortally wounded, Julio slouched over; the motor smoked momentarily and sputtered to a halt.

Pellet was the first to scream, "Holy Shit!" Matty clutched her face in horror. Oscar stumbled backward and fell down, almost falling off the boat. He immediately sprang to his feet and scurried around until he found a club in the cabin below. In complete denial of reality, he ran back up to the deck, ready for battle. Once Pellet stopped screaming, Matty slouched against him and wrapped her arms around his waist. Oscar took a deep breath and let the club gently drop from his hand as they all began to accept what was coming next. They had no illusions that they could stop it. It was amazing how quickly their buzz had worn off and how fast one could sober up when faced with the reality of imminent death.

As soon as the shooting at the Zodiac stopped, one of the executioners hopped into the Zodiac and tied the anchor chain around Julio's neck, cut the rope that attached the anchor to the small boat, and then threw them both overboard. After he climbed back into the cigarette boat, the crew opened fire on the Zodiac until it began to sink.

Once again the engines roared and the cigarette boat headed back toward the *Aqua Vita*. Matty clung to Pellet as if she had accepted their fate and didn't want to face it alone. Oscar regained his fighting spirit and grabbed a four-foot-long gaff used for hooking fish. He had no plan other than to put up a fight. Glancing over at his friends, he felt a slight wave of jealousy pass over him; he realized he was standing in what were the last moments of his life, and he was alone. Then he looked down at the gaff in his hand and wondered what in God's name he intended to do with the pointed stick against a boatload of heavily armed drug runners. In a moment of perfect clarity, he realized what was about to happen. He wondered what Iggy was doing at this very moment. Then he wondered what she would do after he was gone.

Matty's heart began to sink as the boat headed toward the *Aqua Vita*. With a slight whimper of resignation, she buried her face deep into Pellet's neck. Pellet stood and looked at the drug runners with complete apathy. It was as if he were back at the eraser factory and everything seemed pointless. He turned and gave Matty a kiss on the top of her head and told her it was going to be all right. But he had no illusions; he understood that they were all going to die in a few moments.

As the executioners neared the sailboat, they throttled back to quarter speed in order to stare down Julio's bewildered crewmates, just to make sure they received the message loud and clear. A tall, strong-looking island man with more muscles than God, long dreads that hung down his back, and a machine gun hanging from his shoulder motioned like he was shooting at them with his index finger. Then he put his finger up to his lips, indicating to them that they should remain quiet. He turned to the guy driving their boat and said something to him. The motor immediately roared up to full throttle as they sped off.

"What just happened?" Oscar mumbled.

"A second chance. A chance to get it right this time," Pellet said as he watched the boat go until it disappeared over the

222

horizon. He was already imagining a sober, more fruitful life.

"My God," Matty whispered.

"I think I peed my shorts," Oscar added.

Both Matty and Pellet instinctively looked down at their crotches to see if they were wet or dry. For the next ten minutes all three of them stood on the deck without moving. Finally a gust of wind grabbed the sail and the boat lurched to one side.

"I guess we need to figure out how to work our way back home," Pellet said as he turned to the wheel and grabbed it as if he were the Captain of the *Aqua Vita*.

CHAPTER EIGHTEEN

THE JOURNEY HOME

Matty looked like a woman who had just come from shock therapy. "Which way do we go?" she asked Pellet, who was standing at the helm but didn't seem to be clear about what he should do.

"I dunno. What do you think, Oscar?"

"I think we're screwed if you're asking me for sailing advice, that's what I think. You'd be better off asking Julio or Pablo or whatever his name was."

"Are we closer to Anguilla or Tortola?" Matty asked.

"About halfway between the two. Guess that's no help," Pellet answered.

About an hour had passed since their lives had changed forever, and Oscar was rebounding a bit more quickly than the other two. The most obvious sign was that he was smoking a joint and brainstorming how to handle their situation. The first thing he had done after all the excitement, after they had all stood like statues for an undetermined length of time, was to go below to change his shorts. Right after that he came up and threw his soiled underwear overboard. Now he stood on the bow of the boat, burning one while contemplating. "I've got an idea," he blurted out. "We passed the lighthouse, heading north, about an hour ago. The sun's going to go down soon and we're obviously in the middle of the ocean, so dropping anchor is out of the question. Let's head south until we see the lighthouse.

Once we find it, we'll sail in a big circle all night long and use the light as our reference point. Tomorrow morning, when we can see something, we'll head back to Anguilla."

"Wow, I can't get my brain to have one clear thought, and you came up with an entire plan," Pellet responded. "But I didn't shit my pants," he added without emotion.

He had hoped his added comment would lighten the mood, but it didn't.

Matty sat on one of the seats with her head hanging low and her hands covering her face again. "Jesus Christ, they killed him. I can't believe I just watched a man get murdered." She started sobbing as reality began to set in.

Nobody said anything while Pellet brought the boat around and began heading south. All of them were thinking about Julio and the fun they'd had with him in the few days that they had known each other. Pellet wondered what Julio thought or said in the last moments of his life.

They had been too far away to see the big grin on Julio's face or see his nonchalant demeanor as he flipped off his killers. His last words were, "Give me another million dollars and I'd steal it again." They were also too far off to see that one of the men had a video camera and recorded the whole thing. It was most likely a proof of death type thing for someone higher up in the food chain.

Once the sun went down, the island dogs found the lighthouse with ease. Presuming that the lighthouse was built on some sort of rock foundation, they kept the *Aqua Vita* a couple of miles away, just close enough to keep the beacon in sight. Two nights ago they'd dropped anchor because they were afraid nobody would stay awake. Tonight nobody went to sleep.

The next day was clear and calm with a slight breeze.

They sailed with the small front sail up for a while and then they ran the engine for a while. They would have run the engine the entire journey, except none of them knew how far a sailboat could travel without being refueled. Even with sails, they feared running out of diesel. After fourteen hours of near silence, Oscar finally broke the ice and started asking questions.

"So just what the hell did Julio tell you anyway?"

"Not much."

"Could you be a bit more specific?" He hadn't slept for thirty hours and hadn't smoked in a couple of hours. He was getting punchy.

"I'd feel better if I knew a little more," Matty chimed in.

"All he told me was that he wasn't a diplomat's son and he ripped off a drug cartel for a million bucks. Said he's been on the run for eighteen months."

"You guys were talking for a while; I saw you. There must have been more than that," Oscar snapped.

"I'm telling you that's all there was," Pellet shot back. He hadn't slept in a day or two either and didn't like the accusations. "He was telling me how to sail the boat and I kept ignoring him. I thought he was trying to impress me with sailing shit. Then he got mad at me because I wasn't paying attention. That's when I knew something was wrong. That's when he spilled the beans."

Oscar took a deep breath and interlocked his fingers behind his head as he looked up into the sky. "This is fucking unreal. I gotta tell you this is really killing the buzz," he added, trying to lighten the tension.

Matty stopped crying and looked up at Pellet, "What do we do with the boat when we get back? I mean, what do we do?" Her crying had stopped, but panic was starting to set in. "What if

Customs wants to see its papers. What if they want to know where Julio is? What are we going to do?" Her voice was tense and her brain wasn't working.

"Calm down, Matty," Pellet answered. "Everything's gonna be all right. First we gotta get back to Anguilla. We'll just take things one-step at a time. I know we're not that far away, but we're too far to swim, that's for sure. Between here and there we'll figure it out. Right now we need to make sure we don't run aground on any reefs or anything."

Oscar walked over and stood beside Pellet and looked out over the boat from behind the wheel. "We could still be in some deep shit, you know. If anyone sees us with this boat, shit, who knows what would happen."

"I know we can't be talking to any police or Customs guys or anyone official like that," Pellet added.

"So what do we do?" Matty asked again.

Nobody answered for the next ten minutes, until Oscar spoke up. "When we get back to Anguilla, we stay offshore until after dark. Then we make sure all the lights are out before we sail to the south side of the island and drop anchor near the Hut. Once we get there I'll go talk to Desmund to figure out what to do. He'll know someone who can help."

"No, you go home to Iggy and tell her you love her. Matty, you go home and keep quiet about this, OK? I'll go see Desmund to take care of what needs to be done. Sound good?" Pellet knew that Matty was in no shape to handle things, and Oscar had someone in his life. If anything went wrong, it would be best if the shit-bucket dropped on Pellet and Pellet alone.

"Sounds good to me," Oscar answered. All he could think about for the moment was making love to Iggy and making as many babies as she wanted to have.

Matty was pulling herself together when a puzzled look came to her face. "How do we get ashore?"

"We swim," Pellet said as he pulled the boat east to head around the island off in the distance. The winds were in their face now. He decided that they had gone in the wrong direction, but the sails were down and the motor was running so he wasn't going to worry about it or make any changes. The seas were getting choppy, but they didn't care about that either. All they knew was that they were almost home and the cigarette boat hadn't returned. They were well aware that just because they didn't get killed before, didn't mean the boat couldn't come back to finish the job.

"Do you think Julio was scared? I don't mean in the end. Do you think he was scared the whole time we knew him?" Matty asked.

"Matty, you heard me say we've got to keep this quiet, right?" Pellet asked again.

"I know," she whispered, "I was just wondering about him. He seemed like such a nice guy."

"I think being on the run from people who are trying to kill you for an extended period of time either makes or breaks your character. I think it made Julio's character," Pellet said, as if he knew. But he really had no idea one way or another; he was just hoping, for Julio's sake, that he had made peace with everything somewhere along his journey. "He seemed to have it together right to the end. He wasn't surprised to see them coming for him. He knew they were coming sooner or later and he knew his time was running out. When it all went down, he thought of us first. That says something about who he was."

"He was a great guy," Oscar added. "Glad I met him and happy I got to party with him a little bit."

"I can't believe he got in that little boat and went off to die just to try and save us," Matty said as she once again began to cry.

"I can't believe them island boys didn't shoot our asses," Pellet added as he numbly looked forward at the horizon. "I can't believe they didn't kill us and sink our boat. My god, they never would have found us or known what had happened to us. I mean, we hopped on a boat and sailed off not knowing where we were going and nobody knew who we were with. Hell, even we didn't know who we were with. We should be dead right now," he added.

He spotted something in the distance. Immediately his heart raced as he thought about the cigarette boat, but over the waves that were beginning to break all he saw was a catamaran that was sailing north. It took twenty minutes for Pellet's heart to slow down and for his brain to compose his thoughts. Once again he thought he might have to look to see if he had peed in his shorts.

"You know what *vaya con dios* means?" Oscar asked. At one time he'd studied Spanish for a year because someone had told him that it was an easy language to learn, and he just had to know for himself.

"I dunno. Good luck or see you around or something," Pellet mumbled.

"*Go with God*. The last thing he said before going off to sacrifice himself in order to save us was to tell us to go with God. People sure confuse me. He was obviously in a drug cartel. He puts us at risk by not telling us he's on the run. And then in the final moments, he sacrifices his life and asks God to take care of us. What a trip."

The sun was just beginning to set when they saw the first

couple of twinkling lights from the houses on the north shore of Anguilla. In less than an hour they'd be on the south side, looking for a safe place to drop anchor. They rounded the end of the island; the waves began to chop as the currents picked up between Anguilla and St. Maarten. Normally they may have cared about the strong currents and choppy seas, but they were almost home now; the only thing they cared about was getting to shore. They'd jump off the boat right now and swim to shore if they thought they'd make it. A couple of more miles, maybe another half-hour, and they'd be anchored for an hour or so waiting for dark to fully set in.

Matty stood up and held on to the aluminum canopy frame as she stared out over the stern and smoked a cigarette. Up until yesterday, there was a Zodiac being towed behind the boat every time she looked to see where they had just come from. It struck her as odd that she never really noticed it there before, but now it seemed strangely empty without it floating behind them.

"I think I'm going to go to rehab," she blurted out without turning around.

"What?" Oscar asked, not sure he'd heard her correctly.

"I said I think I'm going to go to rehab."

"You think it's that bad? I mean, I know we party a lot, but don't you think you could just cut back?" Pellet added.

"You of all people, Pellet? Do you think you can just cut back? Or how about you, Oscar? Iggy told me about getting all turned on and throwing herself at you, and what did you do? You got drunk with us," Matty responded. "Shit... if I had the choice between drinking and having sex with Iggy, I'd probably go to bed with her. And I'm straight."

"I think you're exaggerating," Oscar said in weak defense.

"I don't know, Oscar. I'd probably stay sober for the night if Iggy offered to sleep with me," Pellet added.

"And I suppose that you don't think kissing some strange guy and then insulting his wife was pushing it too far either. Right?" Matty snapped at him.

"I dunno. Not really thinking about it, to be honest."

"Well, I'm thinking about it. I think you two are in denial. I got trashed last week and almost went home with Clive. Jesus Christ! Clive!"

"Maybe," Pellet said as he looked at the island and tried to decide where to drop anchor. "Maybe I'll think about it, but no promises," he added.

Twenty-five minutes later they dropped anchor a couple of hundred yards offshore and a couple of hundred yards west of the Hut. They talked about the details of their plan one more time before they took one last look around and dove in. Ten minutes later they were on the beach and walking toward the Hut.

Matty and Oscar stayed outside on the lawn; Pellet walked into the bar and went straight to Desmund. There were a couple of people sitting at the bar along with a few more eating dinner.

Pellet motioned for Desmund to come over to the corner. "I need to borrow your truck keys so Oscar can take Matty home, and then we need to talk. Got some serious shit."

"Everyting OK?"

"Just give me your keys, then we'll talk," he whispered.

Desmund reached into his pocket and pulled out the keys. He handed them to Pellet, who nonchalantly strolled outside and gave the keys to Oscar.

"Not a word to anyone," he said sternly. "Not even to

Iggy." They both nodded in agreement as they turned to walk away.

"I'll see you sometime tomorrow," he added.

Oscar waved acknowledgement without turning around as he headed for the truck. Matty gave no response at all.

Returning to the bar, Pellet sat with Desmund at the corner table that was usually occupied by Helmut. Then he quietly reconstructed the entire trip, and left out no details.

At one time or another Desmund had heard it all, but this story rated up there with the best of them, or the worst, depending on how he looked at it. "So whatcha gonna do?"

"Nothing. I'm here to get you to do something for me."

"Cool. Whatcha need?"

"Our boat's got to disappear and it's got to go tonight."

"No problem, I'll call—"

Pellet cut him off. "I don't want to know who you call. I don't want to know what they do with the boat or if they find money or drugs on it. I don't care what happens, as long as it disappears and nobody can ever trace it back to us."

"Dat's cool," Desmund said. "Where's it anchored?"

"A couple hundred yards down the beach. All the lights are out and it needs to go before someone gets curious."

"You better get out of here. I got calls to make n' tings to do. Go home n' get some sleep."

"Desmund, the only thing I want to hear about is that it's done. Then I never want to talk about it again."

"OK."

"It's got to disappear for good, understand? I don't want to see this thing in St. Maarten, got it?"

"Go home, Pellet," he snapped. "Nobody's gonna see dis ting again."

With that last reassurance, Pellet headed up the driveway toward the road and began his stroll home. For the first time in three days his feet were on land and he had the luxury of pondering what had happened yesterday. He saw everything as if it were all happening again. He saw Julio smile and say *vaya con dios* as he motored away from them. He saw Oscar with a gaff in his hand, ready for battle. Then he not only saw Matty, but he could feel her body against his, he could smell her hair, and he remembered thinking that he was glad that he was holding her when he thought he was going to die. But mostly, he saw Julio say something and do some kind of gesture, then die. For the first time since he was a boy, Pellet cried. He walked and he cried. When he arrived at home he cried himself to sleep.

About noon the next day he wandered down to Da Hut for a burger and a beer. Looking out over the bay, he found some relief at seeing that the *Aqua Vita* was nowhere in sight. He didn't know where it had gone and he didn't care. Dez knew, but would never reveal it; so Pellet had no knowledge or concern about the $250,000 found stashed under one of the seats, and he had no idea who took it. He didn't know and he didn't want to know.

A short time later Oscar and Matty pulled up in Desmund's truck and walked in, tossing the keys on the bar. Oscar sat down, and just like Matty he tried to pretend he wasn't looking to see if the boat was gone. They both let out a sign of relief at the same time. Oscar blurted out, "Barkeep, one ice-cold beer please."

"Make it two," Matty followed.

The three of them raised their bottles. Oscar said, "To our friend," as they clinked their bottles together and never spoke of him again.

CHAPTER NINETEEN

ANGUILLAN SKY

You cannot love another until you love yourself, and Helmut could not conceive of loving himself while carrying the guilt of the past. But hate is an exhausting emotion, so somewhere along the line, when he got too tired to hate any longer, he had simply stopped having any feelings at all.

Fatisha made him feel worthy of love for the first time in longer than he could remember. After discovering her, or perhaps after being saved by her, he finally forgave himself for letting Samira go off into the jaws of war. He finally forgave himself for allowing her to be killed. He finally forgave her for dying. Forgiveness allowed him to love again. It allowed him to look in the mirror and be all right with who was looking back at him. It allowed him to fall in love with Fatisha. And love her he did. Loving her gave him absolution from his past. His love for Fatisha would have made Samira smile down upon him and perhaps whisper in his ear, "Life is good because I say it is; that's all I need to know."

For a short while, perhaps just a few minutes, or sometimes much longer, he would disappear. The weight of time, the screwed-up, loveless childhood, then loving and losing Samira, war, work, the dysfunctional world that surrounded him—they all evaporated in the heat of the moment. Without warning, the man he had become evaporated along with it. The taste and the texture of her tongue and the soft sweetness of her lips overtook every sense that his mind could experience. Her kisses became his salvation, and nothing else mattered. He savored the hardness of her nipples in his mouth as he kissed her body. Her aroma overloaded his senses to the point where nothing else existed except for her skin, her flesh, and her love. When she rolled over on top of him and gently slid him deep inside of her, everything else became a blurred outline or a colorful backdrop that turned into a sea of emotions surrounding her perfect golden-brown body. His senses sharpened. He breathed in the fragrance of her perfume and her scent until he felt dizzy. He tasted her passion until he couldn't tell where he stopped and she began. Her long dreads draped down as she leaned over, rocking her body against his skin. He tingled with excitement each time the colorful beads or silky hair skimmed across his face or chest. His hands explored and his mind drifted as his emotions focused on her breasts, her long legs, and her slender fingers. Her eyes were dark when she looked at him, and even more inviting when she closed them. When her eyes were closed, she escaped to the same erotic paradise he had drifted to. Their hearts, their souls, their bodies became one.

Each time they made love, she was his brief escape from the burdens of life on earth. She became his gateway to heaven. She was the one warm, soft, passionate, shining light that shone in his otherwise cold, gray existence. Fatisha did not just give Helmut a reason to exist. She gave him a reason to live, to love, and to dream of possibilities. Making love, and being in love with her, gave him hope and, more importantly, a reason to have hope.

Like a young man having sex, he felt the adrenaline rush and surge of having an orgasm. He felt the enormous power that came from bringing physical pleasure to another human being.

As a weathered, hardened man making love to an angel, he felt redeemed. She was his savior. For the second time in his life he had found someone whose beauty, kisses, voice, love, and life were all reasons for Helmut to risk the tragic lows that could possibly follow the euphoric highs.

As for Fatisha, when her best friend Amelia asked how Helmut was in bed, she smiled and said, "Writing is not the thing he does best." They both giggled and then she added, "When we finish, my body tingles so much I feel like I'm paralyzed." They burst into another shameful laugh and gave each other a high-five.

"Details please," her friend added.

"You've got all the details I'm sharing, sweetie. He's all mine," she said in a polite but possessive tone. Even though she had shared big-picture information between girl friends, the truth was she had fallen for him as hard as he had fallen for her. All the remaining intimate details would remain strictly between herself and Helmut.

In truth, Helmut had been her savior as much as she was his. She could have had any man on the island, but who she wanted and who she typically found were two different animals. Mostly, Fatisha wanted the one who sparked her flame. She wanted to love and be loved. She wanted to be inspired and excited. She wanted to trust. Only once in her life had she truly loved. She had given everything to the man she had dreamed of, and he gladly took everything. Then, unlike Samira, he did not sacrifice himself for the greater good. He did not leave her scarred because he gave of himself to all humanity. He simply cheated on her and then left her soul wounded far more than anyone would ever know. Even Fatisha didn't know she was scarred for life.

When they first met, Fatisha and Helmut had three things in common. They both lived in Anguilla, they both loved poetry, and they had both built fortresses around their hearts that weren't likely to ever be penetrated by anyone else. She had no idea that she stayed away from the highs to protect herself from the lows, just as much as he did. Helmut was well aware of the wall he had built, and he went out of his way to fortify it. Fatisha foolishly believed she was simply waiting for the right one to come along before she would ever be in a serious relationship again. The truth was that she had set unattainable standards no man could ever meet—and she did it in order to protect herself from ever being crushed again.

Helmut caught her off guard. He wasn't the tall, strong, black man she always presumed she would one day find. He didn't have a smile that radiated a room, nor did he have a contagious laugh. Those were traits she always thought were prerequisites for her man-to-be. Helmut was solid, but on the short side. His smile was slight; his laughter nearly silent. Most notable of all, he was white. Logic was nowhere to be found. But thanks to Pellet and his "plan" on that fateful night, she had read his words and had taken over to him the glass of wine. When she had leaned over and kissed his face, her lips surprisingly wanted more as they touched his day-old whiskers. When she breathed him in, she wanted to bury her face in his neck and breathe in deeper. When she wrote her phone number and said, "Call me," and then walked away that night, she had almost grabbed his hand and taken him home with her.

***

Mimi's Beach was a remote strand near the east end of Anguilla.

It was ordinarily unoccupied during the day and was always empty at night. The half-moon cove, surrounded by dunes, was secluded and hard to get to. It was a perfect place for a couple to linger for an evening. They arrived just as the sun was setting, and laid their blanket on the beach along with a cooler that held a bottle of wine, a loaf of French bread, and cheese. A couple of minutes later, the blanket also held all their clothes as they strolled, their bodies naked, into the cool, refreshing water.

After a few long kisses, Helmut took the washcloth he had carried into the sea and began gently washing the sweat of the hot August heat from her body. He patiently washed her as if she were his Princess and he was there to take care of her every need or desire. Time slipped away as they lingered about, taking in the beauty of their world.

"Someone asked me once, if I had to leave Anguilla forever, what would I miss the most," she said as she floated in the sea, looking at the light of the moon that shimmered off the ripples in the water.

"Why would you talk about leaving?" he asked as he floated on his back and took in the universe.

"It was easy to answer. I didn't even have to give it any thought," she said.

"Bring yourself over here and I'll make you stop thinking of leaving," he said as she drifted away from him.

"The stars. I'd miss the stars most of all. I swear, sometimes I feel like if I could just find a tall palm tree to climb, I could reach out and touch them. They seem so close to earth, don't they." It was a statement, not a question. This time he didn't respond for a while as he watched her gaze upon the heavens.

"So if you could reach the stars, what would you do with

them?"

"I'd pick one out of the sky and give it to you," she said without hesitation. Then she turned and looked at him with one eyebrow raised and a smile on her face. "Come with me," she said as she reached out for his hand. They waded to the shore. The air was warm and the sand was warmer. The coolness of the water quickly gave way to the heat of Anguilla and their bodies.

Fatisha lay on her back with one arm thrown over her head and her eyes only half open. She gazed up at the stars as he lightly kissed her neck and worked his way to her breast. His hand lightly brushed her thigh and then explored its way down her. She was aware that her body was growing impatient, but she savored the desire. He delicately fondled her, but he was not clumsy and he wasn't fumbling about aimlessly. His lovemaking came naturally and he knew what to do, where to touch her, how to touch her. Reaching down, she held his head in her hands and pulled him toward her until their lips met and they seemed to kiss forever. They kissed lightly so their lips barely touched. They kissed deeply and passionately while their tongues tangled. Then they kissed lightly again.

Helmut smoothly climbed on top of her and she cradled him between her long legs while his shoulder and arm muscles rippled under the tightness of holding himself up as his head hung down, his eyes closed.

He rocked his body back and forth just enough so he repeatedly touched her but didn't go in. Each time he moved, they touched, she rose with anticipation, and each time as they almost reached the point of no return, he pulled back. Her frustration began to grow along with her passion; when she couldn't take it any longer, she opened her eyes and punched his shoulder at the same time.

"Stop teasing me, Helmut!" she snapped in a whisper.

"Oh, you want me," he said with a smile of satisfaction of being wanted so much by a woman he loved so much.

"Yes!"

He stopped smiling and rocked further this time, and easily entered her body as he lost himself in another world. Fatisha pulled with her strong arms while he held himself up with his. Her legs wrapped tightly around his thighs while he pushed deep inside of her until neither of them could last another moment. Her body trembled with pleasure for what seemed like forever as every muscle in his body tensed and he exploded inside of her.

Both of them were motionless for a time. Then Helmut gently laid his chest down upon her breast and put his head on the blanket beside hers. They silently lay in each other's arms, with the waves lapping on the shore only a few feet away, until she stretched her arm over his shoulder as far into the air as it would reach. Just for a moment she was certain she could reach out and touch the glitter. With a sigh of disappointment, she wrapped her long arms around his neck, pulling him tightly against her.

"I love you," she whispered, without looking at his face.

"I love you too," he whispered back and kissed her lightly on her neck.

She was surprised at his response. He was a man of few words, and she was contented with the way he was. She hadn't expected him to respond; she certainly didn't expect him to say those words. She pushed him away so she could see his face.

"I didn't think you'd say those words to me," she said with a pleasantly surprised expression. "At least not yet."

He rolled over and pulled her back down on top of his

body and gave her a long, slow kiss. It was a big step for him to say the words in the first place. He was not going to discuss it any further.

They made love again. When they were both satisfied and exhausted they ate cheese and bread and drank wine before falling asleep on the blanket beneath the glittering Anguillan sky.

CHAPTER TWENTY

THERE AND BACK (PART 1)

Matty sat at the bar with tears rolling down her cheeks, and a rum drink, untouched, in front of her. "He dumped me, Dez," she said, almost choking on the words. "He said he really liked me, but I party too much. Then he dumped me."

Desmund listened and said nothing. Bartenders in Anguilla are the same as bartenders everywhere else in the world. They listen, they nod, and when the subject is too painful, they try to get their customers to think about something else.

In this case, Matty and Desmund had become good friends. To be honest, he thought her doctor might be right. Guys like Pellet and Clive were hell-raising, fun-loving guys, and Oscar had been his running partner since they were both five years old. All three of them were good-hearted, good-timing dimwits who could typically be counted on to use bad judgment. They didn't really hurt anything or anyone, other than themselves; on the other hand, they weren't going to do anything in particular that could be classified as "for the greater good of mankind."

Even though they had adopted Matty and had a blast with her over the last couple of years, there could be no argument that she really was out of their league. Even when she was drinking, she wouldn't have seriously considered dating any of the guys. It may not have been clear to Matty, but it was obvious to Desmund, that she was attractive, smart, and classy.

None of the traits one would envision in a woman who would end up with Pellet or Clive. And Oscar had already won the love lottery; he was a completely undeserving soul who found a beautiful woman with a kind heart, who for reasons known only to Iggy and God, had claimed the drunken hobbit to be her husband. Even having less than stellar intellect, she was still far better than he deserved.

Matty pushed the drink away and buried her face in both hands as she started sobbing. At least twice over the past few months she had mentioned giving up drinking, and once she had even talked about going to rehab. Now she was kicking herself hard. Given the choice between partying or being with the man she was falling in love with, she had made excuses and procrastinated until he was gone. Now it was just the island dogs, the rum, and herself. Clearly, at this point in time she had not made the best of life decisions.

Helmut was the only other person in the bar. Even though he showed no outward emotion or judgment, his heart went out to Matty. She seemed like a sweet woman stuck in a vicious loop of self-destruction. She was punishing herself for her past, punishing herself for sins that didn't belong to her, and whether she knew it or not, she had built a wall that kept people away from the good places in her heart. In the case of her new doctor friend, she had slipped up. In her double life she partied with her compadres at the Hut; then the other Matty, the real Matty, struck up a relationship with someone who was probably a good guy. It was inevitable that sooner or later her two worlds would collide and she would be forced to choose between safe and easy, or dangerous and possibly painful. Over the past few months she had been standing at a crossroads in her life. As she stood at the intersection without picking a direction, her friend grew impatient and made the decision for her. Now she was in the valley, where she had tumbled when she carelessly crept too close to the edge. The only people left to comfort her were the same people who helped to get her into this mess in the first place.

"Dese tings have a way of workin out, Matty," Desmund said in a moment of reassurance. "You're smart. You'll figure tings out."

The words *You're smart. You'll figure tings out* would rattle around her brain until she couldn't take it anymore.

"What's happening?" Pellet blurted out as he hopped over Shlomo, bounced into the bar and plopped onto the stool beside Matty. Desmund set a cold Carib down in front of him as he looked at Matty with a puzzled look on his face.

"Hey, lil sister, what's wrong?" he asked.

"Everything, Pellet. Everything is wrong," she answered without looking up.

"Come on now, it can't be that bad," he said.

"Her doctor friend dumped her today," Desmund injected.

"His loss," Pellet shot back.

"No, Pellet, it's my loss!" Matty snapped. "He's a good guy and I couldn't do a couple small things to make him happy. In fact, if I had done just one small thing we'd still be together, but I was too pig-headed," she said as she again laid her head face down on the bar and continued crying.

"So what's this thing you were supposed to do?"

"Quit partying," she mumbled.

"Hey! That's no little thing, Matty," Pellet answered.

"Pellet, you dumbass, when's the last time you got laid? I mean when's the last time you had sex with a woman when you were sober enough to remember the intimate details of it?" She glared at him through her red, tear-filled eyes as she waited for an answer.

"Damn, Matty, how the hell did I get myself into the middle of this shit?" he said, leaning back defensively.

"You're a guy, and tonight that's enough to put you on my hate list. And more importantly, when we were out on the sailboat, you know... after." For just a moment she stopped talking and all three of them looked around to make sure no one was listening. "After that day," she continued, "I told you I wanted to go to rehab. We fought about it that day, and I'm telling you again, I need rehab. And guess what, you need it more than me." She looked at him for a few more seconds then turned back to Desmund when Pellet had no answer.

Pellet sat on his stool looking at the beer in his hand and didn't say anything for a long time. Finally he mumbled, "You're not ruining this beer for me. I'm sorry about your guy and all, but I worked hard today. I'm hot and tired and thirsty." He took a long drink then set the bottle back down on the bar. "We can talk about rehab later," he added as an afterthought.

Clive and Oscar walked in together with the same happy-go-lucky, clueless demeanor that Pellet had entered with. They both promptly went through a similar conversation and a well-deserved scolding. When things settled down after they had a couple of drinks, the four of them started to reflect on the idea of rehab.

"Look," said Oscar, "if we can find a place in the Caribbean that offers some kind of rehab, I'm willing to talk about it. But I'm not making any promises," he added.

"No shit? You'd go to rehab?" Pellet asked.

"Why not? Iggy's going to hound me until she figures

out how to get me to cut back on the partying. The truth is I think I'd like having kids." He stopped and took a drink as he drifted off into deep thought. "And I know I enjoy sex with Iggy. As of right now I have no children and very little sex. I gotta do something."

"Hmmm. This just may be something to consider," Pellet said as he looked over to Matty. "You mean to tell me that my odds of seducing a woman that I desire to have sex with would increase if I were sober?"

"Yes, Pellet. We generally enjoy having erotic sober sex as opposed to drunken sloppy sex." She showed the first sign of a smile for the evening.

"Interesting. I've never considered that."

"I ain't going," Clive blurted out. "I don't have any desire to stop drinking. In fact I've been thinking I might need to pick up the pace." He held his empty glass toward Desmund. "Only in the Caribbean could you go to a bar and get drunk with a group of friends who only want to talk about how much they want to be sober. It's like diving in the sea to discuss how to keep from getting wet."

Desmund poured a Rum Punch and slid it over to Clive, and noticed Matty was silently staring at him. He started to ask her if she wanted another drink. Then he realized what she was silently asking him.

"Hell no, mon. I'm a bartender. Far as I'm concerned, everyone should drink more. I tink you're a lovely girl n' maybe dis ain't da life for you, but dese guys, dere ain't no hope for dem. Might as well be me dat takes da money," he said with a tone of sarcasm.

"It's good to have such good friends," Oscar replied. "Pellet, don't you think it's nice that Dez looks after us like he's our big brother or something?"

"Hey, I only come to this bar because I feel bad for the guy. He'd starve if not for us. It's like we're humanitarians or something," Pellet said with a grin as they all raised their glasses and drank up.

They continued to drink into the wee hours of the morning as they discussed their impending dry out at rehab. Matty was officially put in charge of rehab research. Clive adamantly abstained. Other than Matty, none of them seriously considered going to rehab while they were sitting at the bar and draining it dry.

A few short hours later, though, when the Godzilla-sized hangovers kicked in, both Oscar and Pellet thought that rehab was a splendid idea. Clive was hung-over, but he was unwavering in his commitment to continue drinking. He had been sober all the years that he worked at the septic tank factory. He had been sober when his fugitive girlfriend robbed him at gunpoint, and he had been sober in Seven Winds when the inbred mafia family fed him pig slop, cleaned out all his money, and stole his truck. Sobriety was overrated, from what he could see. Hung over or not, there would be no rehab for Clive. Desmund had no hangover but he still owned a bar. Besides, who would pour drinks for Clive if Desmund went off to the sober house with the other three?

Matty's doctor friend had finished his rotation then vanished on the wind for a few months. She didn't know where their relationship might or might not go, but what she did know was that if it was going to end, it wasn't going to end because she was a drunk. She could bear the load if he couldn't bring himself to be in a relationship with a descendent of the legendary Charles M. Stodgy. She could understand if he thought she was damaged goods due to being tossed aside by her gay proctologist ex-husband. But she'd be damned if she was getting dumped because she couldn't stay out of the Hut. That's where she drew the line. Or maybe it was simply she wanted some say-so in this bad situation. The other incidents were dumped on her through no fault of her own, but this time there was nobody to blame but herself.

Four nights later she walked into the Hut where the others already had a head start on her.

"Drink up while you can, boys," she announced as she threw brochures onto the bar in front of Pellet and Oscar. "You put me in charge and I'm making this thing happen."

Pellet looked down at the picture on the front of the brochure that said "Island Refuge" in big letters at the top. As was typical with Pellet, the details of the earlier rehab conversations were at best moderately foggy, at worst... he had no idea what the hell she was talking about. "Did we put you in charge of organizing a vacation?" he asked with a bewildered look on his face as he continued to inattentively scan the document. "I didn't already give you money or a credit card, did I?"

Oscar clearly recalled their conversation. He quickly realized he had once read about Island Refuge when he was on one of his research projects, after someone grumbled there weren't any legitimate rehab centers in the Carib. Oscar then spent the next few days reading about every clinic and retreat that could possibly be construed, or misconstrued, to be a rehab center. Island Refuge was one of them.

"Well, it looks interesting. I'll have to give it some thought," Oscar said as he pushed the brochure away.

"Think all you want. I've already given Iggy a copy.

And I'm guessing you won't be making any babies until you go on this little trip with me," she said. "You won't even be practicing making babies."

"That's just not right," Oscar mumbled as he continued to stare at the brochure.

"Ohhhhh, this is starting to sound familiar," Pellet mumbled as he stared at the brochure lying in front of him. Just below the name of the retreat, there was a black-and-white photo of a small, Gandhi-looking man with "Dr. Keshva" written underneath it. Pellet had no idea if that was his first or last name, but he quickly concluded he seemed to look like a good doctor. That would be the total research Pellet ventured into.

The remaining pictures were of a wide range of visitors of all types: men, women, black, white, Hispanic, Indian, Asian; and as in all brochures, everyone was attractive and apparently heading in the right direction in life. Alleluia!... they had been healed! Senior citizens looked rejuvenated, teenagers looked contented as if they were hovering on the edge of utopia, women looked to be euphorically in love, and men carried stoic looks of humility and wisdom. None of them looked like Pellet, Oscar, or Matty on the end of a three-day bender. They didn't even look like Pellet and Oscar on their best days.

"What the hell is this nonsense?" Oscar mumbled to himself. If Matty had gotten to Iggy, which she apparently had, he was screwed. It was a done deal.

***

Dr. Keshva had arrived in St. Lucia from Mumbai fifteen years ago and bought a failing hotel that lay halfway between Anse La Raye and Dennery, just a couple of miles outside the small village of Dame De Traversary. Anyone who tried to research Dame De Traversary would simply find a map of St. Lucia with a dot near the middle of the island, and perhaps a weather report for the local area. But nothing more.

At one time, the lovely complex was a hotel owned by a developer from Orlando.

Regrettably for the developer, the hotel was built on a Caribbean island, but it was not close to the water nor did it have a distant view of the blue Caribbean Sea. It was also not on a mountainside and had no view of the mountains. It had no view of anything other than trees, thus making it a nice set of buildings in the middle of a hot, muggy jungle. Quite predictably, not many customers came to the jungle hotel, and more often than not, the ones who did come, didn't return. Keshva, a shrewd businessman, bought it cheap after the Florida man ran out of cash and customers. Kesh, as he was called by those who knew him, immediately opened up what had since grown into a thriving business.

***

"'Island Refuge, cleansing the soul, the spirit, the mind, and the body for fifteen years. Come witness firsthand what Dr. Keshva and his dedicated staff can do for you,'" Pellet said as he scanned the paper. "Sounds good. Wonder if they have a bar," he added with a grin.

"I'm going to do this thing. You guys in or not?" Matty asked and then smiled at Oscar. "Actually I'm just asking if you're in, Pellet. Oscar's already committed."

"Have you checked this place out? I mean, this guy could have his degree from Domino College or something. Do you have any idea of the costs and what dates are available?" Oscar was grasping at straws. He already had an idea of the costs because it had only been a couple of years since he had read about it. How much could the rates go up in two years? As for availability, what were the chances of a rehab center in St. Lucia being booked up? Besides, Iggy had already made up her mind. He was certain of it.

Clive smirked at the panicked look on Oscar's face. "Desmund, a shot of rum please." When Dez set it down in front of him, he raised his glass to Oscar and toasted, "To rehab."

"Shit. You'd better pour me one of those," Oscar mumbled in a daze.

"Me too," Pellet chimed in.

"What the hell. Make it three. We're going to rehab," Matty announced. Standing with a drink in her hand, she could almost see her new life. She could imagine living the wonderfully sober times with the good doctor. Convinced that she was practically there, she raised her shot into the air, downed it, and then slammed it onto the bar. "Beer please," she uttered as the rum stole her breath and voice.

"Stairway to Heaven" played quietly in the background on Desmund's iPod.

CHAPTER TWENTY-ONE

THERE AND BACK (PART 2)

There were no direct flights to St. Lucia from Anguilla. In fact there weren't many direct flights to anywhere from Anguilla. At 8:30 Thursday morning all the good-byes were said as they checked in at the ferry terminal that would take them to St. Maarten. Oscar was the contented recipient of a long passionate kiss from Iggy. She wanted to leave him with a taste of what was awaiting his return. A couple of nurses who worked with Matty came to see her off. They wished her luck and threw in a couple of comments like "You'll do great" to boost her confidence. Pellet looked at his watch and decided it was probably a bit early to pop into Big Jims for a beer and a Jonny Cake. After giving a halfhearted wave to Iggy and the two nurses he didn't know, he put out his cigarette, turned, and headed into the terminal to get his passport stamped to begin the journey to his new life.

The passage across the channel between the two islands was uneventful; less than forty-five minutes after checking in at the departure gate in Anguilla, they were exiting the ferry in Marigot Bay. The quiet laid-back life of Anguilla had given way to the hustle and bustle of St. Maarten. Matty was excited, Oscar was scared shitless, and Pellet, as always, was clueless. As soon as they checked though Immigration, they crossed the street and stepped into a French café for coffee. An hour later they crossed the same street to the taxi stand and hopped into a van that took them to the airport.

Matty momentarily wished she had drunk a Rum Punch

in lieu of sipping a cup of coffee at the café. She knew getting a taxi in St. Maarten was always an interesting proposition. There was typically about a 50-50 chance you'd end up with a driver who apparently scored extra points if he could make one or more passengers soil their pants before arriving at the airport. While his efforts failed on this particular morning, it was not due to his lack of effort. Matty tightened her seatbelt and cringed each time he sped around a corner, passed cars where there was no room to pass, then drove at the speed of light when the road was clear for more than a few hundred feet.

After getting out of the cab and paying the Caribbean version of Jeff Gordon, the first thing Pellet needed was a cigarette. Once composed, they all headed inside the terminal and checked in. And once they cleared Customs, they headed upstairs to their gate. Walking out of the screening area into the terminal, Pellet grinned and said, "Hey, a bar. Who would have thought?"

"I'm in," Oscar added as if he were a man on death row being granted his last request.

"What the hell," Matty said with a shrug, and followed them into the bar.

One hour and two drinks later, they were boarding their flight and heading toward sobriety. Forty-five minutes later, they landed in St. Kitts for a twenty-minute layover before continuing on to Antigua, where they would have four and a half hours to kill before moving on to Saint Lucia. In Antigua, Pellet stood in front of the terminal, looking off in the distance toward the sea as he smoked a cigarette and jingled the keys in the pocket of his baggy cargo shorts. His somewhat ragged, faded yellow T-shirt had "I break for goats" written across his chest, with "Anguilla" written on his back; it screamed *I am not a tourist*. Expats who lived in the islands for more than a year or so seem to lose the look of confused intimidation or the outward appearance of awed amazement as they stand among the locals. Pellet looked like he belonged in the Caribbean as much as any Rasta that an American tourist might run into. After scanning the buildings that surrounded the airport, a large grin came to his face and he once again said, "Hey, it's another bar. Who would have thought it?"

"I'm in," Oscar added as if he were still a man on death row being granted his last request, for the second time.

"What the hell," Matty said with a shrug and followed them to the bar. This time she rolled her eyes at the absurdity of them drinking all the way to rehab, but she wasn't particularly surprised. In the end, as long as they got there, that was all she cared about. She'd probably be dreaming about a drink in a couple of days.

At 7:25 that evening the three happy souls stood in front of the terminal in Saint Lucia. The sun had set over the horizon an hour ago and the stars sparkled as brightly here as they did in Anguilla.

"You need a taxi?" an older black man asked as he was reaching toward their bags.

"In a few minutes," Pellet answered. "Gotta smoke a cigarette first."

"Cool," the driver answered as he grabbed their bags and began toting them to the back of his van. "Take your time. Just let me know when you're ready to go."

"All right," Matty answered with a smile.

"Where you headin?" he asked.

"Island Refuge."

"Ohhh," was all he said, and then left the three expats

standing in a cloud of smoke.

This taxi driver, like most of the locals, knew little of what actually took place at Island Refuge. He had heard it was a rehab center, but he and his friends had often thought it to be a Middle Eastern cult or something else along those lines. Of course that rumor was started and then spread by folks who admittedly didn't know the difference between a devout Hindu and a devout Muslim. As one of his friends had put it, "Dey all look da same to me." All the taxi driver knew for sure was that he was going to make forty dollars for taking these customers to the middle of the hot, muggy jungle on a night that he almost had no customers at all. Tonight he simply considered himself to be one of the fortunate few drivers to have a fare and a potential tip.

Pellet and Oscar finished smoking and they all climbed into the van. The driver slid the door closed and slowly walked around to his door. He talked to one of the other cabbies for a minute before getting in. Matty was pretty sure she heard them both chuckle a little when he said he had a group heading out to Island Refuge.

"First time to Saint Lucia?" he asked as he pulled out of the terminal parking lot.

"Yes," Matty politely answered. Oscar seemed to be growing more and more stressed with every mile that passed by. Pellet was looking around and had the same look that he almost always had on his face: the look that indicated his motor was running, but the gears were not quite engaged.

"Nice place. Quiet, people are friendly. Hope you have a good time while you're here," he said as he continued with the small talk, working his way to a good tip.

"Thanks. Glad to be here," Matty answered again, while the two men she had snared into her trap looked out the open windows as they slowly drove through the night.

"I'm from Martinique originally, but moved here twenty-three years ago. My wife is from here. All my kids were born here."

Matty smiled, the others drifted.

"Here's my card," he said, reaching into the back seat as he drove, holding the card up for anyone to take. "You can call me anytime and I'll come and drive you around. If you want me for the whole day, I'll give you a good rate, OK?"

"I appreciate it, but I think we're going to spend most of our time right at Island Refuge," Matty said as she reached up and took the card.

"What's your name?" Pellet blurted out.

"Sacha."

"Well, Sacha, what is Amos's that I see over there?"

"Just a small hotel with a bar and restaurant. Local food and drinks. Not too much price," he answered. "Amos's Bar and Hut is its full name."

"Sacha... I believe we'd like to stop there. Just for one drink, OK? I'll pay you a little extra to wait for us."

"No problem, mon."

"Ah, come on, Pellet," Matty snapped. "Enough's enough. You cannot put this off forever. I mean, we're going to be there tonight either way. Let's just keep going." She was pleading, but she already knew the outcome. He had that stupid-looking teenage-boy look on his face. He was stopping at the bar, with or without her.

"One drink isn't going to hurt anything," Pellet snapped back.

"Pull in to Amos's Bar and Hut, Sacha," Oscar added, breaking the tie and ending the conversation.

Sacha thought for a moment and then decided to go with the offer of being paid more money for waiting for them at the bar. It was a dead night and this would likely be his last fare. "Come on," he chimed in, "Dis guy has a point. What could one drink hurt?" Matty glared at the back of his head and considered reaching out to slap him for casting his vote, making it three against one in favor of stopping at Amos's Bar and Hut. Oscar felt like a guy standing in front of a firing squad, and when they pulled the triggers, all the guns clicked and failed to fire. He wasn't out of the woods yet, but he had gotten a reprieve for at least a few minutes.

At half-past midnight, after Sacha got paid, he left the three of them still sitting at the bar. Jeremy, the bartender, had set them up with two rooms and had one of the waiters take their bags up. While Oscar and Matty sat at the dimly lit outdoor bar with local characters keeping them company, Pellet walked to the parking lot and made arrangements with Sacha. He was to come back to get them tomorrow morning so he could take them to Island Refuge, so Matty could finally straighten herself out to keep from being rejected by another doctor.

Ten days later, Sacha pulled into the dirt driveway at Amos's Bar and Hut, picked up the three friends and took them to the airport. Keshva kept the fifty-percent deposit they had paid up front without ever meeting them. He never heard from Matty again.

Nine hours later the three weary travelers wandered off the ferry, through Customs, and back onto Anguilla. Pellet was a happy camper because he just took a great ten-day vacation in Saint Lucia and was still drinking. Matty was mad at herself and frustrated that she hadn't gone to rehab, even if they did make new friends and had a great time. Oscar was thrilled and scared to death. He didn't make it to rehab, which meant he could continue going to the Hut to hang out with Desmund, but had no idea how he'd be breaking the news to Iggy. He was pretty sure what her reaction was going to be. That scared him.

"Carter, what's going on, man?" Pellet said to the young taxi driver as they walked out of the terminal into the late afternoon sun.

"Cool, mon. Everting is good. Need a ride?"

"We need three rides, thank you very much," Pellet said as he reached out and shook his hand.

Carter grabbed Matty's bag and let the guys carry their own as they headed for his van. "You hear the news yet?" he asked as he slid the side door open.

"What news might that be?" Pellet said.

"Da Hut's gone, mon," he said with almost complete indifference, as if he had said, "Looks cloudy today."

"Gone?" Oscar asked. "Where the hell can an entire building go?" he added.

"Went to a pile of ashes, mon. Up in smoke and down to ashes."

"What are you talking about?" Matty asked, as if she had been told that her best friend's home had just burned down— which in some ways was exactly what had happened.

"Two nights ago. Was a big fire and there's not nothin left."

The three looked at each other in shock. Oscar wondered about his best friend. "Anyone hurt?"

"No, mon. No one hurt, no one killed. Just the building's gone."

"Take us over to the Hut," Oscar ordered, as he climbed into the van.

Fifteen minutes later they were sitting on an old picnic table in the yard near the Hut, when there was a Hut. Desmund, who had just finished smoking a joint, sat in stoned bewilderment at the table, looking like someone who didn't know what the hell had hit him. He could clearly recall coming in to work on Tuesday afternoon and everything was cool. After that, it all went to shit pretty damn fast. The fire was just the last of it.

CHAPTER TWENTY-TWO

THERE AND BACK (PART 3)

A few days prior to "up in smoke and down to ashes," an old white gentleman strolled in and sat down at the bar.

"Good afternoon, sir," he said to Desmund as he pulled himself up to the bar and adjusted his stool.

"Hey, hey," Desmund responded as he set a coaster in front of him. He could read people good; what he saw in this guy was someone who was either retiring or thinking about retiring to Anguilla, but hadn't spent much time in the islands, at least not yet. His shirt was a short-sleeve flowery thing, obviously bought just for the trip to the Caribbean. His cargo shorts were the correct shorts to be wearing, but like the shirt, they were ironed and stiff as a board. Desmund figured the guy had years of island experience, most of it from books and the Travel Channel. In the end, though, it didn't make any difference to Dez the Keepa, as long as the old dude had money and planned on spending it at the bar.

"So, what do you recommend for a good island drink for a newcomer to Anguilla?" he asked with enthusiasm.

"Rum Punch. Everyone's gotta start off with a Red Stripe or Rum Punch. If you get hungry we've got baked snappa wit peas n' rice. Good stuff," Desmund answered, already pouring the elderly gentleman a glass of punch.

"Rum Punch it is then," he responded.

Desmund set the drink in front of him, welcomed him to Anguilla, and moved off to check on a scattering of customers throughout the bar.

Clive sat in his usual spot and only seemed slightly put out that his three compadres had abandoned him when they had flown off to rehab land. He was optimistic that at least one, if not all, would fail at rehab, hence he believed the island dogs would all be back together in a few days. For now he sat and sipped while he made small talk with Desmund and a few locals.

Helmut had been conspicuously absent for the past several days. It was unusual for him to miss coming to the bar to write. This week he had missed the past four days. Anyone who noticed he was missing simply presumed he was in Fatisha's sweet company, and that he no longer needed to write poetry to her when he could lie in bed next to her and whisper the same words into her lovely ears.

"Get you another drink?" Desmund asked the old guy as he returned to his side of the bar.

"No, thank you, but I'll try some of that snapper you were talking about."

"Cool, be out in ten minutes," Desmund said as he headed back to the kitchen. When he reached the kitchen doorway, he yelled "Snappa," and returned to the bar and started wiping it down.

"Augustus Burton," the overdressed tourist said as he reached out to shake hands with the Rasta bartender.

Dez reached and gave him a firm but friendly handshake. "Dey call me Desmund," he said with a smile. "Enjoying Anguilla?"

"It's beautiful. I just flew in from New York and I've got to tell you, it is absolutely breathtaking here. Even better than I imagined."

"So dis your first trip here?"

"Yes. I've read a lot about the place and watched what I could on the Internet, but it doesn't do the island justice," he answered.

"Just visiting, den?" Desmund asked, making conversation. He presumed the old guy was probably staying at Cuisinart or maybe Cap Juluca, or one of the other high-end places. He'd seen thousands of them come and go, escaping the pressures of work, maybe the pressures of marriage, the pressures of life, all of it. It was all an easy read after a while.

"No, I've bought a place here. I'll likely only stay for a few weeks this time, but hope to stay longer when I come back."

"Cool," he said again. It was his canned answer that he used for almost anything that someone told him. Unless of course it wasn't cool. Desmund was surprised at himself for misreading this guy, not that it mattered one way or the other. If he was going to live here, then maybe he'd become a regular customer. Visiting, staying, it didn't make any difference to Dez.

It was late for lunch, but because Augustus had arrived before the cook left for her afternoon break, he was in luck. He tapped his hand on the bar in a light-hearted effort to keep beat with the reggae music playing as background noise on the bar's iPod. He had the rhythm of an old white guy who had obviously spent the better part of his life in a bank or law office, something along those lines.

Desmund poured him another punch even though he hadn't asked for it. "Dis one's on the house. Welcome to da island."

Augustus stopped tapping on the bar. He raised his glass and offered a toast to Anguilla, the Hut, and Desmund. Dez smiled then nodded and returned to the kitchen to see how his lunch was coming. Five minutes later he came back out carrying a plate of food, a basket of bread, and silverware. He set it all on the bar.

The old man leaned forward and breathed in the aroma of the steaming food. "Smells fantastic," he said, looking up with the lenses of his glasses steamed up from leaning so close to the hot food.

"Wonderful! I see you two have met," a woman's loud voice called out.

Desmund froze in his tracks and turned as white as a black man could turn. His blood ran cold. He wasn't sure if his heart stopped beating or simply exploded in agony. As soon as she opened her mouth, her voice made Desmund cringe as if her fingernails were loudly screeching down a long, long chalkboard.

He hadn't heard from her in over two and half years. The last he had heard she was still over lording France, with her eyes on the remainder of Europe as if she were some kind of Caribbean Conquistador looking to take over the world. It was his understanding that she loved living in France and had no intention of ever moving back to Anguilla. Or perhaps, he thought, it was his misunderstanding.

Still facing his customer, who hadn't yet taken a bite of his food, Desmund looked horror-stricken.

Augustus watched the bartender, with a genuine look of concern on his face. He feared Desmund was experiencing the early moments of a heart attack or stroke, as he stood in front of the old white guy with his mouth hanging open and making sounds as if he couldn't breathe. He was trying to speak, but Queenie had rendered him speechless.

Queenie came around the bar and kissed Augustus on the cheek and told him that it was good to see him again. Then she looked up at Desmund. "Close your mouth, you silly old man. You look so happy to see me dat you be in shock," she said sarcastically.

"What?" was all he could utter as she pulled her chubby little self onto the barstool that was far too small for her big bottom. She sat in front of him, grinning from ear to ear, savoring the shock of her arrival that had hit him like a thunderbolt.

"You miss me?" she asked with an even wider grin.

Desmund poured himself a shot of rum and downed it. After he savored the warmth of the rum and closed his eyes for a few seconds, he began to compose himself. "Astra, what da hell?" he snapped. "I thought you said you were never coming back."

He didn't even try to imply that he was glad to see her. She owned a whole damn country, and was working on taking over a continent. All he wanted was to be left alone on one tiny little island in the middle of the Caribbean.

"Well, dat's not da same as saying 'nice to see you,' but no matta. Only gonna go downhill from here anyway," she said, looking over at Augustus. Desmund looked at the two of them and tilted his head like a confused puppy.

"You two together?" Desmund asked tentatively. Envisioning Astra running off with any man made him feel liberated. But envisioning his wife with this old white guy kind of creeped him out. Just for one moment, he felt a twinge of pity for the old dude.

"Don't be stupid, old mon. You haven't gotten any smarter since I left, have you?" she said, completely apathetic. "No, Mister Burton n' I have been doing some business. N' I am glad to say dat I just left da attorney's office n' it's all finalized."

She turned to Augustus and congratulated him then shook his hand and gave him another kiss on the cheek.

"Couldn't do your business somewhere else?" Desmund asked.

"Da man just bought da bar n' I tought I'd better come here to let you know."

"Bought what bar?" Desmund blurted out.

"Dis bar, Da Limin Hut," she said smugly.

"He bought me bar?" Desmund yelled back.

"No, you ole fool, he bought *my* bar. What's wrong with you? You tink I'd ever put someting like this in anyone's name but mine? Besides, ten years ago I suggested dat you start sending me some of the profits from the bar. You know what you said? Noting! Dat's what you said. Didn't even bother to answer me. Well, I got my money anyway, didn't I?" This time she gloated when she finished speaking.

"Woman, you're still da same lousy bitch you were when you left here. You come all the way back jus to give me misery n' steal me bar?"

"No, not *just* dat. Here's one more gift for you," she said in her sweetest voice, as she dropped divorce papers on the bar and walked out with her head high and her chubby butt sashaying back and forth.

"Have fun, boys!" she called out. It was her parting shot as she walked out of Desmund's life. Or what was left of it.

After she waddled out, Desmund stood at the bar in silence for a few minutes. Then he picked up a bottle of Appleton Rum and a shot glass and drank a shot. He then poured himself another. With the bottle still in his hand he walked over and faced Augustus, who by now was in shock. His untouched food was still in front of him; he sat looking at Desmund, not knowing what to say. Desmund reached down and picked up a clean shot glass, poured it full to the top and pushed it in front of the old man. Augustus promptly picked it up, drank it to the bottom and slammed it on the counter as he tried to catch his breath. Desmund easily drank his second shot and then refilled both glasses.

"How da hell dis happen, mon? What made you want to buy me bar? Ain't got no business. Ain't got no assets. Jus me n' da beach, n' a few customers here n' dere. Why dis bar?"

Augustus swallowed hard and then downed his second shot and again gasped for air. He pushed the shot glass forward and motioned for him to fill it again.

"You need to understand, I was not told that you were in the dark on this whole thing. With that said, there's probably more you don't know." Augustus had sat in stunned silence while Astra had put on her show. He was trying to savor the momentous occasion of buying the bar, but the Waddling Witch had failed to tell him that her husband had no idea of what was coming. Or that Desmund was about to be the *ex*-husband. All she had told him was to not say anything because she wanted it to be a surprise. Clearly he didn't know Astra, the Queen of France. And clearly Astra had deceived yet one more man, without really telling any lies at all.

Desmund took a deep sigh, poured two more glasses, and pulled up a stool before the drinking or the flow of information continued. "What else?"

"Do you know a gentleman by the name of Helmut Brandt?" he asked.

"Ya, mon. Sits right over dere most of da time. Always writing. Never says much," Desmund answered.

"Always writing," Augustus said with a smile and then

downed his third shot. "Do you know what he writes?"

"No, mon. Never asked. Wouldn't have told me if I did."

"Well, Desmund, it seems that Helmut has written a book. And he's not only written it, but he's already sold it."

Desmund shrugged; he didn't see any connection between the book, the sale of the bar, and his impending divorce.

"The book was about Da Limin Hut and the people who hang out here. Not only did a publisher buy the book, but it was a package deal."

"What kind of package?" Dez asked.

"A book-movie package. Within six months the book will come out. Six months after that, the movie should come out. If things go as planned, this place will be a goldmine. As soon as the ball began rolling, I had an attorney find out who owned the bar. He said it belonged to Astra. I contacted her and we worked out a very lucrative deal. She did quite well for herself."

"How'd you know about da whole book-movie ting?" Desmund asked.

"I worked for the publishing house. When I advised them to buy the bar, they passed. Once they passed, I stepped in. Obviously if the book and movie do well, business will boom for years." His words were beginning to slur a bit. He wasn't a drinker; nonetheless he downed another, as did Desmund.

"So let me get dis straight. Astra is richer than she already was, n' Helmut is going to be rich soon."

"Oh, he's rich already. He's already received the first check, and it was a big one."

"OK, I stand corrected. Astra's richer. Helmut's richer. You own my bar, n' I..." He didn't finish the sentence simply because there was nothing for him to say.

"You're apparently soon to be divorced," his new

drunken bar-owner friend said.

That was the only bright spot in Desmund's day.

Clive moved around the bar and slid onto the stool beside Augustus. He had watched and listened as the entire drama unfolded and would have come over and introduced himself a few minutes earlier, but Queenie scared him. He didn't want to be sitting with the two bar owners, one present and one past, if she happened to return with more bad news. He didn't want to become collateral damage. Feeling he'd waited long enough so he could safely assume she wasn't returning, he motioned to Desmund to pour a shot for him.

"Hey, I'm Clive," he said as he shook hands with a now half-drunken bar owner. "Guess we'll be seeing each other a bit. I'm sort of a regular," he mumbled.

"Pleasure's mine," Augustus slurred.

"Seems like he's becoming one of us already," Clive said to Desmund, who didn't look up or smile.

His wife was gone and he couldn't care less. Dez wished they'd gotten divorced years ago. He was tired of her kicking his ass, but this last blow was too much. She took his bar. That mean-assed bitch took his bar from him. That was one step too far. He poured another and slid the bottle to Clive.

"Pour your own. Ain't my rum anyway," he growled.

Clive picked up the bottle and poured a shot, then held it up in the direction of the old guy to see if he wanted another. He nodded as Clive poured and grinned. He was certain that Augustus was already too looped to understand that they were drinking his own liquor.

Desmund walked over to the bar and picked up two bottles of Appleton 12-year-old rum. Then he went and sat down with Chatta and the domino boys. One bottle he opened and didn't share. The other, he set in the middle of the domino table with a handful of plastic shot glasses.

"On da house, fellas. Better enjoy it."

For the rest of the night he drank and said nothing. Clive went behind the bar and waited on the few customers who came and went throughout the evening. Augustus passed out at Helmut's corner table. The cook got disgusted with all of them and went home for the night.

***

Matty, Oscar, and Pellet had been sitting at the picnic table listening to the entire story in disbelief as they watched light wisps of smoke continue to rise out of the ashes of what just two days ago was the Hut. Oscar tapped Desmund on the shoulder and got a joint from him, fired it up and passed it around.

"So how the hell did the fire start?" Pellet asked.

"Don't know. Two nights later Boatmon call me n' said he could see da flames shootin way into da air all da way from his house. Jumped in my truck n' came down to see. When I got here, cops, fireman, everybody were all lookin at the bonfire. Nothin nobody could do."

"That's so sad, Desmund. I'm so sorry that your bar burned down," Matty said.

"Not my bar," he answered with a crooked little smile on his face.

"Ain't that a bitch," Pellet added, laughing at the new owner whom he hadn't met yet. "First week he owns the bar it burns down. Bet he's sorry he ever met Astra."

"No, mon. He's collectin da insurance money n' buildin a new bar. Said he can build it so it would fit better with the book n' movie. You know, like some kind of theme-park bar,"

Desmund mumbled, still rocking his head back and forth.

Carter the taxi driver had long since left them behind. After another thirty minutes of talking, consoling, and smoking, the three rehab-failures picked up their luggage and headed down the road. Desmund had no place else he wanted to go, so he sat and listened to the sea as he watched the smoke continue to drift into the air.

"Seems like God answered your prayers, Matty," Oscar observed. "Your goal was to stop spending so much time at Da Hut. There you go," he said, motioning back at the pile of ash and cinder behind him. "Happy now?"

"Shut up, Oscar! I just spent twenty-five hundred dollars on rehab I didn't go to, and another fifteen hundred on a vacation that I didn't want to take. You think I'm happy now?"

Oscar knew he was going to hear "Shut up Oscar!" a few more times over the next couple of days. He couldn't begin to imagine how he was going to break the news to Iggy that he was sidetracked by a bar on the way to rehab. He could easily imagine what her reaction was going to be and he knew it wasn't going to be a pretty weekend.

"Jesus Christ. We go away for ten days and Helmut sells a book we didn't even know he wrote, then he sells the movie rights. Queenie sells the bar and divorces Desmund. Then someone burns down the bar, and they've already made plans to build a new one," Pellet mumbled as the three of them walked side by side up the road, carrying their suitcases.

"That's more excitement than has happened on my previous twenty-eight years of living here," Oscar added. "Good thing we didn't go for the whole month."

"I need a drink. Anyone else?" Matty chimed in.

"Yes ma'am. Let's head to Big Jim's and grab a beer

270

and some chicken. By the way, I would like to say for the record that Iggy is going to be pissed off when she finds out I blew off rehab and partied the whole time."

"Hell of a time though, huh?" Pellet said with a grin as he dragged his exhausted carcass up the road.

"Can you believe we're going to have to find another bar to hang out at?" Matty asked.

"Everything changes," Pellet added as if he were some old wise man.

It all seemed to happen fast, but it was a tsunami that was years in the making. Helmut had been submitting one version or another of his book for the past three years and steadily receiving rejections. Then a couple of months ago he received a call from a guy in New York. Three weeks later the book deal was signed and a week later the movie rights were signed. Augustus Burton quickly moved to scoop up the Hut and made Queenie a generous offer that she promptly rejected. She presumed if he was willing to pay a high price, then he'd be willing to pay even more. She was right. Queenie had been planning on dumping Desmund for years, but there'd been no hurry. She didn't have a schedule to meet, and he wasn't going anywhere. When the whole book and movie thing came up, it was all just perfect timing. If she kept Desmund, she knew she'd have to give him money. If she dumped him, she knew him well enough to know he wouldn't chase her or her money. He'd lackadaisically go back to being a semi-unemployed carpenter. That's just who he was.

In a nutshell, the book-movie was sold. The bar was sold. The divorce papers were issued, and last but not least, the Hut burnt to the ground.

The final act was a mystery to everyone.

PART III

CHAPTER TWENTY-THREE

MATTY

Matty was the first to leave.

She cried. She swore to herself she wouldn't. She was certain she'd hold it together. But when she met Clive, Oscar and Iggy, Desmund, and, of course Pellet, in front of the ferryboat terminal on the day she was leaving, she sobbed. And seeing even Helmut standing in the wings, almost as if he were still sitting at his table in the corner, with Fatisha by his side, was the final straw. All the people who had become her life over the past couple of years had come to see her off. She was heartbroken to leave them behind; she was saddened to leave the clinic and her co-workers; she was regretful that she hadn't gone to rehab in Saint Lucia. If she had gone then, she might not be leaving now.

Since she'd returned from Amos's Bar and Hut a few months back, everything had been different. Some of the reasons were obvious. First, the Hut was gone, as their taxi driver Carter had said, up in smoke and down in ashes. Then Clive stopped drinking when he started going to church, which was probably a good thing, but it threw everything out of kilter. Perhaps most importantly, the sand had slipped through the hourglass of her life and the view had become clear: It was time to make a change. She and her doctor friend were cordial to each other, but he had no interest in being with a woman who drank a lot, and she had no interest reforming just to chase him. At least that was what she told herself for quite a while. Until one morning when she looked in the mirror and realized *she* had no interest in being with a woman who drank a lot either, especially if that woman was herself.

Calls were made to friends who were former co-workers back in Little Rock. Rehab and counseling was set up, and a job was secured. It was nearing time to accept her life and release her demons. The legend of the Stodgy family as well as the stain of her first husband had haunted her for long enough. For Matty, it was about time for her to find some inner peace and let go of her past.

Oscar and Iggy were the first to say good-bye. Iggy was beautiful as an angel and dingy as a bell, but to Matty's surprise, she was strong as iron. With her head held high along with a warm smile on her face, Iggy gave her a big hug and then kissed her on both cheeks.

"Life is good. Learn from your mistakes, and don't look back with regrets," Iggy said, looking Matty square in the eye. Matty was taken aback and thought to herself, *who is this woman?* Not once, in all the time she had known Iggy, had she thought words like that existed within her head. Iggy was full of surprises.

"I can't believe you wouldn't go out for one final blowout," Oscar said as he hugged her, and then stood back to take in one last look.

"Maybe next time, huh," she whimpered as she wiped the tears out of her eyes. She didn't really think there would be a next time.

"The next time, we'll all come up to Stodgy and show them how it's done," he answered.

"Oh God, I don't think Stodgy is ready for you guys yet. Besides, I don't have enough money to bail you out of jail." She smiled, but it was a heartbroken smile as her tears flowed like a river. He smiled and gave her a little kiss and then took his place back at Iggy's side.

"I ain't never gonna forget you, lil sister," Desmund said as he wrapped his big arms around her and she nearly disappeared in a cloud of black arms and black dreads.

"Who's going to be my advisor from now on?" she said, clinging to him as if he were the safety blanket that protected her from the demons of this big, bad world.

"Must have bartenders where you're from. We're all full of shit, ya know? You keep buyin drinks, we jus keep tellin you dat everyting is cool." He was still hugging her and holding on to her as if she were his security blanket. Perhaps for the first time since he'd known Matty, he realized he loved her. Not like getting-married love, but certainly he loved her like she was family, and he was going to miss her. When he finally let her go, Matty reached up and wiped the tears from his face.

"I'll always be your lil sister, Dez," she said. She couldn't believe how hard this was. She had known it would be difficult, but this was brutal.

Clive had never parted ways with a woman on good terms. From his mother to Tina and everyone in between, they all had ended badly. He never had the opportunity to hug them and give a heartfelt good-bye. He stepped up to Matty who wrapped her arms around his neck and squeezed tight as tears continued to run down her cheeks. Clive stood stiffly with his hands at his side for a moment and then patted her on the back as if he were burping a baby.

"Take care, Matty. We'll be here if you need anything," is all he said. He turned around and looked at Pellet, shrugged and added, "They usually have a gun or something."

Pellet walked over and he and Matty looked at each

other with stupid grins on their faces. Of all of them, they were the closest to each other. Pellet and Clive drank a lot together, but Pellet and Matty were connected. They clicked the first time they met each other, and they had been laughing or fighting since that very first moment. Taking a deep breath, still fighting but losing the battle with her tears, Matty stepped forward to give Pellet a hug. Much to her surprise, he took her in his arms, leaned her back like in an old movie, and gave her a huge French kiss. For a split second she was in shock—so he had a moment that he fully enjoyed the taste of her mouth and the softness of her lips, before she recovered. With a surge of energy she punched him beside the head and pushed herself away.

"God damn it, Pellet! What the hell is wrong with you?" she yelled.

"I just thought I'd let you know what you'd been missing all this time," he said, still grinning. He was proud of what he'd finally done, especially after her many rejections. It had almost worked. Almost. He had hammed it up and stunned her enough so that she cussed him out and would leave without a bunch of tears over their good-bye. But she realized what he was trying to do. He was trying to keep himself from having a sad good-bye. He was trying to keep himself from feeling the pain of losing her. He was trying to keep her from feeling the pain of losing him. For all his faults, and there were many, there was only one Pellet in the world. Matty was going to miss him most of all.

"You stupid ass," she said as she grabbed him and gave him a kiss that he'd never forget. When she finished, Matty had succeeded in easing the pain for Pellet, instead of the other way around. It was the best and the worst good-bye he'd ever experienced.

For the first time since arriving in Anguilla, Helmut came out of the shadows and into the light of the island dogs. Matty didn't quite know what to say when he approached her. She didn't really know him, even though he'd clearly been a part of her life over the past couple of years.

"I watch people, and I don't say too much," he said, then paused for a moment as if he were absorbing what she looked like so he wouldn't forget her when she was gone. "I watch people and I see all kinds of things. I see all kinds of people. You, my friend, are one of the good people. Unlike these clowns," he said, gesturing toward his friends, "You have a lot to give to the world."

He handed her an envelope. "I wrote something for you. You can read it later. Thank you for being who you are." He leaned forward and kissed her on the cheek and turned to walk away. "I would have given her a real kiss, but not after you kissed her," he added, as he glanced up at Pellet. Everyone stood in mild shock at the absurd idea that Helmut might have a sense of humor—or any personality at all, for that matter.

"Hey, that had better not be a poem, God damn it," Pellet snapped at Helmut.

Fatisha and Matty were casual friends and nothing more. Out of respect for all the others, she stood in the wings and flashed a peace sign and a smile to Matty, who returned the gesture. Helmut returned to Fatisha's side and put his arm around her waist while he continued doing what he always did: He watched from the distance.

Matty put her hand to her lips, and through her tears, she blew them all a kiss, then turned and headed into the ferry terminal. She did not look back until the boat was well away from the shore, when she could no longer make out the faces of the people on the beach who watched her sail away. She was afraid if she looked back, she wouldn't be able to leave. As the boat chugged away from shore, she sat on the upper deck, letting the wind hit her face and dry the tears that continued to flow. Once they had gone far enough from shore, she turned around to take one final look. She saw her band of friends, standing on the beach beside the terminal, waving beneath a brilliant Anguilla rainbow that extended from one end of the island to the other. Pellet was bent over with his pants pulled down, shooting her the moon.

When she arrived in Little Rock she relaxed for a couple of days before heading off to rehab for two weeks. In the end, she may or may not have actually needed the rehab, but it was good for her. It gave her time to adjust to being back in the real world. She never went to Stodgy to make peace with her ex-husband. She didn't know if she would hate him forever or not, but she was certain that it was a real possibility. He could have come out of the closet in college. He could have come out of the closet after college, while they were living in Little Rock. But he didn't have to drag her all the way back to Stodgy and make her look like a complete ass in front of all her friends and family. He was still on her shit list, and she was OK with that.

She took a job as a nurse in a children's cancer ward when she went back to work. A year or so later she met the father of one of the children, and the sparks flamed up almost instantly. Less than a year later they were married in a civil ceremony at the Little Rock Courthouse. The three of them, Luke, Matty, and Luke's daughter Paula, moved into a comfortable house with a pool in the suburbs. He was an architect, not a doctor, which weighed heavily in his favor.

He wanted to take her back to Anguilla for their

honeymoon, but Matty said no. Despite all of the trials and tribulations, and despite her memories of the excessively good times, her time in Anguilla with some of the best people she had ever met was *her* time. It was a private window of time in her life, which she was well aware could, and should, never be repeated. After she politely refused his offer to visit the blue, tranquil waters of Anguilla, they headed off to Colorado to ski for a week.

***

Ashley Belmont was a close friend and co-worker of Matty's who had been helping the children in the cancer ward long enough to see too many children come and go. A few weeks earlier, she had asked for an extended leave of absence. She told Matty she just needed a break from the weight of her work for a little while. Matty suspected she needed more than a little break. It was a Tuesday evening when Matty knocked on her door and was promptly invited in. After an hour of talking and a little crying, it was clear that Ashley probably wasn't coming back any time soon, or perhaps ever. She just wasn't up to it any more.

"Ashley, I don't know how you'll feel about this, but I'm going to leave you this brochure. There's a clinic; it's on a small island in the Caribbean called Anguilla. The pay is lousy, the place is hot and at times you will dearly miss the comforts of home, but if you go there, you won't regret it. Anyway, take a look at it when you get a chance, and if you're interested, give me a call."

As Matty drove through the freezing rain toward her home, Ashley looked at the brochure with the white beaches surrounded by blue waters, and wondered.

Chapter Twenty-Four

Clive

A tiny woman with a great big voice stood in front of the Anguillan Parish, and gloriously sang an impassioned rendition of "Ave Maria." Her voice floated in the air as she musically proclaimed her love for her God and the Holy Mother. Parishioners sat, some with their heads bowed in prayer and meditation, and others with their heads up as they listened to the woman whom God had undeniably blessed with the voice of an angel. The shutters were open on the glassless windows, allowing an ever so slight warm breeze to flow through the church. For the third Sunday morning in a row, Clive Higgins sat in the back row listening to the music, absorbing the sermon from the priest and grappling with the conflicts that existed between his life and the words of Mathew, Mark, Luke, and John. He had by no means committed his life to God or the church, but he was for the first time in a long time accepting the fact that he might possibly be traveling down the wrong road in life. Whether this new one was the right road or not, he didn't know. For the moment he was simply enjoying another Sunday morning with a clear head, no hangover, and a Caribbean angel singing "Ave Maria." Her voice, the Latin words he did not understand, and the lightly strumming acoustic guitar in the background all touched him more deeply than he had been touched for longer than he could recall.

After Communion was finished, Father Hernandez performed the Catholic ceremonies and said some prayers that were formalities that, up until a couple of weeks ago, Clive hadn't experienced since the last time he went to church. He was eight years old then. That was the year that his mother, a devout Catholic, died in a car accident. His father never once stepped into a church after the day of her funeral. Clive was a good son who loved his father, and obediently followed the man who set the example for his boys. As far as Donald Higgins was concerned, God had ruthlessly stolen the love of his life and left him with three sons to raise on his own. In one tragic week, Clive lost his mother, the strength and compassion of his father, and the support of his church and his God. Since she had died, he had emotionally been on his own.

Decades later in this hot church in Anguilla, Clive patiently listened to the homily, the sermon, the hymns, and everything else that went on during mass. As the service began to wrap up, his butt began to go to sleep from sitting on the hard wooden pews. He tried to lean discretely to the left to give his right cheek a break, then to the right to give his left cheek a break. Suddenly, as a wave of nostalgia ran through him, he could have sworn he felt the chastising gaze of his mother, indicating he needed to stop squirming and listen to the priest. It was the first time since he was eight that he had felt close to his mother. He sat up straight, with a smile on his face, and unintentionally glanced around to see if she might be sitting somewhere in the congregation. He did not see her, but he was still pretty sure she was there.

"Go with the grace of God," the old priest said as he began to walk to the front door with an altar boy in front and another behind, while an organ bellowed a parting hymn. Following the priest and altar boys, the congregation poured out to do whatever it was they all did on Sundays. Clive stood, shuffling his feet in the background, waiting for the majority of them to leave so he could speak to Father Hernandez in semi-privacy. Several of the parishioners recognized his face from seeing him around the small island, but few of them actually knew who he was. His circle of friends and their circle of friends didn't often cross paths, even in a little place like Anguilla. Eventually, almost everyone had either moved to their cars and driven away, or had strolled away, heading to their homes. Clive eased his way over to Father Hernandez after he had meekly shuffled out of the church.

"Clive, it's good to see you here again," Father Hernandez said, putting one hand on his shoulder and warmly shaking Clive's hand with the other. "You're becoming a regular face in the crowd."

"Don't jump the gun, Father," Clive answered defensively. "I guess you could say I'm just testing the waters."

"Feel free to test all you want," Father reassuringly added, not wanting to make Clive feel pressured.

Clive politely smiled at the priest and looked around for a few seconds while he reconsidered if he wanted to do this or not.

Father Hernandez had seen plenty of people on the fence over the years, and the signs were obvious to him. Clive was a newcomer to the church, who had waited around to see the priest after the mass, and then got defensive when he was invited to become part of their community. Pretty typical stuff. Now he silently stood with Father as he awkwardly searched for the words he wanted to say.

Finally he just blurted it out. "I've got a question for you, Father. I think I need to go to confession, but I'm not sure how the whole thing works. I mean, I know how it works, but do

I need to make an appointment or what?" he asked, not sure if confession worked more like a walk-in clinic or does the patient need to schedule an appointment to meet with the healer.

"Well, we usually do confession here at the church on Wednesday afternoons or Saturday mornings. You just come in and have a seat. Sometimes there are a few people here. Other times there's only one or two."

In truth there were typically only one or two, or fewer. The ones that did show up rarely confessed anything other than impure thoughts and such. Father often thought that, for an island that had a high rate of teen pregnancy and an ever-increasing crime rate, there certainly weren't many people fessing up to much, not even to God.

"I know I'm new to the church, Father, but do you think it's possible for me to kind of get a private meeting with you? I'm pretty uncomfortable with coming to church instead of going to a bar, and I'd appreciate if you could help me out here," he said, with his head hanging down like he was an eight-year-old boy again.

"It's no problem at all. How about tomorrow at three?" Father asked with a warm smile.

"Sounds great," Clive answered. With the warm welcome and reassurance, he felt his comfort level growing. He shook the priest's hand again and said good-bye. Leaving the church, he drove toward Shoal Bay to take a walk on the beach and grab a bite to eat. On the way out to that end of the island his thoughts drifted as he began to wonder what he would say once he got inside the confessional. Would he give the short version of his life, or the long version? How detailed should he get? Should he confess to everything, or just the things that were bothering him? Suddenly he felt as though this process might be a little more difficult than he anticipated.

It was hot and muggy when Clive walked into the church at five minutes to three the following afternoon. Father Hernandez was standing just inside the front door. As soon as he entered, Father reached down and locked the deadbolt on the door behind him.

"I'd prefer that we are not disturbed," he said with a polite smile. "You'd be surprised how many people think interrupting a priest is completely acceptable behavior, even when I'm in the confessional," he continued, surprising Clive at how human this man of God seemed to be.

Father Hernandez walked toward the confessional with Clive one step behind him. He motioned for him to go into the half with the curtain as he stepped into the side with the door. Clive walked in and looked down at the kneeler in front of him that faced the metal screen that symbolically obscured the view between the confessor and the priest. After adjusting to the confined area for a moment, Clive knelt down and blessed himself as Father said, "In the name of the Father, the Son and the Holy Spirit."

Clive was surprised that, after all these years, he still clearly recalled the process. "Bless me, Father, for I have sinned. It's been... a couple of decades and then some, since I last confessed," Clive said.

"Uh-huh, uh-huh," the priest mumbled in little choppy syllables, acknowledging Clive's statement. "Please continue."

"Well... to be honest, Father, I don't really know what to do next. When I was a kid I just said that I swore a couple of times and took my brother's baseball and made him cry. Then I had to say some prayers, and that was it."

"Uh-huh, uh-huh," the priest said again, then continued,

"Just go ahead and tell God your sins. Everything remains private. Only you know what sins you have to confess," he instructed. "Well, you and God," he added.

"All my sins?"

"Whatever you feel you need to be forgiven for. This is to cleanse your soul and for you to be forgiven. This is to lighten your burden."

"I got a lot of stuff, Father. You got a lot of time?" Clive asked. He wasn't sure how long these things were supposed to last for grownups, but he was pretty sure that "I stole my brother's baseball" wasn't going to work with God this time.

"Uh-huh, uh-huh, well, let's start with some of the bigger ones and work our way down the list, OK?" he answered, realizing this probably wasn't going to be a typical confession.

"OK, here goes," Clive said and took a deep breath. "A few years back I slept with another guy's wife. I know that's against one of the commandments, plus it's just not a cool thing to do. So I guess that's the first thing I want to confess," he said, and then hesitated before continuing. "But to be honest, I think she slept around quite a bit. I mean, I was by no means the only guy she cheated with." He instantly felt a little better, getting that one off his chest.

"I'm sure you understand that her sins do not relieve you of responsibility for your own sins. Today we are here to cleanse your soul, and not to pass judgment on the sins of others."

Now Clive felt like he needed to confess that he had passed judgment on her, but he moved on. "There's been a lot of sex over the years. You know, not being married to the woman sex, and I'm pretty sure that premarital sex is against the rules too, right?"

"Uh-huh, uh-huh," Father Hernandez mumbled once

again and said, "Continue."

"A lotta drinking and smoking. Way too much to go into. I'm just going to list that item as one, long, extended party. Bars, strip clubs, parties, you name it."

"Uh-huh, uh-huh, continue."

"After my mother died, me and my brothers and my dad, we all kind of told God to piss off and turned our back on him. I'm guessing that wasn't cool either. He probably doesn't like stuff like that, huh," he said more as a statement than a question.

"Uh-huh, uh-huh, continue."

Clive tried looking through the screen at the priest to check out the expression on his face. Mostly he was wondering if the guy was even listening to him, or was he half asleep and mumbling "uh-huh" at him.

"I burned down Da Limin Hut," he blurted out. Silence followed. Silence from Clive, and silence from the priest. There was no "uh-huh". He presumed that if the priest had been sleeping, he just woke him up.

After a long stretch of silence, Father Hernandez finally responded. "Please continue," he said in a very serious tone, in place of the tone of indifference he'd been using. Clive knew he touched on some kind of holy nerve when Father said, "Please" instead of "uh-huh."

"Just how did this happen, my son?"

Things were suddenly feeling holy to Clive. Suddenly he had become "my son." Apparently he had gotten God's attention—or at least His secretary's attention. He began to smile a little bit on the inside. Then he realized that getting God's attention like this may not necessarily be a good thing.

"Well, Desmund's fat-ass wife came back from France and stole the bar from him and then sold it to some guy from the

States." He knew he shouldn't be swearing in church.

The priest knew that he should probably remember to say something to him about swearing later on, but for now he just wanted to hear the entire story.

"So at first I felt bad for Desmund, but it wasn't really my problem, right?" he asked, as if Father Hernandez was going to answer him. When he didn't say anything, Clive continued. "So anyway, that first night when Desmund found out about everything that was going down, we all got pretty drunk and stoned. Even the old white dude that was buying the bar got trashed with us. I really thought everything would be cool once the dust settled." He stopped talking and took a deep breath to compose his thoughts.

"Continue," the priest said in a tone that made it clear that this story was more interesting than "I drink a lot."

"So the next day, after I recuperated from the night before, and just around dinnertime, I drove over to the Hut, you know, to get a drink and something to eat, but it was closed. I hung out for a while, figuring that someone would come to open it up soon, but nobody came. Then I called Desmund to ask him what was going on and he gave me hell. Asked me why I'd call him to ask about the bar that he didn't own any more. Called me a dumb son of a bitch. After that, I went down to the Pump House to get something to eat, and maybe a drink or two." He stopped talking again and waited for the priest to say something.

"And the fire?" he asked.

"Yeah, the fire. Well, while I was eating fish tacos and working on my third or fourth drink, Chatta came in. I presume you know Chatta?"

"Yes, yes. Continue."

"Chatta said the guy who bought the bar was going to

change everything. Said he was going to do a kind of theme-park bar like you'd see in Vegas or Florida or someplace like that. I shrugged it off, but after a few more drinks, I started getting kind of worked up."

"Did you think that perhaps you should have stopped drinking and gone home for the night?" the priest interjected.

This irritated Clive. He had come for a confession, not the foreordained advice. "I did go home, as a matter of fact," he snapped back. Then he decided that snapping at a priest in the confessional was yet one more thing he was going to have to add to his confession list for the next time he came in for a cleansing.

"I don't understand. If you went home, how did the fire start?"

"When I got home, it was hot and muggy and I didn't really feel like going to bed, so I went to the cabinet and got a bottle of rum. I swear, I was just going to have one nightca Turns out I had quite a few nightcaps. Sometime after midni wandered down the beach, which of course led me to sta the Hut. My plan was to go sit at the bar and drink. Tha brought my own bottle." Saying the story out loud human being turned out to be pretty damn exha bowed his head, not in prayer, but to rub his tem beginning to throb in pain.

"So what happened next?" the pries as if he were some busybody who wanted

"What happened was when looking at the empty bar, it pissed me of rum all over the place, lit it on home. Didn't really give it much when suddenly I remembered

There was another l

prayed for guidance from the higher power as to what the penance should be for burning down a bar. Clearly, this was not a ten- "Our Father" deal.

"Also—" Clive added. Before he had the chance to say another word, Father Hernandez interrupted, "There's more?" with a surprised tone in his voice.

"No, Father, there's no more. I was also thinking that I might go see Desmund and tell him the whole story; you know, get it off my chest. What do you think? I mean, I told God, now maybe Desmund deserves to hear it too."

Once again there was silence while Father contemplated what he had just been told. After a few moments, he said, "Say fifty 'Hail Mary's' fifty 'Our Fathers,' and do not drink any for one year." The not drinking part was an arbitrary on the fly, going with the assumption that drinking completely. A year was a

ssing your sin to Desmund, this unless you want to go out for a e never known Desmund to be anyone who burned down his indly to a drunken white guy very least, I'd pray for a long

on."

bar anymore," Clive rything more palatable. . He had either burned uy's bar. Either way, he n. As for Desmund not ike a good idea to test pray long and hard e other than God. If

292

telling Desmund is the right thing to do, then you will know. There's no hurry."

"OK, whatever you think, Father. Do you want to hear the rest of my confessions?"

"Are any of them worse than the last one?"

"No, that was about as bad as I've done. Most of the other stuff is just... you know... women and drinking and shit like that."

"You are forgiven, my son. Say your prayers and sin no more. Do as I instructed, and go with the grace of God. Your sins are absolved.

"And Clive, you really shouldn't use profanities in church."

Clive blessed himself, thanked the priest again for seeing him on a day that wasn't his scheduled day for hearing confessions. Then he went to a pew and started praying.

After listening to the confession, Father Hernandez remained in the confessional for a long time and prayed. He prayed for guidance on how to deal with the situation. He prayed for Clive and his well-being. He prayed for Desmund, that he would be guided into a better life now that the bar was gone.

Mostly though he prayed for forgiveness for being so thoroughly amused and intrigued by Clive's story.

***

Much to the surprise of Clive and Father Hernandez, Clive's confession was not the end of his rejuvenated Catholic faith. First of all, after he said his Hail Mary's and Our Fathers, Clive did not drink for one year. He spent that year religiously attending mass, and was taken in by Father as a sort of protégé.

At the end of the year he volunteered for a position as a Catholic missionary in Honduras, to spend the next several months working in a poor village that desperately needed a school built for their children.

Helmut, who didn't particularly believe in this type of stuff, made a sizable donation partly because he liked Clive. When Clive had originally approached him for a donation, Helmut's response was as logical as always: "If *you* can give up drinking, then perhaps there is a God after all." Then he wrote the check.

Pellet wanted to give Clive a going-away party, but Clive knew how that would end up. After a little persuasion, he convinced Pellet, Desmund, Oscar and Iggy, and Helmut and Fatisha to go out for a nice dinner at Blanchard's. He was smart enough to know if they didn't go someplace a little upscale, the night would not end respectably. After a lot of prayer, he convinced them all to attend mass on the last Sunday before he left the island. Not to anyone's surprise, Pellet went up for Communion and asked for seconds when they gave him a sip of wine.

Once he got to Honduras, Clive's missionary schedule was demanding; he often wondered if God would grant him the strength and desire long enough for him to accomplish his mission. But no matter how tired he became, no matter what burdens the day piled on his plate, he always found time to pray for Oscar and Iggy, Matty, Pellet, Helmut and Fatisha, and Desmund, each and every day. On a good day, he even prayed for Queenie. Of all the messed-up people he had hung out with in his old life, they were the best of the best.

With the exception of Queenie, of course.

CHAPTER TWENTY-FIVE

OSCAR AND IGGY

Iggy Srebotnik's father was a drunk, and a hard-core one at that. From what she could remember of her grandfather, who passed away when she was only five, he was a drunk also. Probably every man in a long line of men in her family, reaching back a thousand years, perhaps reaching back to the point where the first of them discovered alcohol, were all drunks. She accepted their drunkenness as a reality that could not be altered and she didn't lose one minute of sleep over that reality. Occasionally she thought of her little brother, who still lived in her small village in Slovakia, and she presumed he had taken up drinking too. They wrote letters to each other from time to time, but he never said too much other than he was happy for her. She knew that his future lay in his hands and there was no point in agonizing the point any more than she did.

There were two things that she knew with certainty: All the men in her old family, the Srebotnik men, were nearly worthless drunks. And none of the men in her new family were going to be drunks. More to the point, if Oscar Duncan was going to continue his non-stop partying ways, then he would be the last Duncan in his particular line of the Duncan family heritage. There would be no little Duncan's watching their father stagger into the house. Their children wouldn't be embarrassed by their father as he stumbled around while people laughed at him. They wouldn't watch him lie around the house the next day, too hung-over to go to work.

If that wasn't enough reason for Oscar to tone it down and wind the partying level way back, then Iggy's little speech caught his attention and drove the point home. When he returned from Saint Lucia and dragged his tired carcass into the house, he was prepared to catch hell from his lovely wife. Whether the rest of the gang knew it or not, Iggy Duncan was one tough woman. She had been raised poor and she'd worked hard to save herself. Oscar was no match for her.

He sat at the kitchen table and told the whole story of going and drinking at the airport and ending up at Amos's. He told her how Matty was indifferent to going to rehab, and Pellet was the guy who instigated the ten days of partying. She believed the second part, but knew the first part, about Matty's indifference, was complete bullshit.

He told her how bad he felt, and that he was going to cut way back on his partying now that he was back home. This time she believed the first part, and knew the second part was complete bullshit.

Oscar sat at the kitchen table, rambling on endlessly, trying to save his hide; while Iggy stood with her arms folded, leaning on the kitchen sink, listening without saying a word. After twenty minutes of non-stop groveling, he finally finished. Iggy stood there and said nothing for a long time.

"Oh come on, Ig. Say something," he pleaded.

Iggy took a deep breath and gave Oscar a sad smile, then stood up straight and began unbuttoning her blouse until it was completely undone. She let out a little sigh, almost a whimper, as she slipped it off and tossed it onto the floor. With a flick of her finger she loosened her bra, and it went onto the floor too. Her eyes were half closed. He couldn't quite tell if she was fantasizing about something, or simply avoiding eye contact as she bent her lean body back and made a cat-like stretch. She was putting on quite a show for the stupid man sitting in front of her. When she finished her lingering stretch, she slid her long skinny fingers into the sides of her shorts, pushed them down to her bare feet, and then whimsically kicked them aside, standing in only her panties.

Oscar watched in erotic bewilderment. This wasn't what he had expected at all, but he liked it. Iggy softly licked her lips with her tongue, and gently bit her bottom lip; and repeated it as she slid her panties to the floor and kicked them off in the same direction as her shorts. By now Oscar was beginning to get hard. Iggy eased her way over to him and stopped just inches out of his reach. He began to lean forward to take her in his arms; she put her hand out, signaling him to stay right where he was.

She was not yet finished. "Do you smell my perfume, Oscar?" She feigned leaning in close to him, then stopped.

"Yes," he said, like a teenager trying to contain himself.

Iggy smiled a crooked smile and put her fingers against her lips as if she were thinking of some very provocative words to say to her husband. Just when he believed he couldn't take it any longer, and just as he was about to spring to his feet and go to her, she began to speak, very calmly and with absolute authority. "My father was a worthless drunk. All the men in my family have been worthless drunks as far back as anyone could trace our family history. Listen to me very carefully, Oscar Duncan. I will not bring a child into this world so they can know the pain of being ashamed of their father."

"Iggy—"

"Be quiet, Oscar. I'm not done. If you're going to keep drinking like you do, then we will not be having children. And if we're never having children, then there's really no point in ever having sex. Ever!"

Oscar sat with his mouth hanging open, half in awe of her beauty, half in shock over what he was being told. Her skin was tanned and flawless. Her breasts were perfect. Her muscle tone and her curves were breathtaking. She was a Tinker Bell sex goddess and she was driving her point home.

"So take one last long look, Oscar, because from now on if you want to see this, you'll have to steal a glimpse or a peek like some kind of Peeping Tom. If you want to have this," she said, motioning her hands to her whole body, "you'll have to sober up."

Oscar sat motionless in the chair. Iggy gave him one last arrogant look that seemed to last forever, then picked up her clothes, making sure that she bent over right in front of him, and lazily walked toward the bedroom.

Oscar had never been so aroused in his life.

***

The twins were just over one year old now. Desmund Pelletier Duncan and Maria Rosaleen Duncan were gifts from God. As it turned out, Oscar's fear of having hobbit-like idiots for children was an unfounded anxiety. While it was not quite clear yet if they'd be as beautiful as Iggy, they were by no means unattractive little tykes. Besides, on the day they were born, Oscar quickly realized his children would have been beautiful no matter what. As for his concern that they might not be too bright, he was beginning to suspect that Iggy was not the lovely imbecile he had thought her to be. While she may not be well-read, and her head may not be filled with all the useless facts that filled Oscar's head, she had found her way from being a poor girl on a pig farm in eastern Europe to living well on an island in the Caribbean. Then she somehow fixed Oscar, a man who clearly needed fixing. Last but not least, she was an incredible mother and wife. She was twice as good as he deserved, and Oscar knew it. It took him a while to figure it out, but he came around.

Dezzy was obviously named after Desmund and Pellet, and his mother would make sure he did not end up like either one of them. Maria was named after Iggy's mother, whom Iggy held only one slight notch below the Virgin Mary. Rosaleen was Oscar's mother. Even though he wasn't keen on the name, Iggy was smart enough to know it would be an insult to snub her mother-in-law, especially if the other grandmother was included. Taking a closer look, Oscar couldn't quite make up his mind if he was the smartest one in the family or not, but he knew for certain, he was the luckiest one. He was blessed with a beautiful wife and two precious children, and the only price he had to pay was to stop spending so much time with Desmund and Pellet. He still spent time with them, just not as much as before. And he never came home drunk, because the price was simply too high to pay. There was just too much at stake to take the chance.

CHAPTER TWENTY-SIX
DESMUND

Dezzy's Beach Bar, or *Dezzy's* as the regulars called it, was Desmund's replacement of his beloved Limin Hut. Less than a mile from where the old—now the new—Hut stood before being sold, burnt down, and then rebuilt into a theme-park-like bar, Dezzy's, just like the old Hut, became a humble island bar where the service was OK, the food was local, the drinks were strong, and the company was good. Dezzy's was open from noon until ten p.m., Monday through Saturday. However, sometimes they opened earlier, or later, depending on... whatever. They also frequently closed pretty much whenever they felt like closing; sometimes early, sometimes late, sometimes very, very late. And if a customer was to show up on a day when it was supposed to be open, but the liquor was locked up and nobody was around, well, apparently something had come up that outweighed opening the bar or worrying about customers. The view was almost the same as the old view; most of the customers were the same as the old customers, just as the food, the drink, and the bartender were all the same. The entire lot had simply drifted a little to the east and landed on the beach again.

Behind the bar stood a Rasta-looking character, who occasionally sort of washed beer mugs, lazily poured drinks into clear plastic cups, made small talk with the patrons, and continued to live the same life he'd lived in his old bar. In an effort to keep the place from looking new and shiny like the new theme-park bar that had just been built down the beach,

Desmund had gone out of his way to find used and somewhat worn-out furniture when he furnished the place. He wanted it to feel settled in on the first day, and didn't think anyone should have to wear things out before they felt at home.

Pellet sat at the end of the bar, sipping on a beer, and complained—everything was quickly almost back to normal. "Jesus Christ, man. Did you ever consider that the reason the last people got rid of these stools was because they're so damn uncomfortable? It's like I'm sitting on a piece of coral with a hump in the center of it. I'll probably have hemorrhoids by the end of the week," he grumbled, but wasn't so disgruntled that he actually moved to another place to sit, or to another bar. Just like old times at the Hut, Pellet settled in and immediately felt at home enough to bitch about anything that came to his mind.

"Not a problem for me, mon. I ain't sittin dat stool. Mine's got a cushion," Desmund answered, patting his hand on his stool and grinning at Pellet.

Voices carried a little better in this bar than the old one, which meant tourist were easily entertained while they listened to Chatta constantly running his mouth as he sat at the domino table, either taunting the guys he was beating or accusing them of conspiring against him if he was losing. The downside was that the regulars found it more difficult to ignore him than they once did. Not that it was such a downside that any of them stopped coming to the bar. They grumbled and told him to shut up, but they came just the same. The beer was still cold, the drinks were still strong, and the relationships among them were all interwoven, dysfunctional, and binding. They may not have been all the island dogs that once lounged around the Hut, when Matty and the gang were still hanging around, but they were still nearly as useless and entertaining as island dogs could be.

Matty had been the first to coin the term *island dogs*. It was when Desmund told her about Pellet's incident of waking up with a mutt peeing on his back. "Just a couple of island dogs hanging out and peeing all over the place," she had said while sipping on a beer. They all laughed and drank, and the name stuck. Eventually it grew to include just about anyone who hung out at the bar long enough and often enough.

The new bar, Dezzy's, was a bit smaller than the old bar and a lot smaller than the new version of Da Limin Hut, but for the most part, Desmund was good with the way things turned out. Everything, including the new location, just felt right. A couple of faces were missing and a couple of faces were added, but all in all, the song remained the same. They continued to have iPod Fridays, although it was considerably more civilized than the old ones. Boatmon still came around, dominos still slammed, Pellet was still useless for anything other than entertainment purposes, and Helmut still sat in a corner table pretty regularly, but not as often as he used to. Fatisha occasionally came in to paint her kaleidoscopic personality into the evening crowd, and add a breath of fresh air to what was often a stale rehash of the night before. Just as often as not, she simply sat with Helmut for a while and made small talk while he tried to write. He didn't mind the distraction. Pellet cringed every time he saw them together. There was no sign that his bitterness toward the two of them would ever end. On average, Pellet reminded Helmut about once a week that the poem thing was his idea.

"Hey Helmut! Yeah you, hiding over in the corner. That wasn't cool, man. You stole my idea and my dream girl. And you owe me two hundred bucks." He had probably yelled those words across the bar seventy-five times over the past year or two.

"You hired me to write the poem, and I wrote it. I told you up front I wasn't responsible for the results of your silly plan," he repeatedly yelled back after Pellet drank a few too many. "And if you'd stop being such a horse's ass, you'll recall I said no refunds. Count your blessing that Fatisha told me I should give you a finder's fee. That's the only reason I gave you the three hundred." The real truth was that for the most part, the only reason he didn't pay Pellet any more money, other than he didn't actually owe it to him, was because he looked at the argument back and forth as an ongoing story line of the sitcom called *Pellet*. Helmut enjoyed being part of the show.

"What da hell you writin over dere?" Desmund occasionally yelled in Helmut's direction, and then added, "Don't be writin bout my bar. You already ruined one. You're lucky I even allow you to come to dis one."

Helmut typically smiled and nodded. Sometimes he didn't even bother to look up from his writing, as he waved his hand to shoo Desmund away and to tell him to stop being a nuisance. If he answered at all, there was of course only one answer he would ever give: "It's personal."

After the book was sold and the movie was released on the big screen, Helmut was what Desmund and the gang would refer to as "Oprah rich." The plain truth was he had more money than he knew what to do with. Since he felt badly about the whole Hut thing, he had bought Desmund the new bar. Or to be clearer, he let Desmund buy it and Helmut simply paid for it. This time there was only one owner and he didn't live in France. For Helmut it was a win-win. His conscience was clean; he had a place to write the new book that he was working on, and which he had already signed a contract on. Nobody knew what it was

303

about yet.

Ashley Foster was the newest member of the gang. She stole Pellet's heart the first time he laid eyes on her, but she was by no means Matty. She was funny and easy to talk to. She stopped by once or twice a week for a meal and a couple of drinks, plus she usually showed up for iPod Fridays. But that was about it. Unlike Matty, she never drank until sunup; she didn't match Pellet, Oscar, and Desmund drink for drink, downing rum shots for rum shots; she rarely smoked hooch at all; and the odds of getting her to go sailing for a long weekend with the guys and a perfect stranger were a million to one. Still, given the option, Pellet would have gladly taken her completely into the fold, and probably would have elevated her to a status higher than Matty had ever reached, if it were up to him. Of course, as always, he would have done this for ulterior and obvious reasons. The one thing she had over Matty was that while Matty was good-looking and nice, Ashley was drop-dead gorgeous and nice. The drop-dead gorgeous thing immediately took Pellet out of the running. He had as much chance of going on a date with her as he ever did with Fatisha, which perversely meant he would pursue her relentlessly. But he definitely would not be asking Helmut to write a poem for her.

The dance Pellet chose to do with unattainable women was mind-blowing, but all would agree his taste in women was impeccable. Ashley was a tiny little woman, less than five feet and certainly less than a hundred pounds, with flawless proportions. Intellectually she was as sharp as a razor, and emotionally—well, she was in Anguilla because the weight of reality was lying too heavy on her shoulders. She was one of those people whom friends would refer to as "too nice for this world." To top it off, she was a hoot. The first night she met

Pellet, he held true to form, and poured it on way too thick for far too long. As the evening wound down for her, even though it was too early for him to be leaving any time soon, she asked him, out of the clear blue sky, if he liked his lovers soft or rough.

"I'm guessing I like them soft," he answered with an excited twinkle sparkling in his eye. "Don't get me wrong, if you're rough I can adjust," he continued, immediately allowing his naive imagination to spin out of control.

She laid her hand on the bar and said, "Let me see yours," as she reached into her little purse sitting on the bar. The back of his rough hand lay helpless in her tiny, fragile fingers as she pulled out a small tube of hand cream and squirted it into his palm and gently massaged it with her soft fingers. Unsure of what to think, Pellet simply went with it and enjoyed the moment as Ashley smiled at him like an angel sent from heaven for no other purpose other than to save him.

"There, it should be soft now. I hope you enjoy it." She picked up her purse, winked at Desmund as she headed out of the bar.

Pellet sat in a confused state of shock while Oscar, Desmund, and complete strangers laughed so hard they nearly fell off their stools.

"What the hell, man? Does someone slip 'bitch pills' to women who sit with me?" Pellet asked, unaware that he was holding his hand up to his nose, smelling the fragrance of the lotion she had left with him. It took a few seconds for him to register what she had implied. The most painful part was that he knew she was right. If he was going to have sex tonight, it would be with his hand. Then he smiled as if he were going to get the last laugh.

"Hey," he yelled as she neared her car, "You didn't even

put it on the correct hand."

"You're an idiot, mon," Desmund said as he set a Red Stripe in front of him. The last thing Pellet remembered, much later in the evening, was Big Daddy O singing "I Don't Drink Much" as he danced by himself and sang along, word for word.

***

"What da hell you doin in me bar?" Desmund snapped at Augustus Burton, the one and only time he came to visit, about a year after the fire. "Didn't you build a bar down the beach? Go sit down dere n' drink," he mumbled, without offering to serve him.

"It seems I no longer own Da Limin Hut, Mr. Kingston. So, I thought I'd come here to spend some of my money before going back home," he said in a cheerful mood. He looked around the bar and noticed that the Tuesday night crowd, typically the busiest night of the week at Dezzy's, was lively and looked to be in a drinking mood.

"What do you mean, you don't own it anymore?" Desmund mumbled, still not serving him.

"Desmund, do you think if I paid for everyone's drinks for the entire night, that you might serve me?" He promptly threw his credit card on the bar and said, "Rum Punch, please."

Desmund looked at the card without picking it up, and then slowly started pouring him a Rum Punch. "You serious bout paying da tab? Gonna cost you a bit, you know."

"It seems the company that I previously worked for, the ones who originally had no interest in buying your—Astra's—bar, changed their minds. I typically don't like to brag, but since the movie has been making millions, I did quite well. I suspect there will be tours and the whole nine yards by the time they get done."

"Hey Dez," Pellet chimed in, "what you gonna do if this bar becomes famous and it's overflowing with customers all the time?"

"Gonna raise me prices and give em lousy service till dey all go back to where dey came from." He wasn't joking.

Just to make sure Augustus wasn't joking, Desmund inquired once more to make sure that he was serious about picking up the tab for the night. "Food too?" he asked before spreading the news.

"Food, drinks, and good times all around tonight, Mr. Kingston," Augustus said, smiling from ear to ear. He was not the kind of guy to unwind in a bar, or anywhere else for that matter. The only time he had completely loosened up in all of his years was the night he passed out at the Hut with Clive and Dez, while the gang was out on Julio's boat, and Queenie was beheading her soon-to-be ex. He thought it was appropriate that his last celebration in Anguilla was going to be at Desmund's bar.

"Listen up, people. Dis man over here, Mr. Augustus Burton, stole my last bar from me." Desmund hesitated long enough for his friends to boo and curse and mumble at the out-of-place, uptight-looking guy at the end of the bar. "But... me n' him are cool now. Everyting is good, n' just to show what a good guy he is, drinks n' food is on him tonight. Everyting! Drink up, my friends."

Augustus instantly changed from villain to hero, and like any bar where free drinks and free food are announced, the stampede immediately ensued.

"Hey, you caused dis problem, get over here n' get to

work," he said to Augustus once it became apparent there was no way Desmund was going to keep up with the rush. Augustus quickly scurried around to the backside of the bar. Desmund had one of the best business nights he ever remembered, certainly the best since Dezzy's had opened. As for Augustus, being a hero in a small bar in the Caribbean felt almost as good as selling, what was not long ago a burned-down bar in the Caribbean, for a ton of money.

Queenie, who had waddled her chubby little self back to France dragging even more bags of money than she had swindled from Pierre, would have been outraged if she knew that Augustus made twice as much as she did when he sold the bar the second time in a year. In the end, though, she hadn't done badly for herself, and she had earned every penny of it. Desmund and Pierre were really the only two who believed she was an evil woman sent from hell to torment them.

She didn't instigate evil. From Pierre's point of view, she was, after all, supposed to be the mark in some big royal scam when it all began. And from Desmund's point of view, she may have been an evil bitch, but he was by no means an innocent victim. Once upon a time he had promised to work hard and give her a good life. That was a promise he only worked on for about the first six months of their marriage. These days Queenie lives happily in the luxury of her Paris apartment and doesn't particularly bother anyone. Occasionally she still attends royal functions put on by the SLRF just to remind them that their little black Queen is still lingering around, lest they forget.

Pierre, the poor bastard who got the whole ball rolling in the first place, slipped away in his sleep one night a few months after Dezzy's opened. Toward the final months of his life, he considered writing and publishing the whole truthful story, just to let the world know that Astra had been a willing participant in an absurd ruse for the past fifteen years. But when all was said and done, he proudly clung to his last shred of dignity and took the secret of Astra, the black queen of France, to his grave. She attended his funeral and sobbed and wailed for all to see the agony that gripped her total being. She convulsed in physical pain from losing such a loving and generous friend. Not a tear was genuine, not a sob was sincere. Her royal act would continue long after Pierre was gone.

From Desmund's point of view, the saying "absence makes the heart grow fonder" was a pile of crap. He loathed her wherever she was, no matter how absent.

***

Mama stood in the same kitchen she had stood in since the beginning of time and kneaded the dough for her Jonny Cakes.

"How's your girl doing over there in France?" asked one of her church friends who had stopped by to visit.

"That girl's gone plumb crazy," she answered with a big smile, followed by a loud laugh. "Got more money, clothes, and stuff then she'd know what to do with in ten lifetimes," she chuckled.

"She ever come home to visit?" her friend politely asked.

"Last time was a couple years ago. You know, when she came to beat up on Desmund."

"You ever see him?" she asked with indifferent curiosity.

"Yeah, he still comes around. I like him. Always been good to me, even when he was living with Astra, you know... before she was the Queen of France." They both laughed.

"And your boy? How's he doing?" she continued inquiring about Mama's family for no particular reason. Mama stopped kneading the dough and looked around as if she wanted to make sure nobody was listening.

"That boy's got a stick up his ass," she said just louder than a whisper. They both burst out into a roar of laughter this time. "Ebenezer Scrooge ain't got nothin on Alfred Lancaster. Cheapest man I ever seen. Gonna die rich though, one day he's gonna die rich." They were both happily quiet for a minute as Mama thought about her family while her friend likely did the same.

"Family is family, though. Gotta love your children," Mama said with a sigh and a warm smile. She was remembering them when they were small and running around under her feet in the kitchen. Little feet, little hands, little giggles, big joy. "Gotta love your children," she mumbled again, lost in distant memories.

Chapter Twenty-Seven

Helmut

Rain fell rhythmically onto the tin roof while Helmut sat on his front porch, gazing out over the whitecaps crashing on the distant reefs of Shoal Bay. His feet were propped up on the concrete porch railing and the song "Who'll Stop the Rain" popped into his mind, followed by Fatisha's name, and then by a smile that ran across his contented face. He had waited for what seemed like a lifetime—from his last sunny days until now—for the gray dreariness to drift off over the horizon. She was a long time coming, but she was worth the wait. Through an act of emotional self-preservation, he had long ago forgotten what it was like to be loved; and to the best of his ability, he forgot about giving love to anyone else. But these days love flowed like a river and he focused on savoring every moment of every day.

Reflecting on way back when, was something he had avoided for years. Once upon a time he believed that time would not heal everything. Now he was thinking maybe he was wrong. Maybe time heals. Maybe love conquers all. Maybe, where there's life, there's hope. For the first time in years, Helmut had no regrets, or at least no regrets he was clinging to or hiding from.

Dr. Brandt stood at the end of the porch with his hands folded behind his back, looking like he was waiting for the next train to arrive. Engineer Brandt was in the kitchen, sipping wine and trying to help Fatisha make a mango salad and to pan-fry some fresh snapper. They had arrived three days ago. Helmut had feared it would be an awkward and uncomfortable visit, but he was once again pleasantly surprised. Being pleasantly surprised seemed to be happening a lot lately. Fatisha had become the magic serum that made his life good. She made everything she touched become good.

After not hearing from their son for over five years, the Brandts, who were aware he was still alive because they had hired a detective to confirm his continued existence, jumped on a plane and flew to Anguilla as soon as they received the call from Helmut. Once upon a time, they had believed he was a disappointing blemish on their genetically superior intellect. Surprisingly, after hearing of Samira's death through an engineer that Frieda Brandt had worked with, and subsequently losing him to the darkness that consumed his existence, they finally realized that Helmut was not their failed project; he was their son. But by the time the light came on in their attic, the light had shut off in his. When they finally began dreaming about spending their golden years with their son, he was gone.

"So, what are the plans for this evening?" Dr. Brandt asked.

"Well, I thought we'd have dinner here and then take a drive over to Dezzy's Beach Bar for an after-dinner drink," he said as he continued sitting with his feet up and a smile on his face.

"Ahh yes, Dezzy's Beach Bar," the good doctor answered, trying not to give any obvious sign of disapproval. He had read the book about Da Limin Hut and, to say the least, it wasn't to his taste. He presumed Dezzy's was similar in most ways. Still, he was putting his best foot forward because he didn't want to have anything come between them ever again. Not to mention that his wife would make his life a living hell if he allowed his obsessively anal view of everything to take her little boy away from her again. She blew it the first time around, and nothing would prevent her from getting it right this time—not even her husband.

"You look happy, Helmut," his father said.

"I am happy. I am very happy," Helmut answered out loud, as he glanced over his shoulder towards the women.

"I am sorry to say these words, but I think this is the first time that I've ever actually seen you content with life," his father said without making eye contact.

"Don't be sorry. It may be the first, but it will not be the last," he answered as he got up and patted his elderly father on the back. "Come on. Let's go help in the kitchen."

"Helmut, you know I do not cook," Dr. Brandt answered.

"Never too late to learn. Look at me. Besides, they're not going to allow us to interfere with their cooking anyway. Just going in to enjoy their company."

They walked into the kitchen. Fatisha was cooking with the same graceful ease that she radiated when she walked or talked or made love. She possessed smooth, sweet, fluid beauty, no matter what she was doing. She was the most beautiful creature Helmut, or perhaps even Frank, had ever seen or imagined.

"Frieda, would you like a little more wine?" Fatisha said, holding the bottle up.

"Yes please," she answered with a giggle. Years ago his mother would have never touched alcohol for any reason, but in the recent days and weeks, something had changed. She had taken life far too seriously for far too long. Her priorities were not the same as they once were; without consciously realizing it, she had decided to reach for some of the highs and say to hell with the lows, whether they came or not. Her cheeks were flushed, as they often were when she had a drink or two, and she giggled like a schoolgirl doing something just a little bit bad.

"Dr. Brandt, or would you prefer Frank?" Fatisha said, holding the bottle up.

He hesitated for a moment. Relaxing and enjoying himself did not come as easy for him as it had for Frieda. He could not comprehend that *trying* to enjoy oneself almost always prevented one from actually *succeeding* at enjoying life. He did not have the foggiest idea of how to simply relax and go with the flow. But he was still determined to make the best of reuniting with his son and getting to know Fatisha. If that meant he should have a glass of wine, then that's what he would do.

"Yes, a little white wine would be nice. Thank you. And please, call me Frank. It feels like a nice change." He stood stiffly at the end of the kitchen counter as Fatisha poured him half a glass of wine. She corked the bottle and set it down, then picked up the glass and walked over to where he was standing. As he reached for the glass she set it on the counter and wrapped her long arms around him and gave him a spectacular hug.

"Welcome to our home. Helmut and I are wonderfully happy that you're here," she said softly and then kissed him on the side of his face. He was exhilarated, scared, thrilled, and perhaps a little confused all at the same time. *So this is what family love is supposed to feel like,* he thought, as he blushed at her. He was full of joy and sorrow all at once. He felt like he had walked into some kind of cleansing light, but then again felt like he should have made sure some of that light had shone on his family over the years.

"She's something, isn't she?" Helmut interjected as he

handed the wine glass to his father.

"She is at that," he said as he looked first at Fatisha, then at his wife. He had never seen her look so happy. For a split second, he was thankful to a God that he did not believe in for reuniting his family and filling their hearts with so much goodness.

Dinner was pleasant and uneventful, and the drive to Dezzy's was an adventure for Dr. Brandt and his glowing wife. The bumpy island roads wound through small hills and valleys, with an occasional bar-shack with men playing dominos on front porches. Now and again they passed villages that were spattered with clumps of houses with lights dimly burning behind dirty windows. But if they had thought they were experiencing new flavors of life with every passing hour they spent with their son and Fatisha, they were about to get a blast of flavor stronger than biting into a ripe island lime.

They were about to meet Pellet.

They walked into the bar where "Have I Told You Lately," by Van Morrison, was softly playing on the iPod. Helmut was mildly relieved by the music selection, but Fatisha wasn't the least bit surprised. She had called Desmund an hour ago to let him know they were on their way. In fact, she had spoken to him more than once over the past few days and told him how important it was to Helmut that his parents relax and enjoy themselves. He and Fatisha did not want them to leave the island disappointed in the life their son had chosen.

Fatisha fluttered into the bar like a dove and quickly began introducing Frieda to her island friends. The old German woman was beaming like a kid in a candy store. Desmund made her a Rum Punch with only slightly more than no rum at all. He had been told they were very proper folks; getting them drunk, and putting them in an embarrassing circumstance during their visit to the bar, would not likely go over well.

Dr. Brandt and Helmut began to head to his table in the back corner when the doctor stopped and asked if they might be able to sit at the bar.

"Certainly," Helmut said as he motioned toward the hard, uncomfortable stools. He had no way of knowing his father had never sat at a bar in his entire life. Tonight the doctor was committed to doing some of the things a Hemingway man might do.

"I'm Desmund. Welcome to da island," he said as he set two coasters—*new* coasters—in front of his friend and his friend's father. "What you be drinkin?"

"Well, I don't drink all that much, so I guess I'll take whatever you recommend," he said as he looked at the wall full of liquor behind Helmut's friend.

"Two Appleton's, iced," Helmut answered. "This is sipping rum. It starts off a little warm, but it gets smoother with each sip," he politely told his dad.

"Starry night," his father said as he looked off to the sky in the distance.

"Stars sparkle bright round here," Desmund mumbled as he slid two drinks across the counter.

"Bow down to da domino king!" Chatta bellowed from the other side of the bar, slamming down the final domino for probably the millionth time. His friends laughed just as they always laughed, and dominos clinked as they were mixed for the next round. In a little while, Chatta would be grumbling about the domino gods turning on him, but it never really mattered what he was saying. He was part of the color of the bar and all that mattered was that his voice remained as constant as the waves on the shore.

Ashley arrived and gravitated to Fatisha for an introduction to the Brandts. When she leaned forward and kissed Fatisha on the side of her face, Pellet immediately had an indecent thought, which was not uncommon for him. After the introductions, and after saying hello to a couple of the regulars, Ashley worked her way over to the stool beside Pellet. She wasn't sure if she sat near him to torment him or simply because they were friends of sorts. She had taken him in as somewhat of a favor to Matty. It was as if she were protecting Matty's dimwitted little brother who was living in a strange land all by himself. As the evening pleasantly passed with everyone mingling and having an easygoing time, Ashley sipped her third glass of wine—which made it a wild night for her—and Pellet sipped on rum drinks that he had long ago lost count of.

"Hey you, old guy over there," he yelled across the bar toward Dr. Brandt. "Yeah, I'm talking to you," he added, as the doctor looked at Helmut as if he were analyzing Pellet and trying to figure out why a complete stranger would act out with such odd behavior.

"Hey, mon, be cool," Desmund mumbled, knowing there wasn't any possibility that his instructions would have any effect on Pellet once he began to stew again over the whole poem, Fatisha, two hundred dollar incident.

"Hey, are you HIS dad?" he continued as he waved his index finger in the direction of Helmut.

Dr. Brandt was honored someone had referred to him as *Helmut's dad*. He sat up straight and raised his glass of rum in acknowledgement. For the first time in his life, he downed a shot of liquor in one gulp. "Yes. Yes, I am his dad," he answered proudly.

317

"Well, let me tell you something. That son of yours," he stopped and took a long drag off his cigarette then began again, "that's right, that man of questionable character sitting right beside you, owes me two hundred dollars and a girlfriend. What do you think of that, huh?" Pellet threw the same old accusation once again, but for the first time ever; he said Helmut owed him a girlfriend. In the past he had always spoken of just the money and Fatisha. This time he was less specific about who the girl would have to be. It was almost as though there was a crack in his armor and he seemed to imply Helmut simply needed to supply the two hundred dollars and a woman, not necessarily Fatisha.

"Well, I'm sure if my son owes you money, he will pay it to you." Dr. Brandt felt warm all over as he not only said the words *my son*, but said them while defending his honor. "And as for a girlfriend, what is wrong with that beautiful lady sitting right next to you?" He smiled warmly and nodded in a friendly way in Ashley's direction. Complimenting a woman he did not know was new to the doctor, but he was beginning to feel the effects of the couple of glasses of wine at dinner, followed by the rum, and he thought he had thrown the compliment quite nicely, without being awkward, too forward, or offensive in any manner.

Ashley didn't agree. "Hey! Don't be giving me away. First of all, I don't even know you, and second of all, I do know Pellet. So I'm not yours to be giving away, and nobody is giving me to him." She shoved her empty glass of wine towards Desmund to fill. She was probably pushing the limits of her drinking ability and would regret it in the morning, but for now, she seemed to be going with the flow.

"Give em hell, Ash," Pellet mumbled. Desmund just looked at him, shook his head, and poured wine.

"Damn right," she responded with a smile of vindication.

Oscar and Iggy had arrived a few minutes earlier and had been introducing themselves to Frieda when the Pellet-Helmut feud began to erupt. Iggy promptly connected with Helmut's mother and the two of them, plus Fatisha, were standing off to the side, laughing, talking and admiring the lights of St. Maarten as Oscar worked his way over for an introduction to the good doctor.

"Dr. Brandt, I'm Oscar," he said, extending his hand out to him. "Pleasure to meet you, and welcome to Anguilla." Oscar had researched everything ever written about, or by, the impressive Dr. Brandt. "I heard Pellet introducing himself," he said with a grin. "Glad to see you're meeting the gang."

"Poor fellow. He seems to have some anger issues. At least, that's what my observations indicate."

"He's got more issues than just anger issues," Oscar answered. He and Desmund both laughed. "What can I say, he's like a dog you just can't housebreak, but you can't help but love him."

"So he's like a stray that wandered in, and you decided to keep him?" the doctor asked.

"Exactly," Oscar responded emphatically.

"Hmmm, interesting," Dr. Brandt said as he jingled the ice in his glass toward Desmund.

The twins were home with Mrs. Srebotnik. Oscar had flown her in two weeks ago as a surprise to Iggy for her birthday. It seemed that against all odds, Iggy's mother had finally escaped her desolate existence at the pig farm, and her drunken husband, at least for a short while. If Iggy had her way, her mother would stay with them forever. Much to Iggy's disappointment, however, and despite her mother being awestruck by the beauty of the Caribbean as well as overwhelmed by the beauty of her daughter's family, she knew where her home was. She had no intention of leaving it forever. She would stay four more weeks and then return to her home and her friends. She would talk about her visit to the beautiful Caribbean Sea, the people of Anguilla, and her daughter's lovely family for the rest of her life.

The feud over the two hundred dollars, and Ashley being given away, faded amid the music and laughter of the bar that was slowly but surely gaining patrons. Frieda was giddy with wine, family, and her newly acquired friends when she walked over to the bar and introduced herself to Desmund. Two weeks ago she would have expected to be quite uncomfortable in a bar, especially in one where there were more black men than white, but things in her life had changed. She had her son back, she was being properly introduced to island life, and perhaps most significant of all, she was slightly inebriated. Tonight she felt at home.

"Desmund, I want to request a song, please," she said as if he was a DJ and making a song request was a normal thing at Dezzy's.

"Cool," was all he said as he motioned for Fatisha to come over. This seemed like something she should handle. He didn't quite know the logic behind his thought process, and he didn't really care. To him it just seemed simpler if Fatisha came over and found the song while he drank rum with Helmut and Frank.

"I want to hear the 'Quack Quack' song," Frieda said. "You know the one where everyone flaps their wings. It's just always looked so fun, and I always wanted to dance to it," she announced to Fatisha, who eased in behind the bar. Fatisha knew this was a delicate moment that could make or break the night. Frieda was letting her hair down for perhaps the first time ever, and the last thing Helmut would want for his mother was for her to be embarrassed or to have regrets tomorrow. That was Pellet's job. On the other hand, she was having fun and Fatisha didn't want it to stop the evening in its tracks.

"I have an even better idea, Frieda. Since this is your first true island bar experience, how about if we put on some Reggae and let you feel the full experience?"

"Oooh, that sounds even better," she answered excitedly. Moments later Fatisha turned the volume up just a little bit as Bob Marley's "One Love" came over the speakers. Frieda glowed as she swayed to the music and basked in the warm Caribbean air under the sparkling stars. *All of this,* she thought, *is with friends and family! Life doesn't get any better than this.*

Pellet had left his stool and was leaning against the railing, talking to island friends who were coming and going. Helmut had quietly slipped off the stool and settled down in his corner of the world. He watched his father laugh and talk with Oscar and Desmund. It was as if they were all old friends. Ashley had decided to slow down on the wine and had moved to a table with a couple of other nurse friends. They had ordered conch fritters and red snapper and were laughing about something that had happened at work.

Frieda and Iggy were off to one side chatting about Germany, Slovakia, and Iggy's mother. Frieda was hoping they would meet each other; she couldn't help but believe she would like anyone with a daughter as nice and as beautiful as Iggy.

Helmut pulled a notepad out of his pocket. He never went anywhere without it, just in case there was something he felt inspired to write. Swirling the ice in his glass, he took a long look around the bar and breathed in everything that was going on. A small crooked smile came to his face as he looked down at the pad and wrote, "Life is good." He didn't have any idea where the line would take him, but it was a good place to start.

More often than not, no matter what the opening line in a story at Dezzy's was, Pellet eventually came into the picture dramatically and quickly. This time was no different from a hundred other times.

He was still leaning against the railing, talking to a couple of guys from work about nothing worth talking about, when Fatisha glided towards them. The problem for Pellet was not that he thought of things to do and then pondered them for a moment, then still made the wrong decision. The problem was he didn't think at all. Sometimes it seemed like his entire life was a long series of impulses. No thought process, no pondering, just doing. As Fatisha approached Pellet and his friends, Pellet did not yet know it, but this was going to be one of those impulsive moments. She turned and slid past a couple of tourist who were standing near the bar. For a split second, she was just a foot in front of Pellet with her back, or more to the point, her backside, facing him. A stupid-looking grin came to his face as he impulsively reached out and grabbed a handful of Fatisha and did not let go. For a single moment in time he relished the feeling of her flesh being held firmly in his hand.

But that moment did not last long at all. She did not need to look or think or wonder who would be stupid enough to grab any part of her without her consent. She instinctively knew it was Pellet. Pellet's friends did not have time to be shocked or humored or, for that matter, to have any reaction whatsoever before Fatisha spun around. Her perfect cheek had barely slipped from his grip when he caught a mere glimpse of her right hand, in the form of a fist, flashing like lightning and then exploding like thunder, directly on the end of his nose. He had only enough time for his eyebrows to rise slightly in acknowledgement that he was going to be in pain. When her fist landed, it landed with the force of an angry island woman, and not that of some prissy little American girl giving him a symbolic slap across the face. It was a barroom punch.

He tried recoiling, but it was too late; the damage had been done. He jerked backward against the railing and immediately lost his balance. His feet flipped up into the air, his drink spilled down onto the ground, and he landed full-force in a large thorny bougainvillea bush. The entire bar momentarily froze.

But as always, Fatisha made everything all right. With a brilliant smile she leaned down toward where he had flipped and looked at her friend with blood running out of his nose. "How did it feel, Pellet?" she said. Of course she meant all of it: the handful of her backside that he had grabbed, the punch, and the thorny bush: *How did it feel, Pellet?*

"Rum Punch, please, Desmund," she called as she easily strolled away from the scene of the crime and over to the bar. Life instantly returned to the gang. Pellet's friends were so mesmerized by Fatisha, they paid no attention to him bleeding in the bushes.

"That's the sexiest thing I've ever seen," one of them mumbled. The other stood with his mouth hanging open and said nothing.

The next morning, as they sipped coffee and nibbled pastries at the kitchen table back at Shoal Bay, the Brandts talked and laughed and smiled with only slight embarrassment about what a wonderful time the night had been. Helmut and Fatisha beamed with satisfaction about memories they knew they would cherish forever. This time was a long time in coming, but late was better than never. Helmut had never seen his father laugh so hard in his life as he recounted Fatisha whirling around and punching Pellet.

The crowning moment for Helmut was when his mother asked with all sincerity, "Does this mean we are island dogs now?"

Fatisha smiled warmly at Helmut and squeezed his hand as he answered his long-lost mother and father. "Yes, Mom, you are both officially island dogs now."

After all, they drank too much rum, sang and danced to island music, laughed with their friends, and saw Pellet make an ass of himself.

The last item sealed the deal.

CHAPTER TWENTY-EIGHT

PELLET

Insanity: Doing the same thing over and over again and expecting different results.

—Albert Einstein

With his eyes closed, Pellet listened to the early morning surf splashing onto the sandy white shores of Anguilla. A warm Caribbean breeze blew soft sea air off the water and eased its way onto the island, but he paid no attention to it. His mind was occupied with more pressing issues. Clearly, Desmund was up and about; Pellet could hear *Comfortably Numb* by Pink Floyd quietly playing on the bar stereo. He presumed the song was a mocking jab being thrown in his direction. If he could have lifted his head, he would have seen his friend drinking a cup of coffee and looking out over the white waves and blue water, paying no attention to Pellet.

Unfortunately, Pellet was in too much pain to move. Other than the predictable pounding headache, the first thing he noticed was that neither of his arms had any feeling from the elbows down. Without opening his eyes, he felt as if both of his arms had been cut off at his elbow joints; but even in his foggy hung-over state of mind, he believed that to be highly unlikely. And if possibly missing limbs struck him as uncomfortably odd, the knife-cutting pain in his back raised just as much concern. After not moving for the first thirty seconds or so of consciousness, Pellet, who was lying face down, considered rolling over. But as he moved less than a centimeter, sharp pain shot through every inch of his body that was still capable of feeling anything.

His brain was functioning in the lower operating range even for him, and once again he seriously thought he really should consider making a life change. Of course he had been considering this very issue since working in the eraser factory in Waldoboro Maine many years ago. He had considered it when he realized his antipodal point was near the Antarctic. He thought he was making a life change when he drove from Maine to Florida. He believed he was taking a giant step in the right direction when he left Zoe, the bitch, and envisioned her standing alone in enraged befuddlement in Royal Palm Beach. He considered making a life change on at least a dozen occasions when he woke up like he was waking up this morning. When Julio died, he took some time and seriously reflected on the shortness of life and he was certain he would somehow make his life take a turn in a more productive direction. Watching a friend get executed would seem like an obvious motivator. When he, Matty, and Oscar journeyed to St. Lucia, they almost made a life change together, but they didn't. In the end, Matty ultimately made a conscious choice to stop being held prisoner to her past, and Oscar was motivated by the love of his life to make a change, but Pellet was still Pellet. He continued to live in his perpetual loop of being committed to making a life change... soon, or perhaps just a couple of days after soon.

Taking a deep breath, he attempted to open his eyes. He was surprised that even the act of eye opening was painful, until he had a quick flashback of Fatisha's fist connecting with his nose, which was connected to his stupidly smiling face. In a single snapshot that zipped through his brain, some of his pain was clarified. But the clarification was not a Hallelujah moment. That one single punch did not explain the total body pain he was currently enduring. With one more deep breath, he forced his eyes open, only to realize he was lying face down in the loosely hanging rope hammock Desmund had hung between two palm trees, partly for occasions just like this one.

It was bad enough that Pellet's nose was broken, and dried blood hung off the tip of it like some kind of miniature stalactite; but to add insult to injury, the nylon mesh hammock had been cutting into his face for several hours. The little diamond-shaped pattern crisscrossed from one side of his face to the other and would likely remain visible for at least a couple of days, but that wouldn't be his concern until after the blood returned to these depressed areas of his skin. That would be yet one more shard of pain racing through his haggard body.

Apparently when he initially tumbled face first into the hammock under the bright night sky of Anguilla, he fell in a sort of spread-eagle fashion, leaving his arms hanging over the side of the outside ropes. After several hours of not moving, and the ropes cutting off the blood to the bottom half of his arms, they had eventually lost feeling to the point of not existing at all. It was highly likely that they were going to throb with the intensity of rapidly growing new arms, once the blood was allowed to rush back into his lifeless limbs.

Of course that led to the immediate problem of not being able to move due to the incapacitating pain shooting through his back. It would be reasonable to think flipping over the railing last night and landing in the bushes below may have caused the excruciating pain. Perhaps he landed in a twisted position or slammed against the stump of the bougainvillea, causing some sort of vertebral damage. Or maybe the pain stemmed from the thorns of the bush poking into his skin and tearing little cuts all over his back and arms, as he tumbled backward while clinging to a brief recollection of the grab and the punch.

While it was highly likely the fall, the stump, and the thorns were adding to his current condition, the majority of the pain was being caused by the fact that he had slept face down on a loosely hanging hammock that was shaped somewhat like a horseshoe. Pellet was bent nearly in half in the wrong direction; the human back was not meant to bend like that. It damn sure wasn't meant to stay in that position for five or six hours.

Pellet continued to lie face down, moving nothing but his eyelids, as he greeted the bright morning daylight of Anguilla. As his vision slowly came into focus, what he should have been looking at, given his location and position, was the white sandy ground covered with spattering's of island weeds and grass. But as the morning world came into focus and the mind fog thinned out, the first spectacle that manifested itself less than two feet from his face was a dirty, sprawled-out island dog lying on its side and enjoying the quiet of the morning. His skinny, bony body lay flat with legs stretched out as if he had been run over by a steam roller; and his unblinking eye, at least the one that Pellet could see, was open and looking up toward the pathetic view that hung in pain above him.

"Jesus... you again?" Pellet mumbled as he stared straight down without moving. Shlomo was thinking the same thing.

Pellet was stuck in a bad position. He was enduring horrific back pain that was certainly going to get worse when he tried moving. He was screwed whether he moved or not. The first thing he did, with a mighty groan of agony, was to use the upper part of his arms, the parts that were still functioning, and flail them around long enough and hard enough to get his arms completely inside the confines of the hammock. This movement shot excruciating pain through his pretzeled back, but it had to be done if he ever hoped to get out of the rope coffin that was holding him. On the bright side, his back was much more painful than the rebirth of his lower arms, so he barely noticed the throbbing in his elbows as the blood rushed into his missing limbs.

Still lying face down, with the rope cutting into his face and the stalactite hanging from his nose, Pellet began concentrating on regaining control of his hands. He wiggled his fingers and repeatedly clenched his hands into fists until he felt confident they would be of some use to him. With a superhuman effort along with a mighty groan of agony, he reached up and grabbed the hammock ropes as he flailed, flopped, and twisted until his face was looking up into the blue skies of Anguilla and his back was bent in the direction that human backs were meant to bend. Most of his body was experiencing some level of pain, and his head was pounding, but there was a bright side. Fatisha's mighty right hand had brought an abrupt end to Pellet's drinking for the night, and even though he had drunk enough, he had not drunk too much, or at least not way too much. So the good news was that his hangover was not the worst one he had ever had. It wasn't even the worst one he had experienced in recent weeks.

For the next twenty minutes he drifted in and out of consciousness, as much of his pain began to subside. With his eyes closed, he listened to the hypnotic sound of the waves lapping at the shore, and the sleepy sounds of Shlomo lightly snoring just below the hammock. Music continued to play in the background. The thought of rinsing off and having a cup of coffee sounded inviting; but first, just a bit more rest. As he gently swung between the palms, a fly began buzzing his face. He shooed it away a couple of times, but it was being drawn in by the scent of dried blood, so the pesky bug quickly returned. His peaceful, slightly hung-over, rest came to an abrupt end when he haphazardly waved his hand at the fly and accidently caught the side of his nose with his swinging hand.

"Son of a bitch!" he moaned as the blood began to flow again. Frustrated, he sat up and swung his legs over the side, then promptly flipped over face first on top of Shlomo. The poor old dog yelped and jumped up, perhaps for the first time in his life, then looked at Pellet as if he were considering peeing on him once again. Like a wounded warrior, Pellet climbed to his feet with sand and blood on his face, with scratches and scars on his back and arms, and hobbled toward the sea like a man who had been wandering the desert for forty days. The cool sand beneath his feet was the only thing that wasn't causing pain. As he stepped into the water, he fell forward in anticipation of the cool cleansing feeling one can only experience in the blue Caribbean Sea. Of course one can only appreciate this cool, comforting salt water, if he does not have a hundred shredded cuts on his body. Still wearing his bloodstained shirt and ragged cargo shorts, Pellet paid no attention to this newest burning sensation. It was so minor in relation to everything else, he barely took notice at all as he floated face down in the water. He considered just staying in that position until he drowned and brought everything to an end, but eventually he flipped over and began to contemplate how well his life was coming together.

A few minutes later he slowly swam to shore and unsteadily climbed up the incline from the water to the beach. Deciding against drinking any coffee, or more to the point, deciding against facing Desmund in his current condition, Pellet walked over to the hammock, slipped on his flip-flops and headed to his truck. On the short drive home he smiled as he revisited the look on Fatisha's face when she spun around with her fist drawn back, ready to fire. There was a split-second picture frozen in his mind when he caught every feature of her beautiful face, and he was certain he didn't imagine it. She was as beautiful and graceful when she was readying to punch him, as she was when she was flirting with him in the bar, back when she would flirt with him. Of course that was before Helmut stole two hundred dollars and his girlfriend.

As he sat behind the wheel of his truck, his back pain was fading, the cuts were only slightly burning, the diamond pattern on his face was actually becoming more visible; but more important than any of those things, regret was once again beginning to set in.

"I really gotta stop drinking," he said out loud. "Guess we shouldn't have stopped at Amos's when we went to St. Lucia." After a few more seconds of riding along, he wondered if it was a bad sign to be talking out loud and having an actual conversation when he was the only one in the truck. Then he shrugged and mumbled, "I guess that's the least of my problems." Three minutes later he pulled into his driveway, went into the house and took a shower before he fell into a bed that had a mattress, pillows, sheets, blankets and everything.

Seven hours later, after he had slept, showered again, nursed his scratches and taped his nose, he made a pot of coffee and cleared most of the remaining fog from his head. Upon opening his refrigerator, he would have been surprised if there was food in it. He was not surprised. Feeling the need for something to eat and not feeling the need to explain to anyone what had happened the night before, he was left with only one choice of where to eat. After slipping on a bloodless shirt and gathering his wallet, keys, and cash, he headed out to his truck to venture back to Dezzy's. A few minutes later he sauntered up the steps, climbed over the dog, and sat on the stool facing the bar. Desmund stood on the other side of the bar looking at him.

Chatta was running his mouth, and a couple of tourists were quietly sipping on their drinks, as Pellet smoked in silence after he asked Desmund for a cheeseburger and a beer.

"You need me to fill in last night's details?" Desmund asked.

"No, I pretty much remember the whole damn thing, or at least the important parts. Wasn't really that drunk. Guess I'd just waited so long to be with her, that for one brief moment in time, grabbing her ass seemed like a good idea."

"How's it seem now?" Desmund asked with a grin. "Can't be grabbin no woman who don't want to be grabbed, mon," he added.

"No shit," Pellet answered. He sat for a few seconds and stared down at the bar and then kind of smiled. "Man, I have never seen with such clarity in my life. When she whipped around and our eyes locked, I knew I was about to get my ass kicked. Didn't even see her hand. I think I actually smiled like a man who's made peace with his impending execution. Damn. You should have seen the look in her eyes," he added as he shook his head back and forth.

"You over her now?"

"Don't really get over a woman like that, do you? I mean, I guess it's time to accept reality, but she's one of a kind. What's that old Clint Eastwood line? 'A man's got to know his limitations.' She made it clear last night, she's out of my league."

"Amen to dat, Pellet. I tink you've finally seen da light."

"Hey..." Pellet added, "If I'm gonna get my ass kicked by a woman, she's the one I'd pick every time." They both laughed and clinked their beers together. Desmund walked to the other side of the bar to wait on some New Yorker who had just come in and sat down.

When the cheeseburger arrived, Pellet tried to scoff it down, but winced in pain when he tried to chew. Each time he took a bite, it seemed as though his face muscles were all connected to each other and they all came together at the point of his nose. It took him twenty-five minutes to eat the burger, one tiny nibble at a time.

A medium-size afternoon crowd was drifting in. Pellet had nursed a couple of beers and was trying to avoid conversation with anyone, especially with anyone who wanted to know what happened to his nose, his face, and his scratched-up arms. His empty bottle sat in front of him as he puffed on a cigarette, and he looked as though he were contemplating life in general.

"Hey Goat Turd, you want another beer?" Desmund called out while he had the cooler open.

"What'd I tell you about calling me Goat Turd? It's Pellet or Pelletier, whichever you prefer, Rasta Boy."

"Dat be a yes, or a no?"

"Yeah, I'll take another one, but this is the last one. I'm gonna cut down on my drinking for a while, I guess."

"Tink so?"

"Yeah, definitely. Well, probably. Maybe. Hell, I don't know. Just give me the damn beer. It's like I'm here with my wife or something. What the hell kind of bartender are you anyway? When I tell you to give me a beer, just say OK and give me a beer."

"OK," Desmund said with a shrug as he set an ice-cold Carib on the bar.

About the Author

B.M. SIMPSON was born in rural Maine. He joined the Air Force at 18 and lived and moved across the U.S. and Europe. After retiring, he spent many years living, working and traveling in the Caribbean. On the islands of Anguilla, St. Kitts and Grand Cayman, he discovered a passion for island life and formed friendships second to none. After 30 years of writing poems, songs and short stories, he wrote his first novel, *Island Dogs.*

Today Simpson calls St. Petersburg, FL home. He enjoys periodic trips back to the Caribbean to visit friends, share island stories, and soak up the peaceful vibe, sun, sea and warm breezes of the islands. And of course, a good rum punch made perfect by a local. He is currently writing his next novel, *Avis Humphrey.*

www.BMSIMPSON.COM
www.facebook.com/BMSimpson.author

67248210R00211

Made in the USA
Charleston, SC
09 February 2017